THE
Girl
WITH THE
Golden
Scissors

ALSO BY JULIA DROSTEN

The Lioness of Morocco
The Elephant Keeper's Daughter

THE
Girl
WITH THE
Golden
Scissors

JULIA DROSTEN

Translated by Deborah Langton

AMAZON **CROSSING**

Previously published as *Das Mädchen mit der goldenen Schere* via the Kindle Direct Publishing Platform in Germany in 2017. Translated from German by Deborah Langton. First published in English by Amazon Crossing in 2020.

Published by Amazon Crossing, Seattle

www.apub.com

Amazon, the Amazon logo, and Amazon Crossing are trademarks of Amazon.com, Inc., or its affiliates.

ISBN-13: 9781542007825
ISBN-10: 1542007828

Cover design by Shasti O'Leary Soudant

Cover photography by Richard Jenkins Photography

Printed in the United States of America

Contents

Chapter One

Vienna, 1889

"I'm frightened," whispered the young woman.

Her companion's mouth twisted in reply, but the young woman could see nothing in the darkness of the hired carriage that bore them through the icy winter's night.

The young woman shut her eyes to concentrate on the muffled clatter of horses' hooves and the crunch of wheels on the compacted snow. The nearby shrilling of a bell made her start. An unfamiliar male voice bawled out, "What the hell's going on? Damned idiot! Think you can outrun a tram?"

The carriage jolted and jerked to a stop amid the frozen tracks on Schwarzspanierstrasse.

"Holy Mary!" The young woman's hands flew to her belly.

"Pull yourself together," hissed her companion. "If you'd given Mary a thought nine months back, we wouldn't be rattling through the night in this dreadful old crate!"

"I just want to get there," gasped the younger one.

The older woman snorted in disgust but rapped her knuckles on the side of the carriage. "Hurry, coachman!"

At the crack of the whip, the horses hastened through the night.

The pain in the young woman's belly eased. In an attempt at distraction, she watched as her breath formed icy little puffs, seeming then to freeze against the window.

The carriage turned right and then quickly left. They lurched on for a short distance and then stopped.

"Rotenhausgasse! Thank you, ladies!" The coachman jumped down from his stand and opened the carriage door with a flourish. Light flooded in from the gas lamp he'd stopped beneath, and, in its yellow glow, white flakes danced. Since the start of Advent, it had snowed almost every day in Vienna.

The pregnant woman's companion rather brusquely gestured to her to climb out first. The young woman's movements were awkward and cautious. It was with gratitude that she accepted the coachman's hand as he helped her keep her balance on the treacherous surface. Her ample fur cape shielded her from the freezing air, as did her fur hat. A dark chiffon veil concealed her face from prying eyes, including the coachman's. He was not to know whom he was helping down from his carriage.

Then the older woman followed close behind. She was dressed exactly the same, right down to the veil. The only distinction between the two was the visibly swollen belly under the cape and the travel bag over the companion's arm. She delved into it for a moment and then held out several banknotes.

"I expect you to treat this journey in strictest confidence."

"You can trust in me, ma'am." The man gave the folded notes an appreciative glance before tucking them away in his coat pocket. "I'm honored." He clambered back to his position, took up the reins, and urged the horses away at a trot.

The women stood together at the intersection of two narrow streets. They were alone. Even the guards from the gate of the Alser

Barracks across the way had withdrawn to the relative warmth of the guardroom.

To their left rose the elegant buildings that housed many of the doctors and professors from the General Hospital and the adjoining Faculty of Medicine. It was not long until midnight, and only a few lights still glowed in the windows.

Along the right-hand side of the street ran the walls of the General Hospital. The birthing house was just one part of the hospital complex, which extended from Sensengasse to the north, Alser Strasse in the south, the surgical Military Academy to the west, and Spitalgasse to the east. Beyond the cone of light, they could just make out a closed wooden double door set in the wall.

"Come away from the light!" The woman with the bag firmly nudged the girl toward the door and then knocked vigorously with the heavy bronze ring in its center. Soon they heard a bolt sliding back, and the porter opened just wide enough to let through one person at a time.

At that very moment, the bells of the nearby Votive Church rang out for Midnight Mass. The young woman gave a weary sigh, then stepped through the door behind her companion.

The two women now stood in a passage lit by a single lantern hanging from the vaulted ceiling. The porter bolted the entry again and led them down a door-lined corridor. Gas lamps cast a flickering light on the flagstones and whitewashed walls.

"Frau Pfeiffer is expecting us," announced the older woman. "Where is she? I made a point of sending a message about our arrival."

Just then, a door opened and a reassuringly sturdy little woman stepped out. She wore a black dress and a starched white pinafore that made a crinkling sound as she bustled toward them. A white cap covered her hair, but strands of gray escaped across her forehead. Her round cheeks were pink with exertion.

"Good evening, ladies. My name is Josepha Pfeiffer. I am the matron of the foundling home." She gave both veiled women a long and careful look, then let her gaze rest on the expectant one. "I'll take you to your room." She picked up the travel bag that the companion had put down on the floor.

"Can't let you through without collecting the admission fee," remarked the porter. "Can't let the lady into the private areas without that."

The young woman nodded and turned to her companion, but before she could speak, a fresh contraction tore through her, making her cry out. In a blink, Josepha was at the girl's side. "Please allow me to deal with the formalities, ma'am. But now I'll take this lady to her confinement."

The older woman turned to the younger. "I'll be here to collect you tomorrow afternoon. Three o'clock sharp."

Josepha escorted the young woman down the corridor. "Not so far now," she said soothingly as the girl moaned with every step, and they came to a halt outside a door on the right. Josepha pushed firmly on the handle and stepped into the dark room. There was a crack and a whoosh as she lit the gas ceiling lamp. "Please, do come in."

Moving with difficulty, the woman made her way to the bed in the center of the room and heaved a sigh of relief as she lay down. She remained still for a few moments. Then she took off her gloves and fur hat, dropping them to the floor. But she didn't remove the veil. Women who had arranged to give birth anonymously were permitted to remain so throughout the proceedings.

Setting the travel bag down on the floor, Josepha went to the window and closed the curtains. Then she checked the washbasin for soap, clean towels, and carbolic disinfectant. One glance in the cupboard confirmed there were enough extra towels and sheets. A huge pan of water simmered on the stove in the corner. The housemaids had made a good job of preparing the birthing room.

Josepha turned back to the woman gasping and whimpering on the bed. "I'm sure you won't be waiting for the babe too long now. I've told the doctor and the midwife. They'll be here any moment. Here now, let me help you undress."

Josepha went over to the bed, picked the gloves and hat off the floor, and placed them on the bedside cabinet. Then she helped the young woman out of her cape made of sable, the same silky fur as her hat, and hung it over a hook on the wall. Last of all she undid the girl's soft woolen dress and slid it down over her rounded belly, her legs, and her feet, revealing delicate cambric underwear, silk stockings, and the prettiest of leather button boots. The nightdress that Josepha found in the travel bag was, she noticed as she slipped it over the young woman's head, finer than any Sunday frock she'd ever owned.

Of the twenty-five unmarried women arriving at the Viennese Maternity Clinic on this Christmas Eve to be relieved of the unwanted fruit of their indiscretion, only this unknown figure had the means to pay the considerable sum of 720 crowns for a comfortable birthing room. Most of the women Josepha had cared for in her thirty years had been chambermaids, factory workers, or day laborers unable to afford the protection of anonymity. They were permitted to give birth free of charge in the maternity ward, but in return, had to give their names and addresses and also be subjected to their deliveries being used as a means of visual instruction for medical students. On top of this, they were then required to act as wet nurses for other foundling babies, often up to four at one time.

Josepha draped the blanket over the pregnant woman's belly. "I need your emergency envelope. Is it in the bag?"

The young woman nodded weakly. If she were to die in child-birth, this sealed envelope would give up the secret of her name and the address of the relatives to be informed of the child's existence. If every-thing went well, the envelope would be returned on her departure.

Yet another little mite who'll never know where he comes from or who his parents are, thought Josepha.

She found the envelope beneath a clean bodice in the bottom of the bag. As she took it out, her fingers felt something raised, as if embossed, on the back. The young woman behind her started whim-pering louder, so she quickly tucked the document in the breast pocket of her pinafore and hurried over to the bed.

The pregnant woman was now sitting up and seemed to be looking down at her belly. Josepha put her hand on her shoulder and said, "Are you alright?"

"I don't think so!"

Josepha threw back the blanket to reveal a large wet mark, yellow in color and giving off a sickly sweet odor.

"Your waters have broken," Josepha explained. "This is quite nor-mal. The birth is starting."

A few minutes later, a young man came into the room and intro-duced himself as Dr. Fuchs. Following him was the senior midwife, an older woman with years of experience. The doctor took a quick look at the admission papers he'd collected from the porter. "First-time birth."

He observed the pregnant woman trembling on the edge of the bed while Josepha covered the mattress with a clean sheet and cast the wet linen into a corner of the room. Her role was to receive the baby after the birth, give it the appropriate immediate care, and then take it to the foundling home only a few minutes away on Alser Strasse. But so few staff had access to these anonymous deliveries that she tended to take on other duties as well.

Meanwhile, the midwife was ready to examine the young woman. "Please lie down again, bend your knees, and place your feet hip-width apart."

Instead of doing as she was asked, the young woman drew the blanket right up to her chin, so it was the midwife who had to place her legs in the correct position and then reach beneath the blanket to palpate the birth canal.

"Everything's as normal," she informed the doctor.

The young woman had endured the examination with a degree of indifference, but now she suddenly sat upright.

"I don't want any pain!"

"I'm afraid I can't prevent that." Dr. Fuchs came over to the bed.

"But I know there's something you can give me!"

"You're referring to chloroform. I can only administer that in the final phase of the delivery. And it's not without risk."

"Do it anyway! Aargh!" The pain of the next contraction swept through her. "Holy Mary, mother of God, I can't bear it! I should have put an end to it right at the start. Then I wouldn't have to suffer this torture."

You stuck-up little thing, thought Josepha. *All you're thinking about is yourself. You don't give a damn about the poor mite. If you did, you'd have sought out a good home for it and not left it to the foundling home.*

"The babe's head is already coming!" cried the midwife. With her left hand, she pushed aside the mother's knee, checking the position of the baby again with her right.

The young woman screamed and thrashed from side to side.

"Hold her, Matron, so she can't fall off the bed!" exclaimed the doctor, himself grabbing the flailing arms.

Josepha pressed down on her shoulders as the young woman fought them with every ounce of strength she had.

"Chloroform," she gasped. "Doctor, I beg you!"

The doctor frowned. Going over to the bag he'd left by the wash-stand, he took out a small glass bottle with a pump device attached to a tube that led to a leather mask. Without dislodging the woman's veil, he placed the mask over her mouth and nose and used the little pump to release a fine mist of chloroform. This should have given her immediate relief, but her body remained tense.

"More!" she gasped, the mask distorting the sound.

"Only a little." The doctor was firm. Too high a dose and the contractions would weaken or stop. In the worst case, the woman could become too numbed to push the baby out.

Even after this second burst of chloroform, the woman was demanding yet more relief, but Dr. Fuchs would have none of it. This set the woman off again, and she wildly rocked her body from side to side. Even the midwife found herself saying, "Sir, can we just give her the stuff for the sake of peace? Then we can get the babe out."

Half an hour later, there was still no progress with the delivery. The midwife did another examination and realized the baby was face up. "No wonder she's been screaming. This one's going to be a stargazer!"

Dr. Fuchs looked alarmed. "In that position, the head's too big for such a narrow pelvis."

"The lady's fit for nothing now, after so much chloroform," observed the midwife.

Josepha, the doctor, and the midwife stood and looked at the young woman, now in a stupor. The contractions had already stopped.

"If mother and child are to survive, forceps are the only option," Dr. Fuchs declared.

Josepha was shocked. She'd attended a number of forceps deliveries and knew the process was both dangerous and painful for the baby. Even when the tool was used by an expert, it always caused bruising, sometimes lacerations and nerve damage. The ordeal could even result in the baby's death.

"Matron, you will be in charge of the anesthetic pump." The doctor's voice jolted her out of her musings. "If the patient shows any sign of waking during the operation, give her three doses immediately."

"But my responsibility is the baby. Who'll see to the child if I'm busy giving anesthetic to this lady?"

"Just do what the doctor says," snapped the midwife. "You know what a drama there'll be if this lady wakes too soon. Then the only baby you'll be seeing to will be a dead one."

Josepha knew the midwife was right but felt uneasy as she took the glass bottle and pump from the doctor.

Dr. Fuchs took the forceps from his bag. At one end were two handles for opening and closing the instrument, at the other, the two slightly curved spoonlike structures.

You'll need to be really strong and be ready to fight for your first breath, thought Josepha as she watched how carefully the doctor placed the spoons inside the woman. He had to rely entirely on feel in order to take hold of the baby's head. Once he had positioned the forceps, he would normally wait for the next contraction, but the contractions had stopped and the baby could die if left too long in the birth canal, so he started immediately to pull and turn the baby with the utmost care.

"The head's out!" confirmed the midwife, the relief in her voice almost palpable.

Josepha put the anesthetic down on the bedside table, hurried to the cupboard for towels, and positioned herself at the foot of the bed. She felt she'd done her duty by this woman who refused to take responsibility for the new life inside her. All that mattered now was the child.

Her throat tightened when she saw the little one's head. Thanks to the doctor's skill, the face no longer looked upward but to the side. The eyes were shut and the head covered in a pale mucus as was normal, but the bloodied bruising was clear to see. Josepha hated to think what this innocent creature had had to go through even before taking that first breath.

At least the worst was over. Putting the forceps aside and using just his hands, the doctor pulled the little body free.

Now the baby lay between the mother's legs, still splayed across the mattress. The midwife bound the umbilical cord with thread she'd previously sterilized in the water still bubbling on the stove. Dr. Fuchs used scissors to cut the only remaining tie between mother and child. He unbuttoned his gown and took his watch from his vest pocket.

"Half past five in the morning," he announced. "The first child born this Christmas Day and the 6,572nd child born in the year of our Lord, 1889. And it's a girl."

"She's so quiet." Josepha leaned over the little bundle that lay motionless on the bloodied sheet. The wet and reddened skin, wrinkled and coated with debris, seemed too large for the little body. Using the corner of a towel, she dabbed muck from the newborn's nose and mouth.

"You'd do better with a good smack on the backside. Then you'll know if it's alive." Josepha was used to this advice from the midwife, but it made her throat tighten yet again.

For her, there was no question of striking this little girl after such a difficult and painful journey into the world. Instead, she gently massaged the little body with the towel, clearing away all the blood and streaks of mucus. Still the child didn't move. So, Josepha wrapped her in a fresh towel, picked her up, and held her close. With just her index finger, she stroked the baby's damp hair, forehead, cheeks, little ears, and tiny mouth.

"Breathe, little mite, breathe," she whispered.

The child's lips gave a little twitch, her eyes blinked and opened, and she stared fixedly at Josepha. There was a croaky whimper.

Laughing with delight, Josepha put her index finger close to the baby's tiny right hand and was overjoyed to feel it gripped and squeezed.

"Has the lady disclosed what her Christmas angel's going to be called?" The midwife asked as she set about getting the bloodied sheet out from under the young woman's body.

Josepha looked at the newborn's mother. She was just coming around. Dazed and exhausted after the delivery, she lay flat.

"You have a healthy baby girl, ma'am," Josepha told her. "What shall we call her?"

But the woman just stared at the ceiling in silence.

Chapter Two

Vienna, 1890

Children's footsteps clattered down the corridor and came to a noisy halt outside of Josepha's office in the east wing of the foundling home.

"If you tattle on me, I'll give you a smack in the face!" This was the high, clear voice of a young boy.

"You wouldn't dare!" shot back a second.

There was an exclamation of anger, then loud wailing. Josepha sighed, pushed back her chair, and went to the door. As she looked out onto the corridor, a grunting mass of four arms, four legs, and two disheveled mops of hair rolled toward her feet.

"Stop that immediately!" She bent down and got hold of one protruding ear.

"Ow!"

The mass stopped rolling around, and the second voice moaned, "Matron, please, Paul—"

"I'm not interested!" Josepha snapped. "Stand up and make up."

Grudgingly the boys got to their feet and stared at one another, their lips stubbornly sealed.

"So? What're you waiting for? Shake hands."

They managed a brief handshake.

Josepha nodded. "Now go to your rooms, and no more fighting. It's lunchtime. Quiet time."

She watched the lads as they trotted away, then closed her door quietly.

When she sat back down at her desk, she thought how welcome the little interruption had actually been. Updating the records for all the permanent residents of the foundling home was not among her favorite tasks. She'd much rather be caring for the children and, whenever time permitted, playing with them, singing, or reading aloud.

She adjusted her spectacles and took a new folder off the pile on her desk: "Number 6,572."

Fanny, thought Josepha. As always, her heart seemed to melt at the thought of this little girl, the first baby to be born last Christmas morning.

Josepha had selected the name because that's what she'd have called her own daughter, if the dear Lord had seen fit to let her have one. The biological mother had raised no objection. She'd refused even to look at the child.

Josepha gazed out of her office window at the west wing, enjoying the sight of sunlight playing on the newborn ward. She could just make out the indistinct babble of female voices and crying infants that always accompanied the daily throng of up to two dozen caretakers, foster mothers, coming to pick up babies. These women received money from state coffers to care for a babe, plus extra for laundry and diapers. They came from the families of tradespeople and workers in Vienna and the immediate surroundings. The wages their menfolk brought home didn't go far, so the additional income was a relief—and not always used for its intended purpose. Although there were inspections, these were, to Josepha's mind, few and far between. What she'd have liked was to keep all her little charges in the foundling home under her protection. But they only had just over one hundred places, and these were for sick babies not ready to go into care or for returning children who had been neglected or mistreated.

Once her forceps injuries had healed, even little Fanny had been placed in the care of a foster mother. That was three months ago now, and Josepha had often wondered how the little one was faring. She doubted very much whether the natural mother had ever given a moment's thought to her daughter's fate.

Sometimes the wrong people are blessed with children, she mused as she opened Fanny's folder.

The baby's birth certificate and smallpox vaccination document were safely filed here. There was only one further paper, a blank sheet ruled into columns. Josepha started to fill in the spaces with place of birth, date of birth, the baby's first name, and the name and address of the foster family. In the column for the surname, Josepha wrote that family's name: Schindler. The "parents" column remained blank because it had been an anonymous birth.

During her many years of service, Josepha had never come across a woman as indifferent to her own flesh and blood. Fanny's mother had even turned down a certificate of admission when she left. This document bore the child's designated number—the only means the mother could ever have to find her daughter again.

And yet, someone beyond the walls of the foundling home was clearly not indifferent to the child's fate. Josepha recalled how taken aback she had been when the first payment had appeared in her bank account. It was an anonymous cash deposit specified for child number 6,572.

The amount was not lavish, but it was generous.

Josepha had questioned the bank clerk, but the man insisted that he had no memory of the person who had made the payment.

On the first of the following month, the payment came again, and yesterday, Josepha had received the third monthly sum. Her spine tingled with unease at the thought of how someone could possibly have discovered the details of her personal bank account. It must be someone influential and well connected, that was for sure. Someone who knew about child number 6,572.

How is that little soul getting on?

Josepha had been sure to pick out a reliable caretaker for Fanny, one who had already raised children from the foundling home without a blemish on her record. She hoped this woman would take good care of Fanny and perhaps even love her, but it had still been painful when she'd put the baby in her foster mother's arms.

Josepha knew full well that she wasn't supposed to feel like that. She was there for the welfare of all the children. She wasn't supposed to be more attached to one than the others.

But somehow, she mused, *that little mite hasn't let go of me ever since she first gripped my finger with her tiny hand.*

She looked at the file that held these few scraps of information about Fanny's life and thought about the money from the unknown benefactor.

If there was someone who wanted Fanny to grow up without suffering, then Josepha had to fulfill this wish. She decided that, the next day, she would pay a call on the foster mother. If everything was as it should be, she would give the woman the three months' worth of money. And she would carry on doing so, month by month, for as long as the money arrived.

Suddenly, she no longer minded the mysterious donor. Quite the opposite, she was grateful for the excuse to go and see the child.

The following morning, Josepha stepped down from the horse-drawn omnibus onto Taborstrasse in the Leopoldstadt district. After a long cold winter, the locals were now drawn outdoors by the warmth, light, and sunshine. Housewives were on their way to the shops, servant girls pushed strollers, and craftsmen sawed and hammered in the yards behind their workshops, while traders rushed to the nearby stock market.

Josepha stopped in a baker's shop and bought a paper cone of left-over cake crusts as a gift for the foster family's own two children. Feeling unusually light of spirit, Josepha bustled onward and soon arrived at the courtyard occupied by Johann Spiering, a carriage builder. She knew from Frau Schindler's file that her husband worked here as a carpenter. From the barn came the grating and rasping of saws, and she spotted a number of workmen fitting a newly built carriage onto its chassis. But she didn't know what Frau Schindler's husband looked like, so she didn't stop. Two buildings farther, there was a synagogue. Next to it was an old, narrow house with an oriel window. The ground floor was given over to a small print works, while people lived upstairs. Josepha checked for the house number and nodded to herself. This was where Fanny lived.

She walked through an archway and into the back courtyard. An elderly woman was wrestling a broom, and two boys played with a spinning top.

"Good day! Where will I find the Schindler family?"

"Where d'you think? Where all the racket's comin' from." The old lady continued her angry sweeping. "Them dirty kids is always screamin' their heads off."

From somewhere in the rear courtyard dwellings came the persistent sound of a baby crying. Josepha hurried toward the noise and pushed open the dismal entry door of a dilapidated two-story building. The musty smell of damp hit her the moment she entered the communal hallway. The baby's yelling was now very close. Josepha banged on the wooden door. Nothing. Just as she was about to knock again, she heard footsteps. The door opened a crack, and she made out the figure of a woman—gray-faced, careworn, her hair unkempt, and her dress filthy.

Josepha's mouth fell open. Where was the clean and tidy woman who'd collected Fanny from the foundling home three months earlier?

"Frau Schindler?"

"What do you want?" The woman's hostility was obvious.

Before Josepha could reply, a boy of around four or five appeared from behind his mother's skirts and observed this stranger with a mix of suspicion and curiosity. In spite of the drafty hallway, he wore neither socks nor shoes. His short trousers exposed bony knees and startlingly spindly legs.

"Good day, Frau Schindler." Josepha hid her horror and forced a kind smile. "Perhaps you remember me. I'm Josepha Pfeiffer, matron at the foundling home. I would like to see Fanny." She craned her neck to see past the woman. The inside hall was narrow and dark, but she could tell the baby's crying came from behind a closed door at the back.

"Let's step inside," she suggested. "It's difficult to talk out here."

"That won't do at the moment," said the Schindler woman quickly as she tried to shut the door, but Josepha was too quick for her.

She pushed the woman and boy aside and hurried toward the other door. On lifting the latch and stepping forward, she found herself in a cramped, unlit kitchen-cum-living room. It was cold here, too, and stank of sweat and mold. The only light came through the one window, a pitiful geranium in a pot on the narrow ledge. In front of it stood a sofa with a little crocheted blanket thrown across its back.

But Josepha's attention was drawn straight to the wooden table in the middle of the room. On the tabletop lay Fanny, screaming with all her might. She was so tightly swaddled that she couldn't move, and only her head was visible. Near her head lay a so-called comfort pouch, a small linen bag filled with flour and sugar soaked in liquor that people gave babies to suck on. Josepha viewed comfort pouches as highly damaging for a host of reasons, and no infant was ever pacified this way in the Vienna Foundling House.

The moment she loosened the tight swaddle, Fanny grew calmer. That's when the vile smell hit Josepha's nostrils. She freed the baby, lifted her up, and was appalled to find the little body caked with excrement. There were open wounds on the little bottom, and the infant felt suspiciously light. As Josepha gently handled the child, she noticed with horror the sunken belly and protruding ribcage.

"Holy Mary, mother of God. What have you done to the child, Schindler?"

Her anger elicited a piercing shriek from under the table. Josepha bent down to find a little girl of about twelve months staring up at her with frightened eyes, yellow mucus streaming from her nose. Her arms and legs, like that of her brother, were shockingly thin.

Josepha was beside herself. "When did these children last eat?" She glared at Schindler, incensed.

But the woman just stood silently in the doorway as if rooted to the spot, one arm around the boy.

Josepha struggled to hold back her anger. Was there really nothing to eat in this place?

In the far corner of the room was a cast-iron stove with a kettle and a large, deep pot that could be used for boiling laundry or making preserves. Behind the stove was a shelf full of crockery and more pans. A washing line had been rigged up here, and from it hung various pinafores and shirts. Beneath it was a linen basket overflowing with dirty clothes. Still holding Fanny, Josepha went over to the stove and peered inside the deep pot. It was full of water. She tested it with her finger. Ice cold. One glance in the scuttle told her there was no coal.

She noticed a small door in the corner and guessed it led to the pantry. Inside were plenty of wooden shelves with baskets, glass storage jars, and bowls. All were empty save one bowl, which contained a dried-out bread crust. Two wooden crates stood on the floor. In one of these, Josepha spotted a few potatoes, in the other, three onions. Josepha slammed the pantry shut.

"Where's the baby food?"

Frau Schindler wasn't nursing, so she was supposed to give Fanny a gruel with boiled milk. But Josepha saw neither milk nor oats.

Schindler stared at the floor in silence.

"Can it really be there's no food in the house?" shouted Josepha. "Where's the money you receive for Fanny? She looks half-starved! And when did you last change her diaper? You should be ashamed of yourself, letting an infant get into such a state! And your own children don't look much better."

"I was just goin' to change her when you got here." The woman's voice shook.

"Don't lie to me! I'd bet there isn't a single clean diaper in this place."

Schindler's face reddened, and she chewed at her lips.

"Fetch me some clean towels from somewhere, dammit. Quick or there'll be hell to pay."

The woman shuffled out and disappeared behind a side door, returning with tears in her eyes and a few halfway-clean hand towels.

Josepha snatched them, went back to the stove, and dunked one of the towels in the large pot. Then she lay Fanny back down on the table and wiped her down as best she could. She dried the tiny babe with the second towel and used the third as a diaper.

"I presume you have no clean baby clothes?"

Schindler shook her head. Josepha sighed, took off her own pinafore, and wrapped it around Fanny's little body. Then she tied her woolen shawl across her chest like a sling, lifted Fanny up, and gently bedded her down inside it. The baby girl let out a little sigh and snuggled close to Josepha's ample bosom.

"I'll be making notes in your file about the conditions here." Josepha held her arms protectively around Fanny. "And I shall, of course, take the babe with me. Until further notice, you will not be given another foster child."

Josepha was furious with Schindler, but also with herself. If only she hadn't taken so long to make an inspection visit, she'd have spared the child suffering and hunger. Clearly, Schindler wouldn't now receive any of the cash from Fanny's anonymous benefactor. Thank goodness Josepha hadn't let on that it even existed.

"The kids are always cryin'." Schindler's soft voice sounded exhausted and desperate. "All three of them. But Fanny's the worst. That's why I gave her the comfort pouch, but she won't take it."

"Those pouches are bad practice. Liquor is bad enough for adults. It's disastrous for children." Josepha was still fired up with rage. She picked up the linen pouch from where it lay and tossed it into the cold fireplace. "The children cry because they're hungry and thin as rakes."

She recalled the baker's cone in her basket. She carefully unfolded the wrapping, picked out a little chunk of honey cake, and held it to Fanny's lips. The baby began eagerly sucking at the sweet morsel. Then Josepha bent down toward the little girl under the table. The child had stopped crying now but was chewing at her knuckles instead. Josepha handed her a delicious morsel, too, and placed a couple of other goodies in her lap. The child's eyes widened, and then her face broke into a smile as she munched happily on the chunks of cake. Her brother rushed over, scooted straight under the table, and tried to take it all from her.

Josepha grabbed him by the waist of his short trousers and hauled him back. "Do you want a clip around the ear, boy?" She showed him the cone, still half-full. "You'll get this if you promise me you'll leave your little sister in peace."

The boy nodded readily and stuffed a handful of cake in his mouth the moment Josepha let him have the cone.

She turned back to face Schindler. "Now, tell me exactly what happened here."

"Few weeks back, my husband had an accident with the saw," the woman said haltingly. "Lost his right thumb. Now he can't work. I know it was wrong, usin' the babe's allowance. But I had no choice. An' it didn't stretch for three kids. If the Good Lord's angry with me, so be it." Her voice trailed off.

A carpenter with no thumb? *Look how quickly a family can find themselves in dire straits,* Josepha thought to herself.

"Where's your husband now?"

Perhaps Herr Schindler was over at the railway station or the riverfront trying to pick up unskilled work, prayed Josepha.

His wife's response was bitter. "He's in some hole of a bar, drinking away the tiny bit of money we had. Most of that's already gone to hospital payments. An' we're behind on the rent. Sometimes I can take in a little laundry, but I can't go work in a factory cos then nobody's here with the kids." Schindler broke down in tears. "It's killing me, Matron. It's only cos of them I haven't thrown myself in the Danube."

"Now, now," said Josepha. "Put that kind of thing out of your mind. Could you maybe move in with relatives and save the rent?"

"My sister and brother-in-law would take us in, but they live in Erdberg. It's real hard to find a job out there, an' I don't wanna be a burden."

Josepha thought hard. She couldn't simply walk out with Fanny and turn her back on this family's misery. But the city had a charitable organization for poverty relief, and she knew a couple of staff there. "I'll send Herr Urban to see you tomorrow morning. He's the poverty relief adviser with responsibility for this district. He'll be sure to get you back on your feet."

"Any help at all is good," replied the woman weakly.

But Josepha was relieved to see a spark of hope in her eyes. She rummaged in her basket, pulled out her purse, and put a little bundle of banknotes on the table. "Get the kids something to eat and some fresh milk. And don't ever think about that river again!"

"No, Frau Pfeiffer. May God reward you."

That same evening, Josepha stood by Fanny's crib in one of the infant dormitories. The little girl had had a warm bath, a fresh diaper, clean clothes, and a good feeding and was now in a peaceful sleep, her tummy full and her spirit calm. Josepha reached out and gently touched the baby's soft cheeks with the tip of her finger. She would never give this little mite away again.

Chapter Three

"What a smart miss you've turned into, little mite!" Josepha proudly looked at her beloved girl from head to toe as if she were her own daughter. Or perhaps granddaughter, seeing as the matron was soon to celebrate her sixty-seventh birthday.

At fourteen, the girl she still thought of as "little mite" was such a pretty maid, with strawberry blonde hair, brown eyes, and a body already showing some womanly curves. In her long blue skirt with a matching suit jacket and a white blouse underneath, she looked very grown-up.

And she nearly is, thought Josepha, trying not to feel too wistful. At the end of April, only four weeks away, Fanny would finish school.

The headmistress of the Alser High School for Girls had made a point of seeking out Fanny's unofficial guardian to be sure she knew that Fanny was the very top of her class. She had suggested that Fanny continue her education at the lycée, but Josepha had rejected the idea out of hand. Fanny did not belong to one of those society families that expected daughters to fill the couple of years before marriage with extra schooling, most of which Josepha believed would be pointless. In her view, fourteen was the right age for Fanny to learn a trade and provide for herself.

But that didn't stop her wanting to mark the occasion with a special gift—the fabric for her end-of-school ball gown. Josepha wanted to go to one of the Mariahilferstrasse shops, but Fanny had asked to go to Graben first. "I don't want to buy anything, just window-shop!" The girl had begged for so long that Josepha had given in.

Since then, Fanny had been bursting with excitement and could hardly think of anything else. Graben, with its luxury goods and its elegant cafés and restaurants, seemed like another world, so very different from the Alser district and the foundling home.

Josepha had always tried to raise Fanny to be modest and undemanding, for she knew her girl's anonymous, illegitimate birth would make life difficult for her. She hoped this excursion into the dazzling world of rich folk wouldn't turn her head. The monthly payments for child number 6,572 had remained untouched by Josepha, even when the public money automatically stopped on Fanny's tenth birthday. Fanny knew nothing of this nest egg, which had grown to be a tidy sum. Josepha had decided not to tell her until she reached adulthood in the eyes of the law. That was still ten years away.

Josepha had instead paid for Fanny's upbringing with her own wages. She was fonder of the child than of anyone in the world and was happy to support her in this way. But Josepha's salary was small, so Fanny had to contribute as well. She already worked afternoons in the foundling home after finishing her homework. Her initial forays, into the kitchen and the ironing room, had been unsuccessful. Fanny had grumbled that the work was boring and stupid. The cook had gotten fed up with her constant answering back, and the woman in charge of ironing had forbidden Fanny from returning after she singed holes in the bed linen not once but twice. After all this, Josepha had to work hard to get Fanny into the sewing room, but to the amazement of all concerned, she took right to it. Fanny was quick to learn—with needle and thread as well as the sewing machine. She loved making baby clothes for the tiny residents of the home, turning out little bodices, trousers, smocks, and bibs, and decorating them with pretty ribbon and braid.

Perhaps my little mite will be a dressmaker, thought Josepha as she linked arms with Fanny.

She looked thoughtfully at this beloved child who, with increasing enthusiasm, was taking in the regal shop windows and the profusion of elegant displays. There were shops specializing in corsets, silk stockings, and underwear; others tempted her with hats and gloves. Then there were displays of crystal and porcelain, soaps and perfume, or children's toys and the fanciest of strollers. Here and there were confectioners and makers of pralines with the most exquisite chocolates and miniature pastries on show. Every proprietor proudly displayed their name over the door and, in most cases, also boasted the double eagle, indicating that this shop supplied the royal household.

Fanny stopped and pressed her nose against every window and watched with curiosity as well-dressed gentlemen and ladies strolled from shop to shop.

"How I'd love to have enough money to afford such beautiful things," she sighed. "And to live in a big house and eat cake in a high-class café whenever I want."

Josepha laughed. "I fear you'll have to catch yourself a prince, or a count at the very least."

"Maybe all I need is to find out who my parents are," retorted Fanny with a cheeky look.

Josepha let out a sigh. "We've been over that."

The mystery had gnawed at Fanny's heart all her young life. As soon as the child was old enough, Josepha had explained how her mother had delivered anonymously. From then on, she'd started looking out for passing ladies whom she liked the look of, wondering out loud if any of them could be her mother. For a while, she had persisted in the belief that her father was a prince living under a curse, her mother a princess, and that they were being kept in a secret place by a wicked enchantress who would not allow them to get to their daughter.

Fanny was long past such fantasies, but the notion that she'd never know her parents left her with an underlying sadness—and resentment. "I still think you must know something, and just don't want to tell me. You were even there when I was born."

"What nonsense! If I knew anything more, I'd have told you. But your mother wouldn't even take her admission certificate," Josepha shot back. When she saw the heartbreak flicker across Fanny's face, she added, "I'm sorry, my little mite. Let's not argue on this lovely afternoon. Let's just enjoy it."

Fanny nodded. "You're right, Frau Pfeiffer, and I'm sorry, too. Please don't be mad at me."

Arm in arm, they strolled past the Trinity Column, erected by Emperor Leopold I over two hundred years earlier in gratitude for the end of the plague epidemic. Then Fanny spotted something that took her mind off her background completely: a motorcar parked in front of a shop selling hunting rifles. This new way of getting about, like a carriage but without the horses, was a rare sight in Vienna.

"One day I'm going to have my own car and drive it myself!" Fanny announced as they paused to watch the uniformed chauffeur polish the already-gleaming paintwork.

Just then, the gun shop door opened and a couple stepped out. The gentleman looked older than his years, his face kindly but pale and his nose oddly deformed. He leaned heavily on a stick, but this impression of fragility was to some extent dispelled by his military uniform adorned with braid and medals. The lady accompanying him was young and beautiful. She wore a picture hat and a fashionable dress that couldn't hide the fact she was in "a certain condition." The chauffeur hurriedly put away his cloth, opened the vehicle door, and helped the lady and gentleman climb aboard. Then he set about starting up the engine, fitting a crank-handle under the hood and vigorously turning it. Soon, the motorcar was on its way, thundering and roaring as it went.

"Holy Mary, mother of God!" cried Josepha. "That was Otto the Handsome with the Robinson woman!" She crossed herself.

"Otto the Handsome?" Fanny asked. "Who's that?"

"Archduke Otto, a nephew of the Kaiser."

"I don't think he's handsome. Just old!"

"People just call him that."

"Why?"

"My child, you wouldn't understand." Josepha wanted to continue walking, but Fanny had her by the sleeve.

"Why wouldn't I understand?"

"Because you're too young."

"No, I'm not. Try me. You'll see."

Josepha sighed. "People call him that because, as a young man, he was very attractive."

"You mean he had a lot of affairs."

"For heaven's sake, child. How do you know about that sort of thing?"

"From the magazines you sometimes leave on your desk. There's often gossip about how some society gentleman is having yet another affair with a lady."

"That's enough now, Fanny!" snapped Josepha, resolving never to leave her magazines around again.

But Fanny kept going. "That lady with the archduke, was she his mistress or his wife?"

"Her? Saints preserve us, she's one of those actresses!"

"Is that why you just called her Robinson?"

Josepha was fit to burst. "Enough, child! Let's just get your shopping done. Or do you not want the fabric anymore?" She urged her little ward onward, but Fanny had already spotted the next distraction.

"It's so chic!" Fanny had caught sight of a shop window that extended from ground level right up to the next story and ran the full breadth of the premises. Red and gold sun blinds stood open, cleverly catching the attention of passersby. At the immaculately painted black door stood a page in full livery, while eye-catching golden lettering above boldly stated "Sarah Moreau—Couture," the Austro-Hungarian Empire coat of arms confirming the lady as purveyor to the court. A red carpet had been rolled out from the entrance to the edge of the sidewalk to save ladies' heels from catching between slabs as they stepped from their carriage or automobile.

Fanny's pretty mouth fell open as she realized that *couture* must mean the most fabulous outfits anyone could possibly imagine. Instantly, almost reverently, she fell to studying each mannequin draped with a ball gown. These luxuriantly full skirts, impressive trains, and exquisite embroidery were more beautiful than anything she'd ever seen.

What was the material, and how would it feel to put on a dress like that?

"Let's keep going, little mite," Josepha said, bustling on behind her. "Otherwise we'll never get to Mariahilferstrasse today!"

Fanny slowly turned and whispered, "Do you think we could go in?"

"In there? Don't be silly." Josepha shook her head firmly.

Fanny looked at the finely painted door. The page gave her a kindly smile.

"Oh, please! Only for a minute. Just to look!" begged Fanny, taking a few steps toward the door.

"Absolutely not! A place like that's not for the likes of us."

"Please, Frau Pfeiffer! I'd love to go in!" Fanny went a couple more steps closer to the door, now pulling the reluctant Josepha with her.

The page gave a little bow in their direction. "The honor is mine, ladies. Gustav, at your service."

He held open the door, and before Josepha could say a word, Fanny had sailed past him into the fashion house. The older lady was momentarily at a loss, but then hurried after her young charge, set on dragging her right out of the shop. Gustav's additional bow and enthusiastic "I kiss your hand, madam" went right past her.

Fanny stood stock-still just inside the entrance, her eyes popping out. The huge salon was illuminated by a crystal chandelier that cast the bright light that only electricity can, reflecting off the white walls hung with silken wallpaper. There were huge, gold-framed mirrors everywhere and a red Oriental carpet that muffled any undue sounds. Glass-topped cases displayed decorative feathers, braid, lace, and buttons. Covering the back wall was floor-to-ceiling shelving divided into compartments full of fabrics of every type and color. In front of this was a long sales counter. Sales girls dressed in white blouses and black skirts moved quickly and easily up and down little ladders as they took bolts of cloth from the compartments and presented them to clients at the counter. Other clients leaned over the glass-topped cases, excitedly pointing at items they found attractive, or lounged on the sofas lining the walls, sipping champagne as they leafed through thick catalogues.

"I had no idea there were places like this!" Fanny whispered to Josepha in wonder.

Josepha gripped her by the arm and tried to draw her back to the door. "You've had a look, and now it's time to go," she hissed.

But Fanny was unmovable. "Look over there! It's an elevator. Maybe it goes up to the workrooms where they make these gorgeous dresses! And that must be a telephone in that corner."

"That's all the same to me," grumbled Josepha. "Can't you see they're watching us? Let's get out of here!"

They both looked at the woman approaching them. She was strikingly slim and wore a simple black dress, but even more eye-catching was her silvery hair, expertly cut almost as short as a man's, and her cherry-red lip color. Fanny had never seen anything like it. The woman wasn't young, but she was incredibly elegant and modern.

"*Bonjour, mesdames.* How can I be of assistance?" Her voice was dark and husky. Fine lines appeared around her eyes when she broke into a smile, and a French accent confirmed that she was none other than the proprietress.

Fanny found the courage to speak up. "I'm looking for material for a ball gown. For my school-leaving ball."

There was a sharp intake of breath from Josepha, but Madame Moreau was first to respond. "It's perfectly natural that you want a special dress for this special occasion, mademoiselle. I'm sure we'll find something suitable."

"It'll ruin us," muttered Josepha.

Sarah Moreau turned to the older woman. "Please don't be concerned, madame. I shall make you an *offre acceptable*. A little something to drink? A glass of champagne, perhaps?"

Fanny squealed in delight, but Josepha shot her a look. "No, thank you, she's too young for alcohol."

"So just for madame?"

"No." Josepha shook her head. "It would go right to my head and get me muddled when it's time to pay!"

"As you wish." Madame Moreau gave them an amused smile. "Would you like to come this way?" She turned and sailed to the counters in a cloud of rosewater and tobacco.

Fanny almost skipped in her wake. It was like a dream. *Were clients always treated like royalty in shops like this?*

Josepha followed, fearful that this experience would put all sorts of ideas in her girl's head. But when she saw her little mite's eyes shining as she leaned in for a closer look at the fabulous fabrics that Sarah Moreau set out—silk, velvet, tulle, chiffon, brocade—she was overwhelmed with the joy of seeing her so happy.

The little mite really hasn't had it easy in life, thought Josepha. *One little luxury's allowed, after all.*

As Madame Moreau presented the fabrics to her two clients, she explained how Fanny might work with each one, showing her braid, buttons, and lace. At the same time, she asked the girl for her own ideas and listened to her replies with interest. Then she would unroll cloth from the bolt and drape it around her young shoulders, waist and hips, gently nudging the girl in front of one of the mirrors and smiling when this unusual young client exclaimed with pleasure. Fanny eventually decided on pale blue silk for the bodice and lilac tulle for the skirt.

When Madame Moreau got to work measuring out the cloth with a wooden ruler, Fanny turned to Josepha, saying very earnestly, "This must be a lot more expensive than the stuff in the Mariahilferstrasse shops."

Her guardian was touched. "If it will make you happy, little mite. And madame said she'd give us a good deal," she said, looking pointedly at the Frenchwoman.

"Thank you, Frau Pfeiffer, thank you a thousand times over! This is the best day of my life!" Fanny threw her arms around the startled Josepha and kissed her on both cheeks.

Madame Moreau was impressed by Fanny's choices. "A very good decision, superb with your complexion and your lovely copper hair color," she said as she expertly flipped over one of the bolts. "Do you need a pattern? We stock a good range of Butterick."

"Oh no. I can easily do the cutting myself. I know exactly how I want the gown to look."

Josepha frowned. "Are you really sure? You don't want to make any mistakes cutting costly cloth like this!"

"I do all the design and cutting for the baby clothes at the foundling home!"

"But that's tiny smocks and bodices, not ball gowns!"

"Please don't worry, Frau Pfeiffer. It's all in my head, truly," Fanny said reassuringly.

Josepha relented. "Alright, then. Let's look for some pretty buttons and bows for the finishing touches."

Fifteen minutes later, they were at the desk, where the silver cash register stood in all its gleaming glory. In spite of the proprietor's promise, the final figure seemed very high to Fanny. "I'd need to work in our sewing room for a whole month to earn that much," she whispered in shocked tones to Josepha.

"Don't fret." The older woman patted the girl's hand. She knew the price was extremely reasonable for material of this quality. Madame Moreau must have given them a considerable reduction, for whatever reason. "But no slipups when you're cutting," she added.

"Hand on heart," promised Fanny, her voice solemn.

A sales assistant carefully wrapped the purchases in tissue and then finished off with strong parcel paper. Josepha placed the bundle in her basket. Then Madame Moreau accompanied her two clients to the door. "So, you have just completed school, mademoiselle?"

"Yes. I leave officially in four weeks."

Madame paused. "You have a real sense for fashion. Have you ever thought of taking this up professionally, as your *métier*?"

Fanny stared at her. "No. Never."

Sarah Moreau looked at her with curiosity. "And what are your plans?"

Fanny glanced at Josepha. "I'd like to continue my education," she said hesitantly. "Go to a lycée, take the *Matura* exams. I am the top student in my class," she added with pride.

"What's all this? You want to carry on with school? First I've heard about it!" Josepha complained.

Fanny turned to her. "The headmistress said I should try. She thinks I'm smart enough."

Josepha gave a little grunt of indignation, privately noting there'd be a bone to pick with that headmistress next time their paths crossed. How on earth the woman could encourage Fanny to indulge in this nonsense, when she herself had stated loud and clear that the lycée was not on the table, was quite beyond her.

"We'll leave it for now, madame," said Sarah Moreau, placing a soothing hand on Josepha's arm. "Mademoiselle Fanny is a very clever young woman." Turning to the girl, she said, "Your plans are good, mademoiselle, but if you change your mind, you're most welcome to come and see me again."

After lunch on the following Sunday, Fanny and Josepha were ready to start work on the gown.

Fanny was first into the sewing room at the foundling home. She'd already made her own drawing of the dress and placed that first on the huge table in the center of the room. Then she went to the cupboard where they kept all the sewing implements, took out a large sheet of brown paper, and spread that on the table, too. Once Josepha had taken all her measurements, she would sketch the full pattern on here. She unrolled her drawing and carefully studied her design. Since she'd been working in the sewing room, she'd been making her own clothes but was all too aware that throwing together a straightforward skirt and blouse was very different from creating a ball gown. For this reason, she'd decided to go without any stylish pleats or flounces. She'd planned something very simple, with a loose upper part in the style of a blouse and a skirt that fell in two tiers.

The gown will just have to make its impression more through the fabric than a sophisticated cut, she thought as she took the precious bundle from the cupboard and put it on the table. With the greatest of care, she opened it up and looked at the material. She still couldn't quite believe she was now the owner of something so luxurious. The sky-blue sheen of the silk was heavenly and went perfectly with the lilac tulle. Her fingertips caressed the fabrics with the utmost care and respect. At that moment, the door opened and in came Josepha.

Since that afternoon at the fashion house, they had kept out of one another's way and avoided any discussion about the lycée. Their customary warmth had cooled. Josepha viewed Fanny's desire as nothing more than a foolish daydream, while Fanny felt the older woman wasn't taking her seriously.

"Good day!" Josepha swept past her, making a beeline for the cupboard to avoid looking at Fanny, or so it seemed to the girl.

"You don't need to help me with this, if you don't want to," she said rather pertly. "I can make the dress on my own."

Josepha opened the cupboard door and took out a measuring tape, a notebook, and a pencil and then banged it shut. Fanny's impertinent tone of voice loosed her pent-up anger. "And let you mess up all that cloth? You really are being a fool!"

"So I'm not allowed to do anything my own way?" shot back Fanny.

"Not if it's as stupid as that, no!"

Now Fanny's eyes flashed with anger. "For the last eight years, you've told me day after day how I must work hard at school and learn something. And now I've actually got the chance, and you won't let me take it. What's wrong with wanting to study for *Matura*?"

"*Matura*'s a luxury for rich people. And what would you do with it, anyway? Where would it lead? You seem to have forgotten your place in the world."

"How could I ever forget that? You never stop reminding me!" Fanny's voice was thick with tears. "But I'm smart enough to stay in school. The headmistress didn't tell me that for nothing."

Josepha was angry. Fanny had no inkling of the hours she'd spent pondering sending her to the lycée. But that would have taken all the money from the benefactor. School fees and school books really added up, never mind accommodation and meals. Josepha considered it irresponsible to use all her little mite's worldly wealth for such a project. This fund was reserved for other, more important matters that were bound to crop up. And Josepha's wages certainly wouldn't cover the cost of the lycée. Anyway, at the age of fourteen, her little charge was old enough to step out into the world. That's what Josepha had prepared her for—or tried to, at least.

Maybe I'm expecting too much, she thought to herself. *Maybe she's too young for maturity and foresight.* "Here now, let me take those measurements," she practically hummed, feeling calmer now.

The young girl did as she was told, staring sulkily at her feet while Josepha measured her shoulders, chest, back, waist, and hips.

"Listen to me, child. Only yesterday, the director reminded me you have to move out as soon as your schooling finishes. You have no choice but to provide for yourself, can you not see that?" Josepha knelt to measure Fanny's leg length, grimacing as her joints creaked.

"But I have such good grades, you know. Even in math. If we went together to see the director, perhaps I could live here another four years until I've done the *Matura*."

Josepha shook her head. "Your grades won't change a thing. You know the exception has already been made—all the other children are only allowed to stay here until their tenth birthday. Hold the end of the tape here on your hip."

Obediently, Fanny held one end of the measuring tape while Josepha stretched it to her right ankle.

"Not that far down, Frau Pfeiffer," said Fanny quickly. "The skirt is supposed to end here." She took the drawing off the table and held it right under Josepha's nose. This provoked an immediate frown.

"Absolutely not! You'd look like a dancing girl. You'll do me the courtesy of dressing decently for this ball."

"Decent is the same as boring, and I can be boring when I'm old."

"You'll walk out of here in a skirt that short over my dead body."

"It's calf length! And has an extralong train."

"You mean extra-vagant! The whole getup is extravagant!" With more grimacing, Josepha pulled herself back up.

"That's how I want it. And that's how I'll cut it."

"Heavens above, all you do is talk back. That's reason enough not to go to the lycée—it'll give you even more foolish ideas."

Fanny rolled up the drawing, saying nothing but still determined. She got the long wooden ruler from the cupboard and turned to Josepha, saying, "You call out the measurements, I'll mark out the pattern." They worked quietly together. After a few minutes, Fanny said, "If I offer to work longer hours in the sewing room, I can perhaps stay on at the foundling home and pay my own fees to go to the lycée."

Oh, little mite, thought Josepha. "If you go to that kind of school, you won't have any time left for working here. There'll be far more lessons and homework. Look at me, child. I only went to school for six years. I've been working since I was twelve, and it's done me no harm, I can tell you. Look here, missy, that neckline was very different in your drawing! This one goes down to your belly button!" She tapped disapprovingly at the generous triangle that Fanny had drawn on her pattern. "Don't think for one minute I'll let you go to the ball half-naked!"

Fanny couldn't help but laugh. "That's the back view! It's quite high collared in the front!"

"So, everyone's to see your backside?"

"Frau Pfeiffer, you're exaggerating. The cutaway stops a fair bit higher up the back. See?"

Josepha harrumphed as Fanny showed her. "That's still awfully low!"

"But if it's any higher, it'll lose that special effect."

"You and your special effects!" grumbled Josepha. To her mind, Fanny's design was far too revealing. But seeing as her little mite had already had to give up her dream of the lycée, she struggled to deny her this as well.

Fanny sensed a softening in Josepha's mood and felt it was worth another try. "Please, dear Frau Pfeiffer, is there really no chance of my continuing with school?"

Josepha cleared her throat. It was so hard to refuse her beloved child. Just as she wondered whether she should dip into Fanny's savings after all, something else suddenly struck her. "Do you remember that invitation I got last November? To Breitensee? It was for the opening of a new school, that one for girls to become qualified in housekeeping. It's called St. Josefinum."

Not one to be easily impressed, Josepha had enthused about this brand-new educational establishment. Yes, it was a three-year training, but at the end of it, these young women had a profession and didn't have to work in factories or take in laundry. And best of all, her beloved girl would be in safe hands because the school was run by nuns.

"If you are absolutely set on staying in school, then St. Josefinum definitely makes more sense than the lycée."

"Maybe you're right." Fanny was hesitant. She'd never actually thought of doing anything related to housekeeping and wasn't sure she'd like it.

"Of course, I'm right!" cried Josepha. "At a place like that, you'll learn all you need for a housekeeping position in a big house. You could even become a lady's personal maid. Just think of the wages you could expect, too. When I went to that opening ceremony, people told me all sorts of good things."

Fanny was silent but managed a little nod. This wasn't at all what she'd wanted. Maybe an illegitimate child from the foundling home couldn't expect much more than that.

Josepha, however, was overjoyed. As she helped Fanny with the cutting, Josepha nattered on about the wonderful new school building and the range of subjects that included not only housekeeping, laundry, sewing, embroidery, cooking, and baking but also etiquette and conversation. Fanny listened without a word. But when Josepha told her that girls there earned their school fees by cooking, washing, and sewing for the boardinghouse at St. Josefinum, she asked, "Would I be a boarder there, Frau Pfeiffer?"

Josepha stared at her. She hadn't even thought of that. The boardinghouse cost far too much and was out of the question. There was only one realistic solution. "During your training, you'll live with me," said Josepha. "My sofa's big enough to sleep on, and we'll get along alright, won't we, little mite? Then, in three years, you'll be out in the world, and I'll take my hard-earned retirement!"

Of course, thought Fanny, momentarily shocked. *Frau Pfeiffer will be seventy in three years.* She wondered whether the matron had actually hoped to step down this year.

She gave a little start as Josepha nudged her, saying, "Well, what d'you think of my idea?"

"It sounds very good." Fanny sounded cautious. "And allowing me to live with you, that's truly generous."

Josepha gave her a long hard look. "So, is it settled?"

Fanny chewed her lower lip, bothered by her realization about the matron's retirement. "And what if I didn't stay in school but got a job right away? I've heard they need more women for the Edlinger laundry out in Kaisermühlen."

Josepha made a face, knowing how hard the work was in big laundries. The detergents ruined your skin, and the atmosphere was so damp that a lot of the girls fell victim to rheumatism. Whatever happened, her darling girl wasn't going to earn a living doing that. She gently touched Fanny on the cheek. "Don't you worry, little mite. I've planned my pension so that I retire in three years' time. Not one day earlier."

After the evening meal, Fanny stole back to the sewing room and gazed at her gown. She'd already pinned it up and carefully eased it over a tailor's dummy. In the gentle light cast by the gas lamps, it looked a fairy-tale creation fit for a princess. She was bursting with the anticipation of showing it off at the ball.

Will the boys from the council school notice me in this?

It was traditional for the two neighboring schools to have a joint celebration, an exciting prospect for Fanny as she knew no boys her own age. She resolved to enjoy every minute of the evening and not miss a single dance.

Now she went to her worktable and the cloud of lilac tulle that lay there. This was the underskirt, already cut and pinned, too. Picking up the billowing tulle, she moved over to the sewing machine by the window. Outside it was almost dark, and the gas light wasn't really strong enough for such close work. But Fanny settled herself at the machine anyway. She placed a spool on the pin, unwound the thread, and eased it through the eye of the needle. Then she pulled a second thread from the compartment just underneath the metal foot. She eased a piece of the tulle under the machine's foot and pressed her own foot down on the pedal. The material slid gradually over the surface, guided by Fanny's careful hands. As soon as she'd gotten a feel for working the fabric, she increased the speed. The familiar chatter of the machine had its usual calming effect on her, and her concerns about housekeeping training began to fall away.

It's good I'm being allowed to continue with school, she thought to herself. *And I'll go my own way, in any case. Wherever it takes me.*

Chapter Four

Vienna, 1909

As she stood on Florianigasse, Fanny looked up at the three-story housing block. On the first floor, both of Josepha's living room windows were dark, but that didn't mean there was nobody there. Fanny knew the old lady now found walking difficult and rarely went out. She was probably on the courtyard side of the building, tucked away in her kitchen as, unlike the living room, this was always heated.

Fanny took a deep breath and rang the doorbell. Faint noises came from within, but it was a while before a window opened and Josepha leaned out. She looked down at the figure standing on the pavement flanked by luggage.

"Is that you, Fanny?"

"Yes, it's me!" She moved into the glow of the streetlight. It was late afternoon at the end of October and almost dark. "Good day to you, Frau Pfeiffer!"

"Holy Mary, mother of God." Josepha shook her head.

"Would you please let me come up? I'll explain everything."

"Not again!" Josepha drew her head back in and slammed the window shut.

Fanny let out a quiet sigh and waited. A few minutes later, she heard footsteps shuffling down the hall. A key grated in the lock, a bolt shot back, the door opened, and there was Josepha.

The young woman noticed how much smaller she seemed since the last time, and how heavily she leaned on her stick. Her thinning white hair was pushed under a hairnet. Over her nightshirt was a long robe, and on top of that a woolen shawl. Josepha had turned seventy-two in the summer, and age had taken its toll, but her dark eyes were still sharp. "You lost your job again."

Fanny looked pained. "Frau Pfeiffer, do I really have to explain out here on the doorstep?" Then she added very quietly, "I just don't know where else to go."

Josepha frowned. With a fashionable top hat and its jauntily dancing feather, an elegant coat, and pretty button boots in dark red leather, Fanny didn't have the air of a woman without a roof over her head. "You look like you've stepped straight out of the Sacher."

But however critical of her precious girl's extravagant tastes, she would never turn Fanny away from her door. "You'd better come in," she said, stepping aside.

With relief, Fanny picked up first the suitcase bearing all her worldly goods and then the wooden carrying case containing her most treasured possession—a Singer sewing machine she'd bought two years earlier with her first wages.

Once inside, she set down her luggage in Josepha's corridor and followed the old lady to the kitchen. It reeked of cabbage, but at least the stove gave off a welcoming warmth.

Josepha had a real closet of a kitchen, the floor gray- and white-speckled terrazzo, and one small window looking out onto the back courtyard. A single gas lamp hung from the ceiling.

On one wall was a stone sink and a wooden rack for plates, cups, pots, and pans, then the stove. In the back corner, a door led into the pantry. A small table and two chairs stood against the other wall. On the table was a magazine, Josepha's spectacles left on the open page. Next to this was a teapot, a half-empty enamel mug, and a bowl of sugar.

"Hungry? There's cabbage soup left." Josepha went over to the stove and lifted the lid on the large pot, releasing even more of that pungent smell.

It almost turned Fanny's stomach. "No, thank you."

"Then put another mug on the table. I'll make us some fresh tea."

Fanny took a mug off the familiar old wooden rack while Josepha fished the sieve—still full of tea leaves—out of the sink, placed it in the pot, and poured more hot water over it. She muttered in displeasure the whole time, and Fanny caught only snatches: "outrageous," "nothing like it," "a disgrace." As Fanny sat down on the other chair, she took off her hat and placed it on the table.

"If you want to criticize me, then you can do it out loud."

The old lady gave her an angry look before starting to pour out the tea. "You needn't take that tone with me. This is the sixth time in two years that you've lost a perfectly decent post. Are you planning to carry on like this until you've gone through every respectable household in Vienna?"

"This was no respectable household, I can tell you! And nor were the others."

"What nonsense!" Josepha heaped some sugar into her own mug and stirred furiously. "It's only been three months this time!"

Fanny's eyes filled with tears. "Don't you even want to hear what happened?"

"I want to hear a different story this time. I want to hear that the lady and gentleman were pleased with your work."

Fanny ran her hands through her curls. "I really tried. Truly, Frau Pfeiffer. But would you let anyone shout at you for forgetting to close the bedroom curtains?"

"Was it the first time you'd forgotten?"

The girl shook her head sheepishly. "The fifth, I think."

"The fifth?" Josepha was scandalized. "Then I'm surprised the lady didn't lose her temper with you sooner! Why on earth can't you just do what's expected of you?"

"I'm not a machine, I'm only human. It's normal to forget things."

"Not the same thing five times over!" Josepha put the teaspoon down on the table and gave her girl the most severe of looks. "Did you have to leave because you forgot to close the curtains, or because you couldn't hold your tongue again?"

"Must I go on and on just accepting everything? The old shrew was shouting at me, calling me a silly goose, and giving me a terrible earful, so I told her that, in the time she'd been scolding me, she could have opened and closed the stupid curtains herself ten times over."

The old lady tutted in disapproval. "When are you going to learn that you don't talk back to your master or mistress?"

"When I end up biting my tongue so hard that I choke on it."

Saying nothing, Josepha just looked at Fanny while the last two years played over in her mind. Fanny's final report on finishing at St. Josefinum had been more than respectable. While her cooking skills had earned only an average grade, her sewing and embroidery were of the highest standard. Demand was high for those emerging successfully from the institution, and, sure enough, Fanny was immediately offered a position in the household of a well-to-do soap manufacturer. Her future seemed assured.

Eight months later, Fanny appeared for the first time on Josepha's doorstep in floods of angry tears. The soap manufacturer had thrown her out when the lady of the house had caught Fanny in her dressing room, parading back and forth in front of the mirror in one of her evening dresses. Josepha hadn't minced her words about the gravity of this misdemeanor, but Fanny saw the incident as a great injustice. "I have no idea why ma'am made such a drama out of it. She'd cast that dress aside long ago."

Josepha's warnings seemed to fall on deaf ears as Fanny rapidly lost every subsequent post. The second went wrong because she was prone to browsing through the lady's fashion magazines rather than attending to the housekeeping. The third because she set her creative skills to work on her unappealing black uniform, conjuring up a garment fit for any occasion with some clever use of scissors, needle, and thread. The low point of the fourth came when her mistress returned late at night from a ball only to find her napping in an armchair. Fanny protested in vain that she had stayed up half the night to help the lady out of her gown. Then the fifth post came to a close when she refused to continue bathing the lady's Pekinese after it had nipped her hand while she applied the soap.

Josepha had taken her in every time because Fanny never had the money to rent her own room. Instead of being sensible and saving up, she would spend every last cent on fashionable fripperies and fabrics.

For the first time in two years, the old lady felt her usual courage fading. "What on earth's to become of you?"

Fanny was at a loss. "I'm just not suited to being given the runaround for every silly whim."

"Lords and ladies rule, Fanny. If you talk like that about the people who put bread on your plate, it's not going to end well."

"But they set themselves up like they're my masters and I'm their property! I may well be in their service, but I don't belong to them," exclaimed Fanny. "If you'd let me do the *Matura*, I could have paid my own way with a better job."

"There'll always be someone above you. That's the way life works. And you can't go on thinking it's everybody else's fault when things go wrong. That's just not true." Josepha's voice was firm but tinged with sadness.

This made Fanny blush. She reached across the table and took the old lady's hand. "I'm so sorry, Frau Pfeiffer. I shouldn't have spoken to you like that. You're the only person who treats me well."

Josepha nodded wearily. "At least you can see that. Now, drink your tea before it goes cold."

Fanny did as she was told but felt very low as she sipped her way through the mugful. *If only I didn't do the things I do. Then I could stop causing Frau Pfeiffer so much worry.*

"It's going to be tough to find you a decent post in Vienna now." Josepha's voice broke into her musings. "Your reputation will precede you, that's for sure."

Fanny gazed glumly into her tea. If only she could find a job that she enjoyed. But all she'd trained for was running other people's homes, and she had now messed that up yet again. Then something cheering struck her. "I'm going to go and see Madame Moreau! She told me to go back to her if I wanted to get into the fashion world. Wouldn't it be just wonderful if I could earn a living from gowns and fabrics?"

This brought another dampener from Josepha. "All your former mistresses shop with Madame Moreau. They won't be too pleased to cross paths with you whenever they go there. It's no use. You'll have to go back to St. Josefinum. Do it tomorrow. Maybe the headmistress gets inquiries from outside Vienna, too."

"She said last time she couldn't keep on putting herself out for me."

"You'll have to try it. If you can show some remorse and swear to do better, she might help you one more time."

"Well, alright, then." Fanny sounded defeated. "I'll try."

Josepha pushed back her chair and got to her feet. "Bedtime, little mite. Let's see what the morning brings. There are pillows and a blanket in the hall chest. You're used to the sofa."

Just two days later, Fanny and Josepha stepped down from a hired carriage outside the Wiener Staatsbahnhof. This rail station in the Favoriten district served all points east of Vienna. It was midmorning, and the square in front of the departure hall teemed with coaches and motorcars bringing passengers bound for Bohemia, Moravia, and Hungary. Many would continue on to Poland, Rumania, and even the Russian Empire.

The sky hung leaden and overcast above the city, reminding all of winter's approach. A bitter wind swept across the forecourt, sending the autumn leaves dancing, along with men's hats and ladies' skirts. A fine but persistent drizzle drew a gloomy curtain across the station's elegant white façade.

Fanny had asked the coachman to halt right in front of the entrance to the ticket hall. She climbed down from the vehicle first, then turned to help Josepha.

"Do come in, Frau Pfeiffer. You mustn't get chilled out here," Fanny urged.

Josepha nodded. "I'll just quickly pay him."

"Leave that. I've got enough money."

"Alright, then," agreed the old lady. "I'll go and find us a nice bench right on the platform."

The coachman carefully unloaded Fanny's suitcase and the sewing machine. As Fanny delved into her handbag for her purse, she realized her hands were trembling. She'd felt unsettled day and night ever since learning she was to leave Vienna for an unknown city. Vienna was the only home she'd ever known. It was all very fine that Budapest, as capital of the Kingdom of Hungary, belonged to their monarch, but for Fanny, this was still a foreign country with a foreign language. Nor did it help much to hear from the headmistress of St. Josefinum that there were plenty of Austrians living in Budapest and almost everyone spoke Fanny's native German.

She pressed her last banknote on the coachman, bent down to gather up her luggage, and hurried to get inside without taking in just how many young porters were eager to help her.

The route to her departure platform led through the hubbub of the ticket hall. People clustered around the ticket desks and jostled for position at glass-fronted timetable displays. Others pushed and crowded around stalls or hunted the arrival platform for friends and relatives.

Once through the main entrance, Fanny paused to set her bags down and draw breath. She was inwardly cursing her tight girdle when she heard a voice close by. "I'll watch your cases for ten hellers while you get your ticket, and for ten more, I'll carry everything to your seat on the train."

She turned to find herself confronted by a lanky youth with a provocative smile, his flat cap pushed cheekily to one side.

She'd have loved to accept but shook her head. "I bought my ticket yesterday. And I can manage the bags on my own, even as far as the train."

His smile became a grin. "A smart maid like you shouldn't be carting cases around like some packhorse."

This made Fanny laugh. "That's true. But I might need my last heller for something even more important." She bent to pick the two items up again, but he said swiftly, "Leave those, miss. I'll make an exception and do it for nothing."

Before she could say a word, he'd scooped up the suitcase and heaved the sewing machine onto his shoulder.

"Where're you off to?"

"Budapest. On the 10:30 express."

"Platform 3. Are you gonna see your sweetheart there?" He winked at her.

"Do you always ask your customers so many questions?" Fanny asked him rather sharply.

"Only if I like 'em." He showed not the slightest embarrassment.

Fanny's mood lifted for the first time in days.

The headmistress of St. Josefinum had been more than annoyed to find Fanny standing in her office again only three months after the last visit. "I have no desire to put myself out for you again," she had said. "You're ruining this school's excellent reputation."

But Fanny had produced so many excuses, protestations, and promises to do better that the headmistress looked one more time through the file where she kept all inquiries for housekeepers. Prospective clients now came not only from Vienna but from across the kingdom. She eventually came upon one from Budapest, where a Hungarian businessman and his wife needed a maid for the young lady of the house, their daughter. It took one telephone conversation between the headmistress and the family's head butler for the agreement to be sealed. Winter was now approaching, and with it the ball season, so Fanny was expected to start immediately. The young lady would have to approve, of course.

"And get it right this time. I don't want to see you back here." The headmistress's farewell couldn't have been clearer.

"Fräulein? Did you hear me?"

Fanny gave a little start. "Sorry?"

"I asked you twice which coach you're in." The porter gave her a rather reproachful look.

"Oh, forgive me. Coach five, seat number twelve."

They'd already arrived at the platform, but Fanny had been so lost in thought, she hadn't realized. The train stood waiting. Men were preparing the huge black locomotive, replenishing the coal and checking the boiler.

Fanny trailed after the porter as he searched the length of the train for her coach. "Five. There it is." He gestured with his chin toward the dark green coach. Then he clambered up the steps and vanished for no more than a moment before jumping back down to the platform. "Your luggage is on board, fräulein."

"Many thanks." She turned to say goodbye, but he just stood there, looking at her forlornly.

"Don't I get a farewell kiss 'n' cuddle?"

Fanny's eyes flashed. "That wasn't the agreement."

He pushed back his cap. "No harm in askin', is there?"

She looked around for Josepha and spotted the old lady sitting on a bench, watching them with a reproachful air. Fanny turned back to the lad. For the first time, she noticed his manly chin and downy cheeks.

How would it feel to kiss that soft, blonde down?

Banishing Josepha from her thoughts, she stood on tiptoe and swiftly brushed her lips against his left cheek. His skin was soft, as was the boyish facial hair, and to her surprise, he flushed.

"Will you let me in on your name?" he asked softly.

Fanny shook her head. "We won't be seeing each other again." She said a quick goodbye and hurried over to Josepha's bench.

The old lady was the picture of disapproval. "Since when do you give a kiss to every fellow that comes along?"

"He was very kind." Fanny stole another look at the porter, already busy offering his services to other travelers.

"He's got nerve, is more like it. A real gentleman doesn't ogle a lady like that."

"It was only a kiss on the cheek."

"One thing leads to another, and carelessness leads to a wee babe. Just think what happened to your mother. You don't want to end up like her!"

Fanny stared at Josepha. "Listening to you, anyone would think it's a disaster that I'm on this earth."

Josepha bit her lip. "Of course not. You know how fond I am of you, little mite. But your father and mother behaved like fools. And though I'm happy you've been with me all these years, I'm sure you'd rather have been part of a real family?" She wanted to pat Fanny's cheek, but the girl dodged.

"Yes, I grew up in a foundling home and have no idea who my mother and father are, but that doesn't make me a bad person."

"Nobody's saying that, my girl."

"But you are! You think I've got loose morals, and that's because you think my mother had loose morals, too. You don't actually know what happened. Perhaps she had no choice but to leave me on my own." A lump rose in Fanny's throat.

"Now, now, child. You're not on your own. You've got me!" Josepha tried once more to stroke Fanny's cheek, and this time she didn't pull away.

"I won't be a loose woman," she said firmly to Josepha, looking her in the eye. "Never!"

"Calm down. What are your new master and mistress going to think if you turn up in a state!" Josepha glanced at the station clock in the departure hall. "We'll have to say goodbye in fifteen minutes."

Fanny rested her head on Josepha's shoulder. "Oh, Frau Pfeiffer, must I really go to Budapest?"

"Now, pull yourself together and be brave. You know there's no other way. Budapest's supposed to be a wonderful place. What was the name again? The young lady you're going to work for?"

"Izabella Kálman. I really hope I get along well with her." Fanny sighed. "It'll be so strange to wait on someone hardly older than I am."

"Don't think of it like that. All that matters is that you do your duty, whether Fräulein Kálman's nice to you or not."

"But I've never worked as a lady's maid. I have no idea what I'll have to do."

"Your job will be to make sure the young lady always looks pretty! And you certainly know how to do that." Josepha gave her an affectionate smile. In the velvet beret that matched her coat and elegant button boots, Fanny looked so lovely that even Josepha could hardly blame the porter for being so bold.

There was a piercing whistle blast. The platform attendant hurried up and down, calling out, "All aboard! All aboard the express to Budapest! Departing in fifteen minutes!"

Leaning heavily on her stick, Josepha got to her feet. "Take good care of yourself for me, little mite. And don't let any of those fellows talk to you during the journey, do you hear?" She rummaged in her bag and took out a flat package. "That's for the journey, so you won't starve."

Fanny's face brightened. "Nut chocolate! My favorite! Thank you so much!"

With a smile, Josepha reached into her bag again and produced a brown envelope. "And there's enough in here to pay for a train ticket home in an emergency, or if the lady doesn't want you for the job. Look after it and don't spend it on anything silly." She handed Fanny the envelope.

"Oh, Frau Pfeiffer, you're making it even harder to say goodbye." In tears, Fanny put her arms around the old lady.

Josepha patted her on the back. "Everything's alright, little mite."

She was thinking about the way those monthly payments for child number 6,572 had stopped so abruptly. The money had arrived for the last time on November 1, 1906. Josepha had often wondered why the mysterious benefactor had chosen such an odd date, just two months before Fanny's seventeenth birthday, to stop paying. She had waited for six months, then put it all in a fixed-interest savings account on Fanny's behalf. Josepha planned to hand this over to the girl when she turned twenty-four, the age of majority. Were Josepha to pass away before then, a clause in her will would ensure that Fanny received what was rightfully hers.

Fanny's thoughts drifted to the future, to Budapest and her new position with the Kálman family. "I'm going to make a real effort this time. Frau Kálman will have no cause for complaint."

The old lady gave an awkward little cough. "We'll write to each other, little mite, that's for sure. And maybe you can come to see me."

Fanny nodded energetically. "Of course, Frau Pfeiffer!"

But they both knew this was highly unlikely. Domestic staff had one day off a week at the most. They all had to be constantly available to their employers and could only dream of a real vacation.

The whistle trilled once more, and the engine blasted out a puff of black smoke.

"Attention, attention, all passengers for Budapest! Departing in five minutes!" The attendant hurried past.

Fanny hugged the old lady before climbing aboard. As the train slowly pulled out of the station, she waved to Josepha until she could no longer make out the small figure leaning on her stick.

Chapter Five

Budapest, 1909

As Fanny stepped out of the Budapest Westbahnhof hours later, she noticed immediately how much warmer it was than in Vienna. The flagstones outside the station were still gleaming after a recent downpour, and the sun had just burst through the gray clouds.

The headmistress at St. Josefinum had arranged with the Kálmans' head butler for her to be met at the station, and Fanny quickly spotted, in a row behind the bigger coaches, a little two-seater carriage with its driver holding aloft a sign bearing her name: "Fräulein Fanny Schindler."

Soon she was seated next to the elderly coachman, who had introduced himself as András Papp, as they bowled along a spacious boulevard. Fanny was immediately intrigued by the big department stores on both sides, as well as the elegant hotels and magnificent residences everywhere she looked. Although she tried hard to decipher street names and shop signs, she knew not a scrap of Hungarian and had never seen such an unpronounceable ordering of letters.

As they crossed another road, however, she caught a glimpse of the River Danube. The bridge was adorned with statues of lions and supported by huge piers, and beyond this, she caught sight of a green, wooded hill crowned by a host of castle buildings.

"That's odd," she remarked to the driver. "It's so hilly over there, but flat as a pancake here!"

"That's Buda over there on that side. This is Pest. My city is like two beautiful sisters that don't look alike," bragged Papp.

The Palais Kálman was a two-story, cream-colored mansion situated opposite the National Museum on a small square bordered by trees. On the second floor were several big windows extravagantly decorated with reliefs, while in the center of the mansion's façade was a balcony with superbly wrought iron railings, beneath it an imposing arched gateway flanked by pillars.

András gently steered the horse into the cobbled inner courtyard and stopped outside a plain doorway at the rear. Fanny guessed this would be the servants' quarters. As they'd trotted beneath the arch, she had noticed an impressive set of double doors, clearly for use by the master and mistress of the house.

The north wing housed the stables, a carriage shelter, and a gleaming motorcar. Fanny was quick to notice the winged female figurine adorning the radiator. A casually dressed young man was polishing the front windscreen with a sponge, but broke off when he saw Fanny.

"My son, István. He's chauffeur here," explained András, unloading Fanny's belongings for her. "One of the men will take your things to your room. I need to take care of the horse now. You'll be seeing Frau Fischer, I expect." He pointed toward the plain doorway, saying, "First room on the yard side."

Fanny found herself in a long, dark corridor with closed doors lining both sides and what appeared to be access to the servants' stairs. She heard low voices coming from the room András had directed her to, and knocked.

A female voice replied in German. "Yes, come in."

Fanny took a deep breath, remembered all her good resolutions, and stepped into the room.

The housekeeper's workroom was simple yet practical. Apart from one cupboard, a tallboy dresser, two chairs, and a writing desk, there was no other furniture. A tiny window admitted only low-level light.

Fanny saw a woman in middle age, her hair tightly drawn back, her black dress buttoned equally tightly to the neck, sitting behind the desk with a back straight as a ramrod. Lounging against the tallboy was a man of similar age, dressed in the three-piece suit and white shirt favored for butlers. Both looked at Fanny with an expression she couldn't fathom.

"Good day to you. I'm the new lady's maid. Fanny Schindler."

The woman behind the desk raised her eyebrows as she looked Fanny up and down. "Herr Wenzl, I told you things go wrong when you appoint staff over the telephone." Turning to the butler, she added, "A local girl we could at least have had a look at beforehand. But my opinion's not important, of course."

The butler plucked uneasily at the watch chain that hung from his waistcoat pocket. "There were a number of Budapest girls interested in the position. But you know how that turned out. I had no other choice, what with the first big receptions taking place and Rosa saying she couldn't possibly look after both Madam and Miss throughout the whole season."

Both the housekeeper and the butler spoke with a strong Austrian twang, but even that familiar sound brought Fanny no comfort. She had come to Budapest with the very best of intentions, but this was far from encouraging.

"May I ask what it is about me that doesn't suit you?" She was angry. Neither the butler nor the housekeeper had greeted her properly, and now they were talking about her as if she wasn't there.

Frau Fischer rose and stepped out from behind her desk, the large bunch of keys attached to her belt jangling with every step. "So, you're impertinent, as well. You'd better realize right now that we didn't want anyone all decked out for the young mistress. In this house, we value a modest and unobtrusive appearance. The fact that you got this opportunity is entirely because time was of the essence in filling the vacancy."

Fanny struggled to hold back a sharp rejoinder. She'd promised Josepha she would make a huge effort. Did this mean she had to be insulted, too?

The butler stepped in. "Please, Frau Fischer. Fräulein Schindler has only just arrived. Perhaps you could show us your references?"

Fanny raised her chin in defiance. "I don't have them with me."

"Yes, and I can imagine why," observed Frau Fischer. "I've got a bad feeling, but we'll have to give you a try. Provided that the young lady decides to keep you, you are to take all your instructions from me and from Herr Wenzl. Is that clear?"

"Perfectly," replied Fanny sharply.

"Very good," said the housekeeper in the same tone of voice. "Then I'll introduce you to the rest of the staff. After that, the mistress's maid will show you to your room and introduce you to Fräulein Izabella. I expect you to appear before your employers only in clothes suited to your station. You'll find two appropriate dresses in your room."

Stony-faced, Fanny followed Frau Fischer to the servants' dayroom at the end of the corridor.

I hope the young mistress isn't a nasty piece of work like this Fischer woman, she thought to herself.

Homesickness for Vienna and for Josepha overwhelmed her. The only thing that stopped her from catching the next train home was the thought of disappointing Josepha yet again.

The two maids had spent the morning cleaning the master and mistress's living areas and were now sitting at the table, cleaning silverware as they quietly chatted together. The valet was energetically buffing the master's shoes, and another man was busy with a whetstone, noisily sharpening knives. András was at the table, too, lovingly cleaning a bridle. Another member of the staff, a young brunette, had shifted her chair toward the window to get the natural light while she meticulously darned a silk stocking.

As Frau Fischer and Fanny came into the room, they all looked up expectantly. Fanny's chic appearance earned her a couple of surprised glances.

Frau Fischer introduced the staff one by one, some from Austria, others native Hungarians. The valet sharpening knives answered to the name of Franz, the cleaning maids Réka and Eszter, and the master's valet was Karl, while the young woman sewing by the window was Rosa, lady's maid to the madam and mistress herself.

Next, Frau Fischer took Fanny into the kitchen. Preparations for the evening meal were in full swing, so neither the two kitchen maids, nor the cook, Tereza from Bohemia, raised their eyes to say hello.

"How many are in the family?" asked Fanny later on, as she followed Rosa up the narrow staircase to the servants' quarters.

"The master, his wife, and then Fräulein Izabella. The young master, Herr Máxim, doesn't live at home now. He's an officer in the Ninth Hussars and stationed at Pressburg."

"Are they nice people?"

Rosa shrugged. "Provided you do everything the way they want it. But that won't be any different from your previous place."

"Of course," said Fanny with a sigh.

Rosa laughed, and Fanny decided she liked this young woman. "Won't you call me Fanny?" In a household like this, under the iron rule of Frau Fischer, she knew she'd need a friend and ally.

"Yes, and you should call me Rosa. But there's one thing you need to know." Rosa stopped on the stair above Fanny, turned, and looked her straight in the eye. "Keep your hands off Karl. He's mine? Got it?"

"Got it," Fanny assured her. She really wanted to get things right this time, and starting an affair with Rosa's pale, potbellied sweetheart definitely wasn't on her to-do list.

While bedrooms for male servants were downstairs, female staff all slept in the attic. Herr Wenzl and Frau Fischer had a small apartment each on the first floor.

"You are now entering the virgins' floor," said Rosa with a mischievous wink as she opened a door from the staircase to the landing. "Never ever get caught by Fischer or Herr Wenzl when you've got a gentleman visitor or you'll be out on your ear."

"I haven't seen any appealing candidates," retorted Fanny. "Except for Karl, of course, but he's already spoken for." She gave Rosa a wink in return.

"You're sassy, aren't you!" said Rosa with a laugh. "I bet it caused problems at your old job."

"You can say that again," Fanny admitted. "But I'm going to do better this time."

The two young women walked side by side along the narrow corridor. It was cold and the wooden floorboards creaked beneath every step. At last, Rosa opened one of the doors. "Your room's next to mine. It's nothing special, but last year the master had electric lights and running water put in! There's even a flush toilet at the end of the corridor."

Fanny followed Rosa into the room. It was cold, with no heat source to be seen. She thought how hot and stuffy it would get in summer, up there under the roof. Her new room was so small that anything more than a single bed with a thin mattress, a cupboard, and a washbasin wouldn't fit. Somebody had already brought up her suitcase and sewing machine. On the freshly made bed was her uniform: two dreary black dresses. Fanny immediately dismissed them as starchy, uncomfortable, and devoid of style. The same went for the worn-down shoes placed in front of the bed.

"Aha, you've got a sewing machine?" Rosa's eyes lit up. "Now I know how you look so dashing. You make your own things, am I right?"

Fanny nodded. "I've always loved dressmaking." Picking up the sleeve of one of the uniforms, she said, "And I'll spiff these up a bit, too." She gave a little sigh. "If I have to wear one of these, I reckon a white collar and cuffs will stop me looking like some miserable old crow. And I'll take in the side seams a bit, too."

While Fanny took off her velvet beret and coat and hung them over the hook on the back of the door, Rosa sat down on the bed. "I can't wait to see Fischer's face when she realizes you've altered those hideous old sacks," she enthused, drumming her feet excitedly on the floor. "Now hurry. We mustn't keep Fräulein Izabella waiting."

Fanny straightened the little bow under her blouse collar and smoothed down her skirt. "I'm ready."

"You're not going to change?" Rosa asked, marveling at Fanny's daring.

"I'm not going to present myself to the young mistress in a dress that doesn't fit me! And I'm not putting these dreadful old shoes on either!" As she kicked her predecessor's footwear under the bed, she remembered her promise to Josepha. "Or do you think she'll only keep me if I look like a scarecrow?"

Rosa laughed again. "Believe me, she'll like it a lot if you look as pretty as you do right now."

"Really?" asked Fanny. But Rosa was already out the door.

"Are you ready?" Rosa turned and smiled at Fanny over her shoulder. When Fanny gave a silent nod, Rosa knocked on Izabella Kálman's door.

"Come in!" The voice was dark and melodious.

Rosa opened the door and went in.

Fanny followed, uneasy.

In the middle of the room stood a wide four-poster bed strewn with cushions, in front of it a fine Oriental rug. The fire glowing in the hearth gave off a comforting warmth. The deep marble mantelpiece was covered in family photographs flanking a dainty porcelain clock. Beneath one of the two windows was a dressing table littered with little pots and bottles. Seated there was Izabella Kálman.

As the two young women entered the room, she turned. Fanny was taken aback by the silk robe tied so carelessly at her waist that it not only revealed a lace-trimmed bodice emphasizing Izabella's full breasts, but also fell open lower down to expose her naked legs. Embroidered slippers, cast aside with the same studied carelessness, lay near her bare feet.

Rosa nudged Fanny forward and bobbed a curtsy. "Ma'am, may I introduce Fanny Schindler?"

Izabella swept her long dark hair back over her shoulder and looked straight at Fanny. Her blue eyes wandered slowly downward from Fanny's face, over her blouse and skirt, right down to her button boots. Just as Fanny was anxiously wondering whether this scrutiny was a good or a bad sign, Izabella said, "Didn't Frau Fischer lay out a dress for you?" She spoke in German, but to Fanny it sounded strange, with the prominent rolled *r* of Hungarian.

"Two, actually," replied Fanny, feeling brave again. "But they don't fit. I would like your permission to make one or two alterations."

"Do whatever you like with the hand-me-downs," said Izabella dismissively. "But first I'd like to see your skills as a lady's maid."

"Of course, ma'am." Fanny curtsied.

Izabella's full, rosy lips parted for a slight smile. "Good. You can help me dress for dinner. My parents are expecting guests, my father's business partners and their wives, so we need something special. Rosa, you can go now. My mother's bound to be waiting for you."

"Thank you, ma'am." Rosa bobbed again. Before she flitted away, she whispered to Fanny, "Good luck."

Izabella stood up. "Come with me, Fanny. I'll show you my dressing room." She pushed her feet into her dainty slippers and glided over to a door near the mantelpiece, opened it, and switched on the light. "I'm dying to see what you'll choose!" She ushered Fanny into the space that was a good three times the size of Fanny's attic bedroom.

Three of the four walls were fitted with rails from which hung all manner of dresses for morning, afternoon, and evening, not to mention skirts, blouses, jackets, and coats. The fourth wall was decked with two wall units providing floor-to-ceiling shelving. One was full of all sorts of shoes, ranging from silken dancing shoes to fur-lined winter boots. In the other were stacks of hatboxes and handbags, while in the middle of the room was a huge chest of drawers that Fanny guessed was for gloves, fans, underwear, and stockings.

How on earth can one woman possess so many clothes? She was half-baffled, half-envious.

Slowly, she walked back and forth in front of the rail of evening dresses. Every gown was fabulously beautiful. The moment she spotted one that looked perfect for the occasion, she immediately saw another. She had almost forgotten Izabella, lolling in the doorway and watching with amusement. Then Fanny noticed a dress of shimmering silver. Taking it down from the rail, she found it to be a close-fitting garment with long sleeves. Unlike with a ball gown, the décolletage was modest, but it was trimmed with dark blue lace. The whole effect was elegant and different, and Fanny knew right away that Fräulein Kálman would look wonderful in it.

"How about this?"

"That one's brand new. It's based on designs by a Parisian *couturier* called Paul Poiret, and I haven't even worn it yet. But I think this evening would be exactly right for it," mused Izabella. "What jewelry would you suggest?"

Fanny wavered for a moment. Jewelry wasn't her strong point. She quickly cast her mind back to pieces she'd seen in her previous employers' jewelry boxes. "Pearls?"

"A good choice!" Izabella sounded pleased. "I have a pearl necklace. I'll wear that." She turned to go. "And bring some stockings. They're in the chest," she called over her shoulder.

Fanny stole a surreptitious glance at her mistress as she alighted on the bench at the foot of the bed and peeled off her dainty slippers. She'd never seen a woman as beautiful as Izabella Kálman.

As she looked in the chest for a pair of stockings, she noticed a long blue feather in the little drawer of hair decorations. It had a shimmering quality, too, so she took that with her for good measure.

Izabella was smiling in her direction. She had now removed her robe and casually tossed it on the bed. Her magnificent breasts pushed up against the edge of her corset. She had a tiny waist but rounded hips, and her skin glowed a creamy white. "Let's start with the stockings," she said, extending one of her long, slender legs.

Fanny knelt down so she could carefully unroll the first stocking over Izabella's foot. Never before had she been expected to get so close to an employer, particularly not one wearing as few clothes as Fräulein Izabella. What was more, it rubbed her wrong to kneel before anyone at all.

But this is all part of being a lady's maid, she thought to herself as she rolled the stocking up and over Izabella's thigh. Just as she was about to fasten it with the garter belt, a shadow fell across her face. Izabella had leaned forward and was looking into her eyes. "What tiny hands you have," she murmured, gently laying the fingers of her right hand over Fanny's. "And what soft skin."

Fanny lowered her eyes. This moment of contact was not at all unpleasant but left her unsettled. With care, she withdrew her hand from beneath Fräulein Kálman's and fastened the top of the stocking to the belt. Izabella said nothing further, but her eyes remained fixed on Fanny.

Half an hour later and Izabella was ready, looking at herself in the huge mirror fitted to the inside of the dressing room door. In the silver dress with its blue lace trim, she came across as exotic and intriguing. Fanny had combed a perfumed pomade through her hair, fashioned it in a soft knot at the nape, and then completed the effect with a narrow headband that secured the blue feather. The pearls glimmering against Izabella's flawless skin made the perfect finishing touch.

"You've done an excellent job," announced Izabella with a coquett-ish smile at her own reflection. "I am delighted to have you as my personal maid. Will you stay?"

"Of course! Thank you!"

"I'm pleased." Izabella turned to look straight at Fanny, her gaze lingering on the girl's mouth. "Very pleased indeed."

Fanny felt her cheeks redden. She wanted to say something but couldn't think what.

Izabella took a step forward so that she was very close to Fanny. "How old are you, my pretty one?"

"I'll be twenty at Christmas," murmured Fanny.

"So, we're nearly the same age." Izabella sounded pleased. "I turned twenty in September." Slowly raising her hand, she lightly brushed the corner of Fanny's mouth with her index finger. "What do you think, Fanny? Wouldn't it be nice if we could become friends?"

Fanny said nothing, feeling horribly confused and embarrassed. Before she'd first gone into service, Josepha had warned her to watch out if the gentlemen of the house ever started to pay her compliments or touch her. "That means only one thing, and it's that he wants to have his way with you. Don't ever give in to that kind of attention or you'll find yourself in real trouble." Josepha had drummed this into Fanny. But she had never said anything about the ladies of the house compli-menting or touching her.

The mantelpiece clock chimed.

"Goodness, is that the time?" Izabella gave a little shriek. "I had better go down to welcome the guests!" Without so much as a glance at Fanny, she hurried to the door and was gone.

Fanny was left staring at the closed door in a daze. She knew she should be grateful to have the job, but this first encounter with her new mistress had been decidedly odd.

Maybe I'm imagining things. She didn't know what to think. In previous posts, it had always infuriated her the way employers had made her feel the lowest of the low, but the fact that Fräulein Kálman hadn't treated her that way seemed suspicious.

She bent to gather up Izabella's robe from the bed. The silk was so smooth and cool to the touch. She could smell Izabella's perfume, mysterious and intriguing, like Izabella herself.

I'm sure she just wanted to be nice, thought Fanny as she carried the robe to the dressing room to hang it up properly. *She even gave me permission to do what I want with that hideous maid's outfit.*

She neatly placed Izabella's slippers by the bed and pushed in the dressing table stool. Then she, too, left the room.

The servants' dayroom was full to bursting that evening. When the master and mistress entertained, it meant a late night for the staff. Only the two chambermaids had been able to get away for a decent night's sleep, as their duties required them to be up with the lark to have everything spick-and-span for master and mistress alike.

Appetizing smells wafted in from the adjoining kitchen, where the clatter of pans formed the backdrop to Tereza's stream of shouted instructions to the kitchen maids. Every course had to be served precisely on time. Herr Wenzl took pride in ensuring the best wines were available and, to Tereza's eternal irritation, would check every serving dish before allowing it through to the dining room.

The guests' two chauffeurs had sat themselves at the table with Frau Fischer, Rosa, and Karl, both smoking and whiling away the time by boasting of the technical refinements of their masters' motorcars.

Only Fanny was missing. She had disappeared right after the servants' own dinner.

"Where's Fanny?" Frau Fischer said with a frown, looking toward the door for the umpteenth time.

Rosa rested her head on Karl's shoulder and murmured, "I think she just wanted something from her room. Said she'd be back directly."

"*Directly* seems to be rather an elastic concept for that girl. She's been gone half an hour," observed the housekeeper. "I hope she knows that Fräulein Izabella will still need her."

"I imagine so," said Rosa, trying to suppress a huge yawn. "She's not stupid."

"Don't you dare be impertinent with me," snapped Frau Fischer.

Karl had been reading the *Pester Lloyd*, studying up on the latest race day at the Budapest Trotting Circuit, but now spoke up. "Leave my treasure in peace. She ain't the new girl's nanny." He pointedly put his arm round Rosa and drew her close.

Frau Fischer harrumphed with indignation, but before she could reply, there was an angry shout from Franz. He'd been hurrying up the stairs all evening with trays full of food, then hurrying back down with dirty dishes.

"Dammit, are you blind? I nearly dropped the boiled rump!"

"I'm sorry! I didn't see you!"

Fanny had been about to come through the door, and only just managed to avoid a collision. In one hand was her sewing machine case, in the other a little sewing basket and fabric remnants. The loathed uniforms hung over her arm. She had pinned up the seams in her bedroom and now couldn't wait to sit down and alter them.

Everybody turned to stare, and one of the chauffeurs leapt to his feet.

"Alley-oop, darlin'! Don't overdo it!" He swiftly took the carrying case from her. "That's heavy for a doll like you. What you got inside? Gold bars?" He gave her the cheekiest of winks.

She laughed and shook her head. "It's my sewing machine. Would you mind just putting it on the table?" She gestured toward the space next to Rosa.

The man attempted a meaningful look. "Wouldn't you rather sit by me?"

"That's enough!" Frau Fischer's hand came down hard on the surface of the table.

The chauffeur heaved the wooden case onto the table with such an amusing grimace that Fanny had to turn to conceal her smiles from Frau Fischer. The housekeeper looked suspiciously from the sewing machine to the uniforms and back.

"What's going on here, Fanny?"

"The dresses are too big for me, and my mistress has given me permission to alter them." Fanny placed the dresses on the table, careful not to catch herself on the multitude of pins.

"Go for a nice tight fit to show off that pretty figure of yours!" said the man who had helped her with the machine.

"One more crack from you and you can wait for your master in the yard!" hissed Frau Fischer.

"No need to get so worked up, milady." The man made a gesture of mock self-defense.

Now Frau Fischer turned to Fanny. "In the morning, come to my room first thing. We need to go through Fräulein Izabella's invitations for the coming months. There's plenty of work for you to get started with."

"Very well," replied Fanny with composure. She was so relieved she'd gotten the job that she wasn't going to be ruffled by the housekeeper.

She threaded up her machine, and soon its clatter blended with the chatter of the staff and the sounds coming from the kitchen. It wasn't long before she was through and sat checking her work. "Much better," she said with satisfaction. "Now there's just the collar and cuffs left."

She set the dresses to one side and rummaged in the bag she'd brought with her. "What d'you think of this?" Rosa was watching with interest, so she handed her a scrap of white cotton.

"But that's much too soft," said Rosa, puzzled at the choice.

"Not if I make the collar and cuffs frilled," explained Fanny. "Like this." With her dainty hands, she worked the material into even folds.

"That could look really nice!" Rosa nodded. "I'll help you, if you like."

While the two young women worked side by side, measuring and cutting the cloth, they chatted quietly about their experiences in previous households. Rosa told her how homesick she often felt for her family in Graz, and Fanny spoke of her life in Vienna. But when Rosa asked about Fanny's parents, she only said that they'd died long ago and that she'd been brought up by an elderly aunt. Mentioning the foundling home would have meant admitting that she'd never known her parents and that her own mother hadn't loved her enough to keep her. This knowledge hurt Fanny so much that she didn't even want to think about it.

The conversation turned to Fanny's new employers. "Does it bother you that the Kálmans are Jews?" asked Rosa as she tacked on the collar with pins.

"No," replied Fanny in amazement. "I didn't even know they were. Does it bother you?"

"I wouldn't be here if it did," said Rosa. "But there are folk who think it's beneath them to work for Jews. You'd hardly notice it with the Kálmans, though. They're not always traipsing off to the synagogue and don't do anything much for Sabbath. The master always says it's diligence and reason that he believes in. Besides, our mistress and Fräulein Izabella always give us a Christmas tree and decorate it themselves! An' they enjoy it, too—you can tell!"

"So, it was hard to find a maid for Fräulein Izabella because of her being Jewish?" Fanny asked.

"No," giggled Rosa. "It wasn't because of that."

"What was it, then?" Fanny had raised her voice. "Why won't you just tell me?"

"Quiet!"

Rosa's sharp tone left Fanny wondering, and she noticed Rosa checking to see if Frau Fischer and Herr Wenzl could hear. But the two senior staff were busy with their own tasks and paid no attention to the two young women.

"Hasn't it struck you how different Fräulein Izabella is from other ladies?" Rosa whispered as she bent over her sewing.

Fanny was about to pin cuffs to the sleeves but hesitated, lowered her hands, and stared at Rosa.

"Oh, come on," urged Rosa. "Don't act like you don't know what I mean. I saw how she reacted when you first met. She likes the look of you, that's for sure!"

"I don't know what you mean," mumbled Fanny, although she could recall everything about Izabella's touch and flattering remarks.

"Oh, little Fanny," teased Rosa. "Are you really that innocent, or are you just pretending? I'd bet my last heller that Izabella got all flirty with you the minute I left the room. That's why all the girls before you ran for it. They weren't like Fräulein Izabella. What about you? Wanna fool around with the mistress?"

"Don't be dirty, Rosa!" burst out Fanny.

Every head turned. Even Karl glanced up from the racing results.

Fanny pursed her lips and bent over her work once more. Had she liked the way Fräulein Izabella had behaved toward her? It was certainly flattering to have such a beautiful woman, a wealthy and socially superior one at that, pay her compliments. And she did have to admit she was curious about how her next meeting with her mistress would go.

She turned to Rosa. "Are you interested in her?"

"She leaves me cold. I've only got eyes for Karl," said Rosa firmly. "She's never flirted with me either. Maybe she's afraid my sweetheart will go tell the master."

Frau Fischer slammed shut her housekeeping book and glanced at the wall clock. "Fanny! Rosa! Time to turn down the beds for the master and mistress. They'll be finishing dinner soon. And Fanny, I expect you to clean up the mess you've made here before you go to bed."

Fanny nodded, then followed Rosa, even more confused than before.

It's all the silliest nonsense I've ever heard, she thought to herself. *A woman flirting with another woman?*

Chapter Six

Budapest, 1910

"Good morning, ma'am. Did you sleep well?" The clock was striking eight as Fanny carried the tray into Izabella Kálman's room, where the bedside light was already glowing brightly as she read, propped up by pillows. She didn't sleep late but loved to stay in bed with a pot of coffee and her book.

"Thank you, yes, very well. You, too, Fanny? Or did you sit at your sewing machine half the night?" She closed her book, put it on the bedside table, and gave the girl a warm smile.

The whole household now knew of Fanny's passion for clothes and her gift for sewing. Izabella had even given her a few old day dresses she was done with, and Fanny had altered them for herself. She'd also done some work for Rosa, Réka, and Eszter. Even Frau Fischer had come by the previous week and asked Fanny to stitch a new collar to a blouse for her.

In spite of their bumpy start, these two women now had a very good working relationship. Fanny held back her rebellious remarks, even when the housekeeper's strict regime got on her nerves. And Frau Fischer was cautiously tolerant, relieved as she was that the task of finding a personal maid for Fräulein Kálman was finally over—though she'd never have admitted it to the young Schindler girl.

Over the last three months, Fanny had settled in well to the Kálman household. She got along with all the other staff, Izabella did nothing but praise her, and Fanny had found Sándor Kálman and his wife, Johanna, to be kind and gentle people who didn't think it beneath them to celebrate Christmas with their staff around the tree in the entrance hall of their home. And the following day had been Fanny's birthday, complete with more presents. From her master and mistress came a pair of warm slippers, gloves, and a scarf, while Izabella gave her a beautiful barrette. Her colleagues had baked a cake and sung for her, making Fanny feel that she really could have a sense of home here.

The only member of the household she hadn't met was Máxim, Izabella's brother. Fanny knew him only from family photos around the home, astride his horse and in full Hussar uniform. With the fur-trimmed cape and plumed hat, he cut a dashing figure and had the same good looks as his sister, younger than him by five years.

Fanny went over to the bedside table and put down the tray with the utmost care. "I helped Rosa with her costume last night. Tomorrow she's going to the Redoute with Karl for the Fasching Ball."

Situated on the banks of the Danube, the Redoute was a magnificent hall for dance and entertainment.

Fanny was about to pour coffee from the exquisite little silver pot, but Izabella gently reached out to stop her. "Don't worry about that, Fanny. I truly appreciate the way you look after me, but we don't need to overdo things."

"As you wish, ma'am." Fanny bobbed and went to the window to draw back the curtains.

She liked the fact that her mistress didn't want to be waited on hand and foot the way her prior employers had. Down in the street, she spotted the old man who came by every morning to put out all the streetlights. His breath came out in puffs in the bitterly cold air. Snow had been on the ground since Christmas.

"Do you already know what you'd like to wear today, ma'am?" asked Fanny.

In her previous jobs, she had learned that a lady's outfits have to be changed several times a day in accordance with rigid rules. Dresses for daytime wear always had a high neck and collar, and morning dresses were made of wool or cotton with a simple cut and muted colors. In the afternoons, if there were callers or calls to be made, clothes had to be of velvet or satin with braid and bows as decoration. Extravagant ball gowns of silk or brocade, with deep décolleté and long trains, were reserved for evening occasions such as a ball or soirée, the theater, or opera.

Izabella took a mouthful of coffee, then leaned back into her pillows. "Pick something—it's your choice!"

Fanny's talent had already enabled Izabella to stand out as the shining star at the many balls, receptions, *tée dansants*, and sleigh rides that helped local high society while away the dark months of winter.

"I'd suggest the new wool dress in green plaid," said Fanny.

Izabella nodded absently. "And are you off to the Redoute with your sweetheart, as well?"

"No," replied Fanny, opening the door to the dressing room. "I haven't done anything about a costume. And I don't have a sweetheart either."

"Don't tell lies! Surely someone as pretty as you can't be short of a dance partner?"

Rosa had said the same, and István, the chauffeur's son, had actually invited her to the Redoute with him, but this didn't appeal to her one bit.

She'd already gone out a few times with István, Rosa, and Karl to the Orpheum, the dance hall near the Volkstheater. This was where all manner of arty people would drink and dance the night away to the melodies of a gypsy band. Fanny had loved it but for the repulsive stink of beer on István's breath as he'd pressed her for kisses.

"There are two linen bags hanging at the front of the clothes rail," said Fanny as she came back with the plaid dress. "Is that your outfit for the masked ball at the opera tonight?"

"Before I answer your question, my dearest Fanny, you've got to answer mine," retorted Izabella, playfully.

Fanny laid the plaid dress over the arm of a chair. "István asked me out, but I don't want to go."

"So, you turned him down. That's good to hear, as I have another little surprise for you."

Fanny's eyebrows shot up, but Izabella simply smiled and poured another cup of coffee.

Since that first encounter, Izabella had reined in the intimate gestures and ambiguous remarks. She wanted to win Fanny's trust but also, more than anything else, Fanny's affection. Deep in her heart, this outwardly self-confident beauty was lonely. Her looks and wealth meant she had plenty of admirers. But Izabella longed to be loved not by a man but by a woman. In the past, so many women had rejected her, often with revulsion. The few lovers there'd been had soon broken off the relationship for fear of being found out.

This time, Izabella wanted to do it differently. She wanted first to secure Fanny's friendship before gradually introducing her to the idea that two women could love one another. Izabella hoped that if Fanny gave her heart away knowingly, this would mean she'd stay.

She didn't suspect that Rosa had already gossiped to Fanny about her, even less that the conversation echoed in Fanny's mind. When Fanny lay in her narrow bed at night, and nagging homesickness kept her from sleep, her thoughts would drift to Izabella and how it might feel to be kissed by those full, pink lips.

Suddenly setting her cup aside, Izabella slipped out of bed and walked straight to Fanny. "Shall I show you what's in the bags?"

Without waiting for an answer, she took Fanny's hand and drew her into the dressing room, then started to unbutton the first of the two linen bags.

"Holy Mary!" Fanny gasped. "You're wearing that this evening?"

Izabella furrowed her brow. "Don't you like it?"

"I love it! But it'll take some courage!"

Izabella had gotten herself a complete pirate costume. There was a three-cornered hat, a loose white shirt to be worn with the waistcoat hanging open, and red harem pants. Then came red leather boots, a broad leather belt from which hung an alarmingly authentic-looking fake rapier, and a black mask that would fully conceal the face.

"I knew I could rely on you for good judgement!" Izabella's relief was obvious. "I can push my hair into a net, put on the hat and mask, and nobody will know it's me!" She gave a delicious giggle. "Can you see me as a man?"

Fanny gave her a long look. "I can see that very well indeed."

She was a little surprised to see Izabella blush. "And now I'd like to show you the real surprise!" Izabella unbuttoned the second linen bag.

Inside, there was another complete costume. The dress was a glowing burgundy brocade with a full skirt, tight-fitting sleeves only to the elbow, and a lace-covered bodice. Izabella bent down and opened three cartons, one by one. The first revealed a pair of dainty velvet boots, the second a wig of long, silver-white curls, and the third a small velvet purse, a fan and, of course, another mask, but made of gold silk.

Fanny's eyes widened. "It's all just beautiful."

"This one's exactly what a lady would have worn at the French court a hundred and fifty years ago. What do you think of it?" asked Izabella.

"Fabulous! But who's going to wear that?" Fanny was quite overcome.

"You are."

"Me? How d'you mean?"

Izabella closed the last box and straightened up. Solemn all of a sudden, she said, "Would you like to accompany me to the masked ball at the opera?"

Fanny was speechless. She couldn't comprehend how her mistress could consider going to the most elegant of the Budapest Fasching balls with, of all people, her maid.

"Don't look so horrified! Just say yes. I know we'll have so much fun."

Just the thought set off a tingling sensation deep in Fanny's belly. *But how can it possibly happen?*

"We can't just sneak out of the house. Especially not you, without a chaperone. If your parents find out—"

"I thought of all that ages ago!" Izabella insisted. "My parents have been invited to a private party tomorrow evening and told me they won't be back before midnight. As soon as they go out, we'll get changed and then sneak out once all the servants have gone to bed. There are always carriages waiting at the National Museum, and that's not far. We won't be in time for the opening dance at nine, but then we've got all night!"

Fanny took a deep breath, then nodded. "Herr Wenzl and Frau Fischer always turn in early when the master and mistress are out. I expect we can leave without anyone noticing."

"Do you like my surprise, then?"

"It couldn't be crazier, but I do like it. Thank you, ma'am!"

Izabella grinned. "Then there's just one thing to clear up."

"What's that?" Fanny was puzzled.

Izabella gently took Fanny's face in her hands and looked deep into her eyes. "You're not to call me 'ma'am' the whole evening. Promise?"

"I've got something else for you," said Izabella as their coach drew up in front of the opera house on Andrássy Allee. The curtains stood open, and the many lamps outside the opera house cast more than a glow. Izabella took a folded card from her waistcoat pocket and placed it on Fanny's lap.

"How pretty! For me? Thank you!" Fanny timidly fingered the fine white card with its deckled edges, held closed by a slender red silk ribbon.

"For F. S." stood out in curving script on the cover, then: "Masked Ball, Budapest Royal Opera House, February 17, 1910."

"You're supposed to open it." Izabella leaned forward and plucked gently at the ribbon. In her pirate costume, she looked so different and yet so familiar. Fanny could see how men's clothes accentuated her beauty even more than women's and lent her a mysterious air.

"It's your *carnet de bal*, your dance card," explained Izabella. "The gentleman has to give it to his lady at the entrance to the ballroom. And I'm your gentleman tonight. I hope you like it."

"Very much," Fanny whispered.

"Do you see the dance list?" Izabella went on. "The evening began with a polonaise, but there's still waltzes, a polka, a mazurka, a quadrille, and so on. Do you know all the steps?"

"I had dancing lessons in my final year at school and haven't been to a ball since. But the steps'll come back, I bet."

"After the name of every dance, there's a space where you write in your dance partner. With this little pencil." Izabella showed her how the pencil was fitted into a tiny loop on the inside of the card. "I don't want any of the men there to dance with you. So, I'd like you to put my name next to every dance. Unless it's marked as a lady's choice. In that case, you have to ask me!"

"But I can't write Izabella Kálman for my dance partner, surely?"

Izabella clapped her hand to her forehead. "I'd completely forgotten! I'll have to think up a name for myself this evening! How stupid of me!"

"How about using your brother's name? Or will he be here, too?"

Izabella shook her head. "He's spending Fasching in Vienna. But his name's no use. No self-respecting corsair would call himself Máxim." She thought for a moment. "I know, I'll call myself Sir John after the English buccaneer John Hawkins."

"Was he real?" asked Fanny.

Izabella shrugged. "No idea. It comes from a children's book, one of my brother's. Do you want to call me Sir John?"

"Yes, ma'am."

"Shhh! I don't want to hear that again!" Izabella wagged her finger.

"Of course, Sir John," replied Fanny, all innocence.

Izabella laughed with delight. They put on their masks, stepped down from the carriage, and climbed the imposing steps to the opera house.

Just as they entered the foyer, the bells of nearby St. Stephen's Basilica struck half past nine. By now, the place was teeming with partygoers in extravagant costumes and masks, everyone laughing and joking as they raised their glasses to friends. The two new arrivals were quickly caught up in the festive mood.

The auditorium had been transformed into a ballroom for the evening and could be reached only by a broad marble staircase. Doors which, as a rule, only opened to give access to opera lovers now stood invitingly ajar. The two young women saw dancing couples swaying and turning as they waltzed across the space normally occupied by rows of seats.

"Come on, let's dance!" Izabella seized Fanny by the hand, and together they hurried into the auditorium. "Sir John" paused at the edge of the dance floor and gave the most perfect bow to his dance partner. "May I have the pleasure?"

As Fanny eagerly nodded, Izabella took her in her arms, and they slipped seamlessly into three-four time. After the waltzes came a mazurka, a polka, and a galop. Nobody seemed to notice that this pair was actually two women. Fanny quickly saw what a superb dancer Izabella was, although having to do the man's part must have been rather odd for her. But Izabella led with confidence, her arm firmly around Fanny's back, and the lady's maid was all too happy to let herself be guided.

Perhaps she's done this before, disguising herself as a man and secretly going dancing, Fanny thought. The idea that, of all the ball guests, she alone knew Izabella's secret stirred up that tingle in her belly again. When the song came to an end and the dancers paused, she felt as if she was waking from a dream. Izabella's blue eyes, the only part of her face not hidden, were fixed on hers.

"There's a little break now, while the ballet company performs. Would you like to watch that while I fetch us champagne?"

Fanny nearly reminded "Ma'am" that it was her job to arrange drinks, but remembered just in time that everything was the other way around tonight. Izabella was her knight, and his duty was always to serve his lady. The mere thought of it gave her pleasure. "I'd love to," she replied, wreathed in smiles.

As Izabella offered her arm and guided her toward a seating area near the stage, Fanny could hardly believe this was real. Never in her wildest dreams could she have imagined that she, Fanny Schindler, born and raised in the Vienna Foundling House, would one day dance at the most elegant of all the Fasching balls in Budapest.

She recalled the thrill of stepping inside Sarah Moreau's fashion house. This evening brought back that feeling of belonging, if only temporarily, to an exclusive layer of society. And it was intoxicating.

"The champagne bar's one floor up, where the boxes are. It's better for you to wait for me, since it'll be terribly crowded up there," advised Izabella.

She had made a beeline for a little spot with two armchairs, a sofa, and a small table. From here, they had a good view of the stage, but Fanny couldn't help but look longingly at the boxes ringing the auditorium. With the exception of the royal box, all were full of guests having a fine time, scattering brightly colored confetti down on everyone below.

"Could we sit up there?" asked Fanny. "It must be wonderful to have a view from so high up."

Izabella shook her head. "The Kálmans own a box, yes, of course, but you and I can't use it. Remember, I'm here incognito. Oh, don't look so disappointed!" She smiled cheeringly at Fanny. "Don't you think it's fun that most people here know each other, but with the masks, nobody actually knows who's who? Just think what people might dare to get up to when they're in disguise!"

"Like us, Sir John?" Fanny twinkled back at her mistress.

"Yes—just like us!"

Izabella insisted Fanny take one of the comfortable chairs while she herself perched on its arm. Fanny hesitated, then rested her head against Izabella. This made Izabella so happy that she leaned down and breathed a gentle kiss on Fanny's costume wig.

"I'll be back soon." As she stood up, she added, "And don't let any strange men ask you to dance!"

She vanished into the crowd. Fanny relaxed back into her chair, drinking in the sight of so many imaginative costumes. There were any number of sultans and maharajas among the men, but she also spotted Roman emperors and harlequins. Favorites among the women were flower girls, Greek goddesses, and angels, all thrown into perfect relief by the impressive backdrop of the opera house. Above her was a huge candelabrum surrounded by stucco garlands and colorful paintings depicting the gods at play and Graces making music. Gold leaf adorned every supporting column and the balustrade of every box, giving the impression that the auditorium was pure gold. Seating areas had been thoughtfully positioned around the edge of the dance floor, discreetly flanked by potted palms and exotic flower arrangements.

Fanny stretched out her legs to admire her velvet boots. Her feet had never been treated to anything so pretty, but they were now rather too warm, as was her head under the period wig. She took the fan from her little purse and flapped it while watching the ballet troupe complete a round dance. Men and women alike had rustic-themed costumes, and the girls' full skirts and embroidered blouses caught Fanny's appreciative eye. Once the troupe had danced off the stage, the orchestra took a short break before striking up the familiar opening notes of Johann Strauss's Blue Danube waltz.

This brought everyone back onto the floor. Fanny looked hard for Izabella, but in vain. She took out her dance card, unfolded it, and saw that "The Blue Danube" was meant to be a lady's choice. Fanny had, of course, promised it to "Sir John." But he wasn't here. Feeling deflated, she folded the card shut.

Just then, she heard a man talking to her, but in Hungarian.

When she looked up, she saw a man in a mask. A magnificent ostrich feather embellished his three-cornered hat, and long dark curls fell about his shoulders. He wore a white shirt, knee breeches, and eye-catching high boots. A blue cloak completed his outfit. His right hand rested casually on the hilt of the saber that hung from his low belt, while his left lay respectfully across his chest in a traditional show of sincerity. He was studying her more carefully than was comfortable. She felt her scalp get even hotter and tried to look busy as she pushed the dance card back in her little purse.

But when she looked up again, he was still there. A smile played around his full, sensuous mouth. Above his upper lip, finely waxed whiskers twirled upward at each end, while his chin boasted a beard shaped into little more than a slender strip.

She cleared her throat. "Forgive me, sir, but what were you saying?"

His smile broadened. "That I would ask you to dance were it not a lady's choice. So, I'm hoping that you'll be the one to ask me, *gnädiges*

Fräulein," he replied in German. She noticed his rolled Hungarian *r,* the same as Izabella's.

"I'm—I'm sorry." She was taken aback. "I'm already spoken for."

"And by whom?" He looked all around them. "I see no one."

"He's getting me a drink and will be back any moment," she said firmly, sitting bolt upright in her chair.

"If I were your companion this evening, I wouldn't let someone so charming sit around alone. So, if you'd rather not miss this dance . . ." He gave Fanny a smile that made his intentions perfectly clear.

Now it was her turn to look everywhere, but not a corsair was in sight. She'd have liked to dance with this stranger but knew how angry Izabella would be if she came back and saw her keeping three-four time in the arms of another.

"I regret that my answer has to be no."

"You're breaking my heart. You could at least give me a clue as to who you are, my unknown beauty."

Fanny gave a little giggle and flapped open her fan so that only her eyes were visible. "Surely the whole point of a masked ball is that nobody gives away their identity?"

"You're toying with my emotions," came his riposte. "How on earth shall I find you again if you'll give me no clues?"

"Maybe I'll leave a slipper on the staircase when I go."

"That means I'll have to try it on every lady in Budapest? Your cruelty knows no bounds!"

"If you're serious about finding me, you'll have to make an effort!"

"Aha!" His face brightened. "Is that a charming Viennese accent I'm hearing, my beautiful stranger?"

But now more male voices interrupted this little dalliance.

"Hello, D'Artagnan!" called one. "So, this is where you're hiding!"

"I hope you weren't trying to keep this treasure all for yourself, my friend!" exclaimed a second.

Then came the lascivious tones of a third. "It won't do to keep the belle of the ball a secret!"

The man they'd called D'Artagnan turned slowly to face them, snarling with indignation. "You obviously don't know when to get the hell out."

"Come, come!" objected the first man. "What was our motto again? 'All for one and one for all'?"

"Please, no innuendo in front of a lady!" D'Artagnan took one step toward the trio, but they mockingly folded their arms and didn't move an inch.

Fanny leaned to the side a bit to see around D'Artagnan. The three young musketeers were identically dressed and looked back at her with equal curiosity.

D'Artagnan spun back to face her and held out his right hand. "Come with me, my beautiful stranger. Let me whisk you away from the company of this boorish rabble."

"But you already know I'm—" she began to explain.

"The lady's with me!"

The four men whipped around, and Fanny gave a guilty start. "Iza—erm, John, where—?"

"I see I'm back in the nick of time!" Izabella's tone was icy as she pushed her way past the musketeers. Her eyes flashed angrily, and champagne spilled over the rim of the two glasses in her hands.

"Our beautiful stranger has already been captured by some buccaneer," commented the first man salaciously.

"And buccaneers never part with their loot without a fight," added the second man.

Then the third chimed in. "This pirate's come along at just the wrong time for you, hasn't he, my dear D'Artagnan?"

D'Artagnan didn't as much as flinch. He seemed rooted to the spot in front of Fanny, but it wasn't her he was looking at. His eyes were fixed on the corsair.

Izabella slammed the two glasses down on the small table by Fanny's chair, then spun on the four men. "Leave us immediately, or I'll call in the guards of the ball."

"No need to get so heated, sir." The first musketeer gestured for her to stay calm. "We'll make a tactical retreat." He gave a cursory bow and moved off. The two others followed.

Only D'Artagnan remained. Izabella took a menacing step toward him. But instead of following in his friends' wake, he grabbed her by the shoulder.

"Get your smarmy visage out of here, you brute, or you'll get a black eye an' more!"

Both Izabella and D'Artagnan turned in amazement and stared. Fanny stared aggressively back.

"I'm serious!" she hissed.

D'Artagnan nodded almost imperceptibly. Before letting go of Izabella, he leaned close and whispered something to her. For a few seconds, all three stood, glaring at one other. Then Izabella seized Fanny by the arm.

"Come on!"

D'Artagnan watched as they hurried through the ballroom. Only when they'd disappeared from view did he turn to go. That was when he spotted Fanny's velvet purse. As she'd leapt to her feet in Izabella's defense, it had fallen from her lap. Bending to the ground, he gave it a long hard look before slipping it into the pocket of his cloak.

"What was it that man whispered to you?" Fanny asked.

The abrupt end to this wonderful evening had left her shocked, most of all because the two of them had fled the opera house like thieves in the night.

Once they were outside, Izabella had pushed her unceremoniously into the first available carriage. Now it clattered over the bumpy

Budapest cobblestones. But her mistress wouldn't answer her questions, and because she'd closed the curtains, Fanny couldn't even see her face. She heard Izabella's breath, strained and uneven, as if she was fighting back tears.

"What is it about that man that scared you?" Fanny persisted.

Izabella only sighed. "Please don't ask," she said, her voice bleak. "I can't tell you."

This only added to Fanny's confusion. Who was this stranger calling himself D'Artagnan? Her initial regret at not dancing with him had vanished. Instead, she now blamed him for ruining such a lovely evening and for driving her mistress to this state of despair. A muffled sob came from Izabella's corner of the carriage, so Fanny reached out in the darkness for her hand and placed her fingers protectively over it. Izabella's hand flinched a little, but stayed put.

Soon, the carriage drew up outside the Palais Kálman and they stepped down. While Izabella paid the coachman, Fanny anxiously scanned the façade. Curtains covered the windows of the head butler's and the housekeeper's rooms. Fanny prayed that neither one was still up, secretly peering out at her through a crack.

She hurried behind Izabella through the gateway to the courtyard, where the lights were few and far between.

"My parents aren't back yet, but it's only just after midnight." She nodded toward the empty spot where the motorcar usually stood.

They slipped through the servants' entrance, removed their boots before going inside, and then tiptoed through the house. Before long, they'd reached Izabella's bedroom.

The young mistress went in first, waited until Fanny was through the door, and then bolted it. Only then did they remove their masks.

Fanny went to put hers away in its pouch. "Dammit! I lost the little purse that goes with this costume. I must've dropped it when we left so fast. It had my dance card inside. Oh, that's such a shame! I wanted it as a souvenir of tonight."

Izabella turned to face her. In the moonlight coming through the window, she seemed pale, and her dark eyes glowed. She stepped closer to Fanny and placed her hands on the girl's cheeks. "I wanted this evening to be unforgettable, but not in that way. I'm so very sorry."

These words touched Fanny deeply. "But it was a lovely evening, ma'am. Without you, I'd never have been able to go to anything like that."

"You aren't just saying that to console me?"

"It's the truth," Fanny reassured her. "Can't you just tell me what upset you so much? You know that stranger, am I right?"

A sad smile passed across Izabella's face. Then her fingers moved from Fanny's cheeks to the wig. Gently, she pulled it free of Fanny's own curls, now rather flattened and sweaty. "Oh, my dear little Fanny," she murmured. "Do you realize that you've fluttered into my existence like a beautiful butterfly?" She leaned closer until her mouth brushed deliciously against Fanny's right earlobe. "You're right, I know D'Artagnan. But I didn't expect to meet him at that ball."

"He must have recognized your voice! And then he threatened you because you'd gone to the ball in secret and without an escort!"

Izabella shook her head. "He didn't threaten me. But he made it clear he recognized me. And then"—she lowered her head—"then he wanted to know why I was there dressed as a man in the company of a woman."

Fanny hung on her every word, sensing that Izabella was about to confide in her.

Izabella let out a huge sigh. But all she said was, "It's time to get out of these clothes and go to bed."

"Of course," murmured Fanny, disappointed. She went straight to the dressing room to fetch her own dress and the linen bags for the costumes.

She turned over in her mind this new side of Izabella. Her self-assured, rather haughty mistress was sensitive and vulnerable, too.

Fanny didn't fully understand what had upset Izabella so much nor to what extent she'd contributed to it all. But if Ma'am didn't want to talk about it, then she'd respect that. As she came out of the dressing room, she resolved not to say another word about the evening.

Meanwhile, Izabella had removed her own costume and thrown it on the bed. Now barefoot, clad only in delicate linen panties and an equally dainty chemise, she looked straight at Fanny.

"I'll help you get out of your dress." She reached out to take the costume bags and tossed them on the bed. Then she began to loosen the lacing that attached the skirt and the back of the top to Fanny's bodice. It took a while for her to free Fanny from the restrictive garment, but at last the young girl stood before her dressed only in her corset, chemise, panties, and stockings. "Oh, my goodness, how on earth did you manage to squeeze into such a monster without help?"

"Once I worked out how it all fit together, it wasn't so hard," said Fanny, with a giggle. Everything felt topsy-turvy, Izabella helping her undress and not the other way around.

"You caught the eye of many a gentleman this evening, my little butterfly," said Izabella, slipping open the top hook on Fanny's corset as if it was the most natural thing in the world and, as she did so, brushing her fingertips across Fanny's breasts, now covered only by her wafer-thin chemise. "Would you rather have gone to the ball with one of them? D'Artagnan, perhaps?"

Fanny blushed. She'd been so absorbed in the excitement of the occasion and the magnificence of the opera house that she hadn't paid attention to the men—until that D'Artagnan fellow had turned up. When she thought about him, the tingling excitement she sometimes felt in her belly was so powerful that it drove away her earlier resentment.

"But, ma'am, you're the eye-catching one," she replied. "Bet you have lots of admirers."

Izabella laughed softly as she undid the next hook on Fanny's corset. "This is my third season since leaving school. Most of my friends are married now—a few of them, mothers. Mama is quite desperate and is constantly introducing me to what she calls 'promising young men.' For her, it'll be the end of the world if I wind up a spinster. Any woman without a husband and children is, in our circles, a pariah. At best, someone to be pitied, at worst, to be laughed at. If I want to belong, I'll have to marry. But I'm going to put that off as long as I possibly can. And I'll only marry a man who's like me. That's the only way to keep my freedom."

"I'm sure you'll make a good choice," replied Fanny, wondering what her mistress meant by a man like her. But she could see Izabella making a glittering marriage and leading a thoroughly carefree existence. She felt a twinge of envy. All her life, she'd never owned more than what fit inside her suitcase and would doubtless be too poor even to marry. Lady's maids didn't earn much. And apart from all that, she hadn't even begun to find a suitable man. To her mind, someone like István, who had as little as she did, was out of the question. She suppressed a little sigh, thinking how she'd probably have to work all her life, like Josepha. And without the devotion that her elderly guardian had always shown.

"It won't be hard to find a man to marry." Izabella's voice cut across her musings. "But I'd rather spend my life with someone I truly love—and that won't be my husband."

"I don't see how you can be so sure of that already," said Fanny quietly.

"For me, love doesn't mean what it means to most people," confided Izabella. "When I fall in love, it's something very special. For me, love feels like the greatest wonder imaginable, and yet at the same time, I know it can never be fulfilled." By now, she'd undone the final hook on Fanny's corset and let it slip to the floor. "Sometimes I find someone for a while, someone like me. And in those moments, I have to seek out all the happiness that others have their whole lives to enjoy. Do you understand me, my little butterfly?"

She placed her hands on Fanny's hips and looked at her attentively. Fanny was bewildered but guessed that her reaction meant a lot to Izabella, so she nodded hesitantly.

Izabella smiled, her relief obvious. She looked deep into Fanny's eyes as she ran her hands a little higher, placed them around Fanny's waist, and drew her close. Fanny felt Izabella's breath warm on her face as her full breasts pressed against her. Her mistress's body was warm and supple. Yes, it felt good to be this close. As Izabella's face came even nearer, she closed her eyes. Her lips trembled and parted as she thought to herself how she'd never expected her first kiss to be with a woman. Then she felt the soft, moist sweetness of Izabella's lips on hers and found herself enjoying the sensation. But the moment she felt Izabella's hand squeezing her breast, she recoiled.

Fanny Schindler, what d'you think you're doing? Fooling around with your mistress like this!

Pulling free of Izabella's embrace, she grabbed her dress and ran for the door.

"Come back!" Izabella called after her. "Please!"

But Fanny fled without a word.

Chapter Seven

Budapest, 1910

"Fanny, Rosa, come to my office, please," said Frau Fischer after breakfast.

Fanny pushed back her chair, giving Rosa a questioning look. Her colleague seemed equally puzzled.

As Fanny followed Rosa to the housekeeper's office, she worried that something had reached Frau Fischer's ears about the opera house excursion four weeks earlier.

"The master and mistress expect visitors," Frau Fischer began, seated behind her large desk. "I was informed yesterday evening that Baroness Báthory and her daughter will arrive just after Easter." She looked from Rosa to Fanny. "One of you will have to look after Fräulein Helene in addition to your regular duties."

Rosa rolled her eyes. "But the baroness's daughter is eighteen and has already been presented at court. A young lady usually gets her own lady's maid once she's come out. We can all guess why she hasn't—the Báthorys must be short of cash again."

"Rosa! It's not your place to make such remarks, nor even to think them!" The housekeeper sniffed in disapproval. "Clearly I'll have to entrust Fanny with the task. Can you look after the baroness's daughter as well as our own young lady?"

"Couldn't the baroness's own lady's maid do it?" Fanny shifted uncomfortably. "I wouldn't want to displease Fräulein Izabella by not giving her enough time."

"Hardly! You know how the baroness—"

"Rosa! That's enough!" Frau Fischer snapped. "I'm sure you have urgent jobs waiting."

"Just like every morning!" There was no putting down Rosa. "Fanny does, too. She shouldn't have to take care of people from outside."

The housekeeper glared at her. Rosa glared back, then turned and left the room.

Frau Fischer turned her attention to Fanny. "I know I'm asking you to do extra work. But the daughter is not a finicky young woman. In fact, I think she'll be grateful to have someone with your flair and sense of style at her side. Can I count on you?"

"Yes, of course," said Fanny agreeably, but she wondered how on earth she would manage it on top of what she had to do for Izabella.

"Excellent." Frau Fischer looked more than satisfied with the outcome. "The baroness and her daughter are staying a month, perhaps even longer, and their visits to our household are something of a tradition. We already know most of their preferences, but there is much to do in the five days remaining to us before they arrive."

Fanny glanced at the clock on top of the chest. "May I go now? Fräulein Izabella's morning coffee is due in fifteen minutes."

"Fanny, a moment more, please." The housekeeper leaned back in her chair to give Fanny a long hard look, something that left the girl greatly discomfited. What on earth did Frau Fischer still expect of her? Hadn't she just agreed to take on the extra work? The housekeeper gave a little cough. "You know that, until recently, Herr Wenzl and I have been very pleased with your work."

"Only until recently?"

Frau Fischer gestured for her to be quiet. "When the master and mistress were having breakfast yesterday, Herr Wenzl overheard Fräulein Izabella being very critical of you to her mother. She complained that her morning coffee had been cold. And that you're no longer the punctual person you were."

Fanny felt her cheeks flush with anger. "That's not true! I haven't been late, not once, and I'm always careful that Fräulein Izabella has her coffee served piping hot, as she likes it."

"Can I assume from that you're as committed as you were on your first day?"

"You can."

"You have to understand why it's essential that I look into anything like this. And we still haven't seen your references . . ."

"But Frau Fischer, you must know enough about me by now to be certain that I'd give no cause for complaint."

"Fräulein Izabella was more than satisfied with you in the beginning. I'm wondering why she isn't any longer."

"I don't know." Fanny felt quite knocked back.

That Izabella was dissatisfied with her work was something Fanny had indeed noticed. Over the last month or so, not a day had gone by without some reprimand or other. First it was her corset being too tightly laced, then it was her hair too roughly brushed, then it was Fanny's supposed lack of punctuality.

All these accusations were unjust and untrue, but Fanny still tried to make things right with Izabella. She never knew when the next dressing-down would come, and this left her insecure and unsure how to conduct herself in Izabella's presence.

Frau Fischer kept on looking at her thoughtfully. "I know you carry out your work carefully and reliably. However, the young mistress is not satisfied with you. There must be a reason for that."

Fanny hung her head. She knew perfectly well it was because of the night of the Fasching Ball but couldn't possibly have talked to Frau Fischer about that. She hadn't even breathed a word of it to Rosa.

The housekeeper gave her a little more time. But when Fanny persisted in her silence, she said, "I expect you to carry out your duties for Baroness Báthory with no objections and not to hear any complaints whatsoever from Fräulein Izabella or from the Báthorys."

Fanny nodded and hurried from the room.

"So, you're going to look after the baroness's daughter?" asked Rosa, when Fanny came back to the servants' dayroom.

"Yes." Fanny flopped into the first chair she came to.

The appetizing aromas of coffee and fresh-baked bread wafted in from the kitchen. She looked at the round clock over the door. Ten minutes until Izabella's coffee tray had to be on the move, and she needed every one simply to calm herself. In spite of Izabella's recent moods, never for a moment had she expected that her young mistress would make any complaints. And all completely groundless at that!

Rosa was chattering on behind her. "It's really no surprise that the Báthorys have no lady's maid for Fräulein Helene. The baroness gives herself such airs and graces that you'd think she was descended from the royal household itself. The Báthorys just hide behind the high-class name when they're practically poor as church mice. I reckon the baroness is after a good catch for her daughter and that's why they want to stay with us in Budapest. Maybe she's even after our very own Máxim. He's absolutely gorgeous and so rich that any number of Báthorys could live fancy-free on his money. That's why they overlook his being a Jew."

Fanny's mind was elsewhere, but she tried to give the impression she'd been listening. "Are Fräulein Izabella and Fräulein Helene friends?"

"That'd be stretching it a bit! They're like chalk and cheese," said Rosa firmly. "The families only know each other because of the baroness's charity work. A good few years ago now, she founded the relief committee that helps Budapest kids with tuberculosis, and our mistress—well, our master, really—is the biggest donor. It's his money that keeps the sanatorium at Plattensee going. If you ask me, money's the only reason the baroness bothers with a bourgeois Jewish family."

"Oh really?" murmured Fanny, her eye still on the clock.

"You'll find Fräulein Helene nice—maybe a bit colorless," continued Rosa. "But she won't make a lot of work for you. With Baroness Báthory, it's a bit different. She makes a big thing of being descended from the old Hungarian nobility. She's always going on about how before her marriage she was lady-in-waiting to Empress Elisabeth. But everyone knows the empress always had Hungarian staff close to her because she loved Hungary. Listen, Fanny, why are you staring at the clock like that?"

"No reason," muttered Fanny. "Just don't want to be late for Fräulein Izabella."

"But you're never late!"

Fanny looked over toward the door, but all was quiet in the hallway. "Fräulein Izabella's been saying different," she said quietly.

Rosa went straight to the door, closed it firmly, and pulled her chair close to Fanny's. "Something happened, didn't it?"

Fanny thought back to the Fasching Ball that had started out a dream and ended a nightmare. If she hadn't accepted that invitation, she'd never have accepted that kiss.

All this has happened because you won't accept your true place, said Josepha somewhere in her head.

Fanny sighed. No matter how much she wished she'd listened to her old guardian's wisdom, she couldn't ever undo the events of that night.

Since then, everything had changed between her and her mistress. Izabella was no longer kind to her, no longer cheerful or affectionate, but cold and impersonal, and as Fanny had just found out, probably vengeful. She understood that Izabella hadn't forgiven her for running away from her advances. But surely she was entitled to do so? Just because Izabella was her mistress, it didn't mean that Fanny had to do every single thing she wanted. Sometimes Fanny thought she'd like to have a quiet chat with Ma'am about that night but didn't know how to broach the subject, and Izabella certainly never referred to it.

God knows I've tried to show you that I deserve trust, not rejection, thought Fanny. Nothing she said or did could soften Izabella's heart.

Her eyes smarted as she fought back tears. She'd felt so desperate of late that she'd been close to packing her bags and making a break for it. How often had she taken out of her suitcase that envelope of Josepha's with her emergency fund still intact, resolving to get herself a train ticket back to Vienna? But she couldn't bear to tell Josepha that she'd walked out of yet another job, especially as she'd sworn that she wouldn't be any more trouble.

One of the kitchen maids brought her Izabella's coffee tray. Fanny moved to stand, but Rosa held her back. "D'you remember what I told you about the young mistress when you first got here?" She lowered her voice to a whisper. "Is that why you had problems with her?"

Fanny pressed her eyes with the back of her hand and looked unhappily at Rosa. When the kitchen maid had left the room again, she said quietly, "I like Ma'am very much, but not in the way she wants me to, and I'm afraid she's holding that against me." Her hope remained that Izabella would soon go back to being as she was before—kind, generous, and affectionate.

"Forward march, Franz! Or do you expect these ladies to open the door themselves?"

The roar of the motorcar had prompted the head butler and Franz to hurry to the reception hall, and now Herr Wenzl pushed the manservant firmly ahead to open the grand double doors at exactly the right moment.

In stepped their mistress, Izabella, Baroness Báthory, and her daughter, Helene. Behind them was István, barely visible beneath the tall stack of packages and cartons in his arms.

Herr Wenzl gestured to the hapless chauffeur to make himself scarce by taking the well-concealed door to the servants' stairs. Then he executed the perfect bow. "Welcome! I trust the ladies have had a pleasant day!"

"How could it be otherwise? My husband has two department stores boasting everything our hearts desire!" Johanna Kálman was full of good cheer.

The head butler helped her out of her coat, hat, and gloves, while Franz assisted the three other women. Johanna went straight to the silver tray that was always in the hall and swiftly looked through the post and visiting cards that had been left during her absence. The Kálmans had a telephone, as did many wealthy families in Budapest, but for anyone to announce a house visit by phone instead of leaving a card in person would have been considered the height of rudeness.

The lady of the house kept one envelope in hand and told Herr Wenzl to take the rest to the green drawing room. "And bring some tea and pastries, please. We could do with refreshments after such a busy day. Helene!"

She went over to the young girl, who was watching in silence as her mother attended to her elaborately coifed hair, piled high for maximum effect, in front of the mirror. "There's a letter for you from Max. I'm sure you'll want to read it immediately." Johanna held the envelope out to her.

Helene looked pleased as she took it. "Thank you!"

Her mother, however, snatched the letter herself. "As long as you're not engaged, I, as your mother, would like to know precisely what any young man is writing to you, Nelli!"

Helene flushed. "That letter's for me, Mama. Give it back, please."

The baroness only laughed. "What are you thinking of, child! I'm responsible for your reputation until you're at the altar. And I take this duty very seriously indeed." She turned to her hostess. "My dear Frau Kálman, I do hope you've arranged for all the bills from our shopping excursion to be sent to me?"

"And what are *you* thinking of?" Johanna sounded indignant. "It brings me a lot of pleasure if you and your daughter can enjoy a few things from our business."

"My dear friend, you're embarrassing me! I'll accept your generosity, but only for Nelli . . ." The two women went on talking as they walked, Ida Báthory linking arms with Johanna.

The two younger women trailed behind them. Izabella whispered to Helene, "Goodness, Nelli, you're eighteen now. When are you going to stand up to your mother?"

The elegant green drawing room owed its name to the pistachio-colored silken wall coverings and the large Persian carpet with its intricate foliage pattern. Just as the four women entered the room, Franz was carefully placing the tea tray on the sideboard next to a platter of pralines, perfect bite-size chunks of cake, and confectionery, all delivered daily from Gerbeaud, the court confectioner.

The ladies headed straight for the marble fireplace, where comfortable seating had been readied. Ida and Helene Báthory sat down together on the sofa, while Johanna Kálman went to her usual armchair and writing table to give her full attention to the post and visiting cards. Izabella threw herself down into another armchair.

The four women had been out and about all day. Their first port of call had been Waiznerstrasse to make the most of Sándor Kálman's older department store before going on to his other establishment on

Andrássy Allee. This shopping shrine, not far from the opera house, had opened its doors for the first time last year and boasted the first moving staircase in Budapest, as well as the elevator the ladies had taken to the roof terrace with its magnificent view to the other side of the Danube and the castle hill.

They had taken their time and gone around every department in both stores. Only Izabella had been bored stiff. She had never had any interest in protracted shopping expeditions. If she needed anything, she would simply have a collection sent to the house and make a choice. But Ida Báthory had taken full advantage of the excellent service and ordered all manner of things. By contrast, her daughter had asked for barely anything in spite of her mother's enthusiastic suggestions. Most of the time the girl had stood in silence, visibly discomfited by her mother as the staff ran around after her.

Izabella looked over at Helene, hands in her lap, eyes lowered. *What a boring creature this Nelli is,* she thought.

Next to her mother, the baroness, such a stylish, confident woman with strikingly chiseled features, Helene always came across as plain, and more than a little inconspicuous.

Today was different. The color of her dress, peach, complemented both her complexion and her chestnut curls, and its cut flattered her rather homely figure. Today she was not inconspicuous. She was pretty.

This'll be Fanny's work. At the very thought, Izabella's already low mood plummeted.

Things had gone so badly wrong at the Fasching Ball two months ago. She hadn't expected such a decisive rejection. After all, Fanny had accepted the invitation to the ball in the first place, and very enthusiastically at that. They had danced and then kissed in Izabella's bedroom. She had no doubt that Fanny had returned her kisses. And yet when Izabella wanted to touch her more intimately, the girl had fled the room. This had left Izabella feeling she'd done something dirty and wrong. At the same time, she longed so much to be close to another woman, someone she could open her heart to, and she'd hoped that Fanny felt the same. Now Izabella felt she'd never find anyone who would return her love, and this left her unhappy, at times desperate.

Meanwhile, Franz had filled each porcelain cup with tea and served everyone, then done a lap of the room with the cake and confectionery he'd arranged so beautifully. Johanna Kálman glanced over the rest of the post.

"Max has written to us, too!" she cried out happily as she slid the silver letter opener under the flap of one of the envelopes. As she read, her smile grew even broader. "He's been awarded a place at our *Kriegschule*, the imperial military academy! Over four hundred officers sat the entrance examination, and Max is one of the fifty who passed. So, starting this autumn he'll be studying in Vienna! If all goes well, he'll have a glittering career ahead of him! Just think, he could be a senior adjutant on the General Staff, then maybe commander one day!" Glowing with pride, she beamed at her companions.

Baroness Báthory sipped her tea. "Being accepted at the military academy is cause for the warmest congratulations. It is, of course, quite natural that more Hungarians are being accepted there now that my good friend Baron Rohr von Denta is the general inspector of military educational establishments. One countryman helps another."

Izabella's head spun toward the woman. She said sharply, "If Max has been offered a place, it's based on his ability. He doesn't need patronage."

The baroness looked unmoved. "I'm firmly of the belief that we should all rally to protect Hungary's interests. That's of greater use than some certificate."

Izabella was about to retort angrily, but her mother shot her a look and turned quickly to Helene. "So, Nelli, what's the news from Max? Is he coming to Budapest soon?" Although she'd so obviously spoken directly to the girl, Ida replied instead. "We haven't yet had time to read the letter, but we'll do so now, won't we, Nelli?" But she didn't hand it to her daughter. She quickly read it through herself.

"That letter is to Nelli." Izabella's tone was poisonous. "And she's perfectly capable of reading it herself."

"Oh, my child, why are you being so impolite?" Johanna was clearly flustered. Turning to her visitors, she added, "I must apologize for my daughter. It is a mystery to me why she has been in such an intolerable mood for the last few weeks."

The baroness's lips narrowed as she forced a smile. "Izabella turns twenty-one this year, I think. It doesn't suit a woman to have to wait too long to fulfill her natural function. Our dear empress was married at sixteen and a mother at seventeen."

"If it were up to me, Izabella would have been married long ago." Johanna let out a sigh. "There's no shortage of suitors. But she turns them all down. She says she'll only tie the knot with someone she truly loves."

"Love? For goodness' sake!" The baroness raised an eyebrow. "That's of no import in a successful marriage." She turned once again to the letter, then exclaimed with disappointment. "Máxim has canceled his visit! He writes he's off to Galicia on maneuvers with the regiment and won't be back until early in the summer. What a disappointment for my poor little Nelli! She was so looking forward to his visit—weren't you?" She leaned across to pinch her daughter's cheek.

Helene turned her head away. "Please leave it now, Mama."

The baroness folded the letter and placed it in her daughter's lap. "Even if Máxim's had obstacles put in his way, he can still spend the summer with us on our estate! Nelli, you must write back to him straightaway. Tell him how disappointed you are that he's broken his promise. Make it clear that the only way he can make up for it is by accepting our invitation. In fact, it would actually be highly appropriate for Máxim to come while we're staying out on the Puszta—the grassland is so open and invigorating. If all goes well, then we can celebrate your name day the same time as your engagement!" The baroness nearly cackled with delight. She turned to Johanna Kálman. "You and your dear husband are, of course, also invited to visit us there." She paused. "And Izabella, too."

"Why, thank you!" replied Johanna. "It's always a joy not to have to spend the summer in the city, but we have planned a trip to the spa at Héviz on Plattensee. Sándor's badly in need of recuperation and the restorative waters there. He spends so much time at work. And Izabella will come with us, of course."

"This is most regrettable," replied Ida Báthory with a pout. She picked out a nougat praline and held it up between thumb and forefinger to examine the candied violet placed on the frosting. "My dear friend, don't you find it rather chilly in here? Could one of your girls fetch my cashmere shawl from my room? My Zsófia has the afternoon off." With that, she popped the praline into her mouth and chewed it reflectively.

Johanna looked over at Franz. "Please go and find Fanny and tell her to bring the baroness's shawl."

Franz swiftly left the room. He was soon back, followed only a few minutes later by a knock at the door. Fanny entered, bearing the shawl.

"Ma'am." She curtsied to the baroness.

Taking the shawl with only a cursory nod, Ida Báthory flung it around her shoulders.

Helene smiled timidly at the girl, saying, "Thank you, Fanny, you were so quick!"

Fanny curtsied once more. "You're too kind, Fräulein Helene!"

Izabella watched all this in silence. She was angry that Fanny had not once looked in her direction and jealous of the warm smile she had exchanged with Helene. "And where's my wrap, Fanny?" she snapped.

Johanna Kálman couldn't have looked more aghast at her daughter's behavior. Helene gave a little gasp but said nothing, while her mother stirred her tea as if quite detached from the scene. Fanny turned to look at Franz, who gave only a helpless shrug. "Your wrap, ma'am?" she asked in confusion. "I didn't know you wanted one."

"Of course I did!" hissed Izabella. "The green, fringed one."

"Izabella!" Her mother was so shocked she raised her voice. "You gave Fanny no instructions at all. You should apologize."

Izabella swallowed hard. She saw in Fanny's face only hurt and confusion and wished she could take back the lie. But it was too late for that. In fact, the clearer it became to her how disgracefully she was behaving, the more impossible it seemed to apologize. Instead, she heard herself saying icily, "After six months in my service, you should know when I need something. Why else would you be my lady's maid?"

Fanny felt all the old anger rise up inside, threatening the promises she had made to Josepha. "I have always looked after you well, ma'am, and have carried out all instructions. But I'm no clairvoyant." Turning on her heel, she hurried from the room.

"This is shameful, Izabella!" cried Johanna Kálman. "I didn't raise you to treat our domestic staff badly, and I insist that you make amends."

Izabella lowered her eyes. She didn't want anyone to see that she was close to tears.

"Forgive me if I'm overstepping, my dear friend, but that girl shows a real lack of respect for her employers," said Ida Báthory. "If you want to ensure your generosity doesn't lead to your being taking advantage of, then on no account should Izabella apologize. Doing that would show that any impertinence from a servant is tolerated. And then it would be no time before they're running the show."

"Mama, how can you possibly talk about it like this? Nobody should have to put up with every single thing that's thrown at them, especially not when it's unjust!" Helene exclaimed.

Everyone, including her mother, looked at her in utter amazement. Nobody could recall ever hearing an outburst from Helene before. Ida Báthory eventually forced a smile.

"My little Nelli, your democratic ideas are quite out of place when it comes to one's own staff."

"I don't know anything about 'democratic ideas,' as you put it," retorted Helene. "But I do know that since we came here, Fanny has taken care of me, and I know that she goes to a great deal of trouble to do everything right. I'm sure it's the same for Izabella."

Just then, the door opened and in came Fanny. She'd overheard Helene's last remarks and stopped dead in surprise. Izabella noticed her eyes were red, but her face brightened at what she'd heard. Fanny gave Helene a little smile in appreciation before turning to Izabella. "Your wrap, ma'am."

"I don't need it now." Izabella jumped up and ran out of the room.

"So, what have you come up with today?" It had been an hour since the drawing room incident, and Helene now sat at her dressing table, still wearing her morning dress. Fanny had just walked into the room with a supplement from the day's paper.

The Kálmans had invited their guests to accompany them for an evening of piano music by Franz Liszt. Tickets had been in great demand, as every Hungarian revered their fellow countryman and his music. Nobody was looking forward to it more than Johanna Kálman, herself a gifted pianist who had once studied under Liszt.

Fanny came over to show Helene a page. "If you'd like, I'll try this new hairdo for you. It's called the Piskey style."

"Piskey?" Helene was puzzled.

"Here it is. Do you like it?" Fanny held the page out so that Helene could see the picture of a young woman with a beautifully coiled knot decorated with graceful combs, ribbons, and bands. "That's very pretty! But won't it take ages to do?"

"Not at all!" said Fanny warmly. "The curls I did with the irons this morning are still there. I only need to re-pin your hair and decorate it with some pretty things. I'll easily finish in time for your concert. It starts at eight." She peered inside the little vanity chest where Helene kept her barrettes. "That golden band and those two combs with the colored glass butterflies would sit really well with this."

A little smile played at the corner of Helene's mouth. "Please don't be offended if I correct you, but it says here it's called the 'Psyche' hairstyle."

Fanny was embarrassed. "Psyche hairstyle," she repeated. "I didn't know that."

"That's why I mention it, so that you know, not because I'm trying to find fault with you," said Helene quickly.

"Why would anyone choose a silly name like that for a hairdo?" murmured Fanny.

"Well, it's modeled on a figure from mythology called Psyche. Psyche was the daughter of a king, and so beautiful that even the goddess Venus lived in envy of her. But Psyche later married Venus's son, Cupid, and they had a daughter together, called Voluptas. That's like 'voluptuous.'" Helene giggled.

But Fanny didn't smile. "I don't know any of that stuff," she said quietly. "I'm just ignorant."

"Oh, don't be ridiculous!" Helene patted her hand. "I'm only parroting something useless I learned at school. I'd much rather have talent like yours. You're so gifted when it comes to dressmaking and making someone look beautiful. I can only talk about things like that, not do them."

"I've never really thought of it like that," said Fanny pensively. Once she'd started loosely knotting Helene's hair and pinning it carefully around the back of her head in a long coil, she didn't look sad at all.

"Have you already helped Izabella get ready?" asked Helene.

"Yes."

"Did she treat you nicely?" Helene looked hard at Fanny's reflection in her dressing table mirror.

Fanny avoided her gaze. The three-quarters of an hour she'd taken to do Izabella's hair and help her dress had passed agonizingly slowly. Izabella had not apologized as Fanny had privately hoped she would. Only the bare minimum of conversation had taken place, and Fanny felt deeply offended by Izabella's disdainful attitude. But she didn't want to go crying to Helene about it.

"Thank you for your kind words this afternoon," she said as she took one of the butterfly combs from the chest and pressed it firmly on the right-hand side of Helene's hair.

"You don't need to thank me for telling the truth." Helene turned her head slightly to one side to see herself better in the mirror. "How long have you worked for Izabella?"

"Just under six months."

"And was she always like she was with you today?"

"No, not at all. The first few months she was very nice. We got along so well and laughed a lot, too."

"And what happened?"

Fanny took the second comb and placed it on the left-hand side of Helene's hair. "Forgive me, ma'am, but it would be wrong to discuss it."

"You're quite right to chide me. I'm being nosy," said Helene after a short pause. "Your loyalty to those who put bread on your plate deserves respect."

The two young women smiled as they caught one another's reflection in the mirror. Then Helene opened a little drawer in her dressing table and took out a folded sheet of paper. "This is the letter I wrote Max. Mama's going to want to see it. Izabella says it's time I stood up to her, but I don't know how. She's always hovering, wanting to know what I'm doing. There are times when I feel as though she's right inside my head, reading my thoughts."

"So, what you need to do is write a second letter, saying what you really want to Herr Máxim, and then send it secretly," suggested Fanny.

Helene looked at her in amazement but shook her head. "I'd better not. Mama would find out somehow and give me such a difficult time. I'm so sad that Max has canceled his visit," she said after a moment. "I haven't seen him since he joined the army, and that's a couple of years now."

"Are you and he betrothed?" asked Fanny. Straightaway, she heard Josepha's voice. *How often do I have to tell you that it's not your place to pry like that?*

"Forgive me," she said. "Now I'm the one being nosy."

But Helene didn't seem to mind at all. In fact, it seemed as if she'd been waiting to pour her heart out to Fanny. "No, we're a long way from that. Even though our mothers would love it. Max is very well-off and our marriage would lift the Kálmans up the scale socially and put them close to the aristocracy. Izabella, Max, and I have known each other since we were tiny. We often played together, mostly whatever Izabella wanted. Even though Max was the boy and older, he was a real gentleman even then and let his sister take the lead. But at fourteen, he came to cadet school here in Budapest, and I hardly ever saw him."

"So, you don't mind your mother trying to make a match between you and him."

"To be honest, you're right. After all, I like him," replied Helene. "But for once in my life it'd be nice to make my own decision."

"I've finished your hair, ma'am. What d'you think of it?" Fanny asked eagerly.

Helene viewed her hair from every angle using the three adjustable mirrors on her dressing table. "It's lovely! I adore it!"

Fanny was delighted. "And have you chosen your dress?"

"You choose one for me!"

Just like Izabella, Helene was always happy to leave the choice to Fanny and her impeccable taste, and it made Fanny so happy to put together something suitably striking for her mistresses. She went to the wardrobe and took out a shimmering-gold evening dress with a stunning train made of burgundy velvet.

"That's my most beautiful dress, no question," said Helene. "Can I really wear something like it to this concert?"

Fanny smiled and nodded. "You'll be one of the prettiest and best dressed ladies there!"

Helene reached out to touch the gleaming material. "I've had this one since the autumn and wore it to court for the New Year celebration. It's by Madame Moreau, a Frenchwoman who runs a famous fashion house in Vienna."

"I know," said Fanny quietly. "I know the actual salon. It's on Graben." She thought back to the afternoon she and Josepha had spent in those luxurious surroundings. That was one of her fondest memories, and it made her homesick for her city and the woman who'd done all she could to give her a decent life.

Helene looked at her with renewed curiosity. "So, you're from Vienna? I thought I'd picked it up in your voice."

Fanny nodded. "Born and raised." She held the dress out for Helene to slide into. "You look so lovely, Fräulein Helene," she said, seeing how well the dress sat on Helene's figure. "I wish your young man could see you! He'd be bowled over."

Helene looked at her excitedly. "Do you really think so?"

"I've never met him, but what man wouldn't go crazy for you in that?"

"Max is a true gentleman, always so courteous and charming. And he's good-looking." She turned to let Fanny fasten the buttons on the back. "He's a superb horseman, as well, loves the countryside and country life. That's why he'll accept the invitation to our estate."

"He'll accept the invitation because of you, Helene."

"You're too kind, but I know I'm no beauty," said Helene sadly.

"I can't agree with you on that." Fanny took her gently by the shoulders and guided her toward the full-length mirror next to the wardrobe. "Well?"

As Helene stood and looked at her reflection, her unhappiness gradually turned to joy, and she smiled in surprise at what she saw. "My goodness, Fanny! You've made a new woman of me!"

"No need for all that," she said, suppressing a smile. "I've done nothing more than coax out the woman you'd hidden away."

Helene turned and flung her arms around Fanny. "How I wish I could take you with me when we go away next week! I don't know how I'll manage without you." She stopped suddenly and looked hard at Fanny. "Could you see yourself as my lady's maid?"

"Do you really mean that?" asked Fanny in confusion.

"Of course. Unless you'd rather stay with Izabella."

Fanny lowered her head. Would she rather stay with Izabella? No, particularly after what had happened this afternoon. If Izabella had apologized, then perhaps they could have had a fresh start. But Izabella was making it seem as if she wanted to be rid of Fanny. Then she thought about Josepha, knowing she'd have to tell her she'd changed jobs again. Imagining Josepha's response made her sick with nerves.

"Izabella goes from being on top of the world one day to down in the dumps the next." Helene's voice interrupted her thoughts. "When it suits her, she'll put everyone under her spell with her charm and clever remarks. It was like that even when we were in school together. Back then, my family had an apartment in Budapest, and I went to the same convent school as Izabella, the Ursuline. Izabella was two years above me, and we all admired her and wanted to be just like her. But her mood could change like the wind, and we were all scared of her sharp tongue. To be honest with you, I don't think she'll ever be any different."

Helene's comments confirmed what Fanny already feared. And she didn't want to be thrown out of yet another household. Today's incident made her fear that's how it would end.

"I'd be very pleased to be your lady's maid, Fräulein Helene," she said firmly.

"Wonderful!" Helene clapped her hands. "But I'll have to speak to Mama about it." She sighed. "That won't be easy. Cross your fingers for me, will you?"

Her heart pounding, Helene entered her mother's room just as Zsófia was putting in place the baroness's topaz and diamond necklace. This valuable piece of jewelry, in the Báthory family for generations, was now on loan from the head of the family to Helene's father, Lászlo. This wasn't the first time Helene had seen her mother cut an impressive figure, this time in another extravagant Sarah Moreau gown, her hair again styled to add to her height, its abundance and chestnut color so similar to her daughter's. Her posture was impeccable, and the topaz in a diamond setting gleamed against her flawless skin.

"Good evening, Mama." She pecked her mother's powdered cheek.

Ida looked her up and down. "You're quite a phenomenon this evening, Nelli. I particularly like your hair. What a shame that Máxim can't see you looking like that. Did you write to him?"

"Yes, Mama." Helene handed her the folded sheet of paper. "The hairstyle was all Fanny's idea." Anxiously, she watched her mother as she skimmed through the letter. Then she said, "I'd like Fanny to be my personal maid. I've asked her and she's agreed."

Her mother put the letter down on the dressing table. "You know you should have spoken to me about it first."

Helene felt her fighting spirit stir. "I'm grown up now, and I'd like to make my own choices for once."

Ida's eyebrows shot up. "Please leave us, Zsófia." She waited until the maid had left the room. "If you're so grown up, you'll have thought about where the money to pay your maid will come from. My dear child, you have no private means whatsoever."

"You're mistaken, Mama." Helene relished a moment of triumph as her mother's eyes widened in astonishment. "When I'm married to Max, I'll have enough money to pay for a dozen maids if I want. You said yourself how pretty Fanny's made me look. Max'll notice that, too."

"He hasn't asked for your hand yet."

"But Mama, the way you've managed everything, he will."

Ida picked up a flacon of costly French perfume, the one she'd bought at Sándor Kálman's store. She removed the glass stopper and dabbed some drops of scent behind her ears and at her neckline. "Your tone amazes me, Nelli, but you will not influence this. That girl will not be in our employ. I've seen firsthand how forward she is. She doesn't know her place."

Helene had never felt so angry in all her life, and she bit hard on her lower lip to prevent anything untoward slipping out as she racked her brains for a way of persuading her mother.

Ida Báthory rose, picking up her evening bag from the dressing table. "It is high time we went down. We cannot keep our hosts waiting." She made for the door, but Helene stopped her.

"One moment, Mama." She took a deep breath and looked determinedly into her mother's eyes. "My marriage to Max will bring our family money. A lot of money. That gives me the right to decide who I want as my lady's maid. Fanny is a talented girl, and I like her. That's why I've chosen her. And I'm not going to back down. Whatever she costs us in wages from now until my wedding, you'll get back."

One week later, Ida and her daughter, Helene, departed for home. After breakfast, the whole household had assembled in the courtyard to say farewell to the guests. It was a beautiful May morning, almost summery in its warmth. Doves cooed on the roof and window ledges, and horses clip-clopped by on the cobbled street, carriages clattering and rattling in their wake.

István had brought the motorcar around and loaded luggage into the trunk with the help of his father, while the baroness's maid placed a picnic basket on the back seat. Johanna Kálman and her husband stood chatting with Baroness Báthory and Helene, the ladies holding elegant lace parasols against the sunshine.

Sándor Kálman, an imposing man with a gray goatee and bushy gray eyebrows, eyed the front door with increasing irritation. The guests wanted to set off, but his daughter was not there to say goodbye. His wife had assured him that Izabella wasn't sick, although she had asked to be excused from breakfast. Now he wondered why she was being so discourteous as to keep their visitors waiting when they had a train to catch.

All the domestic staff were lined up to wish Baroness Báthory and Helene a good journey. Rosa held a farewell gift for Fanny, a pincushion she'd made herself from the best odds and ends of cloth. But there was no sign of the girl, although András had already helpfully stowed her sewing machine and suitcase safely in the car.

"It's time," said Sándor Kálman, glancing at his fob watch. "I really do wonder what Izabella thinks she's doing."

"Fanny's not here either," added Helene, looking over at the servants' entrance.

"I trust you will not have to teach your new maid the meaning of punctuality," commented Ida Báthory sharply.

"Certainly not, Mama." But Helene looked uneasy. "I'm sure she'll be here in a moment."

Fanny stood looking around her attic bedroom. The small cupboard and chest were now empty, and her brush, comb, and soap were gone from the washstand. Early that morning, she'd stripped her bed, neatly folded the sheets, and left them on the thin mattress. She was to keep the two altered uniforms thanks to Frau Fischer getting permission from Frau Kálman.

Now that she'd packed away all her personal belongings, the room looked even more Spartan, and she wondered how she'd stood it for the six months she'd spent here. Helene had told her that the Báthory Estate was far bigger even than Palais Kálman, but Fanny doubted the servants' quarters would be any less poky. In every household of her hitherto short working life, she'd seen the huge difference between the masters' and mistresses' rooms and those allocated to the servants. She wasn't looking forward to the next rabbit hutch of a bedroom.

Not a day had passed without her wondering if she'd made the right decision. She admired Helene Báthory and felt they'd be able to get along, but it had been like that with Izabella at the beginning, too. Besides, she didn't like Baroness Báthory. The woman came across as so superior and cold, always interfering in her daughter's life. And when Fanny thought about Josepha, she felt even more concerned about the choice she'd made. Yesterday she'd sent her unofficial guardian the letter owning up to the latest job change, so it was too late now. And she wasn't one to give up on a plan.

Light footsteps approached her open door. Before Fanny could turn, two arms wrapped around her from behind.

"Please stay," whispered Izabella, hugging her close.

Fanny froze. When she had informed Izabella of her decision, the mistress had simply replied, "Do whatever you have to do."

From then on, she'd banished Fanny and started to have Rosa help her instead, so Fanny had never expected a warm farewell. Now, her plea was a bolt from the blue. Fanny was thoroughly confused at first but then placed her hands on Izabella's forearms, gently but determinedly pulled them apart, and turned to face her.

"There's no going back." Her voice was steady. "You know why."

Izabella was desperate. "Can't you forgive me? It's because I haven't apologized, isn't it? So, I'll do it right now. Fanny Schindler, I beg your forgiveness." She seized Fanny's hands and squeezed them tight.

Searching for the right words, Fanny cleared her throat. "You've put me down in front of other people. But I don't want to go over old ground."

She tried to free herself of Izabella's grasp but in vain. "Why won't you stay?"

"I've given Fräulein Helene my word, and I want to take the job."

"What on earth do you want with her? She's so tedious, she doesn't bother with her clothes or hair, and the Puszta is an impossibly dull place to live."

Fanny swallowed hard. She still harbored so many doubts that she really didn't want to hear even more arguments against her going. Since the Fasching incident, it had been difficult being anywhere near Izabella. She managed to release herself from Izabella's grip.

"You know I liked working for you at first, ma'am, but it can never be like that again. I'm not the right woman for the kind of love you're searching for."

"You didn't seem to think that when you returned my kisses," shot back Izabella, her blue eyes flashing with anger. "You're scared of my love, aren't you? But you needn't be. You needn't be scared of me." Flinging her arms round Fanny, she tried to kiss her again.

"No!" Fanny pushed her away with such force that Izabella stumbled.

"Then go!" shouted Izabella. "Get out!" She turned her back on Fanny as she brushed the back of her hand across her eyes.

Fanny took a deep breath. She felt for Izabella and didn't want it all to end on a sour note.

"If I gave you false hopes, then I'm truly sorry," she said. "I hope so much that you find the person you're longing for, someone who'll make you happy. But I'm not that person." She stood, every muscle tensed, looking at Izabella's back. As there was no response, she turned away and said sadly, "Adieu, ma'am."

Chapter Eight

The Báthory Estate, 1910

"Are you sure about going riding today, Fräulein Helene? It's already so warm and it's not even ten o'clock."

Fanny was in Helene's bedroom while the baroness's daughter was busy in the mirror, getting her riding hat at exactly the right angle. Both young women loved the close-fitting jackets, long skirts to hide their jodhpurs, gloves, boots, and, of course, top hats. They both looked stunning, if a little warm in the dark fabric. This didn't bother Helene. She was an expert horsewoman, and the long rides across the Puszta got her away from her mother and gave her a sense of freedom she could never otherwise enjoy.

After one last check in the mirror, she accepted her crop and riding gloves from her maid. "Dear Fanny," she said with a laugh. "Are you perhaps looking for an excuse to stay home because you're still new to riding? Don't give up! Soon you'll love it as much as I do!"

"It's alright for you," grumbled Fanny as they left the room together. "You've been in the saddle since you could walk; I haven't been learning for long. I fear I was better suited to Budapest!"

Helene looked at her in alarm. "But Fanny! You didn't want to carry on working for Izabella. And don't we get along well? Almost like sisters!"

Helene loved country life and enjoyed every day in the Puszta, but Fanny was finding it terribly isolated. When she'd stepped off the train a few months earlier, she'd looked around the tiny village in horror. "Oh, my goodness," she'd said to Helene, unable to contain herself, "it's so flat here. You can see your visitors coming four weeks in advance!" When she'd learned they still had to travel for two hours more across the deserted steppe, Fanny felt she'd reached the end of the world.

Vast tracts of grassland stretched as far as the horizon, broken up only by glimpses of traditional wells. The first few nights, she couldn't sleep because she missed the sounds of the city outside her window. Here, she heard only the chirp of cicadas, the occasional cowbell in the distance, and the wind as it swept through the grasses.

On top of that, her talent as a lady's maid was being squandered. Here, there were no elegant social gatherings, and, as Izabella had predicted, Helene scarcely bothered to make herself look nice. Fanny had the impression the lady mostly viewed her as a friend to go riding with and to talk to.

Helene's father had met Fanny on the day of her arrival. Baron Báthory was a warm, uncomplicated character who loved country life as much as his daughter did. The niceties of social class were of no interest to him. He had greeted Fanny with a kiss of her hand as he would a lady, and treated her like his daughter's friend, not her servant. Every morning after breakfast, he rode out to look at his cattle and didn't return until evening. Out on the Puszta with his cattle and horses was where he was at his happiest.

Baroness Báthory was utterly bored by it all. Neighboring residences were too far away for anyone to pay calls, so she passed the days in the garden under a sunshade, reading and writing letters about the lack of entertainment.

Fanny wondered how a snooty, status-conscious woman like the baroness could possibly accept life in a plain and simple country manor. With its whitewashed walls and the thickly thatched reed roof, it looked all too similar to the stables, shed, and other working quarters that, with the manor itself, occupied three sides of the large, dusty farmyard. Modern conveniences like electric light and running water were not available here. Helene had told Fanny that the estate belonged not to her father but to her uncle. As the eldest son, he was sole heir to everything the Báthorys owned and lived with his family in what Helene called the "clan castle" not far from Vienna, but in the old, German-speaking West Hungary.

"Nothing here actually belongs to Papa," Helene had explained. "My uncle permits us a small allowance for our daily needs. He's also transferred to Papa lifelong rights for the use of this estate, and until quite recently we were also allowed to live in an apartment in the family residence in Budapest. When I was presented at court last winter, Mama persuaded my uncle to transfer to us the rights to the Vienna apartment instead. All these concessions will fall away when Papa passes on, though. If Mama and I don't want to be dependent on my uncle's charity, then I need to make a really good marriage. Mama's working on that, of course."

Fanny often turned all this over in her mind as she and Helene strolled through the manor's gloomy halls and out into the farmyard, where their riding boots sent up clouds of dust with every step. Since they'd arrived, there'd hardly been a drop of rain. The sun beat down almost daily from eternally blue skies. This wasteland was not only drier but also warmer than Vienna. Helene warned her the winter was always bitter, but they'd be back in Vienna for the autumn season and its whirl of ball going, opera visits, and invitations to court.

But that was still three months away. Fanny was a city girl, used to buying her food from a shop or a market, and was amazed to discover that the estate provided for their every need. Vegetables and herbs came from the kitchen garden, apples, cherries, and apricots from the fruit trees in the meadow behind the barn. Milk, butter, meat, eggs, and cheese came from their own animals.

When Fanny had first seen the huge herds grazing freely, she was at a loss for words. The estate boasted almost a thousand head of cattle and several hundred horses. Fanny felt in awe of the sturdy, muscular gray cattle with thick horns as long as her arm, but she loved best the herd of broodmares with their charming foals. Mounted herdsmen and their dogs watched over the livestock. Helene claimed the dogs could even take on a wolf, but to Fanny's enormous relief, she'd never seen any. Those gray-coated hunters were themselves mercilessly pursued and had become a rare sight.

As soon as the two young women left the shadow cast by the manor house, they felt the burning sun again—Fanny in particular, in spite of her head covering.

I'm bound to get another rotten headache today, she thought, longing for the cool and shade of the house. But Helene was eager to ride out and see the new foals being branded. And like any correctly brought-up girl, she was allowed to do so only with a chaperone. Fanny had no choice but to go with her.

Helene had taught her to ride. Before coming to the Puszta, Fanny had never even sat on a horse. Every morning after breakfast, one of the stable boys had helped her clamber onto the old pony that Helene had learned on. Then she would trot round and round on the lunge in front of the manor house, riding sidesaddle as was proper for a lady. Helene had assured her the pony was meek as a lamb, but every time Fanny got ready to mount, the creature would try and nip her on the backside. Once, he stopped dead and ignored everything Fanny tried to encourage him forward. The sidesaddle made this almost impossible, as she could apply only one heel on one stubborn flank. If she tried a little tap with her crop, the creature would buck, practically unseating her. But after six weeks of this, she'd felt more confident, and now rode a full-size horse to accompany Helene on her rides.

Even in today's heat, the stable boys had already prepared their horses and were waiting with them in the yard. Just before Helene mounted hers, she looked anxiously toward the windows of the manor. "Mama's doubtless up at the window again, complaining about us using men's saddles."

"Would you rather we didn't?" asked Fanny.

"No." Helene shook her head. "To be honest, it's fun to do something that Mama doesn't approve of. But I dread her ranting about it when we come back."

It was Fanny who'd suggested they use a man's saddle. She was convinced she'd feel safer on the horse with her legs firmly down both sides of the animal. She tried it for herself first and quickly found the broad, deep herdsman's saddle was far more comfortable, and this sparked Helene's interest. Just one try and she was converted. The baroness was horrified and tried to forbid her daughter to straddle the horse in what she described as an indecent manner. But the baron permitted it, and with good humor, saying it wouldn't bother him at all if his daughter rode like a man out here on the Puszta.

The two young women set off from the yard at a walking pace, soon turning onto a narrow dirt track that led out onto the open Puszta. Soon, rows of farmhands came into view, swinging their scythes in time as they moved across the grassland on the first cut of the season, while behind them came the women with long wooden rakes, separating out the mown grass to dry. Helene knew all the interesting features to point out to Fanny on either side of the track.

"That's kale over there," she said, pointing to a plant growing to knee height, its curling leaves green and juicy. "You can cook it and eat it. And that silvery little plant over there, that's wormwood."

"I always thought wormwood was the same as schnapps." Fanny recalled Josepha's usual remark as she enjoyed a tot of wormwood after a heavy meal, explaining it was good for the digestion.

"Yes, sort of." Helene explained. "Schnapps is made using wormwood. Oh, and look, can you see that over there?" She pointed toward a dip in the ground flecked with dashes of magenta, breaking up the uniform green. "That's a bed of cloves. Doesn't it look lovely?"

Fanny shielded her eyes with her hand as she took all this in. "If you know where to look, the Puszta really isn't so dull after all."

"Do you still not like it here?" asked Helene.

Fanny waved a tiresome fly away from her face. "It's alright. But I'll be pleased when we go to Vienna in the autumn."

"I expect you get quite homesick for Vienna?"

As Fanny gave a little shrug, but said nothing, Helene carried on talking. "It's different for me. When we're in Vienna, it's so busy, one thing after another. I can't ever relax and constantly have to be careful about what I say, who to, and how I look. I find it all exhausting. That's why it makes me happy to get back to the country in the spring. Where in Vienna did you grow up, Fanny?"

"In the Alservorstadt." Fanny's tone was flat, hoping that it would discourage Helene from asking more, but to no avail.

"I don't think I know the Alservorstadt," she remarked. "What's it like to live there? Tell me a bit about yourself, Fanny."

"Oh, there isn't much to tell. I was in school there and then went on to study housekeeping. Since getting qualified, I've been in service in various houses, as lady's maid, sometimes in housekeeping." Fanny squinted at two birds of prey circling overhead. "You're so knowledgeable, Fräulein Helene. Do you know what kind of birds those are?"

Helene glanced up. "Hawks. You can tell by the long tail with rounded edges. Fanny, dear, would I be right in thinking you're changing the subject?"

Fanny felt embarrassed and looked down at her horse's mane, remembering Josepha's advice on what to do if questioned about her background. *If people hear you come from the foundling home, little mite, they'll get a whiff of scandal and the questions will never stop. Even worse, they'll be suspicious of you because you didn't grow up in a normal family. So, be crafty and keep all that to yourself.*

This advice had stayed with Fanny, but now she found herself wishing she could speak freely and fearlessly to someone about her past. But was the baroness's daughter that someone?

Then she heard Helene's voice again. "I can tell something's bothering you. Would you like to tell me about it?"

Fanny took a deep breath and banished her usual concerns from her mind. "I grew up in a foundling home." She looked anxiously at Helene's face, but it was blank.

"Foundling home? Is that the poor house?"

"No," said Fanny with a sad smile. "It's a place for children who can't live with their parents. I suppose it's a bit like an orphanage, except the parents aren't dead."

"So, what happened to your parents? Why didn't you live with them?"

"I don't know my parents," replied Fanny softly. "My mother gave birth to me in the General Hospital in Vienna, but she paid to remain anonymous. There are no files anywhere with my mother's or father's names. That's how the matron at the home explained it to me. She was the one who raised me and she's like a mother to me—or maybe a grandmother, as she's quite old now."

Helene looked at Fanny a long time before speaking. "Now I understand why you didn't want to talk about where you grew up. It's so sad."

"It wasn't so miserable, ma'am. Frau Pfeiffer—that's the matron—took good care of me, and I'm very fond of her."

Helene shook her head, deeply shocked by Fanny's revelation. "I just can't imagine not knowing my family. It would feel somehow like missing an arm or a leg, if that doesn't sound too strange!"

"Couldn't have put it better myself," said Fanny, relieved that the baroness's daughter seemed to understand.

The two young women rode side by side in companionable silence. From time to time, one of their horses would give a swish of the tail or a snort of contentment. The conversation had stirred in Fanny all the unanswered questions about her birth. She asked herself yet again whether her parents were still alive, whether her mother had ever regretted not getting the certificate of admission, and whether she yearned for her child as much as Fanny yearned for her.

Has she ever looked for me? Fanny wondered this so often.

"I think every child should know who their parents are. It's a born right," said Helene firmly, interrupting Fanny's thoughts.

"Yes, that'd be fairer," said Fanny. "But I can't find mine, and they can't find me. Even if they wanted to."

There was silence between them again.

Then Helene burst out, "I might be able to help you."

Fanny reined in her horse. "What on earth do you mean?"

Helene stopped with her. "Mama has friends involved in all manner of good causes. I'd bet you anything that one of them has something to do with the foundling home in Vienna. I could ask Mama to write to whoever is its patroness and ask if she can call to mind anything about your mother."

Fanny looked back at her, a flicker of despair already in her eyes. "And what happens if the baroness doesn't know the patroness?"

"Oh, she'd just have to ask around her circle. The aristocracy is pretty small, and we all know each other. It's worth a try, don't you think?"

Tears of gratitude welled up in Fanny as she realized how sincerely Helene wanted to help.

"Thank you so much," she whispered.

Just then, her horse tossed its head and whinnied, and Helene's pricked its ears and gave a little prance.

"They've scented the others. Do you feel like a bit of a gallop?"

"Yes!" Fanny gathered up the reins.

As their horses raced side by side across the Puszta, she felt elated like never before.

Her excitement became tinged with impatience as Fanny waited to hear back from Helene about the promised conversation with the baroness. After one week, she could contain herself no longer and asked for news, but to her great disappointment, Helene had not yet broached the matter with her mother.

"I haven't forgotten," she reassured her. "But Mama is still annoyed with you. She chooses to think that you put me up to riding astride, as she likes to call it, even though it was my own choice. If I'm asking her for a favor on your behalf, I really have to bide my time and seize the right moment—otherwise it could all go wrong."

While Fanny understood Helene's caution, she was still disappointed. Yet another week slipped by, and she started to lose hope.

Late one afternoon, she was helping Helene dress for dinner. At last, it was the day that Izabella's brother Máxim was due to make his appearance at the country estate. The coachman had set off for the station several hours ago, so it couldn't be too long before he'd be back with the long-awaited guest.

Fanny wanted Helene to look special for her future husband, and her work kept her mind off her personal sadness. She had a fairy-tale transformation all planned, but the baroness continued poking her nose in and dismissing Fanny's every suggestion.

"Can't you see how insipid Helene's complexion will look if she wears the green gown? And you can put the blue one away again, too.

It's so unflattering on the hips." She made these critical remarks the moment Fanny came from the dressing room, the gowns over her arm. The baroness stood behind her daughter, lacing the girl's corset so tight she gasped for breath. "Mama, stop! It's making me feel faint."

"Why can't you be more restrained in your eating habits?" The baroness snapped at her. "You'll never have the slender waist of our divine empress. Fanny! Bring me the one with roses on it, the one we bought in Budapest. Máxim will love to see his bride look so young and innocent." She shooed Fanny back into the dressing room.

While the girl searched the racks, the baroness lectured her daughter on how to behave in front of Max. "On no account are you to giggle like an empty-headed teenager. You must at all times be charming and interested, even if he's boring you stiff. You can converse with him about horses—our dear empress used to do the same—but for goodness' sake don't talk about cattle or hens like some country bumpkin. And you are not to mention that you have ridden astride using a man's saddle." She shot an accusing look at Fanny just as she came out of the dressing room again. "That's not going to happen again, whatever your father says. While Máxim is our guest, you will sit on a horse as befits a lady. For heaven's sake, Fanny, do you ever listen? That's not the rose dress."

"No, ma'am," replied Fanny politely, although inside she was quivering with rage. "This will suit Fräulein Helene better than the rose dress, which makes her look like a doll that someone's dressed up."

Helene's hand flew to her mouth to hide her mirth. But the baroness raised both eyebrows in indignation. She was about to give Fanny a thorough telling-off when from outside came the sound of rapid hoofbeats and a man's voice calling out, "Forward!"

"It's Max!" shrieked Helene in delight. She pushed back her chair and hurried to the windows, the baroness right behind her. "Nelli, don't let yourself be seen at the window in your morning dress!"

Helene paused, then inched herself behind the curtain so she could peer out without being spotted. The baroness stood close to her, looking out of the window, too.

Fanny waited before joining them. She was seething at being treated so disparagingly by the baroness and needed to calm down for fear of letting slip another snappish remark.

As she craned her neck to catch a glimpse of Helene's intended, she gasped at the scene outside. The two-wheeled gig that the coachman had trundled away in this morning now careered toward the farmyard at breakneck speed. The coachman clung to the sides with both hands, his face contorted with fear. Next to him was a young man shouting with laughter, holding the reins with an easy confidence as he urged the horse on. The horse's hooves sent up clouds of dust until the gig came to a standstill directly in front of the main door.

"Silly fellow! Drives likes the devil's after him!" said Fanny without thinking.

"Or the horsemen of the apocalypse!" giggled Helene.

The baroness's rebuke was swift. "Fanny! One more disrespectful word and you'll be packing your bags! And Nelli, there's no need to repeat the rubbish you hear from servants."

Fanny felt that burning anger again. It was a struggle not to talk back, but she didn't.

Just then, Helene gently touched her on the arm. When Fanny turned to her, she saw how Helene gave a discreet shake of the head and a sympathetic smile. This made Fanny feel a bit better. *My mistress is such a lovely person. How can she possibly have such a shrew for a mother?*

Helene brought the conversation back to what they'd all witnessed outside. "Max is a real man now, isn't he, Mama?" Fanny heard her say. She looked out, still curious to know more, and saw the coachman climbing down and leaning against the carriage wheel to be violently sick.

Max Kálman sprang down from the coach with an easy grace. "Come, come, dear chap. I told you we wouldn't tip over." He gave the man an encouraging clap on the shoulder.

Then he went over to the horse and gently stroked its black flank, glowing with sweat. "Well done. You're a real Magyar, full of courage."

He was speaking Hungarian the whole time, but Fanny understood everything, so well had she learned the new language.

They heard the front door open below them, and Adam, the baron's valet and the de facto butler, came into sight. He went to the gig and lifted down the visitor's suitcase. "Welcome to the Báthory Estate, Herr Kálman. Did you have a good journey?"

"It's a long haul from Pressburg," replied Max. "There's a damnably long wait at Budapest. I'm in urgent need of a good bath before I make any appearance before the ladies of the house."

"Your room is ready, Herr Kálman. And I've prepared a hot bath. I guessed you'd want to freshen up after such a long journey. Did you not bring your orderly?"

Max shook his head. "I gave him the summer off. He'll come back in the autumn when I go to the military academy. How's Nelli?" The three women could hear everything as he walked beside Adam toward the house. "The last time I saw her, she was just a girl who'd not long given up playing with dolls."

"Fräulein Helene is grown up now," answered Adam. "A real young lady."

Max gave him a playful dig in the ribs. "That's not what I wanted to know. Is she pretty?"

"As firm and rounded as an apricot on one of our trees," Adam assured him as the two men vanished inside the house.

"The impudence of that manservant knows no bounds! I'll be speaking to the baron about this." The baroness hurried from the room.

Fanny turned slowly away from the window. *So, that is Izabella's brother,* she thought.

In the blue jacket of the Ninth Hussars, the close-fitting riding breeches, and boots, he looked young, athletic, and bursting with energy. He had the same dark hair as his sister and an infectious laugh. But what she liked even more than his laugh was his voice. It was melodious and easy on the ear, stirring her to the very core.

Like something familiar that I'd once lost and now found again, she thought to herself in quiet astonishment. She glanced at Helene, fearful she'd somehow given her thoughts away.

But the baroness's daughter was looking down at the empty yard, and Fanny could see Max had already made quite an impression. Now it was Fanny who touched Helene lightly on the arm, saying, "Shall we go, ma'am? I'll make you so pretty that the young man will fall in love with you on the spot."

Dinner was served in a grand room on the garden side of the manor house. The double doors stood open to invite in the light evening breeze after the heat of the summer day. The dining table itself occupied pride of place in the center of the room, while at the end was a magnificent fireplace with a stone surround. Above this hung the Báthory coat of arms, an eagle with a saber in its talons. Ancestral portraits and ornate weaponry decorated the whitewashed walls, while the floorboards were of dark oak.

Although Max had known the estate since childhood, he had always felt a little overwhelmed when faced with this distinguished family history going back hundreds of years. His own forebears had been impoverished Ashkenazi Jews who had migrated from the Carpathians after the Edict of Tolerance and settled in Buda, at that time separate from Pest. His grandfather soon owned a small general store in the Elisabethstadt district and, later, his father the two department stores in the newly created Budapest. Max himself was keen to marry into the old aristocracy and lift the Kálman family to the highest echelon of Austro-Hungarian society.

After centuries of persecution, we Jews belong in Europe at last, thought Max as he finished up his dessert, put down his cutlery, and dabbed the corner of his mouth with his napkin. *Well, almost.* He'd assured the baron and his wife that he would convert to Catholicism if he became engaged to their daughter. It didn't bother him in the slightest. His family was open-minded and forward-looking. Religion was beside the point for all of them.

The baron, at the head of the table, rose to his feet. "I'm going to check the hens are safely in. Adam spotted a fox this morning. Kálman, we'll meet in the drawing room over a glass of something good. I've kept back a couple of bottles of magnificent Tokay. And don't go letting these women charm you too much, or you'll be engaged by midnight!"

"Papa!" Helene was incensed. "You shouldn't say things like that."

"I think I'm entitled to, don't you, my little one?" And he kissed his daughter on the cheek before leaving on his errand.

Max watched him with envy. He'd have given anything to go and stretch his legs and enjoy an after-dinner smoke, far from the baroness and her constant praise of her daughter's virtues.

"Were the dessert pancakes good, Herr Kálman?" Adam asked, leaning slightly to remove his plate.

"Exquisite. My compliments to your cook." Max gave the dutiful praise, but he'd much preferred the main course, beef with beans and paprika.

"Can we persuade you to enjoy another portion of dessert?" The baroness was all smiles.

"That sounds very tempting, but if I eat any more I'll have to get all my shirts altered," said Max, giving his perfectly flat stomach a pat for effect. "To prevent that happening, I'd like to take a short walk."

"Of course!" The baroness was wreathed in smiles. "Nelli will show you the garden."

"I'll run and get something to put around my shoulders." Helene made as if to get up, but Max gestured to her, saying, "No need, Nelli. I really only want to stretch my legs for a minute. You can show me the garden later."

"Whatever you want." Helene looked nervously across at her mother, whose face seemed to have frozen midsmile. In fact, she'd have loved a walk with Max, but the thought of the detailed report she'd be expected to give her mother afterward put her off the idea.

"If you want to be alone, then I won't stand in your way," said the baroness, clearly peeved but attempting to look regal. "But please remember we'll be waiting for you in the drawing room."

"How could I forget!" Max got to his feet and bowed briefly to the two women. As he made his exit through the open terrace doors, he caught Ida hissing at her daughter, "If you'd shown him rather more charm, he wouldn't be wanting to go off to the garden on his own. But if you carry on stiff as a board, he won't have any other option."

Max moved swiftly across the garden. He knew from earlier visits that a gate at the far end led straight to the meadows full of fruit trees behind the animal stalls.

The meadow grass had not yet been mown and was full of wildflowers. He noticed the beautiful birdsong as well as the hum of bumblebees. As a child, he'd run barefoot through these meadows with Nelli and Izabella, trying to catch butterflies in little nets. Happy times for all of them.

Poor Nelli's definitely not happy these days, he thought to himself as he picked raspberries from the bushes behind the gate and popped them into his mouth. *I bet her mother's still taking her to task back there.*

As he strode across the meadow, he remembered the many letters from his mother in which she'd emphasized the benefits of marriage to his childhood playmate.

I can just imagine how disappointed she'll be if Nelli and I don't marry. He stopped, took out his cigarette case, and rested against the gnarled trunk of an ancient apple tree.

He knew that marrying Helene would be highly advantageous to his family. It would open up new business opportunities for his father, and his mother could strengthen her link to the royal family. As for his sister, her marriage prospects would leap from good to superb—if she'd ever accept anyone. Max had his doubts on that score. Ever since he'd caught her dressed as a man at that masked ball, and in the company of that delightful, mysterious lady, he'd suspected she was actually a lesbian. His ambition was a military career on the General Staff of the imperial army, or his own unit, and for him to achieve that, it would be more than helpful to him if his wife came from an old, aristocratic Catholic family. Only those who broke into the immediate circle surrounding the Habsburg dynasty could ever hope for prestige, influence, and power. And for a bourgeois Jew, Edict or no Edict, that was impossible. That was another reason he'd decided to convert.

Max lit a cigarette, raised one foot so as to lean more comfortably against the tree, and gazed up at the swallows as they darted and swooped against the cloudless sky.

In the years he hadn't seen Nelli, she'd become a grown woman but was still in essence the same good-hearted, timid Nelli under the thumb of her domineering mother. He appreciated Nelli greatly, not least because of her sweet nature. She was no beauty, but beauty fades with time in any case. And today she'd looked very pretty with those thick brown curls and her gentle eyes. Her excitement at seeing him again, her shyness and uncertainty, had been absolutely charming. He was sure they'd get along well as a married couple. But a flicker of doubt still nagged at his heart, asking whether this cool, calculating logic could result in two people happily spending the rest of their lives together.

Where's passion in all this? There was the doubting voice again. *What about emotion, sense of devotion, and sensuality?*

Izabella had once told him she'd never give her life away without these feelings. But Izabella was hopelessly romantic and uncompromisingly obstinate. He saw this as no way to find happiness.

At least he and Nelli weren't complete strangers. They'd known each other since childhood. Crudely speaking, he felt he was playing the lottery, not knowing whether he'd end up with a dud or the winning ticket. *Maybe Nelli felt the same?*

He resolved to get to know her all over again before they committed to one another forever.

A gentle rustling interrupted his reverie. *Nelli?* Quick as a flash, he dropped his cigarette and stubbed it firmly with the toe of his shoe. Taking the greatest of care not to be seen, he spied out from behind his tree and saw an unfamiliar young woman headed straight toward his hiding place.

Walking with her head down and hugging close to her chest a little black farm cat, she hadn't yet spotted Max. "Oh, Blackie." She was pouring out her heart to the little creature in her arms. "You have no idea how terribly homesick I am. Country life is not for me, and that's that. It's so dull I could curl up and die."

He was astonished to hear a Viennese twang out here in the Puszta, of all places. Then he realized she'd see him the moment she lifted her gaze, so he swiftly drew back behind his tree.

The young woman carried on telling the kitten her tale of woe. "What's even worse than the boredom is the baroness herself. She's the worst nag I've ever come across, Blackie, picking holes in everything I do. And I can't bear her either. At some point I'm likely to lose my cool and give her a piece of my mind." She sighed.

Max smiled. He loved a Viennese accent, hers in particular. He took a good look at this unknown beauty but shook his head. Viennese girls, yes, he knew quite a few, but this wasn't one of them. The young woman had now gotten as far as his tree, and she sat down on the grass on the other side of it.

"No, darling Blackie," she lamented, "I mustn't even think like that. The baroness isn't going to make me forget myself. I want to prove to Frau Pfeiffer that I can stick it out. She was so disappointed about what I wrote in my last letter. She wrote back that nobody can rely on me to stick to anything, and that it's all her fault for not being tough enough with me. That really upset me, Blackie. Frau Pfeiffer's the last person I want ever to let down—"

Max heard her quietly weeping and gave a worried frown. Any woman in tears made him uneasy, as he had been brought up always to be kind and chivalrous to a lady and to remove all obstacles from her path. If he couldn't do that, it made him feel helpless. And he loathed feeling helpless.

"I've got good intentions, I really do," sobbed the young woman on the other side of the tree. "But something always goes wrong. I made a huge mistake with my education. It's made me 'an eternally dissatisfied wench,' Blackie. That's how Frau Pfeiffer described me in her letter. And she's right." Her sobs grew louder.

Max peered carefully from behind his tree. She was just on the other side, so close he could have touched her prettily disheveled strawberry blonde curls. Her arms were wrapped around the young cat, her forehead resting on his rounded head. Her shoulders shook as she wept.

Desperate to help, he wondered what to do. He took his handkerchief from his trouser pocket and cautiously reached around the tree with his right arm to offer it to her. "Ahem!" he said, waving the handkerchief back and forth.

"Holy Mary, mother of God!" She shrieked and lashed out at his hand. The little cat seized the opportunity to jump from her lap and scurry away across the meadow.

Max stepped out from behind the tree. "Forgive me. I didn't mean to frighten you. But you sounded so sad that I wanted to offer some comfort." He crouched down next to her.

She wiped her eyes with the back of her hand. "You should have told me you were there."

"True. But is there ever a right moment to interrupt a personal confession?"

Looking embarrassed, she remained silent, and he stole a closer look. A pretty girl, that's for sure. Her reddish-blonde hair was drawn up and back into a soft bun. Her neck and cheeks were lightly sun-kissed. Her large, doe-like eyes were framed by long, dark lashes, and her beautifully shaped lips were lusciously full.

Asking to be kissed, those lips, he thought, feeling aroused at the mere sight of them. Trying to distract himself, he said, "Are you visiting the estate?"

She shook her head. "Not exactly visiting."

"So, you live here?"

A smile flickered across her face. "Shouldn't you be introducing yourself properly before firing questions at me? But perhaps I know who you are, Herr Kálman."

"Well now! I deserved that!" He laughed. "Did Nelli tell you I was coming today? Or did we meet before, you and I? I used to come and stay here a lot." He gave her that searching look again.

She shook her head. "This is the first time I've been to the estate." Her eyes were still full of tears, and some stray curls had escaped from the bun.

Good God, what a sweet little thing, was all he could think. He'd have loved to take his handkerchief and dab away her tears. Or better, kiss them away.

He put his handkerchief into her hand. "Blow your nose."

Uneasy for a moment, she looked at him. Then she laughed and gave her nose a good blow. "I can't return your handkerchief like that."

"Keep it. And if you find yourself ever needing a handkerchief again, get this one out and think of me."

She blushed deeply but closed her fingers around the scrunched-up handkerchief. "I ought to go back inside now."

"Wait," he said hurriedly. "I know how you feel."

"Do you?" She sounded highly doubtful.

"Yes, I do," he insisted. "It's not the past I'm wrestling with. My life's at a crossroads, and I don't know which way's right. It's a real dilemma for me."

She tilted her head slightly to one side and looked at him. "Is it that you're afraid you'll miss something on the other road?"

He laughed. "What a wise woman you are. Whichever road I end up going down, I'll always remember that."

"I took the wrong road once, too, and now I'm stuck," she replied pensively. "It's as if I'm stumbling around in the dark."

"You mustn't think like that." He was relieved to find he could offer some sort of answer to her worries. "Just imagine that you're carrying a lantern. Maybe you don't know what's at the end of the journey, but the next step's always lit."

She smiled at him. "It sounds like you need a lantern like that, too."

He gave a long, slow nod of the head. "As I said, you're a wise woman."

They held one another's gaze for several seconds. Then she turned away and stuffed the handkerchief into her dress pocket.

"I'll launder it and return it to you tomorrow."

She began to get to her feet, but he leapt up, extended his hand, and helped her. As he caught her scent of meadow grass and camellia, all he wanted was to take her in his arms. But she quickly pulled her hand away from his grasp and took a step backward.

"Adieu, Herr Kálman." She turned to go.

"Wait!" he called out. "What's your name?"

She glanced back over her shoulder and smiled. "That's for you to find out, Herr Kálman!"

He stood and watched as she walked back across the meadow, and every step she took away from him served only to make him want to hold her close. "I'll wait for you here tomorrow! Same time, same place!"

Chapter Nine

The Báthory Estate, 1910

While the Báthorys and Max dined together the following evening, Fanny sat in front of her washstand on a rickety stool, braiding her hair in the little round mirror that hung from a single nail in the wall. Her eyes were shining, almost as if she had a fever.

I'm going to see Max Kálman again any minute, she thought and felt that tingling sensation again, as if a whole colony of ants were making her lower belly its home.

You silly woman! D'you really think a playboy like him has honorable intentions toward the likes of you? There was Josepha's voice again.

Angrily, Fanny pulled her braids into place. Max wasn't a social climber, and definitely not just some playboy. Look how kind he'd been to her yesterday evening, consoling her and offering such kindly advice.

She heard Josepha again. *Only so he can get inside your undies.*

"I'm not going to listen to all that," muttered Fanny to herself. "She just doesn't know Max."

I don't need to, came that voice again. *Because these men are all the same.*

Fanny straightened up and looked back at her reflection. She was very happy and wasn't going to let anything spoil it.

Lowering her arms, she examined the final result in the mirror. She had pinned the braids around her head like a corn garland and had chosen a white blouse and a brightly colored full skirt to complete the effect. When she and Adam had visited the local market, she'd seen the farm girls dressed like this, liked it a lot, and bought herself some material and got busy sewing. Only an embroidered vest was missing for the full costume, but it was such a warm evening, she wouldn't have worn it anyway.

Is Max already waiting for me by the apple tree? She slipped her shoes on.

He'd been gone all day. Right after breakfast, he and Helene had set off together for a long ride in the Puszta. A chaperone wasn't considered necessary, so Fanny had plenty of time on her hands to try and recall every detail of their encounter the previous evening. She'd wondered if what she was feeling was love, something she hadn't yet experienced and wasn't sure she'd know how to recognize.

When Rosa used to go on about Karl, all she ever longed for was a home and a family and to spend the rest of their lives together. But that wasn't what Fanny longed for when she thought of Max.

No, she mused as she went to open the shutters, closed all day to keep the heat out. *I'm not in love.*

What she did know was that she felt a powerful longing for him, but she could compare it only to a feeling of greed that was all mixed up with that tingling in her belly.

Looking down at the garden, she spotted him walking purposefully through the gate that led to the meadows, turning immediately right and going out of sight behind the animals' stalls.

The tingling intensified. All she wanted was to run after him into the meadow of fruit trees. But she told herself to calm down. Max Kálman mustn't know she could hardly wait to see him again!

Going over to her bedside table, she took the freshly laundered and ironed handkerchief from the drawer and ran her fingers over the embroidered monogram. With great care, she put it away again, closed the drawer, and turned to go.

Max was leaning against the apple tree again. He was smoking a cigarette, but as soon as he saw Fanny coming across the meadow, he threw it down and waved.

Neither of them noticed a figure sneaking around the corner of the stalls, then swiftly ducking down behind a cluster of raspberry bushes.

"You're here," said Max, as Fanny stood before him, slightly out of breath. He removed his dress coat, spread it on the grass beneath the tree, and sat down next to it.

"Do have a seat." He patted the garment with the flat of his hand and smiled at her.

She returned his smile and sat down exactly as he suggested. She loved his courtesy and charm. "I hope your nice coat won't get mucky."

"No other girl has ever said that before." He sounded astonished, and she gave him a sideways look.

"Does that mean you let a lot of girls sit on your coat?"

"Guilty as charged!" He laughed, holding up his hands in mock surrender. "But you, my dear, have the honor of being the first to sit on this particular coat. It's new."

Fanny gave a little giggle, and he gave her that hungry look again. "Did you know you look very happy today and it really suits you?"

She tweaked the hem of her skirt into place. "I've good reason to feel joyful today."

"Do you indeed?" He leaned a little closer. "And why would that be?"

"You know perfectly well!" She was a tiny bit embarrassed.

"Let's just say that I hope I know, yes. And my handkerchief? Where's that?"

"I haven't ironed it yet," she fibbed.

"Aha! So, we'll have to meet again!" He gave her a hard look. "Is that what you want? Or would you rather keep the handkerchief?"

"You're imagining things!" she snapped, annoyed that he'd seen through her so easily.

He slid down all the way onto the grass, leaned on his elbows, and looked up at her. "Anyway, I've solved the riddle you gave me."

"You know my name?" There was that gorgeous feeling again, low down in her belly. He was so good-looking, with those blue eyes, the understated moustache over his beautifully shaped upper lip, and his dark hair. She glanced at his hands. They were tanned and powerful, with long fingers, his nails cut short and square. *How would it feel to be caressed by those hands?*

He broke off a long blade of grass and stuck it behind his right ear. "Your name's Fanny. Fanny Schindler. Adam told me." He grinned. "Did you know your name's a perfect fit?"

"What on earth do you mean?"

He sat up, reached out his hand toward her, and tucked an errant curl behind her ear. "What do I get if I tell you?" He'd dropped his voice.

"Well, what do you want?" she asked, equally softly.

"A kiss."

That was exactly what she wanted, too. For a few moments, the only sounds were the humming of the bees and the chirp of birds in the trees. He sat up and placed his hand under her chin, gently raising it until their eyes met.

Is he going to kiss me? She tingled with excitement.

"Fanny is such a pretty name," he murmured. "Just like you."

"You think I'm pretty?"

"Not just pretty. I think there are many different sides to you," he replied. "And I like that."

His hand wandered from her chin to her neck. As his mouth came closer, she caught the faint aroma of his favorite tobacco, felt his soft breath, then his lips on hers. He hesitated a moment, as if to check her reaction, but she responded by coming closer, so his kiss was deep and demanding.

Holy Mary, this is fantastic, was all Fanny could think as her feelings swept her along like a wave. She wanted more, much more, as she melted inside under this kiss. But then he let go.

"Oh, why have you stopped?" Her disappointment was clear.

He took her right hand in his and brought her fingertips to his lips. "I'd like—" he began saying, then broke off.

"Yes?"

He took a deep breath. "I want to feel you properly, Fanny, your entire body, without all these clothes getting between us. I want to be as close as close can be. Are you feeling the same?"

"Yes," she nodded, although she had no experience of this "feel you properly" business. But if it meant to be naked together from head to toe, to kiss and caress one another, then that was what she wanted, too. "Do you want to come to my room tonight?"

He shook his head. "Too risky. I might be seen. And I can't wait until tonight."

She thought for a bit. "Then let's go to the carriage shed; nobody goes there once it's evening. We could get in the landau. It's big and comfortable, and we won't be disturbed."

"Marvelous idea." He gave her another kiss. "You go ahead. I'll follow."

Fanny hurried away and was soon creeping on tiptoe through the manor house hall and out into the deserted yard. Hugging the wall, she ran to the building where she knew the landau was always kept and slipped in through the narrow door. It was unlit, but the window set high in the roof let her see the way. The landau was in the back corner of the building, next to the handcart, and its canopy conveniently closed. She glanced all around, but not a soul was in sight. Swiftly, she climbed up into the landau and shut the door behind her. Then she closed its curtains, sat down on the softly upholstered seat, and waited.

So, what's going to happen? she wondered.

What indeed? He'll want to get inside your undies, like I said! Josepha's voice came back to her. *And you're falling straight into the trap, you silly goose.*

I'm not falling into anything, Fanny thought angrily. *I'm here because I want to be here!*

But you know he'll get engaged to Helene, don't you? Josepha's voice was still in her head.

This threw Fanny off balance. In her dizzy excitement, she somehow hadn't stopped to consider the fact that she had a lover's tryst planned with Helene's future husband.

But they're not actually engaged, she told herself, feeling a bit abashed. *And if they do get engaged, it's only because it'll be advantageous to both families. It's a business arrangement. Nothing more.*

She certainly didn't want to stand in the way of their engagement. But Max's kisses had stirred her curiosity and her desire. She simply had to know what love and passion felt like.

My God, she thought. *I'm nearly twenty-one and know nothing of all this!*

Someone quietly opened the shed door, then came footsteps across the beaten clay floor. He was there, sliding into the landau, right next to Fanny. Without a word, he took her in his arms and kissed her.

"Herr Kálman, I think you're taking me straight to paradise," she whispered breathlessly.

His arms went around her again, and he ran his hands all the way down her back to her buttocks.

They could hardly keep their hands off one another as he tried to take off his coat. Fanny unbuttoned his waistcoat, he her blouse. As his mouth roamed over her neck and down to the gentle curve of her breasts, he slid himself off the landau seat and knelt between her thighs. With the fingertips of his right hand, he sought out her mouth and covered her lips. The fingers of his other hand slipped beneath her skirt and slowly ran up her legs to the top of her thighs. When he eased aside the crotch of her panties and stroked those yet more intimate lips, she shivered with pleasure, let out a moan, closed her eyes, and let her head fall against his shoulder. Just before the overpowering waves of desire could pull her under, Josepha's threats rang alarm bells in her mind.

Do you want to end up like your mother?

Fanny's overwhelming sense of desire vanished. Fear clawed at her heart, but her innate determination took over. She pressed both hands against Max's chest and pushed him away with every ounce of strength she could muster.

Caught off guard, he tumbled backward, barely avoiding an undignified end on the landau floor. Hurriedly gathering her blouse across her breasts, she was off the bench and out of the carriage door in a blink.

Still confused, he recovered himself in time only to hear her footsteps hastening away, a door opening and closing, then nothing further.

Over the next couple of weeks, Fanny was careful to avoid Max. This wasn't difficult as her work meant she was mostly with Helene, and in Helene's room, at that. But sleepless nights made it hard to banish the incident from her mind. She tossed and turned in her small, stuffy bedroom—and it wasn't because it felt like a furnace in the August heat, but because of Josepha's oft-repeated words going round and round in her head. *Do you want to end up like your mother? One thing leads to another, and from easy virtue comes a wee babe.*

When Fanny thought how easily this warning could have become a reality, she was appalled by her own conduct. In her imagination, she saw herself alone and abandoned with an illegitimate child to raise. The idea of giving a baby away to the foundling home, like her own mother had done with her, was out of the question. Marriage to Max was equally impossible. Fanny wasn't so naïve as to believe that a young man like him, already as good as engaged, could even consider marrying her. He wouldn't risk being shut out by family and friends, losing his position in society, his military career being ruined.

In spite of all her commonsense thoughts, Fanny still longed for him. For his voice, his smell, his mouth on hers, his hands on her skin. When she lay alone in bed at night, she explored those hidden places of desire between her thighs and fantasized that her hands were his. But none of this did anything to quench her passion, and it was only her fear of following in her mother's footsteps that stopped her from running to him and throwing herself in his arms.

Max had been stunned when Fanny had fled the landau so suddenly. No woman had ever done this to him before. He must have done something wrong, he told himself. Should he have wooed her for longer? Did she take fright because he'd expected too much too soon? But whenever he went over the details of their encounter in his mind, he genuinely believed she'd wanted him as much as he'd wanted her.

Every evening for a week, he waited in vain at the apple tree, hoping for a meeting and a conversation that would explain everything. He otherwise saw Fanny only now and then, and never when she was alone. Eventually, he wrote her a letter offering to meet. Just as he was about to push the envelope under her bedroom door, he was horrified to realize the baroness's maid was right behind him. He only just managed to slide the envelope up his sleeve. Later, he burned it and abandoned that plan. A letter could so easily fall into the wrong hands.

A few days later, he saw Fanny and Helene sitting together in the garden, Fanny bent over her sewing while Nelli was absorbed in her embroidery. He hid behind a tall, spreading mallow. They couldn't see him, but he was able to observe the way they talked and laughed together like friends, not mistress and servant. Suddenly, he understood that Fanny had run off that evening out of loyalty to her friend, Helene. He was so relieved to have found an explanation for Fanny's odd behavior and even more relieved that it wasn't because of him.

I need to take a leaf out of her book as far as loyalty goes, he thought as he turned to go. He walked slowly, thinking it through and planning to leave matters as they were. Instead of chasing after Fanny, he needed to pay more attention to Nelli. After all, he was here for her.

The two young women were in the garden together on the afternoon before Helene's name day. The baroness was in the kitchen discussing the celebration menu, while Max and the baron had ridden out together to look at the cattle.

"Are you looking forward to your party, ma'am?" asked Fanny as she stitched a fine velvet trim on a jacket she'd made for herself. She knew that a name day was an important celebration, even more significant than a birthday.

Helene put down the embroidery frame in her lap. "This year I'm looking forward to it even more than usual. There's a special reason why!" She cast a look in all directions before whispering to Fanny, "At the party tomorrow, Papa's going to announce my engagement to Max."

"So, Herr Kálmán proposed! Congratulations!" Despite her own confused emotions, Fanny was sincerely pleased for her mistress.

Helene was in raptures. "It was all so romantic! Max and I were in almost the same spot that we are now. Just there!" She pointed to a wrought iron bench beneath an arch festooned with the blooms of a rambling rose. "He took my hand in his and told me that he respects me and holds me in very high regard. Then he got down on one knee and was really solemn, asking me if I would agree to be his wife. I was so nervous I couldn't speak. Just nodded. It was only when he took me in his arms and kissed me that I fully realized what had happened. Mama and Papa are so happy, especially Mama, as you can imagine. There, now I've told you, what do you think, Fanny?"

"Yes, that sounds so romantic," murmured Fanny as she bent attentively over her sewing. The mention of a kiss between Helene and Max had unexpectedly shaken her up. She knew how it felt to be kissed by Max and didn't want to share that feeling with another woman.

"You don't sound very pleased for us," commented Helene, puzzled by Fanny's reaction.

"Oh, I am!" Fanny responded, rather too fast to sound genuine.

But it seemed enough for Helene. She edged her seat closer to Fanny's and whispered, "I wouldn't resist if Max wanted to kiss me again." She paused, then added, "Was it like that for you, too?"

Fanny froze inwardly, but managed to look up. "What do you mean?"

Helene stared back at her. "Please, Fanny, you know what I mean. Did it feel for you as if butterflies were fluttering around in your tummy?"

Fanny went hot and cold. Was the baroness's daughter asking her about kisses in general, or was she getting at something quite different? She took a deep breath, but had no idea what to say. "I—I—don't know. Doesn't a kiss feel different for everyone?"

"Doesn't it depend on how much you're in love? I would never kiss a man I couldn't imagine being in love with. How about you?"

Fanny tensed all over. Helene must have seen her and Max kissing so passionately under the apple tree.

What a stupid, stupid goose I've been, she thought, horrified by what she'd let happen. *I've put myself in an impossible position all over again. First prize for idiocy goes to me.*

Frantically, she wondered how she could get herself out of this one, but her mind was a blank. Prepared for the worst, she looked at Helene. If the baroness's daughter was about to tell her to pack her bags, then she deserved it. But to her utter bafflement, her mistress leaned across and placed one hand on her arm.

"I'm sorry I've thrown so many questions at you. I just hoped you'd know more about love than I do. Do you know, I'm scared about the wedding night? I know it's really important, but I have no idea what to expect. I've only ever heard about a school friend who ran from her husband on the first night. It caused such a scandal."

Fanny let out a quiet sigh of relief. Her imagination had run away with her because she had a guilty conscience.

"I really can't tell you anything about the wedding night, but don't fret about it, ma'am," she said, trying to sound encouraging. "Herr Kálman is a good man. He'll be gentle and respectful with you."

Helene looked at her in surprise, opened her mouth as if to speak, but quickly closed it again.

Fanny bit her tongue. When, oh when, would she learn to think before speaking? She tried to find the right words. "Well, I mean, that's just what I've always thought when I've seen you together."

Helene smiled at her. "I want him to be in love with me. But I have no illusions on that score. There are plenty of good reasons for him to marry me, and love's not one of them."

Fanny was close to tears. "Please don't talk like that, ma'am. God knows, you have no reason to hide your light."

"Anyway, I do believe I'm falling in love with Max," Helene said with the hint of a smile. "I've always liked him but never expected to love him. My heart's still pounding!" She put her embroidery frame on the table and leaned forward to put her arms round Fanny. "Thank you for listening to me. And tomorrow I'm going to keep my promise and speak to Mama about your mother. You'll see, Fanny, it'll all work out."

Chapter Ten

The Báthory Estate and Vienna, 1910

When Helene walked into the dining room the following morning with Max and her parents, she was thrilled to see her usual seat decorated with fresh flowers. At her place setting stood her baptismal candle, surrounded by cards and prettily wrapped gifts from her godparents, her relatives, and family friends.

Hardly had they taken their seats when the door opened again and the household staff filed in, the head cook bringing up the rear. She looked proud as she carried the tray bearing Helene's favorite, a sugary confection of sponge cake, chocolate cream, and caramel.

As the staff took turns presenting their good wishes to Helene on her name day, Fanny stole a look at the newly betrothed couple. Helene was radiant and Max his usual charming self as he lifted her hand to his lips and smiled at her.

After breakfast, Helene wanted to bathe and have Fanny wash her hair for her. Outside in the yard, the party preparations were in full swing. Helene's name day was always marked by the baron and baroness with a big, lively party attended by the whole estate, everyone from herdsmen to laborers, from grooms to stable lads and kitchen maids.

Adam had moved all vehicles out of the carriage shed and opened every door fully so the staff could more easily set up tables and benches for the party. Then they created a fireplace and put up a stand for the huge iron cauldron, the *bogrács*, to hang from. A stable boy draped garlands over the carriage shed door and placed a torch in every iron ring along the walls of the yard. While the kitchen maids dragged in huge baskets full of crockery and cutlery and busied themselves with setting the tables, the head cook lit the fire beneath the *bogrács* and soon had the traditional spicy dish of chunks of beef, potato, paprika, tomato, and onion bubbling gently. Mouth-watering aromas started to drift across the yard, mingling with the incomparable smell of freshly baked round flat bread, soon to be devoured with sheep's milk cheese and sour cream.

There was *palinka*, an apricot liquor distilled on the estate, as well as ruby-red wine from the vineyards to the south. The baron liked to reserve the first bottle of *palinka* for the servants and always poured it himself, clinking glasses with each and every member of staff.

Around midday, a gypsy band arrived to entertain everyone with music, dancing, and comic skits. This was their way of life, men, women, and children traveling throughout the summer with their horses and covered wagons across the Puszta from village to village and farm to farm. Soon after them, the *csikós* arrived. These were the baron's herdsmen, soon to entertain everyone with their stunts on horseback, performed more often than not at breakneck speed. Their felt hats pulled down low at the front, dressed in brilliant blue trousers and linen shirts, they sat deep in the saddle, cracking the whip as they flashed by. The cowherds arrived on horseback, too, but were not quite so eye-catching.

When the temperature dropped a little in the late afternoon, the baron, his wife, Helene, and Max made their appearance on the steps leading to the main entrance of the manor house itself. In her white linen dress trimmed with lace, Helene already looked the bride, her face radiating a happiness that made her prettier than ever before. Max, in the Hussars uniform complete with red riding breeches and long leather boots, looked every inch the dashing young officer, just like in the picture Fanny recalled from the Kálmans' house in Budapest.

Back then, she'd never have dreamt that, one day, she'd kiss him and come near to giving herself to him, but when she saw the pair now, she was glad she hadn't. Helene and Max looked right together, as if they'd been made for one another.

"Does everyone have a full glass?" called out the baron to the crowd.

"*Igen!* Definitely!" Then the talking and laughter gave way to an expectant silence. The latest gossip around the estate pointed to an engagement between the young mistress and young Herr Kálman.

The baron surveyed the crowd and solemnly made his announcement. "Today is a special day! My darling daughter, Helene, has become engaged to Máxim Kálman!"

Everyone cheered and applauded, making Helene quite flushed at being the center of attention, something she wasn't accustomed to. Max gently took her by the hand, and they walked together toward the balustrade on the staircase's center landing. When Max took his bride-to-be in his arms and kissed her, the shouts and whistles became more boisterous.

"*Eljen!* Bottoms up!" Everyone joined in. "We wish you a long, happy life and lots of children!"

The baron raised his right hand, his schnapps glass full. "Raise your glasses to the summer, to life and love! A toast! *Eljen!*"

After everyone had tucked into spicy goulash with plenty of red wine and *palinka*, the *csikós* began their act. Fanny stood between two of the farm girls, and together they watched the men come racing up to the yard, then lean down off the saddle to swoop up in one hand various bits of colored ribbon that had been placed at intervals on the ground. The winner, a young man who'd not only gathered up the most ribbons but had done so in the fastest time, trotted his horse over to Helene to loud applause and handed her his trophies, bowing deeply as he did.

The high point of the evening was always Hungarian Post. This involved five horses, three hitched up in the front, two behind. A herdsman would climb onto one of the rear horses, stand tall, and then place his left foot on the crupper of one horse, his right in the same place on another. Now perfectly balanced, he'd call up all five and race them around the yard several times, always to thunderous applause.

After the *csikós* had done their bit, the gypsy band started up for the dancing. Their womenfolk joined hands for a circle dance, their swirling skirts adding to the color and excitement. These women gave off a real zest for life and looked proudly independent, but Fanny suspected their lives were tough, traveling across the country year in, year out, living in a covered wagon with no place to call home.

Soon, everybody else joined the dancing. One of the *csikós* asked Fanny to do the courting dance with him, the *csárdás*, and after that she got no peace. After the *csárdás* came the *verbunkos*, the so-called recruiting dance, then it was the courting dance again before everyone joined for a circle dance. Fanny enjoyed the whole evening almost more than the secret visit she and Izabella had paid to the Fasching Ball in Budapest.

She ended up quite out of breath and sought out a bench to rest. She'd barely sat down when she felt a hand on her shoulder. It belonged to the baroness's personal maid.

"My mistress wants to talk to you," said Zsófia, turning on her heel without further explanation.

Fanny, deeply puzzled, followed her. She couldn't think why the baroness would want her, and it annoyed her that Zsófia hadn't given her even a hint. Ever since she'd started work for the Báthory family, there'd been no love lost between her and this severe, older woman, always dressed in black. Fanny was wary of Zsófia's excessive devotion to the baroness and the deliberate distance she placed between herself and young Fanny.

Zsófia led Fanny inside to the small drawing room, where the family often gathered after dinner. She tapped on the door and went straight in. Fanny followed.

Baroness Báthory stood in the middle of the room, stone-faced.

Fanny curtsied politely. "You called for me, ma'am?"

The baroness's lips trembled with fury, but her voice betrayed no emotion. "You will pack your bags immediately and leave this house for good. Adam will take you to the station."

"I'm sorry?" Fanny was flabbergasted.

"You heard me!" retorted the baroness with a disgust that shocked Fanny even more. Accustomed as she was to being disparaged by the baroness, she was taken aback by this display of loathing.

Ida Báthory turned to her maid, waiting in silence by the door. "Tell her what you saw."

Zsófia glared at Fanny with an expression no less cold than that of her mistress. "I saw you and Herr Kálman in an exceedingly improper situation in the orchard. Later, I saw you both disappear inside the carriage shed."

The baroness gave a nod of satisfaction. "Thank you, Zsófia. You can go now."

Her lady's maid turned and left. Fanny, motionless, watched her go. It had never occurred to her that she and Max might have been seen. It knocked the wind out of her. Her first thought was for the baroness's daughter. "Does Helene know?" Her voice shook.

Ida Báthory glared at her as if she were a vile insect to be crushed underfoot. "If you speak of my daughter, you will refer to her as 'ma'am.' She knows nothing of this scandal, of course."

"It's a scandal for Max, too." The words just slipped out. Yet again.

And left the baroness speechless for a few moments. When she next spoke, it was a hiss. "Just who do you think you are? I'm warning you—not one word about this to Helene, or I'll make enough trouble to last you a lifetime."

Fanny swallowed hard. The disdain and hatred emanating from the baroness was almost palpable. She was deeply ashamed of herself because she'd lost yet another position through her own doing. And this time was even worse because she'd risked her friendship with Helene—one of the most lovable people she'd ever met. Her head lowered, she turned and went to the door. Her hand on the doorknob, she looked back.

"Why did you wait two weeks before throwing me out? Why didn't you do it straight after Zsófia saw me with Max?"

"I didn't want to risk the engagement," was the icy retort. The baroness glanced at the mantelpiece clock. "You'll be gone thirty minutes from now. Leave the house via the kitchen. I don't want Helene to see you."

Numb with shock, Fanny stumbled up the steps to her attic room, dragged her suitcase out from under the bed, took all her clothes out of the closet, and stuffed them in the case with a carelessness that was fully out of character.

It's happened again. She felt defeated.

When she opened the bedside table drawer, she saw Max's handkerchief, washed and ironed, on top of her neatly piled underclothes. She took it out and stroked it.

Imagine you're carrying a lantern that always lights the next step. She recalled what Max had said the first time they'd met beneath the apple tree. His words had been a great consolation that evening, but they hadn't come true.

Now I really am alone in the dark. She was afraid and didn't know what to do. One thing was clear. Never again would she go into domestic service. She had to accept that she wasn't cut out for a life of taking orders and being looked down on. But what to do instead?

Maybe I can get factory work? But the mere idea of standing at a machine ten hours a day and doing the same monotonous tasks almost reduced her to tears. She'd never imagined herself with that kind of life.

Leave off that whining, little mite, came Josepha's voice out of nowhere. *Get yourself home to Vienna and let's see.*

The moment Fanny thought about her old guardian, she felt such longing for home. A flicker of hope seemed to shine in the darkness that surrounded her. She dried her eyes with Max's handkerchief and stuffed it back into her dress pocket. Then she picked up her suitcase in one hand, her sewing machine in the other, and headed for the door. She felt so sorry that she couldn't say goodbye to Helene. Her young mistress would be so disappointed that her personal maid had gone off without so much as a word of farewell. But Fanny couldn't face finding a way of seeing her. Right now, she needed all her strength to concentrate on her future.

When she got as far as the hall, she glanced at the sitting room door. It was shut, but she heard muffled voices. Fanny hesitated. She was sure her thirty-minute deadline had expired, but Adam couldn't exactly leave for the station without her. With great care, she looked around for anyone watching, then tiptoed right up to the door.

"I can't believe what I'm hearing, Nelli! How can you expect me to take on nonsense of this sort?"

The baroness's words were hard to make out, so Fanny had to put her ear right against the wood.

"This isn't nonsense, Mama," Helene replied. "I had hoped you would understand why I'm asking."

"Understand? Heavens above! I sometimes think you were at the back of the line when the Good Lord gave out common sense. Do you have any idea what you're asking, child?"

"I'm asking you a favor on Fanny's behalf. She wants so much to find out, after all this time, who her parents are. It would cost you nothing more than a drop of ink and a sheet of writing paper. And it would mean so much to Fanny."

"I'll be damned if I'm going to lift so much as my little finger for her. Someone born of sin doesn't deserve to live." Ida Báthory's voice was shrill with outrage.

Fanny shrank inwardly. This rigid moralizing and torrent of anger made her feel beaten.

There was a deathly silence on the other side of the closed door. Then she heard Nelli again, her voice trembling. "I'd never have imagined you could be so cruel, Mama. Well, if you won't help Fanny, then I will. I can find out from our acquaintances without you."

Fanny heard a chair being pushed back, footsteps hastening across the room, the sound of a slap, and Helene crying out. "Mama!"

"You'll do nothing of the sort! Do you want to discredit us in the eyes of our social circle? Just think of the gossip if you went around asking about something like that!"

"I only want to help Fanny!"

"And I have said no! That brazen hussy doesn't deserve your time and effort."

"I can't tell you how disappointed I am in your reaction, Mama."

Then there was a pause. Fanny held her breath. Ida Báthory spoke again, with greater composure. "You don't understand what you're asking for, Nelli. It's too late, in any case. She's not here."

"What do you mean? Where's Fanny?"

"Gone. You'll never see her again."

"Mama, what have you done?"

"I've dismissed her. She was a bad lady's maid. If I hadn't kept such a close eye on things, she'd have had you looking like a scarecrow. We'll find you someone new, someone who has a better grasp of the work."

"You can't throw her out, Mama. On top of that, you had no right. She worked for me, not you. And I demand that you stop speaking so ill of her. She's done you no harm. And she made me beautiful when I'm not beautiful at all." Helene's voice was thick with tears. "She's been a friend, too. I love her like a sister."

Fanny's own eyes smarted. Did she really have to slink away like a thief in the night just because that's how the baroness wanted it to end? Just then the front door opened and Max called out, "Nelli? Are you there, Nelli?"

Fanny jumped. For a moment, she stood as if rooted to the spot, listening for footsteps. Then she bent to pick up her suitcase in one hand, her sewing machine in the other, and slipped through the narrow doorway to the kitchen in the nick of time, just before Max came around the corner.

"Dammit, I'm practically burstin' out here!" A man was thumping on the door and shouting. "You've been in there near an hour! Are you squattin' in there til Vienna?"

The bolt snapped back on the other side of the door, and Fanny emerged from the train lavatory. "I'm so sorry." She smiled apologetically at the man. "I needed to freshen up after such a long journey."

The sight of this pretty young woman surprised the man so much he stopped complaining. Perched stylishly on her strawberry blonde curls was a jaunty hat with a white lace hatband, while her dress was a beautiful violet silk tulle with a close-fitting bodice that highlighted her charming curves. Its full skirt showed off a fair bit of calf, graceful and well shaped.

"Don't mention it. Quite alright. If I'd known such a lady—" He flushed and raised his own hat. "D'you need help with them bags?"

"You're too kind." Fanny smiled even wider. "Thank you so much, but I can manage."

He goggled after her, openmouthed, as she swept past him with her case in one hand and her sewing machine in the other. She made her way down the narrow corridor of the train back to one of the little cabins.

A few minutes later, the train puffed and whistled its way into Vienna's main railway station, emitting clouds of black smoke as it went.

Porters stood waiting for the train doors to open. "Carry your bags for ten heller!" called out a young man to Fanny.

"Thanks, but I carry my own." As she got down from the carriage, she lost her balance for a moment, but the porter grabbed her to save her from falling.

"Maybe you shouldn't!" Then he looked at her more closely. "Don't I know you? Did Budapest not take yer fancy, then?"

"Pardon? Who are you, exactly?" Fanny pulled free of his grasp and gave him an angry glance, but then stopped short and laughed. "Of course! The young fellow who saw me off! You're a real man now!" She gave his broad shoulders an appreciative look.

He smiled at her and pulled his flat cap down over his forehead. "And you're pretty as ever, ma'am!" He bent to pick up her luggage for her, but she stopped him.

"I'm sorry, but I really do need my last heller."

He shook his head with a grin. "You been gone twelve months to seek your fortune and come back with nothin'? Well, I'll carry the bags for free, but only cos it's you." Without waiting for her answer, he swung the sewing machine onto his shoulder, picked up the suitcase, and was off. Fanny looked up at the huge round clock on the end wall of the station interior: almost half past three. If she was to do everything she'd planned today, she needed to hurry.

"Not outside—to the luggage check!" she called after the young man.

"Shall I fetch you a cab?" he asked once she'd checked in her bags. She shook her head. "I'll take the new tram. But thank you so much." Fanny turned and walked briskly toward the exit.

"Wait a minute, fräulein," he called out, bobbing up again beside her.

"What is it now?"

"Aren't you going to tell me your name this time?" He held open the station door.

"No time. My tram's already here!" Fanny broke into a run, waving her arms. "Stop! Wait!" She jumped on with only a moment to spare, and the tram rumbled off. "Thanks again!" she shouted to the young man running alongside while she stood on the open deck.

"I still haven't had a proper kiss!" he shouted as the tram pulled away.

She waved, laughing. "Next time!"

In mid-August, Vienna was almost as hot as the Puszta. Running in her tightly laced corset had left her quite dizzy, so Fanny was grateful to be offered a seat, hard though it was, on the wooden benches. The city was far busier than she remembered. Carriages, wagons, coaches, and motorcars filled the streets, while the sidewalks were crowded with pedestrians rushing about on errands, and every outdoor café looked full to bursting. Fanny found the traffic noise overwhelming. Then there was the dust in the air, not to mention the stink of motor fuel. But hearing that familiar Viennese twang made her so happy and reminded her how much she'd missed her home city.

But this time she wasn't going to land on Josepha's doorstep asking for help. She'd decided to call on her unofficial guardian when, and only when, she'd sorted out her new life. The long journey back home had given her plenty of time to think. From now on, she was going to earn her living from doing what she loved and what she was best at. Now all she had to do was make this plan a reality.

At Schottenring, Fanny changed onto a horse-drawn tram in order to get to Stephansplatz. From there, she made a beeline for Graben. Parked in front of the gleaming black door were two motorcars and a landau. A lady emerged from the shop and stepped into the landau while her coachman took the boxes of shopping from her page boy and stowed them under the seat.

Fanny looked up at the eye-catching gold sign over the door and then at the dresses on show in the window. In the past few years, she'd feasted her eyes on plenty of exquisite gowns, but it had taken the long trip from the Puszta back to Vienna for her to realize that what she wanted was to learn exactly how these enchanting creations came into being from a length of cloth.

Taking a deep breath, she swept past Gustav as he bowed and opened the door for her. Here she was again, inside Sarah Moreau's salon.

Little had changed since her first visit. Glass-fronted display cases showed off all manner of modish accessories, and clients admired themselves in the gold-framed wall mirrors, while the sales staff trod soundlessly back and forth over the thick red Persian carpet or stood behind the counters to the rear of the salon while they showed fabrics and patterns to other clients. The sparkling crystal chandelier burned bright even though it was broad daylight outside. A new addition was a pair of electric fans that hummed as they turned, keeping a pleasant indoor temperature in spite of the heat outside.

Fanny didn't see Sarah Moreau anywhere. One of the sales staff came over and said to her pleasantly, "How may I help you, madam?"

Madam! Fanny loved that. "May I see Madame Moreau?" she asked in her most respectful voice.

"But of course." The girl gave her a friendly nod. "Who shall I say is asking?"

"Fräulein Fanny Schindler."

"Thank you. I'll inform Madame Moreau right away. Can I offer you a glass of champagne while you're waiting?"

Fanny grinned. "That would be lovely."

She took a seat on one of the stylish sofas and was soon sipping from the elegant champagne glass brought her by a young apprentice. The first time Fanny had come here, Josepha had forbidden her any. All the more reason now to savor the cooling fizziness as she relished a taste of imperial luxury.

Letting every mouthful roll over her tongue, she took a good look at the clients and noted how elegantly turned out every single one of them was. It was a long time since she'd seen any fashion magazines, and she was surprised by how much styles had changed. The upper part of a dress now sat so soft and loose on the hips that Fanny couldn't tell whether corsets were still being worn or not. By contrast, the lower part, the skirt, was now worn very narrow. Admittedly, it looked chic, but it meant that the wearer could only take the tiniest of steps to get anywhere.

She looked discreetly across at a mother and daughter sitting together on a nearby sofa while a sales assistant showed them some pictures of the latest autumn styles.

"This is a Paul Poiret," the young assistant explained. "He's the talk of Paris."

"Why would a girl wear something that makes her hobble along as if there's something wrong with her feet? You'll have to enlighten me, my dear!" said the mother to the assistant.

"Oh, we have plenty of inquiries for this style! Just look at the cut. It creates a beautifully slim figure." The assistant pointed at the pictures.

"Mama, everybody's wearing things like this now!" the daughter excitedly interrupted, and Fanny could tell how much she wanted that particular dress.

Her mother wouldn't hear of it. "I have no idea what you mean by 'everyone.' I've never seen any of my friends in anything like that. Nor do I know how I'd explain to your father why you need a wickedly expensive dress that you can't even walk in."

The sales assistant gave an awkward little laugh. "Perhaps you'll have to persuade the gentleman of the house first."

Not a good answer, thought Fanny. *I bet those two will leave without buying anything.*

And indeed, not long afterward, the two women got up and left. As Fanny watched them go, she heard a husky-voiced woman with a marked French accent addressing her.

"Mademoiselle Schindler? You want to speak to me?"

Fanny turned and saw Sarah Moreau. With her short silver hair and cerise lip color, she came across as flamboyant as Fanny remembered her. Even in this heat, she wore a high-necked black silk dress, her only jewelry a glittering lizard brooch pinned above her left breast. Fanny swiftly put down her glass and stood up.

"Good day, Madame Moreau. Do you recognize me?" She held out her right hand formally to reintroduce herself to this imposing lady.

"Oui, naturellement." Madame returned the handshake but sounded a little confused, and Fanny guessed she didn't actually recall her first visit there.

"I bought the material for my first ball gown from you. Of course, it was years ago . . ."

"Bien sûr. And what can I do for you today?" Madame seemed still not to remember her.

Fanny swallowed hard. "To be perfectly honest, I'm hoping you're still looking for an apprentice."

"Ah." Madame raised her finely plucked eyebrows. "We'd better go to my office. If you'd like to follow me, Mademoiselle Schindler." She turned and headed for the elevator in the rear corner of the salon.

Fanny was quite apprehensive. Not a word was said as they went up in the elevator. Fanny peered anxiously through its lattice gate. On the way she caught a glimpse or two of a long hallway with some exotic rugs, a crystal mirror, and some beautifully arranged flowers on a dainty table to the right and left of which were two elegant lights of brass and crystal. Fanny suspected this was where clients came to try on their gowns or have extensive private consultations.

They left the elevator at the second floor, where, Madame explained, all the workshops were located. "Above us on the next floor are the attic bedrooms. That's where my apprentice girls live."

In the workshops, a functional simplicity and a bustling atmosphere prevailed—none of the serenity and elegance of the fashion house's public face. The floor was wood, very plain but scrubbed clean, and the lamps hanging from the ceiling were gray enamel. It was hot and stuffy and smelt of dust and coffee. Dressmakers hurried here and there with bolts of cloth and half-finished garments over their arms, giving their boss and Fanny only the briefest of glances. An even clattering sound came from a room near the elevator. Through its open door, Fanny spied about twenty women around long tables, each with a sewing machine in front of her. In one of the back corners was a rounded stove made of cast iron, obviously used for heating the many irons, and a board stood ready close by. In view of the extraordinary heat, all windows were wide open, and the street noise mingled with the clatter of sewing machines.

The next room was smaller but accommodated several women bent over their work on square embroidery frames. The third room was full of bolts of cloth and tailor's dummies draped with different lengths of material. Then, in the fourth room, Fanny saw three women chatting as they took a break with coffee and some sustenance brought from home. They broke off their conversation and looked with curiosity at their young visitor.

Can it be that I'll soon be part of this? Fanny wanted it more than anything.

Madame opened a door at the end of the corridor, and Fanny followed her into her office. On one wall was an enormous iron safe and some shelving stacked with books. Beneath the windows on the other wall was a long table with two bulky pattern books, both left wide open, stacks of drawing paper, and a heap of colorful buttons, crayons, and samples of material. She noticed in one of the corners a tailor's dummy with a half-pinned dress on it, then in another corner, four chairs and a small round table with a square ashtray and a small flat silver case.

Madame closed the door behind Fanny and gestured toward one of the four chairs. After she'd taken a seat herself, she said, "I remember you now, Mademoiselle Schindler. You wanted to take the *Matura* exam, *n'est-ce pas?* An unusual plan for a young woman. I take it that this didn't happen?"

"How did you know?" Fanny was taken aback.

Madame smiled. "Would you be here if it had?" She reached for the silver etui. "Tell me a bit about yourself. What do you bring?" Then she flipped open the case to reveal not only neatly packed cigarettes but a lighter, too. Taking out a cigarette for herself, she sat back, lit it, and waited.

Starting hesitantly, Fanny spoke of her training as a housekeeper and the various positions she had held since. She was afraid that Madame wouldn't be thrilled with her checkered employment history and tried to keep it concise. The elegant French lady listened attentively while taking a good look at Fanny.

"Did you make that dress yourself?"

Fanny was pleased at the change of topic. "Yes, and the pattern for it, too."

Sarah Moreau got to her feet, indicated Fanny should do the same, and walked right around her, as slow as slow could be. *"Pas mal,"* she murmured. "Where did you get the idea from?"

"Just my own imagination. But sometimes I get ideas from what's around me. When I lived in the Puszta, I created an outfit based on the local women's traditional costumes."

"Interesting." Sarah Moreau bent to lift the skirt a little so that she could examine the workmanship. She scrutinized the seams, the composition of the lace trim, and the minute pleats at the neckline. "The technique isn't perfect," she eventually announced. "And the cut could be more up to date. These close-fitting tops aren't really *à la mode*, but I have to say, *très chic* overall. How old are you, *ma chère?*"

"Twenty," said Fanny. Her heart was racing. "I wanted to apply to you a year ago, but was advised against it."

The two women sat down again. Sarah Moreau drew deeply on her cigarette, then exhaled, her lips puckered. "I recognize your talent, Mademoiselle Schindler, but your failings, too—you've never stayed anywhere for long."

"But that's only because I've never found the right thing!" Fanny exclaimed.

"And what if you don't find 'the right thing' here either? I'll have invested a lot of time in your training for nothing. On the other hand, I appreciate your *enthousiasme*." She frowned a little and sat looking hard at Fanny. "If I'm honest, you're just a little too old for dressmaker training in my view. I can offer you a position as sales assistant. Then it's a question of just learning quickly. Will you agree to that?"

"No." Fanny shook her head, devastated. "I want to make clothes. I want to learn everything about dressmaking, and I have so many ideas bursting to get out of my head. Of course, I'll be happy to learn how to sell what I have designed and created, but more than anything, I want to be a dressmaker and work with all these beautiful materials." She knew she was near to tears but wasn't about to give up. She took a deep breath to calm herself and looked the French lady straight in the eye. "What must I do for you to train me as a real dressmaker?"

Sarah Moreau smiled. "You're very persistent. I like that. And that you're fighting for your *passion*. Training with me is three years. By then, you'll be at the age when most women are already married and having children."

"Marriage isn't on my mind," Fanny assured her.

"But you have a sweetheart?"

Max's face flickered in Fanny's mind's eye for a moment, but she quashed it. "No," she said firmly. "There's nobody."

Sarah Moreau leaned toward the table to flick the ash from her cigarette. "I don't know."

Fanny stared down at her hands. She could tell that Madame was on the verge of turning her down. Her powers of persuasion were all she had left to stop this chance from slipping away. Fired up by the thought, she held her head high and began to relate what she'd seen. "When I was waiting to see you, I noticed two clients in particular." She told Madame about the mother and daughter, how they'd been shown the latest styles in dresses and then gone away empty-handed. "I'd never have let them leave without placing an order."

"Vraiment?" Sarah Moreau looked at her with keen interest. "What would you have done?"

"I'd have suggested an alteration or two. Nothing that would show, just a little something to make a difference: let's say a concealed pleat, a pretty broad one."

"Pas mal!" Sarah Moreau was impressed. "You never give up, Fräulein Schindler. *Mais ça me plaît,* I like that. And you'd be a good saleswoman. Won't you reconsider my offer?"

"No," said Fanny. "It took me a long time to know for sure that what I want more than anything is to train under you as a dressmaker. But if you won't take me on, I'll try other fashion houses. Someone will take me."

"Not so hasty, Mademoiselle Schindler." Sarah Moreau raised her hand, saying, "You've convinced me. I'll give you a try, but I'm warning you, I expect a lot. Not just talent, but honesty, hard work, and discipline. Do you accept my conditions?"

"Yes! Absolutely." Fanny felt her heart soar. Her face radiated happiness.

"*Très bon!* That leaves only a trifling matter to be settled. Can you find the money to pay the apprenticeship premium?"

An hour later, Fanny got off a horse-drawn bus in Florianigasse. Unlike during her visit last autumn, the shops were still open, and the little street seemed full of housewives bustling along to the baker, the fish-monger, and the greengrocer, while the elderly walked their dogs. Folks who'd just finished work for the day enjoyed a glass of wine and a game of cards at any one of the many taverns, and local children jumped rope or played cops and robbers.

There it was, the same old three-story building where Josepha had her little home. Cooking smells wafted from the open windows as Fanny looked up at the façade, picturing the familiar living room. When she reached the entrance, she spoke to two little girls sitting with their dolls on the steps.

"D'you two know if Frau Pfeiffer's home?"

"Think so," replied one of them. "She don't go out much."

"Cos of her bad knee. She can't do the stairs so good," added the other.

Fanny thanked them and rang the doorbell. It was a while before Josepha's head appeared at one of the upper windows. The old lady stared in disbelief at first, then called out, "Holy Mary, mother of God, what brings you here, little mite?"

It was good to hear her old pet name again. That meant that Josepha wasn't angry. Not yet. "Frau Pfeiffer, can you spare me half an hour? I've got so much to tell you."

The old lady leaned out of the window a bit more and peered at the ground near Fanny. "Where's your luggage?"

"I'll tell you, but not from the street."

Josepha sighed. "You'd better come up, then. The door's open." She mumbled something that Fanny couldn't make out, then disappeared from view.

When Fanny got to the first landing, she saw her guardian standing in the doorway. Josepha's thick spectacles played tricks, but Fanny thought she read a mixture of concern and disapproval in those eyes.

"So, what kind of trouble are you in this time?"

"None at all. Quite the opposite," Fanny assured her. She noticed how heavily Josepha leaned on her stick, but otherwise she looked in good shape. "Oh, Frau Pfeiffer, I'm so glad to see you again!" She flung both arms around Josepha and planted a kiss on her cheek.

"I'm glad, too," said Josepha, hugging the girl warmly. "Now come on in." She turned and hobbled toward the kitchen, Fanny in her wake.

After the grand houses Fanny had worked in over the years, Josepha's place struck her as more cramped than ever. But it was good to be on home ground, all the more so when she saw the jug of summer flowers on the kitchen table and sparrows pecking at the breadcrumbs Josepha had scattered on the window ledge.

"Be an angel and put a couple of glasses on the table and fetch the water jug from the rack, would you? It's a joy to take even one step less." The old lady sank down into one of the two kitchen chairs. "So, you're back in Vienna." She leaned her stick against the edge of the table. "What was it about the baroness's daughter that didn't suit you?"

Fanny served them both the cool water and prepared to tell a version of what had happened. She told Josepha that the baroness's daughter had suited her perfectly well; it had been the baroness she hadn't been able to get along with. She didn't mention Max, of course. Josepha would have no sympathy for that.

But even without that particular detail, Fanny's tale still made Josepha shake her head. "So, here you are again with no job and no roof over your head. What did I get wrong when I raised you?"

Fanny reached out and gently stroked Josepha's hand, her fingers so worn and lined. "You got nothing wrong, Frau Pfeiffer. It's me who got things wrong, taking jobs that don't appeal to me."

"Don't appeal," grumbled the old lady. "That's a new-fangled expression! Did you forget that there's nobody to provide for you? What matters is not whether your job 'appeals' to you, but whether you can put bread on your table."

"But listen, I've found something that does appeal. With Madame Moreau. Do you remember her?"

"Yes, I remember her. Are you going to be her housekeeper?"

Fanny shook her head. "Much better!" She launched excitedly into a detailed account of her visit to the fashion house.

"Learning a trade costs money," pronounced Josepha in her matter-of-fact way after hearing Fanny's plans. "Can you pay?"

"No. But listen to this. Madame Moreau will, as an exception, waive what she calls the apprentice premium. In return, I've committed to working the first three years after my apprenticeship for a much lower wage."

Josepha's thoughts flew to the savings book she'd opened for Fanny all those years ago. The money from the anonymous donor had been invested at a fixed rate of interest until Fanny came of age. There were still three and a half years to go. *Darn it. The little mite could use her money more than ever, just to pay for the apprenticeship.* But there was nothing to be done. She had no access to the funds before that magic coming-of-age.

"Will your wage be really a lot lower?" Josepha looked concerned.

But Fanny was positive about it. "Madame has been very generous." The amount she'd have to forgo was actually less than what she'd have had to find to pay the apprenticeship premium.

"Madame Moreau seems to think a lot of you," Josepha said pensively. "Now then, you've got to see this one through, maybe even stay in Vienna until I go to meet my maker."

"Oh, Frau Pfeiffer, why are you talking like that? Are you sick?" Fanny looked at her with concern.

"Ach, it's nothin'. Other than this awful knee, I'm fit as a fiddle. But I'm not getting any younger . . ."

"You'll be fit as a fiddle for a long time yet!" Fanny interjected fondly. She got up, hurried around the table, and hugged the dear woman who'd raised her from birth. Josepha hugged her warmly in return.

"If I'd known you were coming, I'd have had a decent meal ready. I've only got cold cuts."

"That's perfect in this heat." Fanny busied herself setting the table, fetching the bread, butter, and some cold meat and cheese from the larder. Then she brewed a pot of tea.

Josepha set about making something tempting for Fanny, placing a lavish helping of dried sausage on one hefty slice of bread, cheese on another, while Fanny described the vast expanses of the Puszta, its enormous herds of cattle and horses, the herdsmen themselves, and the gypsies who traveled from farm to farm.

"I'd feel my world had fallen in if I had to live so far away from anywhere," said Josepha, pushing the wooden platter across to her. "I've never been out of Vienna. Now eat up, little mite. You look too thin. By the way, did you know the foundling home's gone?"

"No!" Fanny was aghast.

"It closed in April. That maternity ward where you were born, and the chance to do it all quietly and discreetly, that's all finished. Now a babe can only be delivered under its parents' name. If the parents can't keep the little thing, it goes to a new children's home not far from here in Gersthof. The regional government set it all up. Public money helps with food and shelter only when the parents are too poor to take care of the child themselves."

Fanny listened attentively. "Sounds like it's about reducing need. But before, it was also about helping the mother not be branded for life over an illegitimate child."

Josepha nodded. "But the powers that be can do what they will. An illegitimate birth still brands the mother and the babe for life, and it'll always be that way."

"And what about foster mothers? Do they still exist?"

"It's all taken care of by the children's home now, and the staff there are trained in child-rearing. If you ask me, that's an improvement. The foster mothers I worked with were often so poor that they did it more for the cash than for the child. Look at you, you were half-dead when I took you off that Schindler woman." She paused for a mouthful of tea. "D'you remember how you would come to me when you were tiny and ask to hear again about how I saved you from near starvation?"

Fanny rested her elbows on the kitchen table and placed her chin on her folded hands. "I envy children being born now. Nobody can stop them from knowing where they came from. Look at me: I'll never know who my father and mother were, will I?"

It hurt Josepha to hear that sadness in Fanny's voice still. Swiftly, she reached across the table and gently pinched the girl's cheek. "My little mite, that's how it is with an anonymous birth. You must try and make peace with it." She tried to distract Fanny with practicalities. "Have you got a bed for the night, or d'you want to sleep on my sofa?"

"I'm going to have an attic room at Madame Moreau's! She keeps one ready for any new apprentice. It seemed best to take it right away." Fanny bit into her bread. "Oh, Frau Pfeiffer," she said, relishing the homely food, "you're so right. I'm going to stop fretting about the past and concentrate on the future from now on. And I'm so excited!"

Chapter Eleven

Vienna, 1913

"Holy Mary, mother of God, must your madame drive like a mad woman? It's not doing my old bones much good!" Josepha hung on to her hat with one hand while the other clutched at the arm rest in Madame Moreau's elegant black Bugatti.

At the age of seventy-six, Josepha was experiencing her first trip in a motorcar, the elegant façades in Vienna's Tuchlauben district flashing by.

"Don't be concerned! Madame is an experienced driver." Sarah Moreau's right-hand woman, Elfriede Schubert, attempted to soothe Josepha's nerves while Fanny, sitting between the two of them in the back seat, put a comforting hand on the old lady's shoulder.

"C'est vrai!" Madame sang out, her eyes firmly on the road ahead. "I have to hurry, I'm afraid, if we're to be on time to mark Fanny's success! And remember, I've never had an accident!"

As the vehicle swung left into a narrow alley, Madame sounded the horn at a couple of passersby who had failed to immediately make way for her. The car bumped and jolted over the uneven cobbles the short distance to Judenplatz before braking abruptly in front of a striking white building.

"Just in time!" Madame glanced at the well-groomed guests gathering at the main door, now staring with curiosity at the vehicle and its occupants. Straightening her hat before stepping out of the vehicle, she went immediately to assist Josepha, while Fanny gazed up at the façade. The broad, triangular gable bore the distinctive coat of arms, scissors and a thimble. Running across the front of the building between the first and second floors was a bold inscription to mark the home of the civil tailors' guild: *Haus der bürgerlichen Schneider.*

Today's the day I qualify in my trade, she said to herself, full of joy and anticipation, as she got out of the car behind Josepha.

The old lady had hardly slept a wink and was full of pride to be wearing the Viennese tailored suit that Fanny had made as her final test piece. For Josepha, this was simply the most beautiful item of clothing she had ever possessed. It was made of the finest English cloth, and Fanny had fashioned the buttons from old silver coins.

As the four women approached the wide doorway together, Fanny was aware of whispers left and right. Her own kimono-style gown caught the eye of all the women, while the men ogled the Bugatti and trotted out whatever they knew about pistons, cylinders, valves, and horsepower.

It feels like no time at all since I started out as a new apprentice, thought Fanny as they went upstairs to the hall for the celebration. She marveled at what she had learned over the past three years. Madame Moreau had shown her how to breathe life into clients' fantasies through imaginative fabric choices and flattering colors, always adding a personal touch. And from Elfriede Schubert, she had learned the nuts and bolts of her craft. A hard taskmaster, Frau Schubert had often criticized Fanny's early work as "sloppy," but the girl had bitten her tongue and never talked back. Frau Schubert had served Madame Moreau ever since the fashion house had opened twenty years earlier. She was known throughout Vienna to be one of the best, and Fanny had quickly realized how much she could learn from this woman, whether it was ensuring the accuracy of a pattern or the precision of cutting, right down to a broad range of sewing and embroidery techniques. Frau Schubert's knowledge of the characteristics of different fabrics was second to none, and she showed Fanny how to care for and iron them appropriately. She had been at Fanny's side throughout the tailoring of her final piece and was delighted to be invited to the presentation of the coveted final certificate.

The hall seemed almost full to bursting with successful apprentices as well as their parents and tutors, but Fanny spotted four empty seats in one of the rows near the front. As she glanced all around her, she recognized quite a few faces from other workshops and fashion houses, other apprentices she'd met up with once a week in the classroom for the formal part of their professional training. They were all noticeably younger than Fanny—not that this had ever bothered her, as they'd often asked her advice, knowing that she came from the most respected house in Vienna.

As she took a seat, Josepha whispered, "It's nearly eleven. Time to start. I'm just so proud of you, little mite." She lovingly tweaked Fanny's cheek.

"And d'you know how proud I am of you in my final piece?" Fanny said, beaming at her. "I ought to put you in Madame's window, then the whole of Vienna can have a good look!"

"In all my born days, I've never worn anything so gorgeous." Josepha caressed the fine cloth of her sleeve. "Thank you from the bottom of my heart, little mite."

"Oh, no need for that. It's the very least I can do for you!"

"Shush!" People sitting nearby tutted at them as the president of the Awarding Board, also chair of the Clothiers' Guild, stepped onto the platform. After surveying the hall and all the guests, he began.

"May I start by welcoming all apprentices, parents, tutors, and friends of our guild." Whispers and coughs faded away. "We are gathered here on this beautiful summer's day to celebrate our 1913 cohort of apprentices as they formally qualify in their trade. I'm delighted to announce that all have been successful, some exceptionally so!"

He then continued with a lengthy speech about the current economic position of the clothing business, its expected growth, and the success of the guild in providing training and development. Then it was time for the presentation of certificates. Fanny knew it would be a while, as her surname was late in the alphabet, so she sat waiting, holding tight to Josepha's hand. Then it was her turn. The president's gaze swept the front rows again until it rested on Fanny. He smiled.

"And now I have the pleasure of announcing the name of the best apprentice of the year. With excellent scores in workshop tests, in theory examinations, and in specialized knowledge, Fräulein Fanny Schindler has gained the highest possible grade on her final tailoring examination!"

There was loud applause. Josepha hugged Fanny, and Elfriede Schubert gave her a hearty handshake. Madame Moreau kissed her on both cheeks.

"*Toutes mes felicitations, ma chère.*"

Fanny thought it was all a dream as she stepped up to the podium to receive her certificate. This was one of the best days of her life.

Sarah Moreau had given Fanny a whole day off for the occasion and, after the ceremony, drove them all out of town in the Bugatti to enjoy the vineyards.

They stopped in Dornbach at a tavern near the priest's house, enjoying the view of the city as it lay bathed in sunshine. All the excitement had made them hungry, so they ordered cold roast pork and Liptauer cheese, yellow and spicy, with chunks of crusty bread, all washed down with Riesling and Rotgipfler.

Sarah Moreau lifted her glass in a toast. "I am so proud of you, Mademoiselle Schindler. And I'm delighted that my studio now has another superb woman tailor."

"I agree that Fräulein Schindler's a superb tailor, even if her initial drawings bear little similarity to the end result." Frau Schubert's dry humor provoked a little outburst of fond laughter. Fanny had a wonderful imagination, but drawing was not one of her strengths, something she'd been teased about on many occasions.

They all raised their glasses, and then Madame Moreau took a small package from her handbag and handed it to Fanny. "With my appreciation, Mademoiselle Schindler!"

Fanny unwrapped it and found a little leather case. The moment she opened it, she gasped. "Madame, this is wonderful—I really don't know what to say."

"'Thank you' would be a good start," said Josepha.

Fanny's smile radiated her gratitude. "Madame Moreau, thank you! I've never owned anything so beautiful before!" She placed the open case on the table so that Josepha and her tutor could both see what was inside.

"Holy Mary, mother of God," gasped the old lady when she saw the gold-plated tailoring scissors on a red velvet cushion.

Carefully removing them from the case, Fanny saw the day's date engraved on the upper blade. "I'll cherish these forever," she said, tears in her eyes.

"You've more than earned them," said Elfriede Schubert, giving her arm a little squeeze.

Fanny looked at her three companions and felt her heart swell. *Going to Madame Moreau's was the best decision I've ever made,* she thought.

When she arrived in the workshop the following morning, all her colleagues looked deadly serious. "Frau Schubert's been looking for you. Asked twice where you were," said Elisabeth Nikolic. "You'd better go and see her."

"What did I do now?" Fanny laughed, still elated after the wonderful day of her award.

Elisabeth made a face. "You made your bed. You're going to have to lie in it, I suppose."

Fanny was puzzled now. "Are you sure it's me Frau Schubert's looking for?"

"Oh yes."

One of the other girls added, "Chin up, Fanny! And grit your teeth!"

"Guess I'll go and clear it up, whatever it is," said Fanny, confused, and turned to go.

"She's down in the cellar!" Elisabeth called after her.

Fanny decided it was quicker to take the stairs. Her head was in turmoil as she called to mind every recent piece of work, but nothing had been amiss. When she reached the storeroom, it was dark and silent. Frau Schubert must have taken the elevator back up just as Fanny was on the staircase.

"Frau Schubert wasn't there," she panted when she got back to the workshop. She'd been too anxious to wait for the elevator.

"As soon as you left, she came back up here," said Elisabeth with regret. "Now she's in the embroidery room."

And yet, when Fanny looked through the door, there was once again no sign of Frau Schubert. All the staff were bent over their work, talking quietly to one another. One of them looked up. "Hello, Fanny, who are you looking for?"

"Master Craftswoman Frau Schubert. I was told she's here."

The girl looked at her blankly. "Isn't she in the sewing room?"

Fanny shook her head.

"Well, she isn't here either." She looked down at her work again.

Fanny turned on her heel, now annoyed more than anything. *I hope this isn't going to be one of those days when everything goes wrong.*

As she went through the door to the sewing room, she almost collided with Elfriede Schubert. Their master craftswoman planted her hands on her hips and looked at her accusingly.

"There you are! Where on earth have you been?"

"Looking for you!" grumbled Fanny. "For a quarter of an hour already. You want to speak to me?"

"I do, indeed! It's about the matinée dress you're supposed to be making for Frau Goldberg."

"It'll be ready at the correct time. It's already cut and pinned," Fanny assured her.

"Ready, my foot!" Elfriede Schubert gave her a harsh look. "You got the measurements all wrong and wasted meters of expensive cloth. Haven't you learned anything from me at all?"

Fanny had gone pale. "That can't be right," she said hesitantly. "I checked everything so carefully—"

"So why is the dress too tight across the bust, too loose across the hips, and too short overall? Fräulein Nikolic!" Frau Schubert waved over Elisabeth. "Bring me the miserable item. It's in my workroom."

Elisabeth hurried off. Fanny, utterly baffled, watched her go.

"I don't understand," she muttered.

Nothing like this had ever happened to her before, not even as a new apprentice, still wet behind the ears. Yesterday she'd been awarded her certificate of completion. Now here she stood in front of all her colleagues, feeling like the village idiot.

While she waited for Elisabeth's return, she stared at her feet without a word. The serious look on everybody's faces, their whispering—it was almost unbearable. To make matters worse, the embroidery girls had now joined them, drawn by the chance of a spectacle of some sort.

When Elisabeth eventually returned, she had over her arm Frau Goldberg's dress, all pinned up, and held in her hand the client's card. Fanny snatched at the card first. Then she took hold of the dress and placed it on the nearest worktable. "I need a measuring tape!" She studied the information on the card.

Elfriede Schubert handed her the measuring tape she always had around her neck. Fanny measured the whole garment, then referred again to the client card. "This can't be right!" she exclaimed. "I got it all wrong. How in heaven's name could I have been so stupid? Madame will dismiss me if she hears about it." Close to tears, she rubbed furiously at her smarting eyes.

But then someone touched her on the shoulder. "My dear Fräulein Schindler, don't take our little game so seriously. That client card isn't the real one. We made a second card and put different measurements on it." This was the master craftswoman's voice.

Then Elisabeth Nikolic chimed in. "Don't you remember? We always play a trick on the newly qualifieds, just to send them into a bit of a spin. You did it to me a couple of years ago just after I got my certificate, too!"

"Holy Mary, I'd completely forgotten about all that!" Fanny exclaimed.

Her colleagues laughed uproariously at first, then gathered round to hug and congratulate her.

"I'm pleased you're all having so much fun, *mesdemoiselles*, but I hope you will not forget that your work awaits you." Sarah Moreau's voice rang out behind them. The girls dispersed. But the Frenchwoman smiled as she walked toward Fanny, whose cheeks were now bright red with embarrassment. "Mademoiselle Schindler, I'd like to introduce you to Monsieur Eder."

Only then did Fanny see a man standing in the doorway. He wore a brown suit and a crumpled hat and seemed amused by what he had seen.

"Monsieur Eder writes for our trade paper. You know your final project was outstanding, better than that of any of your male colleagues, so he'd like to interview you."

"Really?" Fanny replied in disbelief.

"Mais oui." Her employer laughed. "It is no prank this time! And when you're done, come to my office. There's something I'd like to discuss with you."

When Fanny got to Madame Moreau's office half an hour later, she found her leaning over a drawing that was spread out on her desk.

"Come and see this, mademoiselle." The French lady turned and waved her over. "What do you think?" She pushed the drawing closer to Fanny.

It showed an ankle-length dress with a broad, swinging skirt. Fanny took a good look, then said, "It's quite a simple style, but I think its elegance comes from that simplicity. If we cut the fabric diagonally against the weave, it'll fall very nicely indeed. I tried that out when I was making one of those hobble skirts. It sat much better like that. And the cloth has more give to it."

"Pas mal!" Sarah Moreau was pleased with this reaction. "Actually, I got my inspiration for this dress from dancing the tango. Its movement means that the woman needs plenty of freedom to move her legs." She glanced at Fanny with interest. "Can you dance the tango?"

Fanny shook her head, although she'd heard of this exotic South American dance, now the latest craze in some of Vienna's bars. "I don't have time. No partner either."

"Work isn't everything, *ma chère.* You should make time for fun, and never forget to make time for love. On Fridays, I always go to the Palm House on Mariahilferstrasse and—"

Fanny interrupted gently. "I have a wonderful job, and that's all I need."

She had no desire to have a conversation with Madame about love or passion. Yes, she adored her work. But when she went to bed at night and thought over the day's events, she was aware of her need for a companion, her need for tenderness, and she was aware as well of her desire. It wasn't loneliness, more a sense of emptiness in those moments between sleep and wakefulness. She found it very lowering at times.

Madame gave her a long hard look, then gestured to Fanny to sit down beside her. Taking a cigarette from her silver case, she said, "I'd like to sound you out on something. Would you like to be Frau Schubert's successor? She'll retire in a few years, and I'll need a new master craftswoman. Then, when I myself want to retire, I'll need to hand the business over to someone capable." She drew deeply on the cigarette and watched for Fanny's reaction.

The girl was quite taken aback. To receive an offer like this only one day after qualifying was beyond her wildest dreams. "That sounds fabulous!" She couldn't think what else to say.

Madame laughed. "Then it's agreed. You'll start your master craftswoman training right away."

The two women shook hands on it. Fanny couldn't wait to tell Josepha.

A knock at the door interrupted them. One of the sales assistants popped her head in to say, "Madame, your nine o'clock client is here. I've shown her to reception on the first floor."

"*Merci.*" Sarah Moreau stubbed out her cigarette in the ashtray and got to her feet. "We've covered everything, Mademoiselle Schindler, *n'est-ce pas?*"

Fanny nodded and stood up, too.

"Then come with me," said Madame. "I'll introduce you to the client, and then you can take over."

"What about Frau Schubert?" Fanny was surprised because it was usually the master craftswoman who attended these meetings with Madame.

"You're starting your training today! This includes listening to clients' wishes and laying out the options for them. Madame Schubert is well aware of my plans and has given them her full support. She thinks a lot of you."

Excited but a little apprehensive, Fanny hurried behind her boss to the client reception area. During her apprenticeship, she had spent most of her time in the workshops and had little contact with clients. What if her ideas weren't well received? Madame's clients were known to be very demanding and difficult to please.

Just before opening the door, Sarah Moreau turned to Fanny as if she had read her thoughts. "*Courage*, mademoiselle. The best moments in our profession are when a client leaves happy." She went into the room, and Fanny followed.

Madame was right in front of Fanny, and her imposing figure, always in black, blocked the girl's first view of the client. But then she froze. Had Madame really said "*Bonjour*, Madame Kálman?" What came next took her breath away. "I'm delighted once again to have the pleasure, madame. And this time your charming sister-in-law and her little daughter have come with you. *Bonjour, petite* Emma." As Sarah Moreau leaned over a little to shake the child's hand, Fanny found herself looking straight at her former mistresses. Helene and Izabella hadn't changed a bit. Izabella was still as beautiful as Fanny remembered. Helene had filled out a little. Between them stood a little girl of about two, with red-brown curls, timidly returning Sarah Moreau's handshake.

Helene still hadn't noticed Fanny, as she was focused on her daughter. Izabella, however, was clearly puzzling over where she could have seen Madame Moreau's assistant before.

"*Mesdames*, I'd like to introduce you to Mademoiselle Schindler, my best trainee *couturière*. She will take excellent care of you." Sarah Moreau turned to her protégée, encouraging her to step forward.

Fanny prayed they magically wouldn't recognize her. After all, she no longer had to dress as a servant, and her whole look had changed in the last three years.

But Izabella had raised those eyebrows. "Well now, it's dear Fanny!" Her voice was still dark and melodious.

Helene looked up and gave a little shriek of surprise. "Fanny! It really is you!" She went straight to Fanny and embraced her. "Oh, my dear, if you knew how often I've thought of you and wondered what had become of you—" She stood back and held her former maid at arm's length. "Fanny—oh, my goodness, Fräulein Schindler, I should say—I'm so pleased to see you again!"

Fanny's mind raced, unable to process this bizarre twist of fate.

"*Très intéressant*, you ladies know one another," commented Sarah Moreau.

"You could say that, yes," Izabella said, her lip curling a little.

But Helene gave Fanny the warmest of smiles. "Oh yes! Fräulein Schindler and I are friends."

"Then I am even more certain of the excellent advice and service you'll receive from us!" Madame turned to Fanny. "And now I'll leave you to get on with your work, mademoiselle. *Bonne chance!*"

Fanny had noticed two glasses and an open catalogue on the table and resolved to do her best. "It looks as if you may already have some ideas? Are you both looking for a dress?"

"I have all my tailoring done in Budapest," Izabella said, then added mockingly, "Mademoiselle Schindler."

"Very well," replied Fanny without warmth. "I take it you need something for yourself, Frau Kálman?"

Helene shook her head. "Not at the moment. I'm expecting again." She placed her hand on her stomach, and Fanny noticed her gently curving belly beneath the loosely cut dress.

Helene carried on. "I need something pretty for Emma, as she'll soon be giving her first tea party."

"A formal dress for such a tiny girl?" Fanny was amazed at the idea.

"Well, Emma's nearly three now and the sooner she learns how to be a good hostess, the easier it will be for her later on! I'm thinking something simple, a good fabric, in white, perhaps?"

"Of course," agreed Fanny, taking her measuring tape from around her neck. She hadn't turned her hand to children's clothes since the foundling home, but if that's what her client wanted, that's what she would have.

Chapter Twelve

Two weeks later, Fanny sat in a cab and listened to the rain drumming on its roof. The summer so far had been either unbearably hot or miserably rainy. Today there was even more bad weather, so Fanny had resorted to the horse-drawn cab to cover the short distance from her work to Helene's home on the Ring.

On her lap was her sewing basket, and next to her on the seat was a flat box containing Emma's dress, ready for today's fitting. As Helene had requested, Fanny had gone for a simple cut that gave the little girl freedom to run and play. She had decided on a fine white cambric for the dress itself and silk for the sash.

Today was to be the second and final fitting. Clients usually came to the salon, as it was so much easier to make alterations there. But Helene had telephoned that morning, explaining that Emma had caught a cold and wasn't well enough to go outside on such a wet day. "Please come to the apartment at three, after Emma's afternoon nap," she had said.

The bells of the Karlskirche were striking three when the cab pulled up outside the newly constructed, superior apartment building. Fanny paid the driver and stepped down.

She found herself worrying as she looked up at the rain-soaked façade. *Are Max and Izabella going to be there?* Helene had mentioned that Izabella's parents didn't have a residence in Vienna, and this was why her sister-in-law lived with her when she was in town. Since the surprise encounter, Fanny had felt very unsettled and had been relieved when Izabella hadn't returned to the salon for the first fitting. Max was the person she really didn't want to run into, especially not in Helene's presence. But she had no control over it and knew she had to find a way of dealing with the situation if it arose. At least the baroness wasn't going to be there. Helene had told her how her mother still spent every summer out at the family estate in the Puszta, coming to Vienna only in September for the season.

Fanny went in through the revolving door, greeted the doorman who sat outside his office, puffing away at his pipe, and took the elevator to the second floor, where the Kálmans had their apartment. Helene had told Fanny how, after the wedding, Max had bought this with a view to it being the family home in Vienna.

A butler opened the apartment door and led her across the hall to a small sitting room. Family photographs and vases of fresh flowers covered every table and chest surface. Through open doors she caught sight of elegant furniture, paintings, and mirrors. A gleaming grand piano stood in one room, a billiard table in another, and somewhere toward the back of the apartment, she heard a child's voice.

It wasn't long before Helene came hurrying in to welcome her. "Dear Fanny! Oh, I'm so sorry. I mean dear Fräulein Schindler! I really will soon learn!" She put her arms round Fanny and hugged her effusively. "Emma's been asking about you all day. She'll be so pleased to see you, as well as the new dress."

"Is Izabella home?" Fanny glanced down the hallway.

"No, she's out at the moment."

"Has she gone shopping?"

Helene shook her head. "No, she's having some medical treatment."

"Oh no, is she sick?"

"Not exactly sick, no, but I'm sure she'll tell you about it."

Helene turned away. Fanny was puzzled but followed in her wake. She remembered how Josepha used to ask if she was "swinging the lead" if a tummy ache suddenly developed when it was time to do the ironing or pot washing at the foundling home. Could Izabella possibly be feigning illness?

As Helene opened the door to the playroom, Emma shrieked with delight. It was as if Fanny had stepped into a toy shop. The large, sunny room was full of dolls and soft toys, mostly cute animals. There was shelving stacked with picture books and wooden storage chests. In one corner was a play grocery shop, in another an enchanting doll's house, something Fanny would have loved as a little girl. The owner of all these delights was squeaking with excitement as she rocked back and forth on a wooden horse in the middle of the room, her nanny patiently keeping it moving with her foot.

"Darling, Fräulein Schindler is here. Be a good girl and say hello," said Helene.

"Whoo-hoo!" All Emma did was continue shrieking, adding an exuberant wave as she shouted, "Look, one hand!"

Fanny turned to Helene. "I thought she was sick."

Helene went red. "She's been much better since lunch."

The nanny managed to remove the protesting child from the rocking horse and handed her to her mother. Meanwhile, Fanny set down her sewing basket and carefully unpacked the dress. To be on the safe side, she'd removed all the pins for the fitting and tacked the dress together instead. Emma was more than a fidget as she tried on the garment, running around and climbing on and off her mother's lap. It was obvious that Helene had made up Emma's cold.

"Goodness me, I feel as though I've been fitting a whole band of children, not just one little girl," Fanny commented afterward. She packed her sewing basket and put the dress back in its box. "The dress will be ready next week. I'll bring it over."

"And now we deserve a pot of tea, don't you think?" suggested Helene.

Fanny wasn't sure. She had tons of work waiting but could see how much Helene wanted her to stay. "Alright. Thank you. But I won't linger."

"Of course. I understand how demanding your profession is."

Helene led the way to a pretty little sitting room, where the table was already set for afternoon tea. She offered Fanny a seat, then rang for the butler. Soon, freshly brewed tea and a plate of crescent cookies, generously coated with almonds, arrived.

"I know you've seen that Emma isn't really sick. But I had to find a way of talking to you in private, without anyone disturbing us." Helene poured two cups of steaming tea. "I've often wondered why you left us so suddenly, without any explanation or warning. Why didn't you just tell me that my mother had questioned your ability and dismissed you?" She gave Fanny the saddest of looks.

"I didn't have a chance," Fanny said, panicked and playing for time. "More than anything, your mother had said so many bad things about me that I just didn't want to stay."

Helene looked taken aback.

"I overheard the conversation between you and your mother on the day you got engaged," admitted Fanny. "And I wish to God I'd never heard what she said about me. About my not deserving to be alive."

Her friend was crestfallen. "If that's what all this has been about, then I completely understand. My mother was cruel. I can't excuse her. But I hope you know I'm not that kind of person. I always hoped we'd hear something from you. Is there some other reason why you ran off like that?" Helene looked at Fanny with an intensity that made her heart sink.

Once again, Fanny had that sense of being caught out, like in the garden on the Báthory Estate when Helene had told her about the engagement. Her voice trembled as she asked, "Other reason like what?"

Helene's look became even more intense. "Only you can tell me that."

A shiver rippled down Fanny's spine. "There isn't any other reason," she forced herself to say.

Helene stirred her tea, and for a while the only sound was metal against porcelain. Then she placed the teaspoon on her saucer. "Good. I wouldn't want anything to stand between us."

Nor would I. But it's too late. Her memories of Max in the landau flooded back.

Then she realized Helene was still talking. "I would like to pick up our friendship where it left off. We could truly be the best of friends. What do you think?"

Fanny reflected on how the kindly Helene had never taken advantage of her position. Quite the opposite, she'd always had Fanny's thoughts, feelings, and welfare at heart.

"I'd like that, too." She meant it, in spite of her fear.

"That's wonderful!" Helene gave a little shout of laughter. "Then let's go back to using first names, like we used to. All my close friends call me Nelli!"

Fanny laughed with her. "And I'll go back to being Fanny!"

They raised their teacups in a toast to a friendship renewed. Helene went on to relate how she hadn't bothered looking for another lady's maid after Fanny.

"You'll remember how I was never interested in getting all dressed up. For everyday things, I can dress myself and do my own hair. And if Max and I are invited anywhere special, I call in one of the hairdressers from the theater here, and that works well. But there'll be none of that over the next few months! The doctor has prescribed complete rest until the baby arrives." As she said this, her hand went protectively to her belly. "I became pregnant again quite quickly after Emma was born but lost the baby. He was a little boy. It happened when I was out on the estate. You'll remember only too well how isolated it is there, and there wasn't a doctor to be found." Her sadness was almost palpable.

Fanny was choked. "I'm so sorry. You must have suffered dreadfully."

Helene managed a brave smile. "That's why Max insisted I spend the summer here in the city. And it's what I want, too." She paused. "I can't stop wondering whether the baby would have survived if I'd been here in Vienna, or at least in Budapest, where there are plenty of good doctors and hospitals."

"I'm sure everything'll be alright this time," said Fanny. "And don't dwell on that. You can't change the past."

"I know." Helene nodded appreciatively. "I'm hoping for another boy and know Max feels the same. Men always want a son and heir, however much they might say a girl is just as lovely." Lost in thought, she started stirring her tea all over again. "But we have a happy marriage. Sometimes I wish he had more time for me and Emma, but that's probably not realistic so close to his finals at the military academy. Once he finishes, he'll spend two years on the General Staff of a regiment. It could be in Bulgaria, Italy, or somewhere on the Russian border, and I'll only see him when he gets leave." She toyed with the crescent cookie, still untouched on her plate. "I asked my uncle if he could use his connections to get Max into a regiment based here in Vienna. But that won't happen, I know." Rain beat against the window as she looked outside. Muted flickers of lightning broke up the leaden sky as thunder rumbled far off. "Enough of that!" She turned to Fanny and managed a smile. "Let's talk about you, dear Fanny! And your search for your mother. Has there been any news?"

Fanny shook her head. "Sadly, no. I pretty much gave up hope three years ago, when the foundling home closed."

Helene gave her a sympathetic look. "Perhaps it's for the best that you stop trying. Or leave it in God's hands."

"I suppose they're one and the same thing." Fanny set down her cup and saucer on the table. "Now it's high time I got back to work." She picked up her sewing basket and the box. "I don't want to walk in this foul weather. Is there a place to catch a cab near here?"

Before Helene could reply, Fanny heard the front door.

"Nelli? Are you there?"

"It's Max!" Helene sounded surprised.

The sitting room door swung open. There he stood.

Helene rushed over to embrace him. "I thought you weren't back until this evening! What brings you home so early?"

"A lecture was canceled because the prof's sick. No wonder in this weather." He bent to kiss her. "And how are you both?" He placed his hand on her belly.

"Very well, indeed!" She glowed with happiness. "Come and see Fanny. She's been here to put the finishing touches on Emma's dress. And we've agreed to renew our friendship." She turned to Fanny. "I've already told Max about how I found you after so long."

Fanny stood motionless in front of the sofa, holding the dress box against her chest protectively. He'd been in her thoughts a lot when she'd first reached Vienna, but as her new life took shape over the past three years, less and less. And yet now here he was, standing there, and all the old excitement came back. He looked so handsome in his custom-made uniform, his dark hair still wet from the rain, that her mind filled with the memory of his lips and the passionate yet tender touch of his hands as they had explored her body.

"Good day, Herr Kálman," she said with deliberate formality. She sensed that Helene was watching her and hoped fervently that her face wasn't giving her away.

He bowed stiffly. "A pleasure, Fräulein Schindler. How are you?"

"Splendid, thank you."

Helene's gaze flickered between her husband and her friend. "Good heavens, you're behaving like total strangers. Fanny, do sit down again, and Max, come and join us."

Fanny shook her head firmly. "I really have to go now."

"Oh, you're being so dull! But alright, let's do it another time. Max, be a dear and get the car so you can take Fanny back to work."

"That really isn't—" Fanny started.

"No arguing," interrupted Helene. "Max, darling, you can drive her, can't you?"

Max showed not a flicker of emotion. "Of course, Nelli, whatever you want."

How did I get myself into this? Fanny was in the passenger seat, staring out of the windscreen at Max, bent over the vehicle in the pouring rain as he turned the starter crank. The engine sparked and roared into life, vying with the drumming sound of rain on the metal body. Max swiftly opened the driver's door and took his seat at the wheel. Rain trickled from his hair down onto his uniform, and Fanny had to restrain herself from wiping a few drops off his cheek. She pressed her hands together in her lap. *For goodness' sake, pull yourself together.*

"The Cadillac has an electric starter button, you know. You just press it from the driver's seat, but we're nowhere near that with our European vehicles." Max pushed his wet hair off his face.

"It's a nice-looking car," she said.

He grinned. "Only a woman could think of calling a car like this 'nice-looking.' It's a Mercedes 38, high performance on the technical side and with seventy horsepower. It's only been around for three years and has won the Vanderbilt Cup twice! Not bad, eh? That's the most important car race in America."

His enthusiasm was infectious, but Fanny wasn't going to fall for that. "Could we get going now?"

Max raised his eyebrows, refrained from commenting further, and set off. They drove in silence. Fanny spoke only as Max was about to make the turn into Graben. "You can drop me at the back entrance on Goldschmiedgasse."

"You're being very formal." Max was brusque in return. "Is this about your sudden exit from the carriage shed, Fräulein Schindler?" He placed a sarcastic emphasis on the last two words.

Noticing how determinedly she was staring ahead, he softened his tone a little. "Is it really necessary now that it's just the two of us?" He turned onto Goldschmiedgasse. "And by the way, the lecture wasn't canceled. I skipped it. Purely and simply to see you. Nelli had mentioned you were coming over for Emma's fitting." He turned to her, but she didn't alter her expression one bit.

This angered him. "Clearly you don't want to talk to me, but if anyone here has reason to be frosty, it's me. You were the one to run off as if a pack of wild beasts was after you. You left me sitting there like a fool. I want to know why you ran away, Fanny."

Suddenly, she turned on him. "Zsófia saw us by the fruit trees. She followed us to the carriage shed, then presented the story to the baroness on a platter." Her face was flushed with anger. "That cost me my job. It cost you nothing. Is that enough of an explanation?"

Max stepped on the brake so hard that Fanny had to grab at the dashboard. "I never knew that! Honest to God. That explains a few things," he exclaimed.

"What things?"

"My mother-in-law is forever making remarks to me about fidelity and virtue. I've often wondered what's behind it all. Anyway, she has no reason to judge. What happened between you and me was before my engagement, and since I've been married, I've been faithful to Nelli." Max put his foot back on the gas, and they moved forward again. "I am so very sorry that you lost your job over it."

"There's no need for all that," Fanny snapped. "I'm doing much better now. I don't have to take orders from anyone, I'm earning far more money, and I love the work. I got the final results of my tailoring apprenticeship two weeks ago. I came top in my year."

By now they'd arrived at the rear entrance of the fashion house, and Max stopped the car. It was still raining, and a few pedestrians hurried by, bent under their umbrellas, while on the other side of the narrow street, the landlord of the Rebhuhn appeared in his restaurant doorway and looked gloomily at the overcast sky before disappearing back inside.

"Congratulations!" said Max, smiling. "Not just for the exam, but for following the lantern light showing you the way on life's journey."

She thought about that summer evening three years ago, under the apple tree. She'd felt so sad and defeated, but he'd consoled and encouraged her. "That was good advice you gave me then," she said softly.

With slight hesitation, he took one of his hands off the steering wheel and reached toward her, but she quickly hid her own hands in the folds of her skirt.

"Did you miss me, Fanny?"

"No!" She shook her head fiercely. "Goodbye, Max, and thank you." She turned to open the door, but he leaned over and grabbed her firmly by the arm. "I don't believe you! I saw how you felt! Your desire for me was just as strong as mine for you."

"Let me go!" She fought to free herself, but he seized hold and kissed her. His passion overwhelmed her all over again. She pressed her body close to his to return his kisses, without caring that his rain-soaked uniform was making her blouse damp. Neither gave a thought as to whether they'd be spotted. Fortunately, the weather had driven most people indoors, and the few passersby hurried on their way without paying any attention to what was going on around them.

Just then, lightning flashed across the sky at the same moment as a clap of thunder sounded. Fanny jumped. Max tried to hold her even more tightly, but she resisted him.

"Stop it!" She had to raise her voice to make herself heard over the rain beating down on the car and the increasing thunder. But he only let her go when she started pummeling his chest with her fists.

"Have you already forgotten what you said two minutes ago about being faithful to Nelli?" She was shrieking at him. "This isn't right, what we're doing. Even Heaven's telling us!" She turned to grab her sewing basket and the dress box from the back seat, pushed open the door, and clambered out, landing in a huge puddle that soaked her dress and shoes. But she was too horrified to care. She was no better than Max. Here he was, betraying his wife, and now she'd just shown herself to be unworthy of the friendship that she and Nelli had renewed only minutes ago. What was wrong with her that she couldn't control herself when she was with him? Was she destined to end up like her mother, with a child she couldn't take care of?

Max stared after her as she hurried across the sidewalk and disappeared inside the fashion house. It was Fanny in his heart and soul, not his wife.

What a miserable louse you are, he told himself as he let his forehead sink against the steering wheel.

Chapter Thirteen

Vienna, 1913

"I'm stopping for lunch! Anyone else?" Fanny put her head around the sewing room door.

Elisabeth Nikolic got up from her worktable. "Definitely. It's past twelve already." She went to the door and two other girls followed.

"Where did you get to this morning?" Elisabeth asked Fanny. "Didn't see you in the sewing room."

"Doing a bit of spying for Madame at the Casa Piccola." Fanny took her lunch tin and coffee thermos off the usual shelf.

Elisabeth was agog. "You were at Flöge's place? Without getting thrown out?"

Fanny laughed and shook her head. "The boss wasn't even there, and her sisters don't know who I am."

Flöge was known to be muse to the renowned artist Gustav Klimt. But she was also Sarah Moreau's greatest rival. They vied to have the most successful fashion house in Vienna. While Madame focused on elegant French couture for the fashion-conscious Viennese society ladies, it was Emilie Flöge who had popularized the new free-flowing, arty "reformkleid" style of dress. She had taken what was basically a shapeless gown and, using fabrics created in Viennese workshops, made it into a variety of exclusive creations favored by women artists, actresses, and indeed any woman who saw herself as truly emancipated.

Sarah Moreau and Emilie Flöge each had a well-established circle of loyal clients, but they watched each other's successes with far more than a passing interest. In fact, each house tried to lure the other's faithful followers to its door.

"Frau Flöge's clothes this autumn are so voluminous they do nothing to show off a girl's figure, which is a shame. But I suppose that's why she uses these fabrics interwoven with gold and silver. To be honest with you, I think it works rather well."

"Madame won't want to hear that," Elisabeth replied.

"You're probably right. But it'll inspire her to some fresh ideas. I have a few thoughts myself."

Fanny opened her lunch tin. Just then, one of the sales assistants appeared. "Ah, there you are, Fanny! There's a lady downstairs asking for you."

Closing the tin again, she pushed back her chair. "Who is it?"

"I don't know. Must be a regular client. She didn't give her name, but asked for you specifically."

Fanny followed her colleague to the elevator. As they stepped out on the ground floor, she saw an elegantly dressed lady waiting near the main door of the salon. She had her back turned and was gazing at the street through the main display window. It was Izabella Kálman. Fanny thanked her colleague and went over to Izabella.

Since the three women had met up again so unexpectedly, Fanny had chatted several times with Helene but had seen Izabella only once, when she'd delivered Emma's finished dress. It had been a brief and impersonal encounter, consisting of little more than passing hellos.

Izabella turned around. Fanny was taken aback to see her looking pale and subdued. "Good day, Fräulein Kálman," she said, holding out her hand.

"Good day, Fräulein Schindler. Can we talk undisturbed somewhere?"

"Of course," replied Fanny.

She led Izabella to one of the smaller salons upstairs. The moment she'd closed the door, Izabella sank down. She took off her hat and rubbed her forehead. Fanny sat down opposite her and waited nervously.

After a while, Izabella spoke. "Nelli lost her baby. I thought you should know straightaway, since you're such good friends again."

"Holy Mary, mother of God," murmured Fanny in horror. "How is she?"

"Weak. The doctor says she'll be alright." Izabella paused. "But she doesn't seem well. She doesn't speak when she's spoken to. She won't touch any food or liquids, not even the medicine the doctor's prescribed. All she does is lie there, staring up at the ceiling."

"I'd like to see her. May I?" Fanny's voice shook.

Izabella looked at her with relief. "That's why I came. Maybe she'll actually talk to you."

Fanny asked Madame for the rest of the day off, then followed Izabella to her cab, still waiting outside. They rode in silence to the Kálmans' apartment. Fanny thought back to her last visit to Helene and couldn't believe it had only been one week ago. Her friend had seemed so relaxed and contented, describing how she could feel the baby kicking. The doctor had estimated that the birth would take place in two weeks' time, in the middle of September, and was confident that everything would go smoothly. Helene had shown her the neat pile of tiny bonnets, little trousers, and baby vests in the lovingly prepared nursery.

How can all that have been in vain? Fanny could hardly believe it.

As she followed Izabella into the apartment, however, the pall hanging over the place quickly drove home the truth. A deathly silence prevailed, the butler's voice was somber, and the large mirror near the door was shrouded to show the house was mourning. Izabella murmured something about needing to lie down and disappeared.

"Where's Emma?" Fanny asked the butler as he took her hat and coat.

"Baroness Báthory came to collect her this morning. It's hard for the child to understand what's happened, of course, and she kept wanting to go to her mother. May I show you to my mistress's room, Fräulein Schindler?"

They walked past the sitting room. The door was wide open. Fanny saw Max standing at one of the windows, staring out at the plane trees bordering the Ring, their leaves just starting to take on their golden autumnal tints.

Since he had kissed her with such passion in the car, their paths had not crossed. She knew from Helene, however, that he had excelled in his final examinations at the military academy and was now serving as first lieutenant on the General Staff, Eighty-Fourth Infantry Regiment, Vienna.

Fanny indicated to the butler that she wanted to talk to Max alone, and the man withdrew with a bow.

"Max." She stepped quietly into the room.

He whipped around and looked as if he'd seen a ghost. His face was drawn and pale, his eyes red and sunken. He hadn't shaved. "How come you're here? Did you—?" His voice trailed off.

"Izabella came to tell me at work. Oh, Max"—she reached out to touch his arm—"I am so, so sorry."

He nodded and wiped his eyes with the back of his hand.

Fanny continued. "Helene must have suffered dreadfully."

He nodded again. "The doctor says her body will regain strength and recover. Whether her spirit will, that's what concerns me. This is the second baby she's lost. I'd give anything to take such sadness out of her life, Fanny."

"Nelli needs time more than anything," Fanny said urgently.

"It started two days ago. She said the baby had stopped moving. The doctor came straightaway and told us he couldn't hear a heartbeat. Fanny, if you could have seen her face at that moment. I'll never forget the fear in her eyes." Max's voice cracked, and he had to take a deep breath before carrying on. "Then overnight she started to lose blood, had terrible pain, and then—oh, Fanny, why wasn't he allowed to live?" He fought to keep his composure. "I saw him, held him in my arms, he was absolutely perfect. But Nelli didn't even want to see him."

"Maybe that would have been too much for her to bear." Fanny tried to sound calm but was deeply shocked by what she'd heard.

Max placed his hands on her shoulders and turned her to face him. "Do you feel able to see him, Fanny? He's in his room, in the cradle that Nelli prepared for him."

Fanny's instinct told her to say no, but when she saw the anguish in Max's eyes, she nodded.

Her heart beat faster as she followed him down the corridor to a closed door. When he opened it, she saw how the sun shone brightly through the window, little specks of dust dancing in its beams. On tiptoe, she followed Max to the center of the room, where the cradle stood. Cautiously, she looked inside. The baby boy was loosely swaddled in the softest linen and lay peacefully on the mattress, as if he were sleeping. Tears came to Fanny's eyes. She reached out and tenderly stroked his cheek with her fingertips.

"We wanted to call him László, after Nelli's father." She heard Max's voice close to her. "He'll be buried tomorrow."

Fanny still felt choked up as she knocked at Helene's bedroom door, but knew how much worse her friend must feel. This made her hold back her own tears and regain her usual composure.

"Would you please leave us a while?" she asked the nurse who opened the door. Then she drew up a chair next to Helene's bed and sat down quietly.

She couldn't tell whether Helene even knew she was there. Her friend lay on her back, motionless, staring at the ceiling, just as Izabella had described. Then Fanny noticed the brown medicine bottles lined up on the bedside table, together with a jug of water. She took a deep breath.

"Nelli, dear, it's me, Fanny. Izabella asked me to come. I hope that's alright." She waited but got no reaction. "If it's not alright, please let me know somehow. But to be honest, Nelli, I really don't want to leave you on your own."

She waited again. Still Helene gave no indication.

Fanny put aside words of sympathy. They felt so hollow in the face of such grief. What Helene needed was warmth and affection, so she gently took her friend's hand and stroked her cold fingers, hoping this would bring her some comfort, however small.

But when Fanny got to her feet half an hour later, Helene still had not said a word. She lay still, almost as still as her dead child.

When Fanny stepped back out into the corridor, there wasn't a sign of life anywhere in the whole apartment. The room where she'd met Max was empty. Nor was there any trace of Izabella.

I need to get out of here, she thought to herself. She'd lost all appetite for work today, so she decided to visit Josepha, who could be relied upon to listen and share her burden of grief.

On completing her apprenticeship, she'd been offered a small apartment in a building owned by Madame Moreau, and it had turned out to be immediately opposite where Josepha lived. As the old lady had increasing difficulty in getting around, Fanny always stopped in before and after work to see what was needed.

The butler had heard Fanny and emerged from the servants' day-room with her hat and coat. Just as she was about to bid him goodbye, a door flew open elsewhere, and Izabella came hurrying toward her.

"Fräulein Schindler! Wait, please wait! How's Nelli?"

"As you said, she's not at all well. I'm afraid my visit hasn't changed much."

Izabella gave her a sympathetic look. "You look weary. Would a cup of coffee help before you go?"

Fanny shook her head. "That's kind, but I want to go home."

"I'll see you out."

"I'm glad you told me," said Fanny to Izabella, as the elevator took them down. "Even though it's definitely been the most difficult visit I've had to make in my life."

"I understand completely," replied Izabella. "It was lucky that I happened to have an appointment with Dr. Freud right after it happened, so I could talk it out a bit."

The elevator stopped on the ground floor. Izabella pulled aside the iron lattice gate and stepped out. Fanny followed.

"Nelli told me a few days ago that you were having some medical treatment. It's nothing serious, I hope?"

Before replying, Izabella checked that they were alone in the entrance hall and that the porter wasn't listening. "That's a matter of opinion," she replied. "It's serious enough for me not to want to have to live with it."

"Really?"

Izabella gave her a sad smile. "You have no idea what I'm talking about, do you? Haven't you heard of Dr. Freud?"

"Sorry, no."

"A Vienna native who doesn't know about the famous Dr. Freud?" Izabella raised her eyebrows mockingly, once again the self-confident young woman Fanny remembered. "He's a doctor like no other," she continued. "He's prescribed treatment for my soul, not my body. His research is renowned. He's considered the coryphaeus in the field of neurology."

"Really?" said Fanny again. That someone like Izabella, always so confident of her own superiority, could be suffering with her nerves left her baffled.

Izabella looked at her for a while, as if wondering whether it was worth explaining. "Do you remember what you said to me on your last day in Budapest about not being the right woman for my kind of love? I've often thought about that. I still haven't found anyone, you know. I'd had so many rejections that I began to despair of life, to be honest. And when you rejected me, Fanny, that hit me harder than anything because I had almost believed—" She paused before trying to strike a lighter note. "But that doesn't matter now. The point is that I could see that my kind of love would mean spending my life alone, and I don't want that." Izabella fell silent and stared down at the stone floor before carrying on with her revelation. "Then I saw an article in the newspaper about the work being done by Dr. Freud and decided to go to him for treatment. I hope so much that he can cure me of my abnormal feelings."

"Don't be so desperate about it!" Fanny's response was quite spontaneous. "You just haven't met the right person yet! It's bound to be harder for you to find someone, but you'll have to be patient and trust the kindness of fate!"

Izabella gave a wistful smile. "Dear Fanny, you're trying to console me. That's kind. It really is." Her voice had lost all its earlier sour formality. "So, have you found someone to love?"

Thoughts of Max flooded back, making her blush slightly. "I love my work. I don't need anything else."

"Well, that's something," said Izabella, a hint of sarcasm there again before she turned serious. "Listen, Fanny, my kind of love makes me lonely and sick, and I can't bear it anymore. I want to be normal and have a happy life."

"And who decides what's normal?" retorted Fanny. "In your shoes, I wouldn't let myself be forced into anything."

"Oddly enough, that's what Dr. Freud said at my first consultation. He said my kind of love doesn't exactly put me in an advantageous position socially, but that it's nothing to be ashamed of and shouldn't be considered an illness."

"Then you don't need to go after a cure, do you?" Fanny felt she could speak candidly to Izabella now that she had such a good profession and her own social standing.

"I don't want to go on being an outsider. I made that clear to Dr. Freud. He actually said I'll only be able to reverse my inversion if I have the will to do so."

"Inversion?"

"It's what he calls my condition. Inversion, or homosexuality."

"Hmm," murmured Fanny. "And how long does he say it will take for you to be cured?"

"A few years," replied Izabella. "It's not done with tablets or drops, nothing like that. I have to put myself through analysis. That means I lie down on a couch and tell Dr. Freud whatever's in my head. Then he gives me his assessment. Sometimes he asks about my dreams, as well, and then he tells me what they mean."

"Sounds like something a nutter thought up!"

Fanny's directness baffled Izabella. "A what?"

"That's what my old guardian, Frau Pfeiffer, always says about something crazy."

Just then the revolving door started to move, and in swept Baroness Báthory, closely followed by her spy, Zsófia, holding Emma by the hand.

Holy Mary! I need these two like a hole in the head.

Emma was all smiles the moment she saw Fanny. She pulled her hand away from Zsófia's as soon as they were through the door, rushed up to Fanny, and flung her little arms around her legs. "Fräulein Schindler! Have you brought me another dress?"

"Not this time, I'm afraid." Fanny returned the child's warm greeting, looking over her head toward the baroness and Zsófia.

Both women had stopped dead.

"And who—?" the baroness began.

"Goodness me, Baroness Báthory, don't you remember me, the woman born of sin? The child who didn't deserve to live?"

Izabella gasped and the baroness's voice was cold as ice. "I've already heard from my daughter how you're trying to put yourself on the same footing as people like us. I see you still have no humility."

"Call me Fräulein Schindler, if you please!" Fanny was equally icy. "I find myself in urgent need of some fresh air. Bye-bye, Emma, my dear. Give your mama a big kiss from me." Her head held high, she marched out through the revolving door.

"Fanny! Wait!" Izabella rushed after her. "What on earth was all that about?"

Fanny was practically spitting with rage. "It's not often I want to give someone a smack in the ear, but the baroness could easily change that!"

Izabella couldn't help but laugh. "Oh, Fanny, I could kiss you for that!" But she added quickly, "Don't worry—figure of speech! I know you're not like me, and that's such a shame. But I'm glad we can put that behind us and be friends again."

"So am I." Fanny hugged Izabella. "And think about whether you really need that Dr. Freud, will you?"

Three months later, it was Christmas and Fanny's twenty-fourth birthday. On Christmas Eve, she'd held a little after-work celebration with her colleagues, and Madame herself had handed out a Christmas bonus to each and every member of staff. Afterward, Fanny had made her way to the Ring to wish Izabella and Helene a happy Christmas and to give Emma the little rag doll she'd made. Helene seemed better and was at least taking part in everyday life again, although she was still rather withdrawn, almost absent at times, and the cheerfulness she'd once radiated was gone.

Fanny's final visit of the evening was with Josepha. They sat down together to a supper of fried sausages, Fanny's favorite small ones, and potato salad. Then they went to Midnight Mass.

The following day, Josepha came to Fanny's for a dual celebration—Christmas Day and Fanny's birthday. The old lady was now very unsteady on her feet and didn't like going out at all but wanted to make an exception. A neighbor boy picked her up from her small apartment and helped her down the stairs, across the road, and then up to Fanny's, as she in turn hadn't wanted to go out and leave the oven unattended.

Fanny was very happy having her own little place, especially because Madame Moreau didn't charge too much in rent. Her employer had given her the idea of getting furnishings from the workshops of the Vienna School of Arts and Crafts. The trainees would sell their practice pieces at reasonable rates, and this meant Fanny could afford some of the most modern and elegant furniture, lamps, and rugs in Vienna.

"Many happy returns, little mite!" said Josepha as she arrived. "Today's your coming-of-age!"

"Good day, Frau Pfeiffer, please come in!" Fanny warmly embraced the old lady, then helped her out of her coat, saying with a cheeky wink as she saw the dark green suit, "Don't you look elegant! Now I wonder where that came from?"

Josepha proudly smoothed down her jacket. "I've got the best dressmaker in all of Vienna!"

Fanny was so pleased. She'd made the new suit for Josepha in the evenings after work, all on her faithful old sewing machine, having bought the fabric from the fashion house as the autumn deliveries started to come in.

She led Josepha into her little sitting room. "You'll see I still haven't quite finished everything! I just haven't had time to do things like hang pictures and curtains. But I've got a telephone!" She pointed proudly at the hall table.

"The bare walls go very well with your furniture," remarked Josepha drily. She'd never made a secret of the fact that she considered Fanny's furniture overly modern and functional, lacking in the old-style ornamentation she loved.

But she greatly approved of the Christmas decorations. "Oh my, now that looks pretty!" she cried. "What an effort you've made, little mite!"

Josepha looked contentedly at everything, from the festively set table in the middle of the room to the dresser where a little Christmas tree stood, adorned with sticks of barley sugar, gold-painted nuts, glass baubles, and candles. On one of the window seat ledges, there were carved nativity figures that Fanny had bought at the Christmas market in the city center, and on the other, a bowl heaped with gingerbread cookies and fresh apples.

"I did most of it after Midnight Mass, to be honest! There's always so much going on at the salon in the run-up to Christmas that I've scarcely been home."

She settled Josepha in a seat, saying, "I need to go make sure the roast's not getting overcooked. But let's have a Christmas toast first!" She left the room, coming back almost immediately with a bottle of wine. "This is the Riesling we had last summer when we celebrated my exam, remember? Out at Dornbach. I liked it so much that I brought a few bottles of it back with me. *Prosit*, Frau Pfeiffer!" Smiling happily, Fanny raised her glass.

"Just a moment, little mite. There's something I'd like to say. Now that you've come of age, it's high time you called me by my first name. So, it's Josepha from now on!"

Fanny's eyes filled with tears. "I'd love that!" They clinked glasses, then she hurried back to the kitchen and its seasonal cooking smells.

While Josepha sat waiting for her Christmas meal, she sipped her wine appreciatively, looking out on the city. Thick snow lay on the windowsills and rooftops, and smoke drifted from the chimneys. Her mind went back to Christmas twenty-four years ago, when her little mite had come into the world. In her bag were two birthday presents. One was from her, but the other she was bringing on someone else's behalf. She knew this would raise more than a few questions, so she'd been turning over in her mind for several days what she should say to Fanny.

A clattering from the kitchen and a little shriek interrupted her thoughts.

"Everything alright, little mite?"

"Fine! Hot roasting tin, that's all!"

Fanny emerged shortly, her face flushed with pride. Bearing a huge tray of meat, roasted to crispy perfection, she walked carefully to the table. "I'll just get the dumplings and the greens. Then we can eat!"

The two women sat together, their plates full of delicious home-cooked food. Josepha picked up her fork and carefully sliced through her potato dumpling, proclaiming it to be light as a feather.

"I tell you, little mite, if dressmaking ever goes haywire, you can always open your own restaurant!"

"Thank you!" This was praise indeed, as Josepha was herself a superb cook. "But it's all thanks to you, really! You taught me how to cook in the first place."

"If the fellers hear what you can conjure up on that little stove, you'll soon be at the altar!"

"Are you hoping to see me with a family?" Fanny asked in surprise.

Her guardian had always been one to preach independence, and yet now here she was saying, "It wouldn't be such a bad idea."

"But I thought you were focused on me sticking with a profession."

"Oh, I am. But I also know what it's like to be alone. Who'll keep you company when I'm not here anymore, little mite?"

Fanny stopped eating. "Please don't talk like that—and just remember that I'm going to take such good care of you that you'll live til you're a hundred!"

"You don't need to worry about looking after me. I'm old now. I don't ask much of life. You just take care of yourself."

Fanny put down her fork and reached across the table for Josepha's hand. "I've got a profession and plenty of women friends. I'm an independent, modern woman."

Josepha looked at her very solemnly, then her lined face broke into a smile. "You're right, my child, and I'm proud of you for it."

There were baked apples for dessert. Then came the exchange of gifts. Josepha presented her with a box of chocolates from the royal confectioner, Demel. Fanny had made Josepha a warm and colorful quilt, all put together from remnants.

"That's just what I need!" The old lady was delighted. "It's so cold this winter." She paused, took a deep breath, then began the little speech she had prepared. "Today's your coming-of-age, little mite, and that's something very special, even if we women still don't have the vote, are still not allowed to study whatever we want, nor do any job we want." She stopped for a moment, smiled wistfully, and then continued. "When I came of age myself, my dear papa put it in writing that he now released me from what was called his paternal authority. His gift to me was liberty. It meant that, from then on, I could make all my own decisions and didn't need to ask a man for permission. He really was a very progressive man and wanted me to have the same rights as all the young men around me." She smiled at Fanny. "You don't need to get anything in writing, as you never had parents." Josepha wanted to stuff those words back down her own throat the moment she said them. But it was too late, and Fanny frowned.

"I'd like to have some family stories to tell, too. But my family history's a big, empty hole."

"Oh, little mite, I know, I know," said Josepha, looking at her long and hard. "But perhaps this is some small compensation for the hand you were dealt." She took a slim envelope from her bag and slid it across the table. "Have a good look. Then I'll tell you what it's all about."

Fanny opened the envelope in wonder and took out the savings book. She flicked through the pages, her eyes like saucers. "Holy Mary," she whispered. "That's a lot of money."

"I'm told with interest and compound interest, it makes 27,919 crowns and 86 heller," Josepha declared. "And I never touched one heller of it for your upbringing."

Fanny was puzzled. "So, it's not from you. I did wonder. It seemed far too much for that."

Josepha cleared her throat before continuing. "The first payment was made into my own savings account soon after you came into the world, and then every month after that. For sixteen years and eleven months, every time with the same reference: Child number 6,572. That was your number, Fanny."

Fanny had gone pale, and her lower lip quivered. "Who did this money come from?"

"I'm afraid I just don't know, little mite. All the payments were made anonymously. I quizzed the fellow at the bank, obviously, but he couldn't, or wouldn't, tell me anything. The final payment was made in November 1906. I waited a while, but when nothing else happened, I opened a new savings book in your name, transferred the money, and left it for your coming-of-age."

"Why didn't you ever tell me about it?"

The old lady spread her hands. "You've always been so sad about not knowing who your folks were, little mite. I didn't want to upset you even more on such a delicate matter."

Fanny nodded slowly, thinking about it. "I'd probably have done the same in your shoes."

Josepha gently stroked Fanny's face. "Any idea what you might use the money for?"

Fanny shook her head. "No idea, to be honest. I'll probably leave it in the bank for now."

"When you get that master craftswoman status, you could use it to open your own business."

Fanny's eyes were shining. "So, all those years, there really was someone who cared a bit what happened to me," she said softly. "Somewhere out there, I've got a family. Parents, uncles, aunts, maybe even a brother or sister."

"I always thought I was your family," Josepha huffed. "After all, I was the one that raised you."

Fanny jumped up, rushed around the table, and flung her arms round her guardian. "Of course you did! I have you to thank for everything that I am! You've always been like a mother to me."

"Grandma more like!" Josepha replied.

Fanny laughed, then collected the dirty dishes and carried them into the kitchen. But she came back quite agitated. "Listen, Josepha," she said, sitting back down. "What was the name of the bank clerk, the one you spoke to about the payments?"

"Ach, I don't remember." Josepha folded her arms rather defensively across her ample bosom.

"I think you do!"

"What's there to be gained from opening old wounds, little mite? If that woman had really been interested in you, surely she'd have taken you back and raised you herself?"

Fanny's mouth was set in a straight line, reminding Josepha so much of little kindergarten Fanny that she wanted to hug her. Instead, she took a deep breath before she spoke.

"It was a Herr Wiesinger."

Chapter Fourteen

Vienna, 1914

Outside it was dark and ice cold, one of Vienna's harshest winters in years, but the fire crackling in Max's study gave off light, warmth, and the comforting scent of resin.

Max was at his writing desk, pondering the wording of a letter to his parents, the only sound the scratch of pen nib on paper, interrupted occasionally by the sharp crack of a log in the flames.

His time in Vienna was almost over. During the January court ball, when he had attended on the Kaiser, his superior officer had given him unofficial warning that the war ministry had planned his transfer. Then four weeks ago, official notice had arrived, stating that Max was to report at the end of March to the fortress commander at Przemyśl, near the Russian border. He wanted to see his parents before leaving. He hadn't seen them once since Emma's birth.

Max rested his pen on the blotter, reached for his glass of wine, and took a mouthful of golden Tokay, sweet as honey. It took him back to warm, sun-filled summers in Hungary and made him long for home.

He'd just picked up his pen and bent over the letter again when a muffled, yet regular, clattering started up in another room, making it impossible for him to concentrate.

Helene! He tried to subdue his irritation with a gulp of wine, but to no avail. The noise became even more intrusive, so he snapped the cap back on the fountain pen and pushed back his chair in one angry movement.

The clattering came from the room that Helene had decked out for the baby. In a few long strides, he reached the door, knocked, and went straight in. All the nursery furniture was gone. Her back to him, Helene sat at a small table with a sewing machine.

Max closed the door behind him. "Do you really have to do that so late, Nelli? You'll wake Emma."

The clattering stopped dead. She turned and smiled at him. "Look! Wouldn't our son look sweet in this?" From under the sewing machine foot, she eased out a matinée jacket still in the making and proudly held it up.

He struggled not to react angrily. Helene, seeming blissfully unaware of his indignation, got up and ran to him, saying, "Max, dearest!" She threw her arms round his neck and tried to kiss him. "Show you still love me, Max!"

"Nelli, stop this! What's going on?" He pulled away from her embrace.

"That'll never get the Kálmans a son and heir," she cried. "Izabella's never going to produce, is she?"

"You leave my sister out of this!"

Helene shrank back. "I deserved that," she said, so downcast that he regretted the reprimand. "Sometimes I think you've stopped wanting a son, Max."

He looked away. It was true he feared the effect on his wife of another pregnancy. He mourned for the two infants who had not survived, and Helene's behavior kept dragging his grief to the surface.

Since losing a second child, she'd become so fragile and her moods so unpredictable. After the period of mourning and seclusion, insisted on by her mother, she'd become carried away with the idea of conceiving again as soon as possible. But he avoided all her attempts at intimacy. He feared another stillbirth could break her, and he himself didn't want more heartbreak either.

"Look, we've got Emma," he would say to her. "She's a happy, healthy child. Let's be grateful for that."

"But we need a son. Every family needs an heir," she would cry out in desperation. "Or am I the problem? Is it that you don't want another child with me?"

"That's ridiculous, Nelli, and you know it. You're the best wife any man could possibly want."

And he meant that sincerely, even though he hadn't married for love. Mutual respect and understanding, common interests, and similar backgrounds were the foundation of their marriage—or had been until that fateful night when she'd lost a baby for a second time. Since then, a gulf had opened up between them and seemed to grow only wider with time.

Helene gave him a long look, turned away without a word, and went back to her sewing machine. The nerve-racking clatter started up once more.

If only Fanny hadn't given her that thing, he thought angrily. *And does it have to make such a din?*

"Sewing is creative, imaginative work, and it'll help Nelli find some joy in life again," Fanny had said. He'd believed her. He'd have done anything to help his wife recover.

At first, Helene showed no interest in the machine, but Fanny was undeterred. She brought over fabric and patterns, showed Helene how to make dresses and pinafores for Emma, and suddenly, the young mother's mood lifted.

Since then, she'd developed a manic devotion to dressmaking but had not made a single item for Emma. It was all about baby clothes. Her matinée jackets, smocks, diapers, and little sleeping sacks soon filled a whole chest of drawers. At the same time, she'd started to pressure Max for another baby. She had grown so insistent that he almost longed for the day of his departure, although life in a grim fortress on the Russian border did not exactly fill him with enthusiasm.

Insistent ringing at their front door tore him from his reverie. Helene broke off her work and turned to him.

"Are we expecting visitors?"

"Not that I know of," he replied, equally puzzled.

He heard the butler's footsteps in the hall. Then they heard the apartment door being opened and the butler's voice saying, "I'm sorry, gentlemen, but—"

There was tipsy laughter and men's voices.

"Don't be that way, my good fellow. Let us in! We know he's here. Where are you hiding, Max?"

The butler's protests were drowned out by what sounded like the men trampling across the hallway. Then, the door of Helene's sewing room burst open and the butler hurried in.

"I can't apologize enough, sir, ma'am, but—" He looked mortified.

"Aha, this is where the first lieutenant's hiding away!"

"He's buried himself at home!"

"A chap can't do that during Fasching! It's Ladies Day! Now that's something to celebrate!"

Six newsboys in peaked caps, sports jackets, and corduroy pants came bursting into the room. These were Max's friends from the military academy in costume, and they had for days now tried to persuade him to join them at the laundry maids' ball at the huge, much-loved *Etablissement Gschwandner*.

Max gestured for them to back off. "I've told you. I'm not going out."

"Not an acceptable answer, comrade! Here's your costume." One of the lads waved a bundle at him. "Quick, get changed. The cab's waiting downstairs. Only if the lady permits, of course." With this, he turned to Helene, pointedly clicking his heels.

Bewildered, she looked from one face to another. "I see I have no choice in the matter," she said, going back to her sewing machine.

Suddenly, Max felt suffocated. He grabbed the package. "Fine, then. Time for some fun!"

"Listen up now! Pretty little Pepi, so they say, is having a wee dalliance.
They say he's a Hungarian baron.
But I say, that's all wrong.
That baron was no more than a tailor's apprentice!"

The young woman's cheeky song was almost drowned out by onlookers' whistling and catcalling as Max and his friends entered the huge ballroom at *Etablissement Gschwandner* out in Hernals.

"Well, I'll be darned if that isn't Lily the Laundry Maid up there!" yelled out one of his group, while another enthused, "I've seen her perform at the Blue Bottle out in Lerchenfeld. Now there's real fun, I tell you!"

Helping themselves to mugs of beer from a passing waiter, they called for a toast. "God preserve our hops and malt!" They all downed the beer. Max's went the wrong way, and he coughed and spluttered.

"Out of practice?"

One of his friends slapped him hard on the back while the others roared with laughter. With a sheepish grin, Max wiped the foam from his lips and thought what a good decision this had been. Before his marriage, he had made a point of taking in all the places like this whenever he was in Vienna. There was no better place for a man to pass the time than these hunting grounds so well stocked with actresses and demimondaines. The crowds, noise, and smoke only added to the experience.

His friends were busy ogling every woman in sight. "God help me, so many good-looking maids, I'm going insane here!" announced one.

All the women had risen to the occasion and were decked out as laundry maids. Their sleeves and low-cut frocks with puffy skirts stopping at the knee were deliberately designed to look like underwear and show off every curve to advantage. From the knees down, there were only red or black silk stockings to be seen, all rounded off with little patent leather boots. The most important part were the laundry maids' scarves, tied around every head in a saucy bow. Like Max and his friends, most of the men were dressed up as newsboys or shoeshine boys, but some had gone in for tails, a walking cane, and a top hat if they wanted to make a really big impression as a gentleman about town.

"Look at them! They'd be good for a bit of fun!" Valerian Brunner, the one who'd brought along Max's costume, nudged him in the side and pointed out a group of girls standing close to the stage, as vocal as the men in daring Lily to lift her dress and show off her red garters.

"They're really not bad!" Max had to agree.

"Charge, comrades!"

The group pushed their way past the packed wooden tables and benches to get closer to the stage. They elbowed their way to the front so that they could get a good look at Lily as well as the group of ladies who'd caught their eye.

"How about that one!" Valerian pointed. "The one with the checked scarf. Bet she's knows a trick or two."

Max stopped dead and stared. Fanny was having a fine time with her friends, whistling through her fingers and shouting with laughter. Her close-fitting laundry maid frock showed off her lovely figure, and the pink-and-white-checked headscarf looked charming against her strawberry blonde hair.

"That one's mine!" announced Brunner, elbowing Max firmly in the ribs.

Max turned on him. "No, she's not."

"Beg your pardon? What—?" But then he gave a knowing smile. "I get it. You want her."

"I didn't say that," said Max, breaking into a sweat.

"No need to feel guilty, Mr. First Lieutenant. I'm a married man, too, but carnival's always time for an intermission in the game of marriage." He gave Max an encouraging slap on the shoulder, took two more beers off a waiter's tray as he hurried by, and handed one to Max. "*Prosit*, comrade. I'm pleased you're showing signs of life again!"

Lily the Laundry Maid left the stage to thunderous applause as the Schrammel-style quartet with two fiddles, a clarinet, and an accordion struck up the Danube waltz. Laughing couples dashed to be the first on the dance floor.

Max put his half-empty beer mug down on a table and pushed his way over to Fanny. She was still talking and laughing.

"Good evening, Fanny."

She turned. "Max! This is a surprise!"

"A pleasant one, I trust." With a charming smile, he reached for her right hand and drew it to his lips.

Fanny's friends were all agog. One of the girls said, "Oh my, Fanny! You've been hiding this one from us, you naughty girl! But we all like a little secret, don't we? Glad you're busy with something that's not work for once! Have fun, you two!" She pinched Fanny fondly on the cheek, smiled at Max, and drew the other girls away to join his group of friends. "Hello there, you newsboys. Buy us girls a glass of wine or two?"

Fanny looked Max up and down. "I nearly didn't recognize you like that. You look pretty good in it, I must say!" She stood on tiptoe and pretended to tap on the peak of his cap.

"Looks like you'll have to dance with me," he said with another of those smiles.

She raised a hand. "I don't think—"

"Surely you wouldn't refuse me a dance?"

And before she could even think how to reply, he had swept her onto the dance floor in three-four time.

She felt his right hand on her back, the fingers of his left hand intertwined with hers. He drew her close and bent his head just enough for her to feel his breath on her neck.

"Do you believe in fate, Fanny?" he whispered in her ear.

"No," she said, her heart pounding.

His body pressed lightly against hers as he led her from one turn into the next, she shut her eyes and let herself be carried by the music. A quiet voice in her head whispered a warning: *Have you forgotten all those good resolutions?*

He bent his head close again. "See that couple to the right of us? The girl's got a blue headscarf on and the boy's wearing yellow corduroy pants. I'd bet you anything the boy's a girl."

Opening her eyes, she stole a glance in their direction. "What makes you think that?"

"Look at his hands. Small, dainty fingers. And anyway, the moustache's painted on. It's running in the heat!"

She giggled. "D'you like seeing a girl dressed as a boy?"

He laughed. "Why not? That one looks very fetching in her peaked cap, and the trousers show off her long legs. Once I caught my sister disguised as a boy. Must have been about four years ago. It was at a masked ball at the Budapest Opera House. Oops! Look out for my feet!"

"Stop a minute, Max! I have to ask you something!"

She was trying to stop, but he led her determinedly into the next steps and turns. "One two three, one two three—"

"Stop, D'Artagnan!" she cried into his ear.

"What did you say?" He stopped so abruptly that the couple behind them crashed into Fanny and pushed her even closer to him.

"It was you, wasn't it?" She searched his face. "You looked different with the long wig and false beard, of course. That's why I didn't recognize you. You were at that Fasching Ball in Budapest. We had a conversation, then Izabella came back and lost her temper with you. Later on, I asked her who you were, but she wouldn't say."

He shook his head in disbelief. "You were the delightful rococo lady?"

As she nodded, they both burst out laughing. He recalled how it had been the ladies' turn to choose their dance partners. "You were about to ask me for a waltz, but my sister turned up."

Fanny narrowed her eyes coquettishly. "What makes you think I was going to do that?"

He paused and said, "Let's find somewhere quiet to talk, over a glass of wine, of course."

She agreed, and he put his arm around her as they made their way to a long wooden table in the corner, where two seats had just become free. When their drinks arrived, he said, "I propose a toast to our newly rediscovered acquaintanceship!"

As they raised their glasses, he gave her a searching look. "The way my sister reacted that evening makes me suspect you weren't there as her chaperone."

Fanny blushed. "I like Izabella a lot, but I'm not like her."

"Knowing my sister, I'll bet she made things very difficult for you once she realized that."

"Izabella's a good person, and her feelings don't exactly make things easy for her," she gently chided.

Max savored his wine. "Maybe I only said that because I'm jealous."

Embarrassed, Fanny dropped her eyes and looked at her glass. She felt light-headed and wasn't sure if that was the wine, finding out they'd known each other far longer than they thought, or this unexpected admission of jealousy.

Watch out, the voice in her head called. *Don't fall into his arms again without thinking!*

"'For F. S.,'" Max said then, looking deep into her eyes. "That's what it said on your dance card. So, my sister gave it to you."

Fanny's eyes widened. "You found that little purse?"

"You dropped it when Izabella whisked you away so fast. It must still be in one of the crates from when I moved back to Vienna from Pressburg." He looked wistful. "I really hoped I'd find that rococo fräulein again, but Izabella always flatly refused to tell me who she was. I asked other people, as well, but nobody seemed to know. To think you were so close by all that time!" His fingers caressed the stem of his wine glass, turning it slowly as he talked. "If you'll let me, I'd love to keep your dance card as a memento of an extraordinary evening." He saw her hesitation and added quickly, "You kept my handkerchief, after all."

"That's my memento of an extraordinary evening," murmured Fanny.

He took her hand. "Do you really mean that?"

"Come on, Max, this can't go anywhere." She tried to pull her hand away, but he only held it more tightly.

"I'd always hoped so much that I might mean something to you. And now I know."

"You know nothing!" Angrily, she snatched her hand away.

"Don't you feel the same, though, that things would have gone so differently for us if we'd met sooner?"

"No, I do not! I'd never have been more than a serving girl for you, the one you'd have seduced without any feeling of obligation at all! You'd have married Nelli anyway, because your families wanted it, and it suited your career. And I'd have ended up with—" She broke off as anger and emotion flooded her.

Lily the Laundry Maid's singing trilled out from the stage.

"I can't help it, I love love,
If that shocks you,

Well, I want only one love,
One that stays beautiful and new."

Fanny felt like laughing. Love might indeed be beautiful, but only for men.

She got to her feet. "I'm going home. Early start tomorrow."

He quickly got up, too. "You can't go home alone in the dark. Whereabouts do you live?"

"Josefstadt. I'm not so stupid as to walk back at night. I'll find a cab."

"I'll get you one."

"I'm pretty good at that myself," came her curt reply.

He stood speechless as she marched off to the cloakroom. *You're not getting away from me this time,* he said to himself. *Not again!*

He caught up with her as she was on her way outside. "Let's not argue like this, Fanny. Surely Helene told you I leave soon? And it could be a very long time before I'm back."

"I don't care!" She hurried out onto the snow-covered sidewalk and called to one of the waiting coachmen.

"Has any man ever managed to win you over?" he shouted after her. "There's got to be some reason why you're not married yet—and probably won't ever be!"

She stopped so suddenly that she nearly skidded on the compacted snow, then whipped around and marched back to stand right in front of him. Raising her hand, she gave him a resounding slap on the side of his face.

All the waiting cabbies, who'd followed the proceedings with great interest, clapped and whistled their approval. "He well an' truly deserves a thick ear!" said one of them, chivalrously opening the door of his cab for Fanny.

She started to get in, but Max held her back. He looked distraught. "I should never have said that. Please accept my apology."

"D'you want me to take care of this for you, ma'am?" said the cabbie, rolling up his sleeves.

"For goodness' sake, no, I don't want that!" Fanny replied.

Max had his hand on the carriage door now. "Let me see you home. What's the address?"

"Florianigasse. Number seven," she muttered.

He turned to the cabdriver, who was eyeing him with deep suspicion, and repeated the address. Then he climbed in behind Fanny and closed the door.

"I don't understand you," he said, as soon as the cab moved off. "First you entice me. Then you push me away."

"That's not true." Her voice came from the dark corner of the cab, all its curtains closed. "It's you that keeps destroying any peace of mind I can get."

"I'll never stop wishing for things to be different between us. But our circumstances mean that I can offer you nothing more than to be my mistress."

"And I'm not so desperate as to want to be nothing more than someone's mistress," Fanny shot back.

"I know, I know," he said, trying to soothe her. "You've shown me that over and over again. But you feel something for me, don't you?"

Fanny was silent for some time. "At first, yes, I was keen to find out what love was all about, and I wouldn't have had anything against finding that out with you," she admitted. "But with you getting engaged to Nelli, who had been such a good friend to me, it didn't seem right, even though it was hard. Even if it weren't for Nelli, the biggest thing standing in the way for me is always fear."

"Fear?" he repeated. "What of?"

"Ending up like my mother."

"Sorry, I'm not following."

He waited patiently as she searched for the right words.

"I grew up in the foundling home. I don't know a thing about my father. And my mother, well, I only know she was said to have loose morals. Whenever I have feelings I'd love to give in to, I'm paralyzed by the fear of the consequences. It frightens me that I might be reckless like my mother. And I absolutely do not want to end up with an illegitimate child, just because I couldn't control my feelings."

Max felt like a fool for not understanding sooner. In the army, he had a few colleagues who had not only a mistress but children with the woman, too. The men were teased but also respected, all the more so if the woman was highly desirable and the man had the means to afford the luxury of a second family. But these men didn't give a moment's thought to the lifelong stigma attached to the children born out of wedlock. Even he hadn't thought through what far-reaching consequences it could have for Fanny to become his lover. All he had in mind was to get her into his bed.

"Thank you for confiding in me," he said eventually. "Just one thing, Fanny. You're a smart woman, and you're certainly neither reckless nor immoral. Quite the opposite—I see you as upright and resolute. You started out from a background that would have held a lot of people back, but not you, and you should be so proud of what you've achieved."

"I certainly am," she said softly.

"Haven't you ever been able to find out anything about your parents?"

"Nothing," she replied. "Sometimes I'm so furious with my mother. All she wanted was to get rid of me. She didn't care what became of me."

"You can't be sure of that. Maybe she just didn't have the means to keep you."

"After I was born, she didn't even take the certificate of admission, the thing that would have allowed her to find me later."

He didn't know what to say to this. They drove on in silence, Fanny in her corner of the cab, he in his, both listening to the hoofbeats, muffled by the snow of another Viennese winter.

"A few times, I thought I'd found some clue or other, but it always fell through. Quite recently, I found out that someone made anonymous payments for my upkeep, and that it went on for years. But when I wanted to go and talk to the bank clerk who'd received the payments, I found out that he died ages ago." She sighed sadly. "I just have to accept that I'll never find out who my parents were."

The cab stopped and the driver called out, "Florianigasse, number seven!"

Fanny didn't move, so Max reached out for her in the darkness and took her hand. When she didn't shake it free, he slid closer, put his arm round her shoulder, and drew her close. "Now that I know all that, I feel closer to you than ever."

She put her head on his shoulder. "I'm pleased you're going away if it means we can't do anything foolish."

He stroked her hair. "It's hard for me to give you up."

"But you'll have to." She freed herself from his embrace and opened the carriage door. "There's no future for us, Max."

Chapter Fifteen

Vienna, 1914

Fanny tilted her head back, all the better to enjoy glimpses of heavenly blue through the canopy created by the chestnut trees. The welcome shade still allowed the sunshine to break through here and there. It was the last Sunday in June, one of the finest days of a season already dubbed by the newspapers "the summer of the century." The sky was cloudless, and Fanny listened appreciatively to the birdsong.

She had on a new dress: apple-green silk. *I've never been so happy,* she thought. *At this moment, everything in my life is perfect.*

For a year now, Fanny had been attending the technical college and working hard toward the status of master craftswoman in tailoring. This was for both gentlemen's and ladies' garments. Next summer, she would take the final examination and, if successful, officially become a custom tailor, maybe even start her own business. But she still loved working for Madame Moreau, who entrusted her with increasingly important client contracts. And the icing on the cake? She was saving up to buy her own motorcar.

Izabella gave her a nudge. "You're very quiet. What's on your mind?"

"My car! I can't wait to drive myself wherever I want, when I want."

Izabella linked arms with Fanny as they strolled along. "We'd better get a picnic basket and a good, big rug!"

"Mama, can I have a pony ride?" sang out Emma, pulling at her mother's hand.

Helene tried to calm her demanding daughter. "Yes, but only when we get to the pavilion. We're going to have a nice coffee while you have a pony ride."

"But how long til we get there?" whined Emma.

Fanny tried to help out. "We're nearly there. Can you see that building? The one with the little tower on top?"

Emma nodded eagerly. "Is that where the ponies are?"

"Yes, near there," replied Fanny.

"Can I go and look now, Mama?"

Helene sighed. "Oh, alright, but don't mess up your clothes!"

"Thank you, Mama!" Emma ran on ahead, squealing with excitement.

"Do you wish you'd gone to the Puszta, after all?" Fanny asked her friend.

"It's my second summer running in Vienna, and I must admit I miss that openness and all the animals. And I miss Papa and all the people on the estate, too," Helene admitted. "The doctor didn't want me to travel. He says I'm not up to it yet."

"But you're a lot better, Nelli," said Fanny, her voice warm and encouraging.

Helene gave a sad smile. "To be honest, I'll never stop wanting a little brother or sister for Emma. But with Max so far away, that's not going to happen."

"We're not letting you give up hope!" chimed in Izabella. "My brother's coming to Vienna in August. Just think, he'll be so pleased to see you, he'll wrap his arms around you, and, hey presto, there'll be a baby due."

"Max hasn't touched me since long before his posting. I'm sure it's because he doesn't want another child. He's scared it won't survive."

Izabella fell silent, embarrassed. She shared the couple's apartment and was painfully aware of their estrangement since the little boy had been stillborn. Helene's fixation on having a son, and the weeks on end when she'd obsessively made little boy's clothes, had unsettled the whole household. But shortly after Max's posting, Helene had packed up the sewing machine and had it stowed away in the attic. She had begun to take part in everyday life again and now showed more interest in Emma, but Izabella suspected this was more out of duty than anything else. Her sister-in-law had not been the same since the day she'd lost that baby boy.

After luncheon, the Kálmans' chauffeur had driven the three women and the little girl here to the popular Praterstern. Now they were walking down the avenue that led to the pavilion, the meeting place much loved by all Viennese. The chauffeur was due to collect them from there later.

The beautiful weather had brought everyone out, and the surrounding meadows and woodlands were being enjoyed to the fullest. The avenue was crowded with walkers, carriages, and those horseback riding for pleasure.

"I always enjoy a cup of coffee," said Fanny, "but I'm going to treat myself to a nice pastry today, as well!"

Now they'd reached the pavilion. In days gone by, this had been the imperial hunting lodge, but now it was for everyone to enjoy. Outside, a little band played excerpts from popular operettas, and the café's proprietor had set up extra tables and chairs in the open to accommodate the extra guests on this fine day. Fanny, Izabella, and Helene made themselves comfortable at a table quite close to the pony rides. Young children eagerly waited their turn for a ride around the little ring in return for a few hellers.

"I'll have my usual hoop bun," announced Izabella, settling comfortably into her seat and savoring the sunshine. "The ones they have here are just the best! What about you, Nelli?"

But Nelli wasn't listening. The band had suddenly stopped playing. The usually cheerful proprietor now stood in front of the musicians, looking stricken.

"What's going on?" asked Izabella.

"He's waving a piece of paper. Looks like he wants us all to be quiet," said Fanny. "I wonder if something happened to the Kaiser. He's eighty-four now, after all."

"I'm sure he's alright," said Izabella. "Only yesterday it said in the paper that he'd gone off for his annual trip to Bad Ischl. But it does look like something's wrong."

Everybody fell silent and looked at the proprietor, now brandishing the piece of paper even more vigorously.

"My dear guests," he began, holding the document high for all to see. "I have just received this special edition of our newspaper, bringing with it the sad and shocking news that his royal highness, the Archduke Franz Ferdinand, and his consort, the Duchess of Hohenberg, have today been subjected to a treacherous assassination attempt in Sarajevo."

Gasps of shock and concern rippled through the crowd. Some jumped to their feet and hurried up to the bandstand. "Are they dead?" called out someone.

The proprietor confirmed that both had been fatally wounded.

"Holy Mary, mother of God," muttered Fanny, instinctively crossing herself, while Izabella and Helene stared helplessly at the proprietor and the knot of people now clustering round him. The press announcement was passed from hand to hand as so many wanted to see it with their own eyes and read it aloud, as if they had to persuade themselves that it was true.

"The emperor's suffered so much already, that poor man," came a fervent voice at a nearby table. "He's had such difficult times in his life. First his son goes and shoots himself, then his wife's murdered, and now this. What more does the old man have to bear?"

Fanny turned to the woman who'd spoken. "But isn't it worse for the archduke and duchess? And their three young children?"

"The kiddies, yes, of course, they'll have a hard time of it," agreed the woman. "But the archduke and his wife, I don't know how to put it, really. It's a tragic way to go, but I can't say it really gets me—" She thought for a while, then shook her head. "No, I can't pretend that. They were both too, I don't know, too remote for that."

"I know exactly what you mean," said Helene. "I was introduced to them once at the opera. They both came across as cold, really aloof. Maybe it was because I'm Hungarian. The archduke made no secret of his aversion to my people."

"Well, maybe that means he's come to a suitable end and saved us all from there ever being a Kaiser Franz Ferdinand!" Izabella's blue eyes glowed with mischief. "After all, he was always trying to weaken our position in the whole empire."

Fanny was shocked at all this. "Hey, he and his wife have just been murdered!"

Izabella shrugged. "That doesn't make what I've said any less true."

The husband of the woman they'd been talking with now returned to his wife and his plate of cake, having rushed to see the paper.

"Did you find out any more?" asked Fanny.

"Not much. But that news story names a Serbian rebel group as being responsible for the attack. They call themselves the Black Hand."

"Why Serbs?" wondered Fanny. "Wasn't the archduke in Bosnia?"

"Yes, but there're lots of Serbs living there, and they're rebelling against our rule," the man explained.

Fanny looked anxious. "What'll happen now? Could there be war?"

The man waved his hand dismissively. "Don't you worry, fräulein. There'll be plenty of shouting about it, like there always is in the Balkans, and when everybody's had their fill, it'll all go quiet again. There's only one real power down there, and that's us—Austro-Hungary." The man seemed more concerned about getting back to his cake. "It was reckless of the archduke to travel over to look at the maneuvers in Bosnia, when everybody knows how those hotheaded Balkan types can't abide the royal family," he said, shoveling frosted sponge into his mouth. "Ever since that lot got rid of the Ottomans, they've all wanted their own countries, haven't they?"

A couple of hours later, the Kálmans' Mercedes arrived to take the ladies home. After the initial shock caused by the tragic news, the mood lifted once more in the idyllic Prater meadowland. Sarajevo seemed distant, the incident unreal. Everybody had made the most of the sunshine and enjoyed coffee, cake, and the music. Izabella had quizzed Fanny about the likely autumn fashion trends while Helene kept a watchful eye on Emma at the pony rides. The only reminder that the heir to the throne and his wife had been assassinated that day was the continuing presence of the newsboys selling extras with the latest news.

Fanny bought herself one and skimmed over it as soon as she got into the car. "It looks like the whole thing was a bit of an unlucky chain of events," she told her two friends. "There'd already been an attack on the archduke's motor convoy, and that was in the morning when he and his wife were being driven to the Sarajevo City Hall. It says here a Serbian high school student called—oh my goodness, not sure how you'd say this: Ned-jelko Cab-rino-vic—anyway, he threw a bomb at their car, but—"

"What's that, Aunt Fanny? What's a bomb?" piped up Emma.

Izabella laughed. Fanny wasn't sure what to say.

Helene replied quickly, telling her daughter it was a dangerous and stupid object that she'd never need have anything to do with. Turning to Fanny, she said, "Please don't talk about such gruesome things in front of the child."

"Don't spoil such a lovely Sunday," added Izabella.

But Fanny was engrossed in the newssheet again. Unlike her friends, she wanted to know more about this incident in far-off Sarajevo. She read how the bomb had actually ricocheted off the royal vehicle and exploded in front of another car in the convoy, injuring two men in the royal party as well as a number of onlookers. It was when the royal couple had tried to visit their two injured staff in the hospital later that day that they had met their end at the hands of nineteen-year-old Gavrilo Princip. Just as the vehicle paused on the bridge called the Lateinerbrücke, he fired two pistol shots. The duchess died instantly, the archduke a few minutes later.

Fanny folded the paper. She'd never had much interest in politics. It was the thought of the three children, so suddenly orphaned, that brought a lump to her throat.

How terrible to lose your mother and father like that, she thought, discreetly rubbing her eyes with the back of her hand.

Izabella stared in disbelief. "Fanny, surely you're not shedding a tear for the archduke and his wife?"

"I'm thinking of the children," explained Fanny. "They're still so little, and now they're alone in the world."

"I'd hardly say alone in the world in their case!" scoffed Izabella. "They've got enough relatives, nannies, and servants to sink a ship." Izabella shook her head in amazement. "I'd never have thought you could be so sentimental, Fanny."

A month passed. In the first few days after the assassination, the outraged press called for revenge, and it felt like war might really come. The Kaiser, however, stayed at his Bad Ischl summer residence, the murdered archduke and his wife were buried quietly and without fuss at Schloss Artstetten in Lower Austria, and the archduke's nephew, Karl, succeeded him as heir just as quietly. The city dwellers headed for summer vacation, and the farmers brought in the harvest. Everything seemed to have calmed down, and there was no declaration of war on Serbia, the country widely viewed as responsible.

So, it was a surprise when, on July 23, the Austro-Hungarian government gave Serbia an ultimatum demanding an investigation into the murders. The mood in Vienna verged on frenzy, whipped up by the aggressive stance of the press.

Five days after the ultimatum had been issued, Sarah Moreau's loyal doorman, Gustav, burst onto the sales floor, waving a special edition. "It's war! We've declared war on Serbia. It's all here in black and white. From the Kaiser himself."

This created a tremendous stir among clients and staff alike.

"About time!" stated one client loudly, carefully removing the latest of the many hats she'd been trying on. "This government's done nothing but dither around!"

"The Serbs need to be taught a lesson," added her husband, sounding very pleased. "They've made a nuisance of themselves for far too long."

Another customer, busily examining different fabrics spread out on the long counter, turned to join in. "To tell the truth, I'm not a big fan of that royal lot up there at the Belvedere, but I'd have felt let down if our Kaiser hadn't followed up his words with deeds."

A man who'd so far done nothing apart from ogle the sales assistants while his wife trawled through catalogue after catalogue, gave Gustav a nod of encouragement. "Now then, young man, what does the old man have to say for himself?"

Gustav positioned himself beneath the chandelier and surveyed his audience. He was rather pleased to see these high-ranking gentlemen and ladies paying attention to him for once. A group had now gathered around him, looking as solemn as he felt. "Ladies and gentlemen, this is what it says: 'July 28 1914—to my people! It has always been my heartfelt desire to dedicate my remaining God-given years, however many they may be, to work peaceably and to protect my people from the sacrifices and burdens of war. Providence has dealt us a different hand.'"

"The perfect tone for a Kaiser, don't you think?" enthused the hat lady, while there was spontaneous applause from everyone else.

"Read on, young man," said the man to Gustav. "I'm sure that's not the only thing the Kaiser's got to say."

Gustav proudly prepared to carry on reading, his script and head held high. "'The kingdom of Serbia, from its beginnings as an independent nation to the present time, has always had the backing and support of my forefathers and myself, but for many years has trodden a path of ingratitude and open hostility toward Austria-Hungary.'"

Murmurs of approval rippled through Gustav's audience as he continued reading of how the Kaiser's tireless work for peace in the Balkans had been rewarded with nothing more than "unacceptable, criminal conduct" and that the only course of action left to him was armed force to reassure hearts at home and achieve lasting peace abroad.

"'I have faith in my people, who have unfailingly rallied to my throne in every storm and displayed unity and loyalty. I have faith in the bravery and dedication of our Austria-Hungarian military, and

I have faith in the Almighty ensuring our victory.'" Gustav's voice cracked with emotion.

There was a moment's silence. Then one of the ladies called out, "Long live our Kaiser!"

A sales assistant took up the cry. "And long live the monarchy!"

Everyone joined the cheering that followed, with declarations of lifelong loyalty to their country and the elderly Kaiser. Nobody heard the creaking arrival of the elevator and the familiar scrape and clatter as the lattice was opened.

"*Qu'est-ce qui ce passe?* Gustav, why aren't you at the door?" Madame Moreau's irritation was clear as she scanned the room.

Fanny and Izabella had come out of the elevator behind her and surveyed the scene, baffled. The three women had been upstairs for the fitting of a pair of brand-new culottes for Izabella.

Gustav looked sheepish. The gentleman who'd claimed that Serbia needed to be taught a lesson was, however, undeterred. He called for Madame to bring out the champagne.

"It's war, Madame! We'll show that Serbian riffraff a thing or two."

Madame's lips set in a straight line. This man was the husband of one of her best clients, so she kept them firmly closed.

Fanny, however, didn't hold back. "Since when was war something to celebrate?"

"Aha! A traitress in our midst?" retorted the man, spoiling for a fight.

"*S'il vous plaît!*" Madame reached for Gustav's paper. She ran her eyes over it, Fanny and Izabella reading over her shoulder.

"So, it's true," said Izabella. "I'd been hoping that Count Tisza would be able to stop any declaration of war."

In the previous year, Tisza had come into his second term as Hungarian prime minister, and the press had repeatedly reported his rejection of any retaliatory action.

"I can't believe it's come to this," murmured Fanny.

She hadn't continued following the crisis in detail, but the last few evenings as she'd made her way home, Fanny had noticed people with placards and loudspeakers, all demonstrating against the "Serbian swine."

Gustav's voice cut across the room. "I'm going to volunteer, Madame!"

"Ah, les conneries!" Madame Moreau said. "I'll hear nothing of it! Now get on with your work."

He stood as if rooted to the spot. "Madame, my sincere apologies, but I wish to resign. I'm going to seize my sword for the fatherland and the Kaiser!" He turned on his heel and made for the door.

Fanny stared after him, openmouthed.

Madame called out, "Don't be foolish!"

"Pardon me, Madame, but what's it to you? It's not right for you, a French national, to get involved in the internal affairs of our country." This came from the man who'd called for champagne.

"Konrad! Please!" His wife swiftly placed a calming hand on his forearm. "The last straw would be for you to fall out with Madame over this silly war. Where on earth would I get my dresses if you spoil our relationship here?"

"It's not the only fashion house in Vienna," muttered Konrad crossly. But he gave Madame a little bow. "A thousand apologies."

"I like to champion diplomacy above all else," replied Madame with dignity. "In this instance, it has failed—*complètement.*"

Before Madame could say more, another of the men cut in. "Serbia's had more than enough time to investigate these murders. Now they'll get the full force of our anger. Let them see just how fast we can bring them to their knees."

Madame looked at him for a long moment. "I'm going to close the salon now. I'll review matters first thing tomorrow."

With that, she went to the door and bid every client farewell. The sales staff went to the second floor to get their bags. Soon after, they slipped out of the back door, together with the girls from the sewing room.

Apart from Madame, only Fanny and Izabella were left on the now-empty premises. Fanny turned to Izabella. "Is it me, or has the world gone mad?"

"I can't stop thinking of Max," replied Izabella quietly. "I'm so glad he's not stationed in the Balkans."

A shiver ran down Fanny's spine.

Izabella leaned forward to kiss her on the cheek. "I'm going home. Let's talk tomorrow."

Fanny nodded dumbly, watching as she said goodbye to Madame and left the building. The Frenchwoman closed the door behind her and turned the key. Her gaze lingered on the spot where Gustav had always stood.

"It'll be strange without him here, Madame," said Fanny.

Sarah Moreau shook her head. "I sincerely hope that he gives it more thought. It's madness to sign up when you don't have to."

"Won't the war be over in a couple of weeks, though?" asked Fanny anxiously.

"Mademoiselle, it's very naïve to think so. Firstly, even a short war brings loss of life. And secondly, remember that Russia is allied with Serbia. If the Tsar intervenes, how can it be over quickly?"

Fanny's heart sank. A vast empire like Russia couldn't be conquered like little Serbia. Her thoughts turned to Max, stationed near the Russian border at Przemyśl Fortress.

"A long war," she said, quietly shocked. "May God prevent it from happening."

Madame gave a harsh, bitter laugh. "Let's hope he listens to you. Austria has bonds with Germany, Russia with Great Britain, as well as my own homeland. Do you see what that means?"

"War all over Europe," whispered Fanny in horror.

Half an hour or so later, Fanny was sitting in the horse-drawn omnibus on the way to Josefstadt. She decided not to go straight home but to call on Josepha. Neither of the two women had ever believed that the assassination would lead to war. "We've never had things so good in our country," she'd said to Fanny. "We've got electricity and running water. We've got enough to eat. Every child gets a basic education and doesn't have to go out to work at twelve like I did. We have peace to thank for that, and nobody wants to gamble that away for some dumb war."

What Fanny saw from the bus window now suggested something very different. Most of the shops had shut. The only lines were outside those selling military equipment. Every street and square was bustling. Every face was joyous, everybody wanting to celebrate and sing patriotic songs: "God save, God protect our Kaiser, our land . . ."

Every young man seemed to be locked in an embrace with a pretty girl. The black and yellow of the Habsburg flag was everywhere. Fanny's bus would normally have crossed the Ring behind the Burgtheater but had to stop amid the horse-drawn cabs forming a procession to celebrate the Kaiser. The square in front of the Rathaus was awash with people chanting in unison, "Serbi-yah must die-yah."

As Fanny stepped down from the bus on Florianigasse, a military band was marching past to the strains of "The Prinz Eugen March." A troop of new volunteers followed in its wake. They waved flags at the onlookers lining the streets, watching from windows and cheering them on. All of a sudden, one young man broke away from the procession. He came over to Fanny and, before she knew what was happening, had slung his arm around her and planted a long kiss on her lips. Everybody laughed and applauded.

"What d'you think you're doing?" Fanny snapped angrily, when she'd caught her breath.

"Just collecting the little kiss you've owed me for ages!" He grinned at her. "Don't say you don't recognize me!"

Fanny stared at him, puzzled, then her mouth fell open. "The boy from the railway station! Don't *you* say you've volunteered!"

"Certainly have." He nodded enthusiastically. "I want to be there when we give them Serbs a good thrashing."

"Can't you find something better to do with your time than go to war?"

He stared back in amazement. "What's better than earning glory and honor for your country?" He gave her a mock salute and hurried away to rejoin his comrades.

Fanny looked up toward Josepha's apartment. The old lady was standing at the open window of her living room. She spotted Fanny and waved at her to come up.

"You're so early today, little mite," said the old lady as she ushered Fanny inside.

"Madame closed up shop early, as soon as we'd heard the declaration. Our doorman, Gustav, actually resigned on the spot and ran to sign up."

"Was he the one who kissed you just now?"

Fanny blushed and shook her head, expecting the customary reprimand and lecture from Josepha. But all the old lady said was, "So, it's really war."

"I was so surprised at what I saw on the way here," said Fanny. "Folk seem to be head over heels for the idea."

Down in the street, yet another band was making its way past, this time playing "Radetzky March." Josepha shut the window.

Fanny's thoughts turned to Madame. "Surely this won't go on for too long, will it, Josepha?"

"Who d'you think I am? The oracle? That I've got a crystal ball?" Josepha's harsh tone softened when she saw how upset Fanny was.

"Now don't you worry yourself, little mite. Our Kaiser will know what needs to be done."

It wasn't long before public enthusiasm for the war was dampened by its effect on everyday life. Factories, office buildings, and workshops stood empty because all the men had reported for duty. The Ministry of War made what seemed like daily demands for clothing, shoes, old newspaper, rubber, bottles, and metal, all to make items that were essential to the war effort. By day and by night, trains rolled out of the city carrying troops and horses to the front. Bread, meat, and butter became increasingly scarce and doubled in price overnight.

The changes made themselves felt in Sarah Moreau's fashion house, too. A number of weaving mills stopped deliveries, and several loyal clients canceled ball gowns on order for the next social season.

Hardly a day passed without another declaration of war. First, Germany declared war on Russia, France, and Belgium. Then Great Britain declared war on Germany. Montenegro declared war on Austria-Hungary on August 5 to be followed on August 6 by Austria-Hungary's declaration against Russia. This was the day when Fanny wondered whether the old Kaiser really knew what he was doing. Unlike Serbia, Russia was a major power with an army never to be trifled with.

Madame had been feeling for a while like an easy target for Viennese skepticism and sourness, but nothing much happened until one evening when she left work to find her Bugatti's tires slashed. That was the first time Fanny had ever seen her boss near to tears, and she was still turning the incident over in her mind as she walked to the Kálmans' apartment on the Ring. Helene, Izabella, and she had decided several days ago to meet for dinner.

The appetizing smell of roasting meat wafted through the door as the butler let her in. Helene and Izabella were waiting in the dining room, smiling and beckoning from the elegantly set table where they sat, beautifully dressed up for the occasion.

"It's so lovely here," said Fanny, warmly returning her friends' welcome. "It's like it was before war came into all our lives."

"My sentiments entirely, Fanny," sighed Izabella. "I could scream every time yet another newsboy waves the latest bulletin under my nose."

"Madame Moreau predicted it all, you know. She said it would be only a matter of days before the whole of Europe was at war," stated Fanny.

"For this evening, why don't we try and pretend there's no war going on?" suggested Helene.

That riled Izabella. "You can't possibly mean that, Nelli? Surely you realize that your husband—my brother—is directly affected as of today? He's stuck in Przemyśl, right under the Russians' noses."

"He's an officer. It's his job to fight," retorted Helene.

"We know he has to serve the fatherland," Fanny exclaimed, "but he could get wounded or even die. You sound almost indifferent."

Izabella looked quite shocked.

Helene, her voice strained, shot back. "How could I possibly be indifferent? He's Emma's father."

Feeling embarrassed, Fanny found herself staring hard at her place setting. The timely arrival of the butler broke the tension as he served the liver dumpling soup with its delicate aroma of fresh parsley. But awkwardness returned as soon as he left the room. Helene toyed with her soup, then put down her spoon, saying, "Max described Przemyśl in a letter. He says it's a huge, well-defended fortress, a stronghold virtually impossible to capture."

"He wrote? When?" Fanny leaned across the table toward Helene. "How is he?"

"His last letter came a couple of weeks ago. He said he was fine." Helene paused. "Would you like me to read it to you, Fanny?"

"Of course not," mumbled Fanny, sullenly stirring her soup.

Then Izabella said, "Nelli, forgive me, but you don't sound terribly worried about your husband."

The trace of a smile played on Helene's lips. "I think Fanny takes care of all the worrying about him."

Fanny went bright red. There it was again. That sense that Helene knew—goodness knows how—about those forbidden moments between her and Max. Guilt gnawed at her as she snapped at Helene. "Well, pardon me, but we're surely allowed to be worried about any member of our circle fighting at the front."

"Max is a staff officer directly under the fortress commandant and won't have to fight on the front line. It's my parents I'm worried about. They're out in the Puszta, alone and defenseless."

"They could easily come to Vienna," said Fanny, starting to lose patience.

"My parents cannot possibly come to Vienna. Civilians are now barred from all trains because they're needed for military transport." Now Helene's anger was showing, too.

Izabella tried to calm things down. "Look, we're supposed to be having a nice evening together, and instead we're arguing because of this stupid war. Nelli, I'm sure you don't need to worry about your parents. The war's being fought a long way from Hungary. My father wants to stay close to his department stores in Budapest, and he's pretty optimistic as far as the war goes. Of all the businessmen in Budapest, he's invested the most in war loans."

"My papa told me the army took away all his cattle and horses," said Helene despondently.

There was a knock at the door. The butler was ready to serve the main course of roast beef with dumplings and pickled cucumber. As he brought in the platters, Emma appeared behind him with her nanny. The little girl was already in her nightdress and cuddled the teddy bear that Fanny had made for her. She bid goodnight to Fanny and Izabella, then went to her mother. Helene leaned forward and kissed her.

"Mama?" asked the little girl, snuggling against her mother.

"Yes, child?"

"When's Papa coming home?"

"Soon." Helene stroked her daughter's hair.

The little girl looked at her anxiously. "Tomorrow?"

"No, not tomorrow, Emma. But every night before you go to bed, you can pray to our Lord that he'll bring Papa home soon. And now sleep well." She ushered Emma toward the nanny.

When the three friends were alone again, Izabella was the first to speak. "And now we really won't discuss the war again. Did I tell you I've managed to get tickets for the first night of *Die Csárdásfürstin*? It's by my namesake, Emmerich Kálmán. I'm so excited!"

The rest of the dinner went smoothly, the war not being mentioned once.

Later that evening, as Fanny prepared to leave, Izabella said to her sister-in-law, "Don't get up, Nelli. I'll see Fanny out."

When they were at the apartment door, Izabella didn't say goodbye but hurried Fanny onto the communal landing, closed the door behind them, and came straight to the point. "What did Nelli mean about you doing the worrying about Max?"

"Nothing." Fanny looked away.

"I don't think I believe that," said Izabella.

Fanny flared up again. "Why not? Is it because you saw your brother flirting with me that time at the masked ball?"

This left Izabella almost speechless. "How on earth did you know? Is that why you didn't want . . . ?" She chewed at her lip, then burst out with, "You're his mistress, aren't you? Oh, Lord, what a mess!"

"Holy Mary! You can't possibly think I'd be his mistress. For goodness' sake!"

Izabella shrugged. "It doesn't matter what I think. But it seems to be what Nelli thinks. That's what matters. And if it isn't true, how did she get the idea in the first place?"

Fanny's face flushed. "I don't know."

"So, it isn't true?"

"No."

Izabella's eyes blazed at Fanny. "Is my brother in love with you?"

The memory of that last encounter with Max flooded back. When he'd escorted her home after the laundry maids' ball, the word "love" hadn't been spoken, and yet, a true sense of intimacy was undeniable.

"'Love' is a big word to use," she replied evasively, glancing at the closed door of the apartment. "And he's married to Nelli."

"And yet."

"Max and I have no future," said Fanny firmly. "But I care about him and pray that he comes back from this war unharmed."

France declared war on Austria-Hungary on August 13. Madame Moreau's staff were dismayed when she called everyone together to convey the news. She concluded by saying, "Things will be difficult for all of us, but I want to carry on with my business and my life here. I'll do everything I can to protect your jobs, I promise."

The relief on the women's faces was obvious. With so many of their menfolk away at war, they were now the breadwinners.

Just before close of business on the third day after the declaration of war, they heard shouting and yelling outside on Graben.

"Out with French scum! Kick their froggy heads in!"

The sound of breaking glass signaled two rocks flying into the salon. Fanny had been putting the finishing touches on a new display, and the missile missed her by a hairsbreadth. With a shriek, she threw herself to the floor, burying her head under her arms, but a shard skimmed her hand.

Panic reigned as clients and staff alike hid behind the long counter. Letting her arms slacken, Fanny cautiously raised her head. Outside on Graben, passersby stood and stared with a mixture of curiosity and shock.

Fanny yelled questions as she got to her feet, her legs trembling. "Did you see who did this? Where did they go?" The onlookers merely shrugged and walked off.

"Thanks for nothing!" Fanny shouted. A soothing hand fell on her shoulder.

"Mademoiselle Schindler, leave them," advised Madame. "You'd do much better to show me your hand. You've been injured."

Only now did Fanny notice blood running down her fingers. "I didn't even notice!"

"It looks far worse than it is," said Madame Moreau. "I'll clean it up and dress it for you. Let's go upstairs."

"That can wait." With her other hand, Fanny fished out a handkerchief and wrapped it around her wound. "We must report this first!"

Madame Moreau gave her most sardonic smile. "You can't really believe that the Vienna constabulary is going to have the slightest interest in a rock coming through a Frenchwoman's window? I'm the enemy now, remember?"

"Then I'll go myself," said Fanny. "Can you give me a quick description?"

Her employer shook her head. "Afraid not. When it happened, I had my back turned. I was putting bolts of cloth up on the shelves."

"Then let's ask the others."

Fanny tried, but it rapidly became clear that everyone had been taken by surprise, and nobody had seen exactly how it had happened.

All the clients quickly made their escape, and no new ones appeared. A smashed shop front with sharp shards protruding all around doesn't do much for business.

Madame Moreau's staff spent the rest of the day helping empty the display space, the glass cabinets, and all the shelving, then stowing their contents in the basement behind a secure iron gate. Once the work was done, Madame Moreau warmly thanked all her staff and asked them to report for work as usual the next day. Thoroughly despondent, the women headed for home.

Workmen were already busy as Fanny arrived for work the following morning. They were knocking the remaining glass out of the frame surrounding the window space before driving nails into the necessary board. There were no customers to be seen. The staff refilled the shelves and display cabinets. When Fanny took the elevator to the first floor, she found herself wondering whether Madame could really keep the business going. Frau Schubert, their master craftswoman, spotted her as she passed the sewing room door.

"The two of us have to report to Madame."

As they knocked at the office door, Fanny asked her colleague if she knew what it was about.

"She didn't say," whispered Elfriede Schubert. "But it seemed pretty important."

Fanny followed Elfriede into the room. An older gentleman in a dark suit sat to the left of their boss at her meeting table. In Madame's right hand was a cigarette. Dressed in black silk as usual, with her bright red lipstick applied as perfectly as her short silver hair was cut, she remained impeccable.

To see her now, you'd never guess what happened yesterday, thought Fanny in admiration.

Greeting the two women warmly, Madame invited them to sit down and introduced the man at her side. "This is my legal adviser, Dr. Strasser." Madame stubbed out her cigarette before carrying on. "I got home yesterday only to find a communication ordering me to report to the office of the district constable at noon on the dot."

"Ordering—you?" Fanny couldn't believe what she was hearing.

"Is it about the attack on the shop?" asked Elfriede.

Madame shook her head and turned to Dr. Strasser. He adjusted his spectacles, cleared his throat, and began to explain. "It's about Madame's enemy status and her permission to remain in our country."

"Do they want to throw Madame out?" Fanny's heart began to race.

"No, on the contrary," replied Dr. Strasser. "Our government has started a process of internment for any citizen of an enemy state. As soon as war was declared on Serbia, the government started requisitioning empty buildings, especially in the Waldviertel in Lower Austria. They've already rounded up and interned Serbs in a storage facility in Drosendorf. Next, it's the French and the English. It's likely they'll be sent to Burg Karlstein, on the River Thaya."

"They want to put you, of all people, in jail like some common thug?" Fanny was beside herself.

Elfriede put a hand on Fanny's arm and asked what the conditions were like.

"Not exactly luxurious, but better than prison," explained Dr. Strasser. "What I'm urgently trying to do, though, is arrange for Madame Moreau's detention to be in Vienna. That would mean Madame could continue running her business. It remains to be seen whether I'll be successful."

"But what would detention here mean?" asked Elfriede.

"Internees are placed in private accommodations and are permitted to move within a specified area only. This is seen as a privilege and is afforded only to those who are not considered likely to abscond and who can afford to meet the costs." Dr. Strasser took out his fob watch and glanced at the time. "And now the reason for asking you both here." He took a leather portfolio from his briefcase and placed it on the table.

"Monsieur, un instant, s'il vous plaît!" Madame raised her hand to ensure she could address Fanny and her master craftswoman first. "I'm turning to you both on a matter of the utmost importance because I have confidence in your ability to handle what's going to be an extremely challenging time."

Fanny and Frau Schubert nodded attentively as they listened to the woman they admired so much.

"For the duration of my absence, I am giving you joint custody of my fashion house and entrusting you with the welfare of all its employees. I realize that I'm asking you to take on a great responsibility, but I want Sarah Moreau Couture to remain open regardless of the circumstances. The order book is nicely full for now, but it won't stay like that. Suppliers have already canceled deliveries, and firm orders have fallen by the wayside. You'll have to use all your experience and ingenuity to break new ground."

"Then that's what we'll do!" Fanny's enthusiasm was clearly shared by Elfriede and brought more than a hint of satisfaction to Madame Moreau's smile as she shook hands with her two lieutenants.

"Merci! Merci mille fois!" That eases such a burden of anxiety on my part." She turned again to her adviser. "Please, do continue, Dr. Strasser."

The lawyer now opened up the portfolio, took out a sheet of paper, and slid it across the desk to Fanny. "Madame Moreau has asked me to prepare a document granting you power of attorney for this business. This means that from now on, you are empowered to carry out extensive transactions on behalf of, and for the account of, Madame herself."

Why me? Fanny was taken aback. *Why's she giving this responsibility to me and not to Frau Schubert?* The master craftswoman was Madame's longest-serving employee and far more experienced in such matters.

Madame seemed to read Fanny's thoughts. "Fanny, do you remember the conversation we had the day after you qualified?"

Fanny nodded.

"Well, circumstances are such that I've had to speed up my plans for you, but I know that you'll be able to handle these unusually difficult circumstances and that Madame Schubert will do everything in her power to support you, *n'est-ce pas?*"

Elfriede gave an emphatic nod.

Dr. Strasser went on to explain more about Fanny's power of attorney. She quickly realized she'd be authorized to purchase goods, hire and fire staff, enter into guarantees, as well as carry out all aspects of running the business. For all intents and purposes, she'd be the owner.

He concluded by asking Fanny if she was willing to accept this. She was overwhelmed and couldn't speak, so nodded firmly instead. He handed her the fountain pen, asking her to sign the document on the table in front of her.

"Madame, I must thank you for your confidence in me," said Fanny, very solemnly. "I'll do my absolute best to run the fashion house as you would want it run." She signed the document, and the lawyer put it safely back in the portfolio.

"To complete the process, I'll be handing this to the court today." With that, the portfolio went back in his briefcase.

"Will we be allowed to visit Madame if she's sent to this Burg Karlstein place?" asked Elfriede.

"I fear not," replied the lawyer. "But you may write. And now, Madame Moreau, it is time to inform the rest of your staff, if you wish to do so."

The elegant Frenchwoman got to her feet, as did the other three. She shook Fanny and Elfriede firmly by the hand.

"*Au revoir, Mesdames.* I know you will represent me with the greatest of dignity."

Chapter Sixteen

Przemyśl Fortress and Vienna, 1915

Hunger kept Max awake at night. All he could think of was food. His imagination conjured up concoctions so appetizing he could almost taste them.

Since the Russian army had laid siege to the fortress, all supplies had been blocked. Only the mail managed to get in, and that was thanks to Austria-Hungary's Imperial and Royal Aviation Troops.

A hundred and thirty thousand men, including the commander and some civilians, had been living on dwindling rations within the fortress's double-thick walls for the last four months and sixteen days. Their daily intake was down to two hundred and fifty grams of bread laced with birch bark.

Max's belly was aching, the metallic taste in his mouth was constant, and he felt irritable and restless. Throwing back his wool blanket, he sat up on the miserably thin straw mattress. He was freezing cold, although he slept in his uniform jacket and trousers. He reached for his gun-belt, always stowed at the foot of the makeshift bed under his greatcoat, as was his uniform cap. He buckled up the belt, pushed his feet into his boots, dragged on his coat, pulled his cap down low over his forehead, then swiftly left the concrete vault that served as a bedroom for him and five other staff officers.

Outside, the cold hit him like a wall of ice, but at least the storms that had swept down from the Carpathians earlier had now subsided. He suspected the temperature was at least minus twenty, even within this inner courtyard of what they referred to as Facility 1, located on the eastern side of the structure. The fortress was made up of forty of these facilities, encircling the small town of Przemyśl. It was often referred to as the Ring Fortress.

Max turned up his collar and headed straight for a corner of the courtyard between the latrine and a squad casemate. The frozen snow crunched under his boots and glittered in the moonlight. He leaned for a moment against the wall, rummaging in his coat pocket for his tobacco pouch. His fingers, numb with cold, fumbled to get at the lighter and cherished cigarette butt. He lit up, then took such a deep drag that he retched. His empty belly rebelled against this cocktail of dried leaves, grass, crushed bark, and a few flakes of used tobacco. But he smoked it anyway. Nausea was still better than hunger.

From dawn until dusk that day, the fortress had been the scene of that frenetic activity that accompanies every clash with the enemy. But this stopped when darkness fell. The besieged, exhausted Twenty-Third Honvéd Division had made a desperate, futile attempt at escape in the face of a far stronger Russian army. Now only despondency hung over them.

Max felt something close to shame as he recalled the thousands of Hungarian lives lost beyond the fortress walls. As staff officer reporting to the commander, his task was to prepare orders and then evaluate the outcome of every military operation. He never had to leave the safety of the fortress.

A soldier came out of the latrine close by and saluted as soon as he saw Max. The man's eyes gleamed in the moonlight as he stared greedily at Max's sad excuse for a cigarette. Max hesitated before handing over the glowing butt, brushing off the man's attempts at gratitude. A piercing, chilling howl rang out.

"Wolves," said Max. He hated the menace of that sound even more than that of mortars, flamethrowers, and machine guns.

"They go after the drumfire," came the soldier's bleak response. "Come morning, it'll be bones and scraps of uniform through the field glasses, just like before."

Max knew what the man meant. After every battle, wolves emerged from the woods in search of easy human prey, tearing apart corpses and attacking the wounded and helpless. Enemy snipers presented a constant threat, making it impossible to rescue comrades left to the harsh winter at the foot of the Carpathians.

The soldier took one final drag and threw down the butt. He thanked Max, then vanished into his sleeping quarters, such as they were.

There was that eerie howling again. Max felt for his pistol and looked up at the observation post on top of a casemate, looming up in the dark between two battery towers. Its dome had been hit by a grenade and was now severely dented, but the thick steel post remained intact. During combat, two men would stand at the observation slits under the dome's edge to check the accuracy of the artillery firing from the neighboring gun turrets. With good aim and a bit of luck, Max hoped to put an end to a few of these bloodthirsty creatures roaming outside the fortress walls.

Soon, he was in position and peered through the swiveling telescope. He spotted the wolves immediately. There were seven in the pack that sped across the wide expanse of ground, always ready to pounce. He saw them come to a halt and gather around a dark figure that lay motionless on the snow-covered ground. Then they fell on their prey, each beast pulling and tearing the body, snarling, yowling, and whimpering in their determination to reach flesh. Rage devoured

Max. He raised his pistol and took aim. But shooting was pointless. The wolves were much too far away.

A door opened behind him, making him whip around and instinctively stand to attention. He quickly realized it was none other than their commander in chief, General Hermann Kusmanek von Burgneustädten, a flickering oil lamp in his hand. His dogged resistance toward the Russians had earned him the soubriquet the Przemyśl Lion.

It had been four months now, and still the Russians had not managed to capture the fortress. The enemy had recently acquired heavy artillery, bigger cannons with a huge range, powerful mortars, and howitzers that could even hit concealed targets. But their strongest ally was hunger. Max knew the fortress would soon fall.

Kusmanek went over to the heavy table positioned between the observation slits and placed his oil lamp next to the telephone used during battle to inform marksmen of their accuracy. Then he took a seat in one of the two chairs and stretched out his legs. The dancing shadows cast by the oil lamp left his face looking even more sunken. He afforded himself as little bread as his men, and was highly respected for it.

"Hunger get you out of bed, Herr Oberleutnant?" asked Kusmanek. "Don't deny it. I know how it gets hold of a man." He took a silver case from his trouser pocket, opened it, and held it toward to Max. "Help yourself."

Turkish cigarettes—the real thing, at that! Max couldn't believe his good fortune. The pungent tobacco aroma alone made his head spin. He took one cigarette, leaned in toward Kusmanek's flickering lighter, and closed his eyes to draw deeply on this unexpected pleasure.

He realized the general had let out a quiet laugh. "Makes even the hunger go away, doesn't it?"

Max opened his eyes. "How long can we hold out, sir?"

Kusmanek tucked the lighter away again. "Two days. Even with the strictest rationing, that'll be the end of the flour."

"Then what?" asked Max.

"I have asked the Kaiser for permission to surrender. Graciously granted."

"So we'll all end up Russian prisoners?"

Kusmanek nodded. "But first we'll use all remaining ammunition to blow up the fortress. There's no need to let the Russians get their hands on anything they could then use against our brave comrades in Carpathia."

Max contemplated the glowing tip of his cigarette. "Herr General, I know our mission is to hold Przemyśl on the orders of Army High Command. But with surrender now a near certainty, the further expenditure of energy seems, if you will permit me to say this, futile. I refer not only to those men here in Przemyśl, but also those very comrades out in the Carpathians, those who've tried to liberate us. Secret reports tell us of the inhuman conditions they're enduring out there in the snow and bitter cold, without suitable clothing, shelter, or hot food. Surely it would be a humane gesture to surrender the fortress even sooner?"

"We've held the mountain passes—with heavy losses, that's true—but without that, the route into Hungary would have been wide open for the Russians," replied Kusmanek calmly. "In one respect you're right, Kálman: our imperial and royal army perished in the Carpathian winter, and we're now fully dependent on the support of our German allies. Whether we like it or not."

Max frowned. What Kusmanek was saying was risky, close to high treason, and he wondered what the man had in mind. Max had always seen him as a strong believer in duty, tough on himself and his men, loyal to the monarchy. Max's only explanation for this was that Kusmanek could be testing the loyalty of his first lieutenant. But why?

Max took a deep breath, then asked, "Where's this conversation leading, Herr General?"

"I was actually going to talk to you early tomorrow after the daily review meeting, but why wait? Herr Oberleutnant, come to my quarters. I have something for you." Kusmanek threw down what remained of his own cigarette, ground it out with his heel, picked up the oil lamp, and got to his feet.

The two men walked together to an inner door of the fortress, beyond which the commander in chief's motorcar was waiting. There was no driver. Kusmanek himself drove them to his accommodation in a private house in the center of Przemyśl, not far from the railway station. Max had never visited his accommodation before, and Kusmanek led the way to his office on the first floor. Once the gas light had been lit, Max looked around what was quite a narrow room furnished with nothing more than a desk, a chair, and some shelves for files. He watched as his superior went to the desk, opened one of the drawers, took out a sealed envelope, and beckoned Max over.

"Kálman, you won't be a prisoner of war." He handed the envelope to Max. "I have a special task for you. Tomorrow morning, the final mail delivery will arrive by air. You will leave Przemyśl in that aircraft. You will land in Kraków and then take a second plane to Vienna. The envelope I've entrusted you with, you must cherish as you cherish life itself. It is intended for the heir to the throne, Archduke Karl, and him alone. You may not speak of this task to anyone, and you must take the envelope to the archduke as soon as you arrive in Vienna. Do you understand?"

"Certainly, Herr General!"

"I knew I could rely on you, Kálman." Looking quietly satisfied, he took two more envelopes out of his desk drawer. He handed those to Max, as well. "Here are your marching orders and your leave pass. Once you've completed the task, you'll have fourteen days off. No argument. You've earned it. Then you'll get further orders from Army High Command."

"Certainly, Herr General!" repeated Max, placing the three envelopes inside his breast pocket. This undertaking meant he would be spared a long imprisonment in harsh conditions. In his heart, however, he felt it was his duty to share the same fate as his comrades.

Kusmanek nodded in a way that indicated business was done. "Good, Herr Oberleutnant. I'll drive you back now. See to it that you get a bit of sleep."

The short drive passed in silence. As Kusmanek applied the brakes at the door of Facility 1, he turned once more to Max. "Would it interest you to know what you're delivering for me, Kálman?"

"As you wish, Herr General," replied Max, taken aback.

"I've been watching you since this siege began," said Kusmanek gravely. "I sense that you feel like I do about the sacrifices being made by our soldiers and civilians in this war. They are out of all proportion to the meager rewards. I know perfectly well that a lot of the men here call the war a death mill. And they're right. In the document I've entrusted to you, I have presented the heir to the throne with proposals for a speedy ending to this senseless slaughter. The most important thing is to start secret negotiations with Russia in order to reach a separate peace agreement with them. Do you agree, Herr Oberleutnant?"

"Who would reject peace?" replied Max with caution. "But if our German allies found out about it, all hell would break loose. They would accuse us of betrayal."

"They would. And they'd be right. But surely betrayal of the confederation is justified if it prevents further needless bloodshed?" The commander looked deep in thought as he spoke.

"At times, a man has to follow reason and not orders," commented Max quietly.

Kusmanek nodded. "I knew I was right about you."

"Do you think your proposals will be respectfully received?" asked Max.

"Let's just say that I hope so. The archduke is young and represents a new generation and the future of our country. The people love him. But the important thing is that he is not overly positive about the war and firmly opposes Conrad, head of the General Staff, the man we can thank for this whole mess. He was the one who pushed for retaliatory action against the Serbs in the summer of 1914 and unleashed the inferno we now find ourselves in."

Three days later, Max stepped down from a cab outside his home in Vienna. He was dog tired but looking forward so much to seeing his family again, most of all the little daughter he hadn't set eyes on for over a year.

He was looking forward to a good meal almost as much.

Once I've got some food in me, I'll take a bath and get some sleep, he said to himself, savoring the prospect of his comfortable bed and the warm feather quilt.

That morning, he'd done exactly as Kusmanek had instructed. Immediately on arrival, he had gone to the Hofburg to hand the archduke the envelope with its secret enclosure. The heir had given him a warm reception and questioned him closely about the siege at Przemyśl. He knew the fortress from his own visit there in the summer of 1914. He even remembered Max. The letter from Kusmanek, however, received only a cursory glance.

"I take it you know what's in this document?"

"I do, Your Imperial Majesty," Max had replied.

The archduke had then ordered him to erase it from his memory with immediate effect. Then the audience ended.

Max now had authorized leave. He had fourteen days in which to live as a free man before he had to report for duty once again in the east at Army High Command in Bohemian Cieszyn.

"Well, good day to you, sir! If it isn't one of our heroes from Przemyśl."

Max was caught off guard, still worrying over the archduke's reaction to the letter. He found himself face-to-face with the porter, standing by the bench near the entrance to his house and clumsily saluting him.

"Greatly honored, Herr Oberleutnant. You look half-starved. I'd hardly have known you."

The porter, too, carried less weight than Max remembered. His suit jacket had previously strained across his belly, but now hung rather loose. The man's cheeks, once round and fleshy, were now quite slack.

"You're right there. That's why I'm hoping our trusty cook still has something nice for me in the larder," said Max, his hand on the revolving door. But what the porter said next stopped him in his tracks. "Your cook's not there. There's nobody home."

Max spun around, puzzled. "What's that supposed to mean?"

"They're all gone. The butler got called up, the nanny went home to her parents after her brother got killed at Bukovina, and the chambermaids ran off, as well. They got factory work somewhere or other. Your cook's still around, but she leaves the house every morning with your family to go and cook for that rabble from the east, eating us out of house and home—"

"Stop there!" Max raised his hand to show he meant business. "What exactly is my family doing, and where's our cook?"

"She's cooking for those Jewish bastards from the Carpathians these past months. Disgusting people, I tell you. All they bring is dirt, lice, and worse. Don't do a lick of work. And listen to this, they live like lords in a hotel that your sister rented for them—spoiled brats. If I may say so, Herr Oberleutnant, it's a blessing you're back. You can get your womenfolk in line."

"This rabble, as you so disrespectfully call them, I consider to be fellow countrymen and fellow citizens, just like you." Max was disgusted by what he had heard. "They've gone through indescribable horror simply because they were unlucky enough to live in towns and villages near the front. If they've made the long trek to Vienna, it's out of sheer desperation."

Max knew only too well how savagely the war had torn through the border region between Austria and Russia, showing no mercy to the towns and villages in its way. The Jewish population in particular was subjected to looting, rape, execution, and pogrom by the Austro-Hungarian army as well as the Russian. Was it any surprise that these people had fled in search of safety? It was, however, clear that not everyone welcomed them.

"As you know so much about what my family's doing, you'll doubtless have the address of the refugee accommodation," said Max coolly.

Looking quite put out, the man stared at him for a moment, then muttered, "The hotel's on Praterstrasse, not far from Nordbahnhof."

Max would rather have driven himself there, but the car wouldn't start, and he realized the fuel tank was empty. Ever since the French navy had blocked Austro-Hungary's ports on the Mediterranean, it wasn't only food that was in short supply but all kinds of raw materials, too. So, he jumped on the electric tram. The driver was a woman. He bought his ticket from a woman, too. On the way, he saw a woman delivering mail. With so many men at the front, women had taken up their work and kept daily life in Vienna going.

He spotted the hotel as soon as he got off the tram on Praterstrasse. It was a drab three-story building covered in scaffolding. Max noticed a number of men working on the façade of the hotel, scraping away the old, flaking paint from the walls and window frames. The men all had dark hats, long beards, and sidelocks.

Over the entrance hung a big sign bearing the name of the hotel, Hotel am Nordbahnhof. Another of these men was up a ladder, paintbrush in hand, as he returned the lettering to its former modest glory. On the sidewalk near the entrance were two benches, one currently occupied by two old gentlemen, deep in conversation. They, too, sported the hats and beards and sidelocks. The other bench was taken up by two women dressed in dark, shapeless clothes, their hair concealed by headscarves. They dropped their eyes when they saw Max. Some of the men nodded in greeting. Their faces were pale and drawn, and they eyed his uniform with mistrust.

Inside, the lobby teemed with people, and Max was immediately struck by the babble of different languages, the stuffy air, and the stink of sweat and pea soup, this last making his mouth water and his stomach rumble. He heard snatches of Hungarian, Polish, and Yiddish as well as what must have been Ruthenian, the dialect used in the western foothills of the Carpathians. He felt himself being observed with a mixture of unease and suspicion. There were chairs and sofas strewn around, and some of the older folk snoozed while others stared ahead vacantly, unaware of their surroundings. Some of the women were nursing young babies, while toddlers played round their feet. So far, there was no sign of his wife and sister, nor his little daughter. As he made his way slowly across the lobby, he noticed how many of the women were at work stitching gray gloves. Army gloves.

By now, he'd reached the reception desk. To the right was a staircase, to the left, a corridor into the rest of the interior of the building. Max was just wondering whether to take the stairs or the corridor when he heard children laughing. Two little girls darted out from behind the counter. His daughter was one of them. Her cheeks were flushed, and her chestnut curls bounced as she ran. She looked healthy and well nourished, while her playmate was pale and wan.

"Emma!" Max called out, but both children simply stopped and stared at him.

Max squatted down to his daughter's level and opened his arms. But she shrank from him.

My God, she doesn't recognize me.

He tried an inviting smile. "Emma, it's me, Papa."

Her eyes widened. Then she cried out, "Mama! Quick! Come here!"

Max straightened up. Helene emerged from the corridor. She wore a starched white cap, a white dress and apron, and an armband with the symbol of the Red Cross. She stopped, unsure of what she saw.

"Max?"

Emma ran to her mother.

"Good day to you, Nelli," said Max. "Have I really changed that much?"

She hesitated before going up to him and kissing him on the cheek. "No, not really, you just surprised me. I read that Przemyśl had surrendered. I assumed you'd been captured with everyone else."

Max was so disappointed, he couldn't speak. This reunion with his family couldn't have been more different from what he'd hoped for.

Helene gave him a hard look. "You're looking thin."

"The cuisine in Przemyśl wasn't too appetizing. We mostly got nothing more than dry bread. So, you're a nurse now, I see?"

She nodded. "When the first refugees came into Vienna at the beginning of the winter, I took a Red Cross course in how to care for the sick and the wounded. Now I work here with Izabella, looking after the refugees." She gazed around the hall with some fondness. "At least we've managed to plump them all up a bit now, but you'd never believe the state of them when they arrived. Undernourished, full of parasites and infection, and their feet ulcerated from the hundreds of kilometers they'd walked to get to Vienna."

"The welfare of these people seems to matter to you a lot." He couldn't disguise his bitterness.

"For the first time in my life, I'm doing something useful," she said quietly, stroking Emma's hair. "How did you know we were here?"

"The porter told me," he said, trying to twinkle at his daughter as she clung to her mother's skirt. "Emma, will you say hello to me now?"

Helene nudged the child toward Max. "Go on, darling."

With a smile, he reached out his hand toward her, and, after a moment of uncertainty, Emma took hold. He could have wept with happiness. It was only his fear of frightening her that stopped him wrapping his free arm around her. "She looks strong and healthy."

"We're the lucky ones. We can pay the ridiculous food prices here. If it comes to it, we'll get the basics on the black market," said Helene.

As he let go of Emma's hand, he sniffed the air, saying, "Speaking of food, something smells good."

She looked away. "We've only got enough for these people."

He bit his lip. "Of course."

"Max!" Izabella came running down the staircase and threw her arms around him. "Is it really you? This is wonderful. When did you get back and how long can you stay?" She shed tears of joy and had slipped naturally into Hungarian with him. After they embraced, she stood back and looked at him with concern. "You've gotten so thin your uniform's hanging off you. You must eat!" She seized his hand and took him back into the thick of the crowds in the hall.

As they made their way, he saw paper notices stuck on a number of doors, announcing in various languages what was behind each one. Latrine, treatment room, dining room, schoolroom, office, it was all there. Outside each door were chairs, mostly occupied. All eyes were on the door at the very end of the corridor. There were people waiting there, too.

"This is all communal space," explained Izabella. "Upstairs used to be the hotel bedrooms, of course, so now it's where the refugees actually sleep. There're so many of them now we have to put whole families in one room. But it's worked so far."

"And you're organizing all this?" Max gestured to indicate the extent of the operation.

She nodded. "I secured the hotel by chance, really. It was standing empty, and I thought, *Look, we could put up refugees in here.* Tracking down the proprietor wasn't so hard, but persuading him to let me have the building took a while. The place had been closed for renovation, but he'd been short of workers, and nothing much had happened. I came up with the idea that the refugees could get some of the work done for him. Eventually, he agreed."

Just then, a door opened behind them, and a large group of chattering, laughing children emerged. They were under the supervision of a pretty young woman with dark eyes and equally dark curly hair. She glanced at Max timidly as they all hurried past.

"Who was that?" asked Max.

He noticed Izabella blush. "I'll tell you later." She stalked off ahead, leading him to the door at the end of the corridor. On it was another paper sign in lots of languages: "Kitchen."

The people lining up there let Izabella through, and Max saw how warmly they greeted his sister and how appreciative their smiles were.

Izabella opened the door, ushered Max in, and then closed it behind her. The good smell went straight to Max's head, and once he spotted the two huge pots simmering on the stove, he had eyes for nothing else.

Two female refugees in aprons were stacking metal bowls and spoons on the huge worktable in the center of the room. A third woman was slicing bread. The family's cook was planted at the stove, keeping watch over the pots, stirring the contents from time to time. At the sound of the door, she grumbled. "Ladies and gentlemen, you couldn't wait til twelve?"

When she turned, her jaw dropped. "Heavens above, is that you, sir?" She crossed herself.

"Yes, it's him," said Izabella firmly. "Half-starved and urgently in need of a bowl of that soup of yours."

"Right away, sir. Right away." She took the big ladle from its hook behind the stove.

Brother and sister now sat together in Izabella's office, her desk a mass of papers and clutter. Without a word, she watched Max wolfing down the thick pea soup, then wiping the bowl clean with a hunk of bread.

"Best meal I've ever had!" He sat back, pushing the bowl away.

"More?"

He shook his head, although he could have eaten another bowl without any trouble. "What about you?"

"I get enough. We need everything here to go to the refugees. They only receive the basics. And now Mayor Weiskirchner is doing all he can to get rid of these poor souls who come to us for shelter. Look what came in the mail today." Izabella passed him a document.

"'This is an official call for refugees from West Galicia to return home,'" he read quietly. "'The enemy invasion has been repulsed and created favorable conditions at the present time . . .' That's absurd!" He broke off, his voice angry. "There's nothing remotely 'favorable' about conditions on the eastern front, especially not for the villagers there. One minute it's the Russian army attacking them, the next minute it's ours. Sending people back there is sending them to their deaths." He rested his head in his hands. "The Jews get the worst of it. In the border region, they're the target of hideous pogroms and mass execution. The Cossacks treat them like cattle, driving them toward the Austrian front positions. Then our own soldiers take care of the rest."

"I've heard," said Izabella softly. "The refugees talk about it. Do you know something? Before the war, I didn't see myself particularly as

Jewish, just a citizen of Austria-Hungary. But since I've seen firsthand how much misery and persecution these Jews have been subjected to, I've started to feel at one with them."

They sat together in silence for a while. Izabella spoke first. "Nelli's a wonderful support. She's here every day, devotedly giving medical care to the refugees. Whenever the doctor comes to examine them, she stays close by and looks at everything with him. And she's donated all those baby clothes that she made after—" She broke off. "Forgive me. I didn't mean to talk about that."

"At least all that sewing had a purpose," said Max.

Izabella watched her brother carefully as she said, "By the way, Fanny's helping, as well. You may have seen the women stitching gloves in the reception hall. Fanny got us that—it's a contract with the army."

His heart beat faster at the sound of her name. All sorts of questions sprang to his lips. But he knew his sister was watching him, and why, so he shifted the topic a bit. "Who's paying for the accommodation and supplies here? I can't imagine Fanny's army contracts can cover all your costs."

"You're right," confirmed Izabella. "We get medicine from the refugee center, but only very small amounts, and I practically have to beg for those. The accommodation is free because the men are working on the hotel, as you've seen. Then there's the food," she said, with an awkward smile. "Well, I pay for most of that from my own pocket." She gave him an anxious look. "Food's in shorter and shorter supply, and prices are going up almost by the hour. Bread ration cards are being introduced in April. That'll make it even more difficult. Refugees will always be given less than the locals."

Max leaned forward and took her hand in his. "I'd like to help you. I'll write a check today."

"That's so helpful, Max, thank you," said Izabella, her eyes filled with tears.

"Any news from the parents?"

She nodded. "It's been ages, but a letter came from Mama yesterday. She said most of Papa's employees have been called up or are in work 'essential to the war effort.' So, he's thinking of closing one of his stores. You really must telegraph them, or they'll assume you've been taken prisoner when they hear Przemyśl fell."

"I'm worried about the fact that Papa invested so much in war loans. It'll hit him hard if we lose."

Izabella looked aghast. "You think we could lose this war?"

He shrugged. "Our army's badly equipped, our weapons are out-of-date. There's a shortage of food and raw materials. We'd be done for without the support of the Germans." His mind went back to the document he'd handed to the heir to the throne that very morning. "But keep your spirits up, my dear little sister. Perhaps this war won't last too much longer."

"Whatever else happens, this war has changed my life in every way," she told him. "Here's one example: I don't go to Dr. Freud anymore."

"Because you're cured?"

"Because I realized I was never sick." She paused and looked him straight in the eye. "I've met a woman who feels, and loves, as I do. I'm in love, Max."

"I'm delighted to hear it!" Max hugged her. "Tell me about her."

Izabella glowed with pride. "Her name's Rachel Mendelsohn. You saw her coming out of the schoolroom earlier on. She's been helping with the refugee children here. She's a teacher by profession, from Lemberg. I met her by chance when she'd stolen a loaf of bread."

Izabella smiled at the memory and started to tell her brother about the day in early January when she'd literally bumped into Rachel outside a branch of the Anker bakery. Rachel had taken a tumble, and before she could get back on her feet, she'd been set upon by a furious bakery worker. The woman threatened to call for police, even after Izabella herself insisted on paying for the bread.

"Rachel hadn't stolen the bread for herself, but for the children who'd made that trek with the other refugees," said Izabella. "She took me to the big synagogue in Tempelgasse, where people were sleeping in the open air in the courtyard. In the middle of winter, Max. Old people, pregnant women, infants, you name it. I felt I couldn't simply leave, as if I'd seen nothing. I wanted to help these people. And I wanted to be close to Rachel, too." She gave an unusually shy smile.

"I can see how happy you are," said Max. "And that makes me happy, too."

A few days later, he found himself on Graben, looking at the shop front of Madame Moreau's fashion house. Gold lettering over the black painted door still spelled out "Sarah Moreau—Couture," but the big display window was boarded up, as were most shop fronts on Vienna's luxury mile. Max tried the door but found it locked.

He went around to the rear to see if he might have better luck there. He had to leave Vienna tomorrow, nearly a full week earlier than expected. The thought of not seeing Fanny at all was inconceivable.

High Command had ordered him back early because the Kingdom of Italy was about to enter the war. This is how Max interpreted the change of instructions. Italy was legally bound to be on the side of Germany and Austria-Hungary, but the Allies had promised the kingdom substantial territorial gains in Tirol and Friuli if they were victorious, and so the Italians had decided to switch sides.

During his brief leave, Max had regularly received secret reports by courier, so he knew the old Kaiser's opinion of the Allies' tactics. For the Kaiser, Italy's action was treason, as simple as that, and he'd sooner have gone down with his honor intact than rely on shady deals. Max found nothing in these secret reports of the peace initiative he'd delivered from Kusmanek.

The back door of Moreau's was also locked. He thought for a bit, then pressed the bell. A voice rang out behind him.

"Kálman! What're you doing here, you old tramp!"

Max turned and was shocked to find himself face-to-face with a severely disfigured man. A black patch covered the right eye, the nose was a shapeless bulge, and across his chin was a broad red scar. The man was sporting the formal uniform jacket of a General Staff officer, bronze military service medals adorning the left side of his chest. The three stars on his collar confirmed his status as a captain, so Max saluted without any idea who this was.

A grotesque grin twisted the face even more. "It's me, Brunner, from the military academy. Don't you recognize me with my new face? I've got the Battle of Kolubara to thank for it. Heavy dose of shrapnel."

"Brunner, you old bastard! I never expected to run into you here." Max gave the man a hearty slap on the shoulder.

Valerian Brunner laughed bravely. "The medics did a pretty good job of patching me up, don't you think? Once they were done, the Kaiser gave me a gong." He tapped at one of the medals on his chest. "Then I was promoted to captain and transferred to intelligence, the Russia desk."

"You're at the Evidenzbüro? Military intelligence? Do I need to be scared of you now, Mr. Secret Agent?"

Brunner teased him back. "Got something to hide?" Looking over toward Gasthaus Rebhuhn, he added, "Shall we get something to eat? They won't have many options, but at least we could talk in peace over a meal."

Max was about to accept when the back door of the fashion house opened. He spun around and saw Fanny. Her hair was disheveled, and she looked tired, with dark circles under her eyes, but his heart raced, telling him how much he'd missed her.

"Max! How wonderful!" She threw her arms around his neck without a moment's hesitation.

Brunner tapped Max lightly on the shoulder. "I'll go on ahead and get us a table."

Fanny watched him go. "Poor man's a mess. I've noticed more and more like him. But what are you doing here? I was so worried when I heard about Przemyśl."

"I got out of there on a special mission before it fell, and I've been in Vienna a week. Today's my last day of leave. Hadn't you heard?"

She shook her head. "I don't see Izabella and Nelli that often. We've all got so much going on."

He gave her a hard look. "Worn out?"

"I could do with a bit more sleep. I'm really busy all the time. Right now I have to go make Josepha's lunch. She can't do much for herself now." Fanny thought for a moment. "Do you want to come back a bit later? We close at five. I can make time for you then before I have to get to my class. I'm still doing the master craftswoman training."

"The shop's open? How on earth—?"

"No, it's just the sewing room these days." She glanced at her wrist-watch. "Time I was off, Max. See you shortly."

"Good. I'll be back at five."

"Wasn't that the girl who lured you away from me at the laundry maids' ball? Is it serious for you two now?" Brunner asked Max as soon as he joined him at the Rebhuhn.

Max only studied the menu. "Do you know what they've got left?"

"Vegetable broth with a nice swirl of egg, then spuds with sausage and cabbage. I've taken the liberty of ordering for us both. It must be serious if you don't want to talk. She's sugar and spice, I must say."

"Don't talk about her like dessert," snapped Max.

"Sorry, buddy, didn't mean to cause offense. Understand completely," said Brunner, changing his tone. "Believe me, I know what it's like to go through it at the front. Then, when you come home wanting a woman's warmth, you realize you've become a stranger to her. Especially when you look like I do now. My wife shrieks every time she sees me. I can't even think about getting close to her, touching her."

Max listened in silence. Between her nursing shifts, he and Helene had barely exchanged a word about anything personal. Mostly, she was too tired and went straight to bed after they'd eaten. He got the impression she had no interest in him. She hadn't even asked about the siege at Przemyśl. It was no better with Emma, who simply avoided him. The war had changed everybody, especially the women. Max found himself wondering whether they still even needed him, or indeed any man, at all.

The waiter arrived with their food. A few chunks of turnip floated in the vegetable broth, and Brunner's "nice swirl of egg" turned out to be a bit of potato flour. The main course was no better. Each sausage was the size of a child's finger and contained more groats than meat. At least it came with a good pile of cabbage. Max ate hungrily. He was constantly hungry, even though he was more than prepared to pay the horrendous prices on the Viennese black market.

Meanwhile, Brunner told him all about the battles he'd fought with the Austro-Hungarian army against the Serbs. He'd been severely wounded when a grenade had exploded right by his dugout in the trenches. And he brought Max news of friends they'd studied with at the military academy, some fallen at the front, others missing or wounded.

"It's been good to see you again, Kálman," he said as they finished their meal. "May God be with you on the next deployment and bring you back safely."

Once they'd said their farewells, Max realized he had a good two hours to fill before seeing Fanny. He ordered a coffee—ersatz, of course—and got himself a newspaper from the rack near the door. He stared at the print, but his mind was full of her.

The last time they'd met, she'd said, "There's no future for us."

Could she have changed her mind?

But why should she? He was married to Helene, and although Fanny meant more to him than any other woman, nothing could alter that fact. Catholics, even converts like him, could only apply for divorce through a church court. And it was hardly ever granted, especially if the couple had children.

Maybe it's better to stay together and put up a show for the outside world. For Emma's sake, too.

And yet he ached for Fanny, and all the reasoning in the world wouldn't stop that.

He looked up when a small three-wheeled delivery vehicle pulled up to the back entrance of the fashion house. A woman in overalls and a peaked cap jumped out of the little cab, stepped up onto the loading area, and lifted down a handcart, like the type a station porter might use. She rang the doorbell and was let in immediately. Soon after, she reappeared, her cart now stacked with crates. Several other women followed close behind her, pushing similarly laden carts that they then loaded onto the three-wheeler.

Women have certainly thrown off those chains they talk about, and in less than a year, he marveled. He couldn't help but wonder if they now felt the same freedom as men when it came to a passing romance. The fear of getting pregnant was no longer such an obstacle now that condoms were widely available, although pricey and mostly obtainable only from a doctor. The army, however, was more than generous in distributing them to soldiers so as to prevent syphilis and other diseases.

Max checked the inside pocket of his jacket for the couple he'd slipped in there earlier.

Fanny got off the horse-drawn bus at Florianigasse, hurried up the steps to Josepha's apartment, and let herself in.

"Fanny, is that you?"

"Of course it's me! Who else would it be?"

Josepha was in her armchair by the window, a woolen blanket over her knees and legs. On the small table beside her were a half-empty water glass and her spectacles. Fanny had brought her the newspaper and now placed it on the table.

For some time now, Josepha had needed help with washing and dressing in the morning, and so Fanny stopped in before work each day. Then she'd come back at lunchtime to heat up the food she always prepared in advance. In the evening, she'd help Josepha get to bed, then make the meal for the following day. Today there was potato soup with turnip, and a bit of fat bacon that Fanny had got ahold of on the black market at Erzhog-Karl-Platz. For what was really no more than rind, she'd paid more than she'd once have paid for a whole pig, but she wasn't going to fret about it. She'd promised herself she'd take care of this wonderful woman as well as she possibly could through these tough times.

When the soup was hot, she filled two bowls and carried them in on a tray. Josepha preferred to stay in her armchair these days, so Fanny pulled up another seat, and they ate together near the window.

"Have another helping, little mite. You're wasting away," commented Josepha.

"A bit less weight doesn't hurt anyone," said Fanny lightly, blowing on her soup.

"It doesn't feel right, you always giving up your short lunch break for this silly old woman."

Fanny shook her head furiously. "How many times do I have to tell you that I don't want to hear all that? You took care of me all those years. Now I'm taking care of you."

Later on, Fanny washed up and tidied the kitchen while Josepha browsed through the newspaper.

"Oh my Lord, look at the size of this death notice. Must be some bigwig." She peered at the print, holding the page right up to her face.

"I'm sure it's the double coat of arms. Fetch me the magnifier would you, little mite? It's on the kitchen rack."

Fanny brought it over. Josepha bent close to the text.

"That's odd," she murmured. "I recognize that crest."

"Of course you do," said Fanny, looking over her shoulder. "It's everywhere."

Bearing the imperial crown of Austria and the Hungarian Holy Crown, this was the coat of arms of the Dual Monarchy and always stood proudly on official buildings, palaces, and the premises of suppliers of goods to the court.

"Yes, but this one's special," persisted Josepha, bent so low that her nose almost touched the page. "You don't see the crest in black and white like that every day. Pity I can't read the text of the death notice. Not even with the magnifier. It's very annoying, getting old!"

She grumbled a bit until Fanny reached for the paper herself. "Perhaps it's in black and white cos the paper can't print in color. Then again, the edges are so sharp that it looks like it's supposed to be this way." She studied the page carefully. "This death notice has been put in here by the imperial and royal Evidenzbüro to mark the death of its old director, a Colonel Edmund von Ostenstein. Isn't the Evidenzbüro like military intelligence? You know, spying and things like that?"

"Never heard of this colonel," muttered Josepha. She put the magnifier down on her table. "But that coat of arms, I've seen that somewhere before."

Fanny folded up the paper. "Josepha, there's a cold supper ready in the pantry for you. I have to get to my class, but I'll be back afterward to get you to bed."

"Don't overdo it, little mite!"

"I'm fine! Bye, Josepha." Fanny kissed the old lady on both cheeks. But as she tried to straighten up, Josepha grabbed her by the wrist.

"I've got it. I remember where I've seen that black-and-white coat of arms before. It was on the envelope your mother brought to the delivery room."

"Heavens! The military intelligence seal was on my mother's emergency envelope?"

"I don't know for sure that it was the Evidenzbüro seal," replied Josepha. "I only saw it for a moment and couldn't read what was written on it. My eyes weren't that good even then. But in all my years at the foundling home, you were the only one to come in with a seal like that."

"So, could this be a clue as to who sent that money all those years?" Fanny paced up and down now in front of Josepha's armchair.

"Maybe we should leave it alone, Fanny. Maybe it's all nonsense. Why on earth would the Evidenzbüro pay money for your upbringing? What does a tiny babe have to do with military spies?"

But Fanny wasn't going to be put off. "Nothing, but a baby's parents might. I'll write to the Evidenzbüro and ask them."

"Little mite, don't bother doing all that. You'll only end up disappointed." Josepha sounded sad at the prospect.

But Fanny was determined. Her head held high, she said, "Giving it a try costs nothing."

"Got something special planned?" asked Elisabeth Nikolic when she came into the washroom and found Fanny in front of the mirror, adjusting her clothes and hair.

Slightly embarrassed, Fanny let her hands drop. "I'm just meeting an old friend. He's on home leave from the front. That's all."

"I see." Elisabeth came over to the washbasin and started to fix her own hair, a few strands having escaped from her usual bun. "So that's why your face is all lit up like one of Madame's chandeliers."

Fanny went red. "You're imagining things."

Elisabeth laughed warmly. "Enjoy it, Fanny. In times like these, we just have to grab at whatever happiness comes our way. I'm heading home now. Everyone else has already left." With a friendly wave, she was gone.

Fanny took one last critical look at herself in the mirror. In her austere white blouse and dark skirt, she came across as rather severe. *No color in my face at all,* she thought, pinching her cheeks.

Ever since she'd taken over the business from Madame Moreau, her life had been ruled by work, worry, and responsibility. There was always something to organize or sort out, even if it was only the next meal.

Elisabeth's right, she thought to herself. *I should enjoy life whenever I get the chance!*

She hurried down the staircase and, her heart pounding, opened the back door. There he was, standing on the other side of the street outside the Rebhuhn. Seeing Fanny, he hurried over.

"Good day, Max." She held out her hand. But he took her in his arms and drew her close.

"Wonderful to see you, Fanny."

They stayed like that, quite still.

Fanny savored the delicious feeling of his being so close. The rough fabric of his uniform rubbed her cheek, and she closed her eyes. If only she could capture this moment forever.

Tutting noises reminded them they were in a public place. A starchy elderly couple walked by.

"Let's go in," said Fanny.

She took Max's hand and led him into the hall. Immediately behind the door were yet more crates stacked against the wall. She gestured at one of them. "This is full of puttees. You know how the soldiers' boots get soaked through otherwise. These days, there's no call for ball gowns and sharp outfits for the court. We earn our money with contracts from the army. The idea came from Frau Schubert. She's our master craftswoman. You'll be even more surprised when you see

277

what the sales room looks like now." Fanny took a bunch of keys from her dress pocket and headed for a door at the end of the corridor. Max followed her.

"Where's Madame Moreau hiding herself? Did she go back to France?"

"No, everything happened too fast for her to do that." Fanny turned the key in the lock. "As soon as war was declared on France, she was interned with other foreigners. She was sent to a castle in Lower Austria. She managed to arrange everything for the business before she left, making me her official representative and deputy. In reality, Frau Schubert and I do it jointly. Without her ideas and experience, I'd never have managed to keep the girls here employed. Madame gives us good advice by letter, too. It makes me sad that we're not allowed to go and see her."

Now Fanny pushed open the door and turned on the light. There was a slight cracking sound as it came to life.

"Good Lord," murmured Max, as he looked around. "It's nothing like a fashion house now."

The wooden boards nailed across the main display window left the once-elegant salon looking as cold and featureless as a warehouse. The Oriental carpet, rolled up and covered in sheeting, now stood propped against a wall. Display cases, armchairs, sofas, and side tables, also draped for protection, had been pushed close to another wall. On the floor were stacks of uniform collars, epaulettes, and field caps, the kind worn by the infantry. On shelving once home to the finest of fabrics, there were now only abdominal belts and undershirts.

"These days we specialize in supplying big manufacturers, as well as making custom items," Fanny explained. "So, this afternoon, for example, we've delivered a load of field backpacks. The goods are made up and machine stitched by Madame's needlewomen, then the sales staff pack them and help with delivery. Then there are smaller contracts that can be stitched by hand, so I give them to Izabella's refugee women."

"The gray gloves. Of course, yes, I saw them. You women are so capable. You're all keeping life going while we men are killing each other."

"A lot of the women here have lost husbands or fiancés," said Fanny sadly. "Our doorman died, too. His mother came here last week to tell us. Gustav was her only son."

Max reached for Fanny again, wrapped his arms around her, and pulled her close. She put her head on his shoulder. As he stroked her hair, he realized he could barely conceive of leaving her again to go and fight in a war that he no longer believed in, not since the fall of Przemyśl.

She raised her head and looked up at him. "Would you like to see something beautiful? Something that has nothing to do with the war?"

He nodded. They took the elevator up, and Fanny led Max to the reception salon, the room where she'd been so unexpectedly reunited with Izabella and Helene almost two years earlier.

"This is my own special place, the workshop where I can dream a little," she said, smiling contentedly as she turned on the light. "Making army stuff is so dreary. Up here I make clothes for when the war's over. It gives me pleasure—hope, too."

He saw a round table with Fanny's sewing machine on it. On one of the chairs were fabric samples, on another lay a notebook that seemed to be full of Fanny's sketches for ball outfits and evening dresses.

She took him over to the middle of the room, where a mannequin boasted an ivory dress in silk. Fanny had decorated it with glossy braid and silver sequins. It was out of this world.

"I made it for the master craftswoman exam. Madame let me have the material from prewar stocks." Her fingers caressed her creation. "I'll put it on if you want. Just for you."

"I'd be honored," said Max with a bow.

With the greatest of care, she eased the dress off the mannequin and went toward the screen behind it. "You'll be the first to see me in it." She vanished behind the screen.

Max heard rustling sounds. He pictured her taking off her blouse and skirt. Those passionate kisses they'd shared at the Báthory Estate and in Vienna came back to him, as did their tryst in the carriage shed. He had to pace a little to distract himself and remain calm. But as he moved around the room, he found himself looking straight at the full-length mirror placed opposite the screen and realized he could see her through a crack between the screen and the wall.

She had bent forward to free up her stockings. A stray lock brushed the swell of her breasts and her naked shoulders. She placed one leg on a low stool and began carefully to roll down first one, then the other silk stocking, slowly baring her delicate thighs. When she looked ready to take off the girdle, he forced himself to turn away.

After a few tantalizing moments, she stepped out from behind the screen. She was barefoot and did a slow turn on tiptoe for him to see the dress in all its perfection.

"Do you like it?"

The hem swirled against her slender ankles. The upper part clung to her body, and the silver sequins glittered in the light. And when she turned her back toward him, he saw how the dress plunged so low it almost reached her shapely bottom. She couldn't possibly be wearing a chemise or girdle under that!

"I wanted to try something completely new," she explained. "Something modern that will suit a modern woman. It's not for a woman who lives like a little doll, sitting around and looking pretty. It's for women who take charge of their lives and don't let themselves feel restricted. This is a dress for freedom of movement. I could play tennis in it if I wanted."

"You look phenomenal." Max's voice was thick with desire.

He moved closer, took her gently by the shoulders, and turned her until she stood with her back against his chest. His arms went around her waist as he covered her neck and shoulders with tender kisses. "Your skin's so delicate," he whispered. "So delicate, so soft. And smells so good."

As she leaned her head back against his shoulder, he ran his hand across the fine cloth barely concealing her breasts. "Do you want more?" he whispered.

"I don't know," she murmured in reply, her eyes closed. "In some ways, yes. In other ways . . ."

"You have nothing to fear," he said. "I'll protect you from what you're so scared of."

She opened her eyes and turned. A smile flitted across her face. "You've thought of everything. Had you planned to seduce me right from the start?"

"I've always wanted you. And you?"

Fanny placed her arms around his neck. "Don't ask," she said in a whisper. "Just make it happen."

Then he kissed her more deeply, more passionately than she'd ever dared imagine possible. As his hands slid down the length of her back, and he felt the little hairs on her skin standing to attention, he was overwhelmed by a craving that he could not control, nor did he want to. He cupped his hands under her buttocks and lifted her onto the edge of the small table. With one hand he lifted the skirt of her dress and deftly stripped off her panties, while she hurried to undo his uniform trousers. He stopped a moment to get rid of his jacket as well as the trousers and swiftly put their protection in place. As he pushed himself inside her, she swung her legs around him, and they made love greedily, feverishly, wantonly.

Afterward, they sat in an armchair together in a corner of the room, Fanny on his lap. She nestled close to him. His fingers played over her thighs, hers over his thick dark hair.

"How much longer will you be in Vienna?" she murmured.

"I'm leaving for High Command tomorrow, then I'll get my next orders."

"So soon," she sighed. "How I hate this war."

He kissed her soft earlobe. "I'll get leave again. Will we see each other?"

"We certainly will."

"You know what I mean."

She stopped playing with his hair and sat up straight. "What we've just done was beautiful, and I'll never forget it. But nothing else has changed, Max. There's no future for us."

He didn't like hearing that but struggled to think of any alternative. He was still a married man, despite the widening gulf between him and his wife. His heart belonged to Fanny, of that he was more certain than ever, but he couldn't offer her more than merely being his mistress. He stroked her hair back behind her ear.

"If you still believe there's no future for us, why did you do what we've just done here?"

Kissing him on the forehead, she said, "Because I've longed for it so much."

Chapter Seventeen

Vienna, 1917

Fanny gazed out of the window from her seat at Madame's smaller meeting table. It was late November and the last brown leaves were fluttering to the ground in the rain. A letter from Madame lay before her on the desk. It had arrived that morning.

A knock at the door startled her. Helene walked right in, furling a wet umbrella. "Hello, Fanny," she said, as she dropped it in the nearby stand. "The back door was open. Your staff are down there, loading crates onto a cart, so I just came up."

"The latest army contract is going out. There'll be more, I bet." After three years of war, there was still no sign of peace, even though hundreds of thousands of men were dying at the front, and women and children in the hinterland were destitute. "I'm just longing to get back to normal, making beautiful clothes out of beautiful material." Fanny pushed back her chair and went over to Helene. "I can't believe that the last garment I made like that was for my master craftswoman exam. Seems a lifetime ago now. But at least I haven't had to discharge a single member of Madame Moreau's staff. That's really something. Now, Helene, what have I done to deserve this visit?"

The two women greeted one another with the customary embraces. But Fanny felt more than a little awkward. Since she and Max had made love, she had gone out of her way to avoid Helene. She was quietly relieved that they were both so busy with their work that their paths rarely crossed.

Helene unbuttoned her coat. "Aren't you going to ask me to sit down? Or have I come at a bad time?"

Fanny's face flushed. "Sorry. Do have a seat." She gestured toward the meeting table and then sat down again in the same place as before.

"There was an attempted break-in at the refugee home last night. They tried to get into the kitchen." She took off her gloves and put them on the table. "Some of our men saw what was happening, thank goodness, and chased them out. But this kind of thing's going on more and more now. Did you know that the little dairy behind the cathedral now has two guards on the door? People lined up outside spit on them and call them names."

"I'd give anything to go back to how it was before all this started," said Fanny. "Do you feel like that, too?"

Helene thought for a minute. "In many ways, yes. But not entirely. When I look back, I was pretty empty-headed, to be honest. My life often felt pointless, and I had nothing to aim for. But now I'm doing something. I'm looking after people who really need me."

"And you're doing a superb job, Nelli!"

"It's good to hear you say that, Fanny." Helene glanced at the letter on the table. "Do you have a couple of minutes, or are you dealing with something urgent?"

Fanny stowed the letter and envelope in her dress pocket. "It's from Madame. But I can get back to it later."

"Is she still at Karlstein? How is she?"

"Not so good, sad to say. She's got typhus, so they've put her in a clinic. In her letter she says she's on the road to recovery but still feels weak." She paused. "Madame's afraid she won't be strong enough to carry on with the fashion house and is asking me to buy it. She says I can contact her lawyer if I want to go ahead. He'll organize everything."

"That really is news!" said Helene. "So, do you want to buy the place?"

"I've been thinking it over all morning. I've pretty much decided, yes. My master craftswoman training goes on another two years, and taking on a business would have been the logical next step. I'd love to run my own business. Provided it's not just supplying military goods."

"But can you afford it? Madame's not going to give away something so successful, surely?"

"Yes, I can raise most of the asking price myself. Then I can pay Madame the rest in installments."

She told Helene about the money paid anonymously into Josepha's savings account over so many years.

"Well, there you have it!" cried Helene. "And you still don't know who it was?"

"I haven't the faintest idea." Fanny looked sad. "I think we need a cup of tea. What do you think, Nelli?"

Nelli nodded. Fanny got to her feet and went off to prepare a tray. Five minutes later, she returned, with two gently steaming cups of chamomile.

"I hope this is alright for you. We haven't had proper tea for ages. There's no sugar either." She placed the tray on the table and handed one cup to her friend.

Helene took a sip. "Fanny, to be honest, I've come for a specific reason. Max has been wounded."

"Holy Mary, now you tell me!" Her cup clattered against the saucer.

She had heard very little from Max since he'd been deployed to the Italian Alps at the end of May 1915. There was the occasional letter, a few lines, that was all. They almost seemed to have been scribbled in haste, but he always wrote of his longing for her and for a peaceful world. Not a word about the war. She didn't even know what his role was on the General Staff.

She picked up from conversations with Helene, or with her staff whose menfolk were in Italy, that the harshest of conditions prevailed for those engaged in combat in the mountains. Both sides had dug themselves into the glacial, rocky landscape, and the front line moved neither forward nor back. Meanwhile, tens of thousands more men had lost their lives.

Putting her cup and saucer down on the table, Helene looked gravely at Fanny. "Max has been hit by poison gas."

Fanny felt all her strength drain away. She'd heard horrific stories about this gas and how it would noiselessly drift in on the breeze. She'd heard how the enemy would first deploy something different to cause vomiting, sometimes sneezing, anything to make the men tear off their masks, leaving themselves exposed to the clouds of poisonous gas that would follow, breaking down their lungs and leading to a slow, agonizing death.

It made Fanny shudder just to think about it. She asked herself what kind of a mind could invent something so barbaric. Josepha had said these "weapons people" were abnormal, sick in the head, and Fanny felt she was absolutely right.

Her voice now trembled as she asked, "How is he?"

"Not so good," replied Helene. "I went to see him yesterday."

Fanny stared at her, dumbfounded. "He's here?"

"He only arrived a couple of days ago. They transferred him to the officers' section of the General Hospital." Her hands around her teacup and her eyes lowered, Helene took a deep breath. "Fanny, Max and I talked about everything. About him, about me, about you. And about our future."

Fanny hardly dared breathe. She put her head in her hands as she stared hard at the surface of the table.

"Why didn't you confide in me?"

"What could I possibly have confided?" Fanny replied quietly. "There's been nothing to say for a long time."

"A long time. Max used the same words. But there was something between you, wasn't there?"

Fanny raised her head. "Yes. I admit that. I've been in love with Max for a long time. That's how it is, and I can't change it."

Helene's eyes flashed. "All the time we've known each other, you've been a friend to me, almost a sister, and now I find out you weren't truthful with me."

"I could hardly go and tell you I'd fallen in love with your husband, could I?"

"Oh yes, you could. You should have, and then we'd all have worked out what to do. Maybe we wouldn't have married in the first place."

"That's nonsense, and you know it. That marriage had always been in the cards for your families." Fanny shook her head in some disbelief. "How long have you known, Nelli?"

Helene ran her finger around the rim of the teacup. "Do you remember that dinner we had at home with Izabella? The war had just begun. And you were so worried about Max being in Przemyśl? I've suspected ever since. But I've only really known since yesterday, when he told me everything at the hospital. We finally got everything out in the open. And that was a good thing."

"Yesterday?" Fanny shook her head in amazement. "And I'd always thought your mother had told you."

"My mother?" Helene was baffled. "Why on earth my mother? What did she know about you two?"

Fanny went bright red. "Her chambermaid saw us together at your estate. It was before you got engaged. She told your mother all about it, then your mother threw me out. That was why I went off without telling you, or anybody else."

"This is unbelievable. And what about after the wedding? Did it go on after that?"

Fanny hung her head. "We met the last time he was in Vienna— and made love. It was the first, and last, time." She struggled to say any of this. "You're angry. I understand."

"I'm not angry," retorted Helene. "I'm disappointed. You haven't been a good friend. You went behind my back."

Fanny thought she might be about to storm out, but Helene went on quite calmly. "Our marriage died with our second baby. But I don't think it ever had much life in the first place. I was given no choice when it came to a husband. That's how things were done. And not just in my family." She seemed lost in thought as she looked down at her hands. "It took me a long time to realize that Max and I are not suited to each other. But now I'm getting a grip on my own life. I'm going to study medicine. I want to be a doctor."

"But what about Max? He's wounded. He'll need you!"

Helene looked at her coldly. "He doesn't need me, and he doesn't want me. I told you that he and I have talked everything over. It's you he needs. And it's you he wants."

Fanny couldn't believe this was happening. "What do you mean?"

"We can't divorce, but we're going to request a legal separation. Max and I have agreed. I ask only one thing of you, and that's discretion until it's all gone through the official channels, for Emma's sake."

Helene drank the last of her tea and got to her feet. Fanny stood up with her.

"Will you go and see Max?" asked Helene.

"Of course," mumbled Fanny, still shocked and wondering what state he would be in.

"Bye, Fanny." Helene brushed her cheek with a goodbye kiss and made for the door. Fanny stood in silence, watching her gather up her umbrella. Helene turned to look at her once more. "Don't ever think I'll forgive you that quickly for betraying our friendship."

The officers' hospital was on Sensengasse, not far from where Fanny had been born nearly twenty-eight years ago.

The doorman barely glanced up from his newspaper when she asked where she might find Oberleutnant Kálman. "Ward three. Up the stairs."

She crossed a large square court with benches lining the pathways, but in winter nobody sat outside for any length of time, if at all. The faded grassy area was bordered by trees, bare of all their leaves. Not a soul was in sight.

Two men in the entrance hall were trying to hang an enormous Advent wreath from the ceiling, one up a ladder, the other holding it firm and giving unwanted instructions. Advent was only two days away.

A portrait of Kaiser Karl I now hung on the wall to the right of the door. Their old ruler had died in the autumn of the previous year, having reigned over them for nigh on sixty-eight years, and thousands had lined the streets the day of his funeral, Fanny and Josepha included. But the public was not overwhelmed with grief. The sentiment among most Viennese was expressed rather well by Josepha as the carriage and its eight black horses went by. "May the old man carry the old world to the grave with him."

Fanny took her time as she climbed the stone staircase to the upper floor. She felt numb at the prospect of seeing Max's injuries. Helene hadn't told her much. But it was common now in Vienna to see war veterans on the street, young men missing an arm or a leg, begging on street corners, often for nothing more than a crust of bread.

It was clear there were a lot of patients here, some on the wards, others moving slowly from ward to stairs, stairs to ward. Some were still dressed in uniform, most in dressing gowns over nightclothes. Some sat in wheelchairs, others in armchairs but with a walking aid of some sort in easy reach. They smoked, or talked in low voices, or just stared straight ahead into nothingness. One man's whole body trembled as he muttered unintelligibly to nobody in particular. When Fanny went past him, he gave a start and cried out like a hunted animal. She hurried on, feeling deeply unsettled.

At ward three, a kindly nurse came over to her. "Good day. Can I help you?"

Fanny clutched at the handles of her bag. "My name's Fanny Schindler. I'd like to see Oberleutnant Kálman." When the nurse gave her a hard look, Fanny added, "I'm a friend of the family."

The nurse hesitated. "Well, alright. But no excitement. He needs rest. Peace and quiet will be his greatest healer."

She led Fanny down the whitewashed corridor to a glass door on the right-hand side. The nurse looked through the glass. "He's in there."

Fanny followed her gaze. Her hand flew to her mouth.

In this small dayroom, with its wicker chairs and a table littered with newspapers, she saw Max. Motionless, sitting bolt upright, he was on the sofa, also made of wicker. His eyes were heavily bandaged.

"Herr Oberleutnant likes to wear his uniform every day." The nurse spoke very quietly. "He likes to have a shave and brush his hair. He's got more fighting spirit left than most of them here."

"Has he gone blind?" whispered Fanny.

The nurse gave her a sympathetic glance. "His eyes were burned by the poison gas. It'll be a couple of weeks before the doctors can tell whether he's lost his sight. It's his lungs that are worst off. They're unlikely to recover fully."

Before she'd finished talking, Max was racked by a fit of coughing. Bending forward, he retched and gasped for air.

"Do something, he's choking!" Fanny was about to rush in, but the nurse held her back.

"He's got pulmonary edema. That's why it's hard for him to breathe. The attacks are less frequent now, but you mustn't get him worked up about anything."

"Edema? Pulmonary edema? What's that?" Fanny asked anxiously.

"He has water on the lungs. It's because of the type of gas he breathed in. They call it Green Cross. His heart's been affected, too. Unlike a lot of his comrades, he managed to get his mask on and survived, but only after taking in a dose of the terrible stuff."

His coughing attack subsided. Fanny watched as Max took out his handkerchief and wiped his mouth. "Is he going to die?" She was still numb.

"He'll probably get through it," said the nurse, trying to help. "You see, most of them die within two or three days of a gas attack. If you can get past that point, you can gradually make some sort of recovery. We know that Herr Kálman suffered the attack nearly four weeks ago. At first, he was treated in a field hospital. Now, the doctors here are doing their absolute best to get him back on his feet. They're giving him morphine for the pain and oxygen to help him breathe. Or they bleed him to reduce the strain on his heart." She turned to look at Fanny. "When you go to him, don't let him sense your anxiety. Try to cheer him up a bit."

Fanny nodded. "I'll do my best." Putting her hand on the doorknob, she took a deep breath. As she entered the room, Max turned his head toward her.

"Are you coming to take more blood, sister?"

She fought against the lump in her throat and replied, as brightly as she could manage, "Hello, Max. It's me, Fanny!"

What she could see of his face lit up with his smile. "Hello, Fanny. You've come to see me on Scythe Street, home to the Grim Reaper?"

She felt like crying but had to laugh at this bizarre display of humor.

"Where are you?" He reached out as he heard her pulling a chair over. "No, come and sit right next to me." He patted the sofa. "I want to be able to feel that you're close."

She sat down next to him. "You smell so good. Sweet. Warm." He felt for her hand and closed his around it.

She glanced over at the glass door and guessed the nurse had gone. Then she put her head on his shoulder. With every breath, there was a rattling sound. "How are you?" she asked.

"I'm well," he said airily. "It's just my eyes. They burn a bit. I've got something to show you." He fumbled for his inside pocket, took out a little handmade card. "I had this with me the whole time I was in the Alps. It gave me strength, especially after I was wounded."

Fanny took the card. "For F. S.: Masked Ball, Budapest Royal Opera House, February 17, 1910."

"Oh, it's my dance card! How wonderful!" She turned the card back and forth in her hands, gazing at it in wonder. Then she gently slid it back in the inside pocket of his uniform "There. Now it can go on giving you strength."

"And do you still have my handkerchief?"

She nodded. Then she remembered he couldn't see that. "It's been next to my pillow at night ever since you got sent to Italy."

He smiled and stroked her hand. They sat for a while in silence. Fanny found herself listening to the rattle of his every breath. *Please let him recover from this.*

"Did Nelli come to see you?" Max eventually asked.

"Yes. Yesterday."

His grip on her hand tightened. "And did she tell you we talked everything through?"

"Yes," said Fanny again.

"Is the friendship between you over?"

"I don't know." Her heart felt heavy when she thought back to the conversation with Helene.

"I'd rather have talked with you first," said Max. "But because I'd been wounded, it followed that Nelli would be their first point of contact." He struggled for breath. There was that rattle again.

Fanny made an effort not to fuss.

Max pushed himself to keep talking. "It's high time to be honest. With myself, with you, and with everybody else." He let go her hand and felt for her face so as to rest his fingers on her cheek. "You've always said there's no future for us. Perhaps there really isn't now. But I feel as if I'm only just starting out and need to relearn everything I thought I knew. What I want to say is that I love you, but you shouldn't feel under any obligation." He hesitated before saying, "I'd be glad if we could stay friends. What's wrong, Fanny?" He touched her cheek all over. "Are these tears?"

"Yes," she said, sobbing. "I'm so sorry, the nurse told me not to upset you in any way. If I'm crying now, then it's your doing." She wiped her eyes. "You can always count on my friendship, and on my love." She placed her hands on his cheeks and kissed him tenderly.

He felt for her wrists and gently pulled her hands away from his face. "You're saying that because you feel sorry for me. I'd end up a burden to you, and I'd feel worse about that than anything. Please understand that I need time to reorganize my life. Everything else, well, that remains to be seen." He lifted her right hand to his lips and kissed her fingertips one by one. "Now tell me about you."

The change of subject threw her, and she didn't know what to say. But then she started, hesitantly at first, to tell him she was thinking of buying the business from Madame Moreau. He was all in favor of the idea, just as Helene had been, and offered to help out if she needed a loan.

She was touched. "That's so kind and generous, but I don't need to borrow any money. Madame Moreau's made me a very reasonable offer, and on top of that, I've still got the money that was sent anonymously over all those years. That covers most of what's needed." She gave a little frown. "By the way, I made another fruitless attempt at finding my parents." She told him about Josepha's sudden recollection of the seal on the emergency envelope that her mother had been obliged to hand in at the hospital, and how she'd then written to the Evidenzbüro about it. "But they didn't even reply to me," she concluded sadly. "They probably thought I was some hysterical woman not worth bothering with."

Max had listened intently. "How long ago did you write this letter?"

"Well over two years. It was soon after we last met." She blushed at the memory of what they had done and was glad he couldn't see her just then.

"And who exactly did you write to there?"

"Nobody in particular," she conceded. "I don't know anyone there. So I just addressed it to the head of the office."

"Hmm." He rubbed his chin. "I do actually know someone who works at the Evidenzbüro. An old friend from my time at the academy. I'll write to him if you like. Well, I'd have to dictate it to you, and then you could help me sign it."

"Oh, Max!" She clapped her hands with joy. "That would be wonderful!"

Chapter Eighteen

Vienna, 1918–1919

Fanny rang the bell at the Kálmans' apartment. She heard footsteps, then Max himself opened the door. He was already in coat, hat, and gloves, smiling down at her.

"Good day, Fanny dear."

"Good day, Max. How are you?"

"Better every day."

He closed the door behind him, and they walked to the elevator together. Max always gave the same answer, and Fanny knew he simply didn't want to burden her with his health problems. Nobody could see the gravity of his wounds simply by looking at him, but Fanny knew better.

She had been at his side when, just before Christmas, the doctors had removed the bandages from his eyes, and she had wept with him when he found he could see again. But scarring on the corneas had left his vision less than perfect. It was like looking through a veil. His lungs weren't fully healed either. Strenuous activity, such as climbing stairs, brought on coughing fits that left him breathless. Medical staff at the officers' hospital took all this into consideration when they declared him unfit for duty. He was, therefore, discharged from the hospital and all further military service early in January. It was now February, and he was living a quiet life with his sister in the family apartment on the Ring. Helene had moved to a little apartment in the Palais Báthory now that their separation was official.

Fanny saw a lot of Max. Their closeness grew by the day. They meant the world to one another but felt they couldn't rush into anything. Max needed time to work out how his new life and career might look. He was interested in diplomacy and politics, but hadn't yet made any firm decision.

The elevator stopped at the ground floor, and they stepped out.

"Are you excited?" asked Max.

"So excited I couldn't sleep a wink!"

He smiled. "It's a big day for you."

"Maybe." He noticed the doubt in her voice. "Or maybe I'm going to be disappointed again."

"Brunner wouldn't say he'd found a clue about your parents if it weren't significant," said Max, determined to cheer her up.

They'd arranged to meet at the Hotel Sacher, not Brunner's office, which was, after all, at the secret intelligence service. The porter gave a mildly disapproving look as they left Max's home arm in arm, but the pair simply nodded in return. They stepped out into the bitter cold, the sidewalk covered in a thick layer of snow.

Fanny thought back to the first inkling she'd had of any developments in uncovering her history. It had been a couple of days before New Year's. She had gone to visit Max in the hospital as usual, and he'd told her that Brunner had written, asking to meet with them. Since then, Fanny had lost a lot of sleep, wondering what Max's old colleague could possibly have unearthed.

Josepha had been equally excited at the prospect of news. "I'm so pleased for you, little mite!" she kept saying, only to follow it with dark warnings. "Let's hope it's not a bad omen that your parents are tied up in some way with this Evidenzbüro. The last thing you'll want is trouble from some bigwig there."

Max's apartment was so close to the Sacher that they were soon standing at the reception desk of the world-famous grand hotel. While the proprietor checked her reservation book, Fanny looked around nervously.

"Here we are. Valerian Brunner, yes, it's a private room. *Séparée* number two. The gentleman is already there. If you'd like to follow me?"

The French bulldog who'd been sitting grumpily on the desk turned out to belong to her. She scooped the creature up in her arms and led the way.

Fanny knew that Madame Moreau had often dined here before the war, but she had never been here herself. She was apprehensive about the meeting but found a moment to admire the magnificence of the building and the décor. Somehow, the horror and misery of the war hadn't permeated the walls of the Sacher. Silk covered the walls, Persian carpets the marble flooring. Rumor had it that ration cards were not to be seen in the restaurant, only cash, and in return, the most exquisite food and drink were always available. No wartime substitutes here, that was for sure.

When two of Madame Moreau's prewar clients greeted Fanny in passing, Max whispered to her, "You wait—soon everyone will know we've been spotted here."

Anna Sacher, her dog now neatly tucked under one arm, turned down a corridor and knocked at a dark wood door framed by a red velvet drape. "Sir, madam, this is *Séparée* number two." She waited a moment before opening the door. "Sir, your guests have arrived."

Brunner got up from the table in the middle of the room. He shook Max warmly by the hand and gave a chivalrous bow as Fanny held out hers.

"Shall I send the waiter to take your order?" asked Frau Sacher. Brunner nodded, and she left.

Brunner pulled up a seat for Fanny and sat down again. "I recommend the Sacher torte with plenty of cream. You won't find anything better. After all, they invented it here, didn't they?" He smiled at his friend. "Kálman, the cake's on you! That's all I ask for helping you solve this mystery."

By now, Fanny was so on edge that she nearly burst into hysterical giggles. But Max's friend was both calming and charming, and she soon collected herself and no longer felt unsettled by his unfortunate disfigurement.

As the aroma of chocolate and fresh coffee tantalized Fanny's nose, she could almost have forgotten why they were all there. She took the first forkful of Sacher torte and let out a little sigh. "Oh, my goodness, this is what fine food really tastes like!"

Brunner talked a bit about the hard times they were all living in, and how important it was to take time to enjoy something when the opportunity arose. When they'd all finished, the waiter appeared and cleared everything away.

"So, Fräulein Schindler," Brunner began, once the three of them were alone again. "There's something I have to say to you before we go any further. You must never breathe a word to anyone about where you got this information. Can I rely on you?"

"Of course," replied Fanny solemnly.

"Good. Now I'm off to smoke a cigar with Frau Sacher. I'll take my time."

Fanny looked at him aghast, but he only laughed and reached for the briefcase he'd left propped against the leg of his chair, placing it on the table. "I'm a bit careless sometimes, you know, and I forget that I'm carrying secret documents around with me." He winked at Fanny. "That's how someone might get to read one of these documents unobserved. But, of course, I wouldn't know." He bowed and left the room.

"What was all that about?" Fanny asked Max.

"He's a secret service man. He'd really be in trouble if anyone had evidence that he'd deliberately passed on confidential documents." Max opened the briefcase and took out one slim folder. "This confidential report tells your history, dearest Fanny." He slid the folder across the table to her.

Her fingers trembled as she opened it. "Oh, look!" she cried. "Here's the letter I wrote to the Evidenzbüro." Then she took out a brown envelope, turned it over, and looked closely at the seal, with its white crest on the black background. "And this must be the emergency envelope that Josepha told me about." Then she murmured, almost to herself, "It's like the crest I saw in the newspaper."

Carefully setting the envelope to one side, she settled down to read the rest of the folder. On reaching the final page, she sat motionless, then collected herself, flapped the folder shut, and looked over at Max. "What it says here is so incredible, I can hardly believe it."

The war dragged on into its fifth autumn. Men continued to perish on all fronts, and more and more soldiers deserted. Entire regiments laid down their arms and turned for home, their superiors unable to stop them.

Vienna saw plenty of its own suffering. Food had been scarce for a long time, but starvation now threatened the many who couldn't afford the black market. Fanny's business now had far fewer army contracts, and she lay awake at night, wondering how to stay solvent for the sake of her staff. Then there was Josepha to look after. But not a day went by without her thinking about the folder Brunner had made it possible for her to see. It was six months ago now, but she still struggled to believe what she'd read.

One sunny October day, she was sitting in the horse-drawn omnibus on her way back to work from Josepha's and found herself turning it all over in her mind again.

"Christ Almighty!" the coachman hollered. "Get away from here and leave my horses alone!"

Fanny gave a little start and peered anxiously through the front window. Men waving red flags were alarmingly close to the horses, chanting, "Down with the Kaiser! Down with the monarchy!" The frightened animals stamped and snorted, then almost reared when one of the crowd grabbed at their harness.

Fanny drummed her fingertips on the bag in her lap. She needed to get back to work, not get stuck here somewhere between the Rathaus and the university. This was a big demonstration, and the marchers were heading along the Ring toward the main theater. To Fanny, the procession seemed endless. Thousands of men and women, some bearing the red flag of the Communists, others waving the red-white-red of the Republicans, strode determinedly along Vienna's once-magnificent main avenue, shouting at the top of their voices. "What'll come of the privileged? And what about the gold star? Let them sweep the streets! Let them chew on dust for a change!"

Fanny caught a whiff of smoke just as the man next to her jumped up, pointing wildly and exclaiming, "Damned crackpots! They're setting fire to the Kaiser!"

Everyone on the bus craned to see what was going on. The square in front of the university was packed with students, some waving banners, others the black-and-yellow flags of the monarchy, now ripped and tattered. Black smoke rose from the middle of the square.

Some portraits of the Kaiser, previously hung in the university's grand hall and lecture rooms, had been torn down and were tossed on the fire amid cheering and applause. The bus passengers were all for calling the police, but the long arm of the law was nowhere to be seen.

"Heavens above, will you look at that girl. She'll get trampled to death by this rabble!" Her shopping basket firmly on her knees, an old lady to Fanny's other side nudged her to look.

Sure enough, not far from their omnibus, a young woman had gotten caught up in the torrent of demonstrators while frantically trying to make her way across. She'd stumbled and fallen and was now trying desperately to get to her feet but kept getting knocked back by the sea of chanting people. She was screaming and shouting at them to stop.

"Holy Mary, it's Nelli!" Fanny was on her feet in a flash and pushed her way to the back of the vehicle to get off. She could just about see Helene, cowering on the ground, her arms wrapped around her head in an attempt to protect herself.

Fanny yelled at everyone to make way, flailing with her arms and fists as she pushed through, managing to reach Helene, grab her by the arm, and pull her to her feet. Helene, so terrified that she didn't realize who was helping her, lashed out, but Fanny kept hold of her, shouting in her ear, "It's me! It's Fanny!" Managing to keep her balance in the crowd, Fanny put her arm around Helene and pulled her into an alley.

There was hardly anybody there, and the hubbub of the demonstration was now muted. Helene sobbed and clung to Fanny in shock.

"It's all alright," she murmured soothingly, her own legs shaking with fear. "Nothing can happen now."

Helene sobbed her heart out. "I'd never have gotten out of that alone."

Fanny thought for a moment, then said, "Let's go to the fashion house. We can rest there and recover."

In her head she'd quickly worked out a safe route avoiding the demonstration, leading Helene behind the public gardens and the Minoriten Church, along Herrengasse and from there to Graben. Within minutes they were at the back door of the fashion house. Fanny took Helene straight to Madame's old office and firmly sat her down.

"I'll make you a pot of tea." She turned to go, but Helene clung to her hand.

"Fanny, you saved my life."

Fanny hugged her without a word and went to get the tea.

"This'll do us good," she said, coming back with two steaming cups on a tray. Putting one cup in front of Helene, she asked, "What were you doing at the university?"

"I went to a lecture. I'm in my first semester of medical school." She ran her hands through her disheveled hair. "It's been a long time, Fanny."

"Nearly a year." Fanny thought back to the last time they'd met, over the same tea right here in this office.

Helene continued. "Mama came back from Hungary two weeks ago. She's living in the Palais Báthory."

"Your mother traveled all that way alone? Did your father stay behind to see to the estate?"

"Papa's dead." Helene burst into tears.

At first Fanny was too shocked for words. Then she took Helene's hand in hers. "Tell me what happened."

Helene held Fanny's hand as if her life depended on it. At first Fanny couldn't follow what she was saying but gradually pieced together the devastating news that Baron Báthory had been murdered. Some deserters, men from their own army at that, had broken into the manor house. Forcing the cook to open up the larder, they'd raided it and shot dead the baron, the coachman, and faithful Adam when they'd put up a fight. The baron's wife and Zsófia had managed to hide away in the maid's room while the murderers rampaged through the house in search of cash and valuables. This was when they'd found the wine cellar, willfully smashed many of the best bottles and then downed lots of *palinka*. Their drunken slumbers had given the baroness and her maid time to escape.

The two women had gone all the way to the railway station on foot, petrified of running into more deserters and robbers. They had neither food nor water and took whatever rest they could under hedges and bushes when darkness fell. After two full days of this, they reached the station. Zsófia exchanged the baroness's pearl earrings for two tickets to Budapest and a bit of food. At Budapest, it was the baroness's wedding ring that got them tickets to Vienna.

Helene's voice had grown quieter and quieter. "I've lost my childhood home. And, worst of all, I've lost my father. He'd have given the deserters whatever food they wanted, right down to his last crust of bread."

Fanny stroked her friend's trembling hands as the tears flowed again.

"Tell me something, Fanny. Anything to take my mind off it."

Fanny cast about. "Oh! Something you don't know yet is that I bought the fashion house. Poor Madame is still interned. First she was at Karlstein, but now she's somewhere smaller. Her lawyer's hoping for her release any day now."

"Will she come back to Vienna?"

"At first, yes, definitely," said Fanny. "But when the war's over, she wants to go back to France." She paused. "It can't go on for too much longer, with so many of the soldiers refusing to go on fighting, laying down their weapons, and making for home."

"They should all have done that a long time ago," said Helene.

"You sound like Josepha," said Fanny with a little smile. She thought for a minute and then said hesitantly, "It's good to have time to sit and talk."

"You're right, Fanny, yes, it is."

Fanny thought back to the day she and Max had met with Brunner. The only people she'd ever discussed the confidential report with were Max himself and, of course, Josepha. She had kept Brunner's role to herself. But she'd been longing to share the news with Helene.

"Nelli," she said, her voice low, her tone urgent. "There's something I want you to know. It's absolutely unbelievable, but it's true." She reached for Helene's hand once more. "Nelli, we are sisters." She looked at Helene, waiting breathlessly for a reaction.

Helene looked back at her uncomprehendingly. After what seemed an eternity, she shook her head. "Fanny, please, I've often wished we were real sisters, yes, but—"

"Nelli, we are! We don't have the same father, but we do have the same mother. Our mother married your father six months after I was born. It was all fixed up by the imperial court."

Helene was still staring at her blankly. Fanny let go her hand and took the brown emergency envelope, now rather creased, from her own bag. With Max's tacit agreement, she had purloined it from Brunner's folder.

"I carry this with me all the time. Inside this envelope is the only document that shows who my mother is. She had to take it with her for the delivery. It gives her name and a contact address so that, if she had died in childbirth, the hospital would have known how to tell her family." She handed the envelope to Helene and watched in excitement as her friend took out the yellowing piece of paper and carefully unfolded it.

"Ida Molnar! That's my mother's maiden name! But I don't recognize the address."

"That's the Evidenzbüro," said Fanny. "I guess they were trying to conceal her family's real address."

"But how did you get from Ida Molnar to Ida Báthory? How did you know it was my mother's name?" Helene refolded the document and placed it back in the envelope.

"It was all in the documents I managed to see. It said how she then married your father and, of course, took his name." Without mentioning Brunner, Fanny told Helene about Max putting her in touch with the Evidenzbüro and how the secret had come out at last. When she'd finished speaking, Helene stood up and went to her.

"I'm so glad that we really are sisters, Fanny."

"Does this mean we can be friends again? Can you forgive me?" Fanny's voice was strained.

Helene replied by flinging her arms around her and holding her tight. "And your father?" she asked, as she released Fanny from the embrace. "Who's your father?"

"Well," said Fanny, a slight smile playing on her lips, "I supposed we'd better ask your mother about him."

The Palais Báthory was to be found between the churches of St. Michael and St. Peter, not so far from the Hofburg. Similar in style to a Venetian palazzo, its magnificence remained undiminished by the destructive war. The family coat of arms above the main entrance was exactly as Fanny remembered it from the impressive reception hall of the Báthory manor house. Helene's uncle, as head of the whole clan, resided on the second floor, or *bel étage*. Above that were further apartments including a small "widow's flat" where Helene now lived with her daughter. Helene's father had previously had the right of abode in the larger apartment on the same floor.

"That right of abode died with Papa," Helene explained as she and Fanny rode the elevator to the second floor. "It was assumed Mama would live with me and Emma, but I refused." She gave Fanny a little smile. "So, my uncle has agreed to let her go on living in Papa's apartment for the time being."

They stepped from the elevator and went down a corridor to an imposing, beautifully carved door. Helene rang the bell. It was soon opened by none other than Zsófia. Her eyes nearly popped out of her head when she saw Fanny.

"Good day, Zsófia. We want to see Mama." Helene seized Fanny's hand and swept past Zsófia into the reception hall.

There was an energy about the determined tap-tapping of Helene's heels across the marble floor as she almost pulled Fanny behind her. She stopped at a door on the left-hand side, knocked, and went straight into the small sitting room.

Ida Báthory sat in an armchair, a fire crackling in the grate. Her somber, high-necked mourning clothes and dark hair contrasted starkly with her ghostly complexion. A Bible lay open on her raised palms, and Fanny heard her quietly reading aloud. "You say unto me: I am wealthy and need nothing. And you know not that you are suffering, poor, blind and nothing more than—" She broke off when they came in, looking first at Helene, then at Fanny. Her eyes narrowed. "What are you doing here, you impertinent baggage? Haven't I forbidden you contact with my daughter?"

Fanny began shaking, partly in fear, partly in rage. Rage triumphed and she was about to give free rein to her anger when she felt Helene's hand tighten its grip on hers.

"Mother!" Helene took a step forward. "May I introduce you to my sister, Fanny? She was born on Christmas Day, 1889, as child number 6,572, an anonymous birth at Vienna General Hospital—but you know the place, don't you?"

Ida Báthory just stared at Fanny. She was speechless for a few moments before furiously slamming the Bible down on the side table and getting out of her chair. "That is a damned lie!"

"No, it is not!" Outraged, Fanny took the envelope from her bag and held it up. "The truth is here in black and white!"

"It must be a forgery. Show me what's inside." Holding out her hand, the baroness approached Fanny, who swiftly stepped back.

"Don't think I'd be so idiotic as to let you have this." She turned the envelope so that Ida Báthory could easily see the broken seal. "This is not a forgery."

"Just admit it, Mother. Fanny's your daughter," chimed in Helene.

Now Ida Báthory really flared up. "I swear I'll never refer to this changeling as my daughter." Her lips twisting with bitterness and loathing, she turned to Fanny and said, "You're nothing more than my misfortune. I was at court, lady-in-waiting to the empress. A moment of weakness with that good-for-nothing, Archduke Otto, ruined my life and my future. I had to leave the court and was married off to your father, Helene, second son of a baron and poor as a church mouse."

"Fanny, that means your father was the old Kaiser's nephew! Heavens above," Helene marveled.

"Don't make too much of that," raged Ida Báthory. "He fathered umpteen little bastards who he never acknowledged, then syphilis put an end to him. And you," she said, pointing at Fanny, her finger trembling with anger and scorn, "you have no claim to anything."

"I'm not interested in claiming anything whatsoever," Fanny shouted back. "I know who I am and what I'm worth—in spite of my parentage. And I must have been worth something to him because, right until his death, he put money in the bank for the woman who raised me."

"That wasn't him, that was the old Kaiser," retorted Ida Báthory icily. "He paid for the results of all those infidelities from his personal fortune. It was all done through the Evidenzbüro to conceal the source of the money." She gave Fanny a long hard look. "Right from the start,

I had a bad feeling about you. I should never have allowed you to insinuate your way into my family."

"Mother!" cried Helene. "You are Fanny's family!"

"I most certainly am not," snapped Ida Báthory, looking at Fanny with utter disdain. "I'd rather you'd never been born, but that avenue was not open to me. Once my condition became obvious, I was kept like a prisoner to avoid a scandal in the imperial household. I had no choice but to go through with the birth."

At that Fanny lifted her chin, held her head high, and looked Ida Báthory in the eye. Her voice shook when she spoke. "You're right. You are not my mother. Being a mother has to be earned."

She turned on her heel and made for the door. Tears stood in her eyes, but she'd rather have fallen down dead than let Ida Báthory see how hurt she was.

Helene stood staring at her mother.

"I loathe you, Mother, and will never forgive you for the way you've treated Fanny. Fanny is my sister. I love her and will always stand by her."

She turned and hurried after Fanny.

Barely two weeks later, on November 3, 1918, the government of Austria-Hungary agreed to an armistice with the Allied powers. The war that had raged for four years, three months, and seven days was now over. This did nothing to stop the fall of the monarchy. Kaiser Karl I abandoned matters of imperial business on November 11 and left with his family for Schloss Eckartsau while the Allies considered his fate. Meanwhile, his empire, once the second largest in Europe and home to people of many different nationalities, broke into a multiplicity of smaller countries. In Vienna, the Republic of German-Austria, a miniature state, was proclaimed but still lacked a constitution or firm borders.

For Fanny, the end of the war meant she could at long last replace the huge glass window at the front of the fashion house. Then she placed newspaper announcements that the house was under new ownership, but deliberately left in place the old sign—"Sarah Moreau—Couture"—in honor of the original proprietress. Madame was finally back in Vienna. Thin and rather frail, she was preparing to move to France.

Fanny was raring to get back to normal business. First off, she made sure her master craftswoman certificate was up on the sales room wall, then she retrieved from the storeroom all the beautiful bolts of cloth that had been stowed away during the war. Elfriede Schubert was much older now but still had plenty of drive and had created new patterns from Fanny's drawings. Soon, the machines were clattering again in the sewing room, and new window displays were in place. The working atmosphere among all the staff, whether in the sewing room or on the sales floor, was stupendous. With the end of the war came hope and confidence, even though many of the women's husbands had been killed or taken prisoner.

Soon, old clients were coming through the revolving door again. Those whose husbands owned factories crucial to the war effort had money to spend and were thrilled to be ordering evening gowns again and making themselves look glamorous. But others had been less fortunate and had lost family properties in Bohemia, Hungary, Galicia, Bukovina, or Croatia. They came in only to browse, but Fanny, confident that their circumstances would gradually improve, made sure to offer favorable credit terms.

It was the first peacetime Christmas in four years, and her twenty-ninth birthday, too. She spent the time with Josepha. When the shops reopened after the festive period, she threw a party in the sales room for all her friends and clients.

A little Christmas tree adorned the long counter, and, with Max's help, she'd created a little wooden platform underneath the candelabra and placed tables and chairs all around it. The Kálmans' cook had taken a trip out to the country and managed to buy all sorts of delights direct from a farmer, including chicken, eggs, cabbage, and potatoes. The dishes may have been simple, but Fanny's guests fell on roast chicken with potatoes and cabbage as if presented with oysters and caviar. All this was paired with wines that had been safely stored throughout the war in Madame's cellar. The prettiest of Fanny's sales staff got up on the platform to model her new designs, while the guests enjoyed the luxury of a decent meal and a glass of good wine.

The clothes were dramatically different from prewar styles. Superfluous frills and furbelows were no longer in favor, and the new designs were simple and yet elegant, with knee-length full skirts that allowed the wearer to enjoy a game of tennis as easily as a dance. The women's pants that Fanny had designed caused a real stir, as they were wide in the leg like men's trousers but partnered with figure-hugging jackets that nicely emphasized feminine curves.

Madame had nothing but praise for Fanny's first collection. "I can see you'll be carrying on my life's work to perfection, Mademoiselle Schindler," she said at the end of the fashion show, embracing Fanny with a wistful smile on her beautifully made-up lips.

Fanny moved from table to table to see all her guests, while they tucked into the much-loved dessert called Kaiserschmarrn, without its usual dose of raisins and vanilla but with plenty of egg to keep it luscious.

Izabella was seated between her dearest Rachel and her parents. Herr and Frau Kálman had come to visit shortly before Christmas and looked very despondent. With the military surrender, Izabella and Max's father had lost his assets, as his war loans had become worthless. It was said that he might have to sell one of his department stores. It was entirely thanks to the support of their son, Max, that they could go on living in their palais in Budapest. He had tried to persuade them to move to Vienna, but they flatly refused to leave their home city.

Fanny saw Izabella was eager to tell her something, so she took a seat near them for a while.

"Today Rachel and I have booked a ship's passage to Palestine. We're leaving Vienna on January 31."

This idea of "going back" to the land of Israel, promised by the British to the Jews as their homeland, had actually come from Rachel. After she had fled Lemberg, witnessed appalling atrocities committed against her fellow Jews, and seen the collapse of the monarchy, she had decided in favor of leaving Europe. She wanted to enjoy kibbutz life on the Sea of Galilee, give up all possessions, and live communally from the land. She had enthused Izabella, as well as many of the refugees, with her vision of a Jewish state for working people, a state without a rigid class structure. Many decided to do the same as Izabella and Rachel. But other refugees opted to stay in Vienna and build new lives there. Very few planned to try to return to their original homes.

"I'll miss you so much," said Fanny. "And I know Max is hoping you'll change your minds."

Izabella shook her head. "We've made the decision and that's it. Rachel doesn't want to stay. And where she goes, I go." She turned to look lovingly at Rachel.

Fanny looked over at Max. Emma was on his lap, playing with the doll he'd given her for Christmas. Max was talking to Helene, who had been seated next to him all evening. Their official separation was now complete, and both had found they could build their own futures as well as a more than civilized rapport as Emma's mother and father.

Max had already started to shape a new career. The damage to his health meant he could no longer pursue military life. However, he was to act as an adviser to the newly elected government under Chancellor

Renner on diplomatic relations with Hungary. Fanny knew how much he relished this new challenge.

As if he'd guessed she was thinking about him, Max looked across, and they smiled at one another.

"Is there a future for us now?" he'd asked her on her birthday.

"I love you," she'd replied. "And I'll always be at your side."

"Does that mean you'll move in with me once Izabella leaves?"

"What about Josepha?"

"There's plenty of room for Josepha, too."

"Good," said Fanny. "I'll ask her."

And she did, that same day. But Josepha couldn't be persuaded to leave the small apartment she'd called her own for decades. Nor did she like the idea of living with Fanny and Max in their unsanctified domestic arrangement.

But the old lady wouldn't have missed today for the world. She sat comfortably in an armchair that Fanny had positioned close to the podium and looked thoroughly contented, if rather weary. Fanny sat down on an empty chair at her side.

"Josepha, are you tired? Would you like us to take you home?"

"Thank you, little mite, but I'm fine here. After all, the only thing I have to do is sit in my nice comfy chair and eat!" She stopped for a moment, then looked up at Fanny with a mischievous smile. "D'you know, I've been thinking about the first time we ever came here. And now this whole place is yours! I'm so proud of you. Not just for that but because of the way you didn't always listen to me! You followed your own stubborn path!"

"It's a good thing I didn't listen," replied Fanny. "Nobody can afford domestic staff these days. And I never liked it, anyway."

"You must have inherited that from those parents of yours," muttered Josepha. "Your father enjoyed the good life, let's put it that way. Then there's that snooty woman who gave birth to you. Really, little mite, there's times I think it'd have been better for you never to have known what kind of parents you started out with."

Fanny leaned forward and took the old lady by the hand. "They're not my parents," she said firmly. "They're just the people who made me. You, Josepha, you took on my parents' job. You've been my grandmother, my father, and my mother. You're everything. And you always will be."

Afterword

The Austro-Hungarian Empire, also known as the Dual Monarchy, was in existence from 1867 to the end of the First World War in 1918 and represents the final period of Habsburg rule.

At the beginning of the twentieth century, the countries of the Empire were distinguished not only by modernity, technical innovation, flourishing art, music, and literature, but also by destructive differences between nationalities and the ensuing social conflict. The army was hopelessly out-of-date, and in terms of foreign policy, the Dual Monarchy had to cede its lead role in Europe to the German Empire. The Empire's figurehead during periods of change for a people wedded to tradition was Kaiser Franz-Joseph—in the eyes of his subjects, a guarantor of order and stability.

The Vienna Foundling House, where Fanny grew up, was founded in 1784 by Maria Theresa's son, Kaiser Joseph II, and remained in place until 1910. It admitted three-quarters of a million children born to single mothers. The objective of the Foundling House was to reduce the number of abandoned babies and the incidence of abortion and infanticide. Its existence made it possible for women to deliver in the adjoining birthing facility in complete anonymity before handing over the newborn. This arrangement, however, changed over the years and was eventually available only to wealthy women who could pay for the service. Shortly after the birth, babies were placed in the care of a woman approximating what we would now call a foster mother. The mortality rate, however, for babies placed in care of this type was high, running at more than ninety percent. This was well above the average when compared with other similar institutions.

A large part of our novel plays out in Vienna. For this reason, we made use—in the German version, that is—of a few Viennese and Austrian expressions. We apologize if any of these are not entirely accurate in the German version. In our English version, there is careful use of some regional words and expressions to add atmosphere, but the translator has deliberately not switched into a dialect of any one specific English language location as this would detract from the essentially Viennese location, culture, and tradition.

We have taken the small liberty of adapting a handful of dates and facts to fit with our plot. In our novel, Fanny grows up with other children in the foundling home, something that is different from what actually used to happen. Only in exceptional cases would a child be raised in the foundling home, examples being special needs or a foster mother being found to be unsatisfactory.

Portable sewing machines made by Singer were first available in 1921. Fanny's Singer was operated by a hand crank and not created as an integral part of a sewing table. It was transportable in its own wooden case. This type of machine would have been quite heavy, but we decided to interpret it as something Fanny would have been able to carry herself.

We invented the Fasching Ball at the Budapest Opera House. Our research gave no indication of a ball of this type taking place in that specific location.

Before the First World War, ladies' fashions made in Vienna had a reputation for their quality and were greatly sought after. The "Viennese tailored suit" made by Fanny as her test piece was an established term for an expertly cut suit made to a very high standard.

The commander at Przemyśl Fortress, Hermann Kusmanek von Burgneustädten, became a Russian prisoner of war after the surrender. He never made an attempt to persuade the crown prince Karl to enter into secret negotiations for peace.

The première of the operetta *Die Csárdásfürstin* took place on November 17, 1915.

The poison gas attack that affected Max is a representation of all gas attacks of the First World War. As a result of such attacks, around 100,000 died and 1.2 million were wounded. In the Alps, there were two gas attacks. The first took place on June 29, 1916, at San Michele del Carso and claimed between 5,000 and 8,000 lives. The second occurred on October 24, 1917 during the 12th Battle of the Isonzo, when approximately 5,600 people died.

The use of poison gas had in fact been outlawed by The Hague Land Warfare Convention before the First World War. It was, however, the poison gas atrocities during that war that resulted in a firm ban on their use in the 1925 Geneva Protocol. Germany ratified this treaty in 1929.

Sources of Quotations

Die fesche Pepi; Leopold Dachs; pub. Verlag J. Neidl, in: Susanne Schedtler, *Von Brett'ldiven und Gelegenheitsbuhlerinnen. Volkssängerinnen in Wien*, in: Jahrbuch des Österreichischen Volksliedwerkes (The Austrian Folksongs Almanac) Band 59 (2010), (Vol. 59) S. 80–93, (pp. 80–93).

"Ich kann nichts dafür . . . !" (Musik: Hans Gerold, Worte: Hans Gerold und E. Patak), in: *Ich leg' mein Schicksal in deine Hände. Lieder von Hans und Fritz Gerold*, compiled by Wolfgang Gerold, Wien 2008.

"To My People." Kaiser Franz-Joseph's address on the occasion of the Declaration of War on Serbia on 28 July 1914. The source used is http://www.sueddeutsche.de/politik/ manifest-von-kaiser-franz-joseph-i-an-meine-voelker-1.2069113.

"Gott erhalte, Gott beschütze . . ." Austrian Imperial Anthem from 1854 to 1918, Text: Johann Gabriel Seidl, Melodie: Franz Joseph Haydn.

The official call to refugees from West Galicia to return home: http://ww1.habsburger.net/de/medien/amtliche-aufforderung-des-magistrates-der-stadt-wien-die-fluechtlinge-aus-westgalizien-zur.

"Was wird mit die nobligen Herren," quoted from: http://webcache.googleusercont ent.com/search?q=cache:5A9xOW4i1YAJ:ww1.habsburger.net/de/kapitel/umsturz-der-werte-das-nachkriegswien+&cd=2&hl=de&ct=clnk&gl=de. Quoted here from Stadtchronik Wien. 2000 Jahre in Daten, Dokumenten und Bildern, Wien–München.

Acknowledgments

We are grateful to a number of people for their expertise. Our warmest thanks are extended to the staff of the following institutions for their help and kindness:

The Vienna Museum, the Museum of Military History in Vienna, the Budapest Opera House, and Kazinczy Street Synagogue, Budapest.

Our thanks are also due to Gerhard Murauer and staff at the Vienna Library and to Reinfrid Vergeiner and Tomasz Idzikowski at the Austrian Society for Fortification Research.

Last but not least, our thanks to our wonderful editor, Bernadette Lindebacher, who gave the original German version of this novel its final polish!

About the Authors

Photo © 2016 Mirella Drosten

Julia and Horst Drosten write historical novels together under the pseudonym Julia Drosten. In their spare time, Julia loves to do yoga, and Horst runs regularly. Horst is also a very skilled cook, and Julia loves to eat the meals he creates. The authors have written many works of historical fiction in German, and they greatly enjoy conducting research for their novels—diving into history and making the past come alive. They count flying in a historic biplane, watching the workers in a butcher's shop, exploring Egypt, and being pampered by a beautician among their research pursuits. The authors of *The Lioness of Morocco*, an Amazon bestseller in Germany and the United States, and *The Elephant Keeper's Daughter*, Julia and Horst live in the idyllic Münsterland in Germany. *The Girl with the Golden Scissors*, originally published in German under the title *Das Mädchen mit der goldenen Schere*, is their third novel translated into English.

About the Translator

Photo © 2016 Chris Langton

Deborah Langton was born in Reading, England. She studied German and French literature at Cambridge and has worked in Munich, Berlin, Milan, Abu Dhabi, London, and Manchester. After a rewarding first career teaching and lecturing, she moved into translation while still working at Munich's Ludwig Maximilian University. She loves translating fiction best of all. Deborah now lives in a rural location not far from London and translates in her study with views toward England's South Downs. She shares her life with her husband, Chris, and their two fine sons, Joseph and Samuel.